Runyo1

A Novel By Edward E. Smallwood

August 18, 2024

Number _____ **Signature** _____

Runyon Falls

Edward E. Smallwood © 2024

CONTENTS

DEDICATION

    PRELUDE

I.   ACT I   TASTE
   1. CHAPTER 1:   Vaurienne
   2. CHAPTER 2:   Hummingbird
   3. CHAPTER 3:   The Donja

II.   ACT II   HOMESTEAD
   4. CHAPTER 4:   Opening Night
   5. CHAPTER 5:   Kickball
   6. CHAPTER 6:   Going to the Storyteller
   7. CHAPTER 7:   The Story of Runyon Falls Begins
   8. CHAPTER 8:   The Tale of the Sherable
   9. CHAPTER 9:   High Pitch
   10. CHAPTER 10: Two Kingdoms
   11. CHAPTER 11: Ruby's Dream
   12. CHAPTER 12: Gravitational Forces & Amusements
   13. CHAPTER 13: Fun In the Park
   14. CHAPTER 14: Clean and Jerk
   15. CHAPTER 15: Cornered
   16. CHAPTER 16: Detour
   17. CHAPTER 17: Explanation

III. ACT III   CLAN GAMES
   18. CHAPTER 18: Gruun
   19. CHAPTER 19: Red Dawn
   20. CHAPTER 20: Finch
   21. CHAPTER 21: Odds On

IV. ACT IV EVOLUTION
22. CHAPTER 22: Pillow Talk
23. CHAPTER 23: Waah-Waahs
24. CHAPTER 24: Soul Vessels
25. CHAPTER 25: Sinister Succession
26. CHAPTER 26: Gram
27. CHAPTER 27: Upgrade
28. CHAPTER 28: Spin Doctor
29. CHAPTER 29: Barrel Roll & The Bard
30. CHAPTER 30: The Demon's Dinner
31. CHAPTER 31: Heartburn
32. CHAPTER 32: Pocket Fail
33. CHAPTER 33: The Offer

V. ACT V PERSPECTIVE
34. CHAPTER 34: Landing
35. CHAPTER 35: Visit
36. CHAPTER 36: Hamada Castle
37. CHAPTER 37: The Summit
38. CHAPTER 38: Adders in the Sand
39. CHAPTER 39: Giant Sapphires
40. CHAPTER 40: Exposed
41. CHAPTER 41: Sunsburn
42. CHAPTER 42: Tough Negotiations
43. CHAPTER 43: Teach's Revenge
44. CHAPTER 44: Treacherous Voyage

VI. ACT VI ARRIVAL
45. CHAPTER 45: Diversion
46. CHAPTER 46: Gravity Park Deux
47. CHAPTER 47: Collision Course
48. CHAPTER 48: Motley Crew
49. CHAPTER 49: Farmhouse Stand
50. CHAPTER 50: Blood on the Falls
51. CHAPTER 51: The Arm, The Watch, The Leg & The Locket
52. CHAPTER 52: Late to the Party
53. CHAPTER 53: Parting Shots

VII. ACT VII ASSUMPTION

54. CHAPTER 54:   Homecoming
55. CHAPTER 55:   Deja Vu

CARTOGRAPHY

PRIMARY CHARACTERS

STORYTRAX

DEDICATION

Dedicated to my sweet angel, Sondra – and the stories and music that inspire us all.

PRELUDE

And then, one green eye opened wide, barely peeking through piles of curly, red hair. That one eye darted back and forth – quickly and erratically. Ruby was in a blurry state of pain and numbness; she losing consciousness.

There were blasts and shouts and commotion all around her. The pain began to crowd out her other senses. She knew she was at Runyon Falls. It was supposed to be a good place – a place of fantasy and stories – but she could barely move. It was a mistake to come here…

****

"Excuse me, Storyteller. We have a new witness for the story. Would you mind starting from the beginning?" The Storyteller glared at the assistant named Sinjin.

"This is a critical part of the story. It is not appropriate to ask me to begin again. It ruins the flow of the narrative. You do understand that, don't you, Sinjin? You do realize the fact that you are interrupting a Storyteller."

"Please accept my apologies. And I understand that I'm asking a lot, but you do always tell me that the point of storytelling is to communicate with others. To share the feelings and the emotions and the history. And now with this new person here… With all due respect, Storyteller, I don't think the story would be shared as effectively with our newbie without starting from the beginning."

"What new person? What are you talking about? What's a newbie?"

"A new visitor – right there."

"Where?"

"Look up, Storyteller. The person reading the book with us. This newbie is ready to dive in and experience the magic and imagination –

the intrigue and adventure – of Runyon Falls. Don't you think we should deliver the full experience?" asked Sinjin, bowing obsequiously.

"Newbie… Hmmmmm. Yes, I suppose you are right, Sinjin. Hey, you, up there… newbie. I hope you appreciate this breach of etiquette. Lucky for you that I value the story itself more than the-uhh…the formalities. Although I do appreciate the benefits of communicating via the printed word across time and space, I am finding it to be different than I imagined. Thank you for joining us. I will begin… (deep sigh) from the beginning."

Fade to black.

STORYTRAX: *Miracles* - Jefferson Starship

ACT I ~ TASTE

CHAPTER 1

Vaurienne

Across the great ocean from Botan – on the continent of Minos – in the green sand of the vast and desolate Donja...

Two gyptos circled in the desert sky. They slowly descended on pillows of thick, almost visible heat, alighting on two tents. They awkwardly stepped down and covered the entrances with their slender bodies and sail-like wings. The first perched and glistened in the suns; it began to pulse and absorb moisture from the occupant of the tent. A few steps away, another was doing the same. The gypto could have wrapped around its prey to suck the moisture out directly, but it can also pull the water without touching – or arousing – an unsuspecting (or sleeping) victim. What a way to go: dehydration in your sleep.

Artax shuffled over to one of the tents and kicked sand onto Vaurienne from the opposite open end while she slept. The messenger warrior coughed and spit sand. As she rolled over onto her knees, the big rammel kicked sand in her face again.

"Hee – eyyyy," she managed to cough out in a gruff voice. "What the vamp?"

Vaurienne coughed again and wiped the sand from her face. Artax snorted. Vaurienne shook her head and sat back. It was so hot in the desert. Her mouth was dry as sand. She reached for her flask and took a long drink. As she drank, she looked at Artax's huge hoof outside of one end of her tent; it was bathed in a greenish haze. Instinctively, she turned her gaze to the far end of her tent. That greenish haze was pulsing slightly. "Gypto," she whispered to herself. She crawled out of the tent and patted Artax on his broad side. "Thanks, boy," she whispered while reaching for her cuttas.

Stealthily, the lone warrior crept around the side of the tent toward the pulsing gypto until she was behind the beast. For a moment, Vaurienne marveled at the creature's translucent body covering the entrance to her tent. Then she remembered that the beast was trying to suck the life from her. She lunged toward the creature – but it swatted her away with its long tail. The barbed edge caught her arm, knocking away one of her knives and sending her sprawling onto the green sand. The gypto turned and snarled at her.

As Vaurienne was now awake – and out in the open – the gypto let go of the tent and closed in on her. It floated toward Vaurienne and began to wrap itself around her. But Vaurienne rolled quickly and sliced the animal's wings with four quick cuts in the shape of X's. The gypto's wings now had little effect as it hopped on the ground flapping the mutilated appendages, but still it spun around and caught Vaurienne's arm with its barbed tail again, knocking her remaining cutta into a puff of green sand. The creature snarled again and spun once more swinging that tail at her head. Vaurienne ducked under the tail, grabbed it with her left hand, then rolled over and grabbed a cutta sticking in the sand. She neatly chopped the barbed end from the animal's tail. The gypto screeched in pain and limped/flew away as best it could, erratically jerking toward the sky. Vaurienne sat back on her knees on that green sand and took a deep breath.

As she wiped her brow, she noticed a second gypto was perched, feeding, drawing water from her companion's tent. Inside the tent was Yuni – and Yuni was clutching her throat, gasping. The water-vampire had already done significant damage. Vaurienne reached for her other cutta and headed toward Yuni's tent. The third Jader with them was Two-teeth. He had heard the commotion and slunk out of his tent.

He saw the first gypto squawking off and noticed Vaurienne headed toward Yuni's tent and the remaining gypto. Not wanting to miss out on the fun, he grabbed his blaster and started shooting! He ran toward the gypto and screamed as he blasted it. "Yaaahhhhh!!" Two-teeth was not a good shot; most Jaders weren't. He fired five or six rounds before he ever hit the creature – even though he was only a few steps away. When he finally managed to hit the gypto a few times, it was probably dead almost immediately. But Two-teeth continued to fire. He not only put several holes in the gypto but quite a few more through Yuni's tent. He scorched the sand in the area around the tent as well.

By the time Vaurienne made her way to him and pushed his arm down, he had fired upwards of twenty shots. The gypto was more than dead; it was mostly annihilated. Yuni's tent was shredded and smoldering. As for Yuni, she was clutching at the sand as she tried to crawl out of the remains of the tent. "I got the water vampire. That quatchee ain't gonna get any more water from anybody else," said Two-teeth, with a disturbing, minimalist grin. (With only two teeth, his grin was...unsettling.) He was clearly pleased with himself as he holstered his weapon.

Vaurienne ran toward Yuni and gave her water. For her part, Yuni downed the flask in several huge gulps. "Get me another water flask," Vaurienne called to Two-teeth. "What? Oh, ok," he responded. He dug into his tent and returned, flinging a flask at Vaurienne's feet. She quickly handed it to Yuni who continued drinking until the second flask was drained. "I think you'll be okay," said Vaurienne. "A few more minutes and neither of us might not have been so lucky. Thanks to Artax; he woke me up."

"I'll be fine," said Yuni gruffly, shrugging Vaurienne's hand from her shoulder. She scrounged around for another water flask in the remnant shreds of her tent. She found it, dropped to her knees again, flipped the top off, and guzzled as much as she could with the excess dribbling down her throat. "You nearly shot me, you quatchee," she shouted back at Two-teeth. "You know, I pretty much saved your life, don't you?" Two-teeth fired back.

"Well... thanks anyway." Vaurienne looked at her colleagues. "Spare," Yuni barely nodded in her direction as a weak expression of appreciation. Vaurienne leaned down to Yuni and put her hand on her fellow traveler's shoulder. "Are you okay?" Yuni shrugged off Vaurienne's hand again. "I'm fine."

"Well, then, we need to head out," Vaurienne said. "It's time we got packed up. We still have our appointment in the Gold Oko." She walked over and hugged the massive Artax. She had to stretch up on her toes to reach the rammel and she still couldn't put her arms all the way around his neck.

****

The three hooded figures rode rammels leaving behind a cloud of glittery green dust. Rammels were large, camel-like creatures with huge, spiraled horns set close against their heads. The horns carried water – which was an essential part of the creatures' innate homing ability. In the Donja, if absolutely necessary, a rider could access rammel water by jabbing small, hard, hollow tubes into the base of the animal's horns. Some say rammel water was a sweet delicacy. Others claimed it to be an aphrodisiac. Although taking horn water won't harm the animal immediately, taking too much horn water can lead to a rammel's navigational confusion and even demise, so few would ever dare to do so – except to save their own lives in the desert.

The hooded figure in the center of the three riders was the leader; she was called Gala Vaurienne. The sides of her head were closely shaved and her black hair was tied back in a braid of braids, ending in a mass that bounced as she rode in the hot breeze. Her hair was slightly tinted green…That Donja sand seemed to coat and invade virtually everything – almost like glitter. Her face was tanned from years in the Hamada sun. Her lips were completely black – as were her eyes – no whites at all. Her lips were also lightly dusted with the glittery, dark, green color of the Donja sand.

Vaurienne worked for Gruun, leader of the Jade Clan. She held the position of "messenger." Each of the four Clan leaders had messengers who acted as their representatives. Messenger duties included all sorts of things. Sometimes she was to act as a spy, other times as a negotiator, occasionally as a delivery person. Usually the expectations had something to do with trade, but, as a messenger, Vaurienne generally did whatever Gruun assigned her to do. Some might call her a 'fixer.' Hers was definitely a position of honor and trust. When

Vaurienne arrived at the home of another Clan leader, she was a respected representative of Gruun. She was cunning, faithful, and reliable. When crossed, she was a harsh adversary indeed – known for her deft skills with a pair of small, curved blades ('cuttas') she carried at her sides.

The trailing cloud of dust changed from green to yellow-gold with lingering, glittery sparkles flickering in the wake of the riders as the shiny dust floated down to the countless grains of colored sand. Vaurienne's current assignment was to deliver a sample of contraband weapons (imported in violation of the planet's technology restrictions) to Oshi at the Gilt Cove Palace in the Gold Oko. Oshi was the leader of the gold clan. Gruun was offering two of the latest advanced blasters to Oshi as a gift – hoping to entice her to buy more.

Vaurienne approached Gilt Cove, accompanied by her fellow Jader escorts, Two-Teeth and Yuni. As her party approached the palace gates, they slowed to be admitted by the Gold guards. She pulled back her hood and the guards quickly recognized Gruun's representative. She was allowed passage with a nod.

She dismounted and nuzzled Artax – her faithful rammel of more than 10 years. Vaurienne was a striking figure with a tiny waist accentuated by rounded hips. Though not very tall, her reputation as a shrewd negotiator and expert with knives was well-deserved – and respected – in all of the Okos. "Would you please get our rammels some water and food?" she asked one of the palace guards. "We've been in the Donja for three days." She rubbed Artax on the neck and patted his nose as she casually handed the reins to the Gold guard.

As Vaurienne climbed the steps, she covered her eyes from the dancing sunslight glinting off the rows of golden ettajays. At the top of the stairs, Oshi – framed by the light from the ettajays – was waiting to greet the Jaders.

"Welcome Gala, so good to see my favorite representative of Gruun," Oshi said. "I'm glad you came. It's always a pleasure to see you." She reached down, pulled up Vaurienne's hand and kissed it gently. Gala focused her attention elsewhere and continued walking on to the covered area of the huge balcony. She turned and looked back at Oshi.

"I hope you don't mind; I just wanted to get out of the suns, your Majesty," she said to Oshi with a slight bow of her head. "And please forgive me, it is wonderful to see you again as well." She made herself comfortable, taking a seat at the table and pouring herself a large cup of water which she promptly gulped down.

"I'm sure you must be thirsty after your trip. Please, make yourself at home," Oshi said with a smile as she walked toward the table to join Vaurienne. Oshi walked up behind her guest and said, "Allow me to take your desert robe," as she reached around to pull it off Gala's shoulders. She handed the garment to a servant who silently took it away. Two-teeth and Yuni walked up but remained several steps behind Vaurienne with a box at their feet, waiting until they were called.

Oshi was the leader of the Gold Clan and a member of the Minosian Council. She was probably the youngest clan leader. Vaurienne guessed Oshi was in her mid 40's. Oshi was tall and thin...an elegant, angular, handsome woman who wore feminine clothing and accoutrements but looked stately and somewhat stern. She usually wore flowing dresses and shoes that made her appear even taller than she already was. She was not afraid to be feminine, but took great pains to project a tough exterior as a leader. Vaurienne thought Oshi was the perfect combination of femininity and masculinity – all rolled up into one body.

"Oshi, would you please provide my comrades with some refreshments as well?" Vaurienne asked. "But, of course, my dear Gala." Oshi clapped her hands twice. Two servants appeared, each carrying a large glass of water, which they presented on trays to Two-teeth and Yuni who greedily – and sloppily – guzzled them down, returning the empty glasses to the trays. (Two-teeth dribbled a fair amount down his chin which he wiped off with his sleeve.)

Oshi sat down across from Vaurienne. "Gala, my dear," she said, "How is old Gruun? I haven't seen him in nearly three months." "He's the same," Gala responded. "Just older and fatter." They both laughed. "...and as mean as ever," she added. "I've brought you something that I think you're really going to like."

"Gala, I've known you for almost nine years now – ever since you started visiting with Gruun. You were just a child when I first saw you, but you never did seem to appreciate the pleasantries. Always straight to business. A woman of few words. I respect that, but would you care to have dinner first tonight?"

"With all due respect, allow me to show you the gifts from Hamada's leader," she said. "Then we can eat, your Majesty."

The leaders of the Okos were each part of the families in their particular geography. They usually rose to their positions by a combination of stealth, cunning, ruthlessness, and some measure of business success. Being genealogically close to the previous, or sitting, leader didn't hurt either as clans were mostly family affairs. Though they weren't royalty, they imagined themselves so. As such, they tended to flaunt their wealth – especially Oshi – and each desired to be referred to with a royal-sounding address. Knowing that preferred reference, and using it liberally, was one of the ways that Vaurienne ingratiated herself to each of the leaders. For Oshi, the preferred method of address was "your Majesty."

"Oh, well, I suppose so," replied Oshi, with a wave of her hand.

"Yuni, Two-teeth, please present her Majesty with the gifts from our dear Gruun," Vaurienne ordered. The two bent down to open the box using the keys each of them wore around their necks. (The keys had to be inserted and turned at the same time – or the box was set to explode.) They inserted the keys, looked up at each other, nodded, and turned the keys at the same time – as they had done many times before.

Two-teeth and Yuni each picked up a gleaming blaster and presented them both to Oshi. She glanced up at a rather large servant, who cleared away the expensive table settings with a sweep of his arm, and the guns were placed in front of her. "On behalf of His Eminems, Gruun of Hamada, I present you with two of the very latest IDC blasters," Vaurienne said.

"I'm listening," Oshi said, feigning disinterest. "These blasters are not available anywhere on Levon – except from Gruun," Gala said. "He has gone to great expense to procure these samples for you. They are 50% lighter than the current models. And these are fueled by ternium chips. They deliver twice the power – with greater distance before dissolution – and can fire more than 1,000 rounds before re-charging is needed," she said.

"That sounds impressive," Oshi said – with a little more interest. "Perhaps a demonstration is in order?" she inquired.

"My pleasure," Vaurienne said. "I'll use the existing model, and you can use the new Browning Vel-T. Do we have a target you'd like to use? Or perhaps you would prefer to go down to the beach, your Majesty?" she added with a smile. "Why yes, that's a splendid idea," Oshi said. "The ocean breeze can be so refreshing this time of day." Oshi clapped her hands twice and a servant appeared. She whispered into his ear and the servant quickly hurried away.

They began to walk around the side of the palace and down the steps toward the golden beach. When Oshi and her visitors arrived down on the beach, there was already a canopy, table, and chairs waiting for them.

"Let's shoot at silver plates," suggested Oshi. "Silver plates, your Majesty?" Vaurienne asked. "Yes," Oshi responded. I have silver plates but I've grown tired of them. I've decided I'll just use gold from now on. This is as good a use as any for the silver ones."

"Have you used these new blasters, Gala?" Oshi asked. "Well, I've practiced with them a few times," Vaurienne answered. "Then I'd like you to show me the difference," Oshi said. She waved over a guard to join them. "You use the new Browning and I'll have my best marksman use his current weapon. I'll just observe."

At the top of the cliff, two servants were waiting with stacks of silver plates. They were ready to hurl them out toward the sea. Vaurienne and Oshi's marksman would take turns shooting them. (The plates, not the servants. Though you never could be too sure – this was Minos after all.)

Oshi sat down and held up three fingers. "Marksman, you go first." The marksman stepped forward. One of the servants threw three plates off the cliff toward the sea. The marksman raised his weapon and shot them: one – two – three. Each plate shattered on the impact of the blasts. Next, the other servant stepped up and threw three plates.

Vaurienne shot as well: one – two – three – all on target. Both weapons seemed to perform similarly well.

"That was too easy," Vaurienne said. "Let's make it a little more challenging."

Oshi smiled and nodded. She held up five – and then two more fingers – for a total of seven. The marksman stepped up. Together, the servants hurled seven plates in quick succession over the cliff. Oshi's marksman fired his weapon: one – two – three – four – were all hits; he managed to partially singe the edge of the fifth as it fell into the water. The sixth and seventh plates fell into the waves before he could fire at them. Still, he was satisfied with his performance.

Vaurienne stepped up. The servants threw seven silver plates for her. She reached across, quickly flipped a switch on the Browning, and fired: one – two – three – four – five – six – seven. All hits – before the plates were halfway to the water. "Oh, the new models have a rapid-fire setting," she said with a smile.

Oshi nodded and smiled. She clapped twice more – with her delicate three-finger clap. Ten servants ran down the dunes and pulled a massive tarp from a huge log just down the beach. It was from a tree almost three feet thick. "What about the extra power you mentioned?" Oshi asked.

The marksman stepped up and fired into the log. The blast made a hole one foot deep and almost two feet across in the side of the log. It was Vaurienne's turn. She pointed the Browning blaster at the log and fired three times at different sections of the log in quick succession. When the smoke cleared, the log had been severed into four different pieces. Each of her shots had blasted completely through the log.

"Impressive Gala," Oshi said. "I like what I see. Now, please sit and drink with me."

Gala sat as she had done with Oshi many times before. Oshi respected a negotiator who could hold up under a steady flow of alcohol. She clapped thrice and more servants appeared with mugs of green beer, serving Vaurienne, Oshi, Two-Teeth, and Yuni. "For the honor of the Jade Clan," Oshi toasted (as she rolled her eyes). "The Jade Clan!" they all said emphatically and raised their glasses.

When they had finished their green beers, Oshi said, "Thank you for the gifts, my Jade friends. The Alpha sun will be setting soon. It's almost time for dinner. I have some business to attend to and I'll meet you in the dining hall in, say, an hour? Faron will see to your needs in the meantime." One servant pulled out Oshi's chair and another escorted her up the steps to the palace. Two other servants packed up the blasters in a different (safer, non-explosive) box and followed discreetly.

Faron held out a hand for Vaurienne and her comrades, directing them up another set of stairs. "If you are ready for your rooms… Unless you would prefer to take a swim first?" Faron asked. They all laughed heartily. Most Jaders didn't know how to swim – and rarely bathed. The habit of not bathing probably had something to do with their conserve-water-at-all-costs desert roots (or maybe not). Two-teeth and Yuni headed up the stairs almost immediately. But Vaurienne…she lingered for a moment, gazing longingly at the waves, before turning to follow her comrades.

STORYTRAX: *Witchy Woman* - Eagles

CHAPTER 2

Hummingbird

Vaurienne was escorted to the Seascape wing and given her usual room with an expansive view of the ocean. Meanwhile, Two-teeth and Yuni were given smaller rooms in the guest wing.

"Why does that loper get treated so special?" Two-teeth said to Yuni. "She's nobody – just a lousy spare."

"You know Gruun likes her," said Yuni. "Besides, she always gets the deals done. That's the only thing Gruun cares about."

"That's not the only thing he cares about," said Two-teeth. "Gruun has … ummm, ambitions. I've heard things." "What have you heard, quatchee?" she asked.

"Don't call me that," he replied. "I've heard plenty."

"Well, I don't believe Gruun would tell you his plans. He thinks you're stupid," she said.

"I'm not stupid. And he didn't tell me. I overhead when I was in the castle kitchen. Gruun was telling Cassius about how he was gonna rule Levon," said Two-teeth. "And when the Jade Clan rules the planet, I'm gonna get rid of that little snit, Gala Vaurienne. She's not one of us and I won't have her leading Jaders."

"I'll be glad to help you with that task, comrade," Yuni replied. She pulled off a boot and dumped green sand on the floor as she walked down the hallway

****

Vaurienne descended the long, curved staircase in a gold-trimmed dress that Oshi had provided for her. She walked gracefully across the huge, gleaming stone floor. "You look lovely, my dear," said Oshi as Vaurienne approached the table. "Thanks, your Majesty. But you know I really don't like dresses," she responded, tugging gently at the waist. "All the same, thank you for indulging me," responded the clan leader. A servant pulled out a chair for her. Six more servants served them dinner – choreographed by Faron – plates and serving trays (all gold, of course) flowed from the kitchen – seven courses in all.

The servants arranged their drinks in a row behind the food plates – as was Minosian custom – from largest to smallest goblets. The five drinks began with the largest, which contained water – critical in the desert but important both physically and ceremonially all across Minos – as fresh water was rarely abundant. (The salt water from the ocean was not potable. And even though the Okos themselves were fertile, all Minosians were keenly aware of the great Donja on their doorsteps and its lack of water. So water was always the first and largest glass.) As the glasses proceeded from larger to smaller, they contained stronger and stronger concentrations of alcohol.

They began to eat – and most important – to negotiate. That was the main course; not just the food, but the business at hand. The pomp and ceremony were for show but the primary purpose of the meal was to conduct trade.

"Do please try the roasted waah-waah. It's a delicacy from Botan," Oshi offered.

"Thank you," Vaurienne said. "Wait, are those puffed pastries?" she asked.

"Yes, with goat butter and sopa jelly," Oshi replied.

Faron approached the table, "We also have saltwater berries, Azuri blue potatoes, red dragon carrots, and romanesco," he added. "And on this side of the table," he continued as he walked around, "we have split-roasted spiny worms – with the poison glands removed, of course – cactus beans, and island gourds, along with rainbow gillers," he said as he bowed deeply while backing away.

Just as Faron stepped away, two more servants approached carrying a golden-domed platter. They placed it in the center of the already nearly-full table. One of them reached out his hand, held it over the dome and waited – while he looked at Oshi. After pausing a few seconds for effect, Oshi nodded her head. The servant removed the cover.

"Clord pie!?" Vaurienne said somewhat louder than she might have intended. "I know that's your favorite," Oshi said. But it wasn't just a clord pie. The pie was cut into slices alternating with bite-sized chocolate cupcakes and sweetwater bell berries topped with sand-apple buttercream icing. Vaurienne had not seen a feast like this in … well… ever. "This is amazing, your Majesty!" she said. "Thank you for your wonderful hospitality."

They ate and stuffed themselves. (No dainty deferments here.) After they had eaten all they wanted – especially of the clord pie – the table was cleared. Next, more servants came to refill their water glasses and re-position the remaining drinks in a line directly in front of each diner.

Faron introduced the drinks, "From left to right, you first have your largest mug with water, next is sand-apple cider, followed by a Minosian Double Sunset, then a Blood & Sand, and finally, the house specialty: Euthanasia. Enjoy." He backed into the darkness yet again.

This was when the real negotiations began. Gruun wanted Vaurienne to sell Oshi 50 blasters, but Vaurienne thought she could sell 100. "Your Majesty, you are far too generous and kind with this feast and these potent libations," she began. "Not at all, Gala. I want you to be happy," Oshi responded with a big smile.

They each took a drink of water from their mugs – the signal the negotiations were to begin. Next, they each began to drink their cider. It was spicy and hot – with the kick of a rammel! They said nothing but studied each other's faces as they drank. Vaurienne was patient; she knew what she wanted to accomplish – and she was sure she could get it.

"I think you need at least 200 of the Browning Vel-T's," Vaurienne opened. Then she slowly took a final sip of cider, draining the glass and turning it upside down on the table. "That sounds a little expensive, even for me," Oshi replied. She slowly drained her cider as well. Servants came out of the shadows and removed their cider glasses. Vaurienne and Oshi each took a sip of water next, according to custom.

On to the Sunsets. A Minosian Double Sunset was made of heavy, burgundy-colored clord rum, coconuts, both red and black light-cherries, and orange juice. These were served in glasses that magnified the bioluminescence of the drink – especially in the soft, low light of the dining hall. Oshi drank first – meaning, according to custom – she was allowed to speak next. Except she didn't speak right away. She savored the drink…and took another sip. Just looking at Vaurienne, almost gazing into her eyes.

"The blasters are impressive. And I'd like to have some for my guards. But if the price you're asking is what I think you're asking, 200 is off the table. Then again, I might not be interested at all. My guards have perfectly good blasters. An enemy can only die once, you know," Oshi said with a wry smile.

Vaurienne took a long, slow drink of her sunset. She knew Oshi was toying with her. "Ten thousand each," she said. "That's only two million levs. A pittance for one as wealthy as you. And I know you want the very best. These blasters would make one guard as good as two."

They stared at each other for a moment, then Faron appeared and whispered into Oshi's ear. "Yes!" she said quite loudly. "Music would be perfect." Oshi waved her hand and soon unseen musicians began creating stringed melodies from the shadows.

The negotiators continued drinking and staring. The conversation veered away from the negotiations. Vaurienne complemented Oshi on her hair and her wonderful taste in food and fashion. Oshi complimented Vaurienne on her reputation as the best messenger that any of the Council members had. "You've also got an excellent sense of style," Oshi added. They finished their sunsets; again they turned their glasses upside down; again servants appeared from the shadows to clear away the glasses. Both diners took another sip of water.

Oshi grabbed her Blood & Sand (a green drink with swirls of red clord syrup and golden sugar crystals around the rim of the glass); she took a big gulp. "Enough with the blasters," Oshi said quickly, taking surprise initiative. "Forget about those. I want you to work for me. You see how I can treat you. I'm sure far better than Gruun. Work for me and I'll make you my chief messenger. I'll even give you command of the guard."

Vaurienne was not easily surprised. But this proposal caught her off guard. One did not move from the service of one clan to another. As someone who wasn't born into the clans, she could choose to switch – in theory – but it was a risky move. One that might come with consequences. Still, Oshi's palace and – well, everything – would be a lot better than Gruun could (or would) offer. It was an honor to consider.

But she only considered it for the slightest of moments; Gruun would never let her go. And if she left without his permission, her role as a messenger would be severely curtailed. There were only four members of the Minosian Council and a messenger's success was based on being able to work with each of the four. Not to mention, there were other consequences that she didn't want to think about.

Vaurienne swirled her Blood & Sand, staring deep down into the glass. She looked up at Oshi and took a drink. "The offer is more than tempting, your Majesty. Working for you would be a great honor – and one that I would certainly relish. But Gruun would never let me switch to another clan." She wanted to change the subject, so Vaurienne reached into her shirt and pulled out a small velvet bag with a small bird-like symbol on the front. She opened the bag and retrieved a tiny blaster.

"What is that, a toy?" Oshi asked with a soft chuckle.

"No, it's a new generation blaster. Called a hummingbird. It's my favorite because it's little but lethal, like me," Vaurienne said as she twirled it in her small hand. It glinted from the candlelight. "There are probably less than a dozen of these on the entire planet," she added. "They weren't supposed to be part of Gruun's shipment, but somehow they were slipped in. I think they're just prototypes, for the utmost in concealed weapons."

"Are you telling me that toy is a real weapon?" Oshi asked.

"Absolutely," Vaurienne responded.

"Show me," Oshi demanded.

"Do you have any more silver plates?" Vaurienne asked.

"Ha ha ha," laughed Oshi. "No, but I have this empty glass," she drank down the rest of her Blood & Sand. "Think you can hit this?" Vaurienne nodded. "Faron!" Oshi called. "Please throw this toward the ceiling." Faron tossed the now-empty glass as high as he could. Vaurienne shot her toy-like hummingbird and shattered the glass. The sound of the blast broke the mood and the light of the shot momentarily lit up the entire hall.

"Only two shots per charge," Vaurienne added.

"Oooohhh. I simply must have one of those – those hummingbirds," Oshi said.

"Oh," Vaurienne replied. "I'm not authorized to sell this; Gruun gave it to me as my personal sidearm. I wouldn't want to offend him by trading away his gift."

"Trust me," Oshi said. "I'm sure that fat, old fool won't care – especially if you come back with an order for, say, 100 Browning Vel-T's now, would he?" "Well, I don't know," Vaurienne said. She drank the last of her Blood and Sand. A servant quietly took away her glass. Oshi and Vaurienne both drank from their water mugs. They were beginning to feel the effects of their libations.

Only the Euthanasia remained. It was a powerful concoction indeed. It contained clord rum, quinoa whiskey, sea salt, blue potato vodka, black mushroom juice, and a hint of spiny worm poison. Euthanasia sometimes resulted in visions; other times it might induce euphoria, and on still other occasions (depending on how much psychotropic spiny worm poison was used), it could cause intense delirium, and even unwanted trips for personal relief. In any event, it almost always led to an earlier-than-expected bedtime – one way or another.

Vaurienne wanted to drink – she was eager to finish up and put her head on an actual pillow for a change instead of the Donja sand – but she waited for Oshi. Oshi, on the other hand, was in no hurry. Oshi's hand meandered around in the direction of her drink. But then she pulled back. This was just part of the dance. Vaurienne participated as well. She brought her hand up but then she passed it over her glass and just moved around some spices. Again, Oshi moved her hand slowly toward the Euthanasia, but then stopped. She looked up at Vaurienne, and then, slowly, painstakingly, inched her hand toward the glass. Then she nimbly wrapped her long, slender fingers around the glass, and gently raised the drink to her lips. She paused for a moment, licked her lips, and then drank deeply.

"My dearest Gala," Oshi began, "I think you're right. I do need some of those blasters. If I bought a hundred of them, would you include the hummingbird, darling?"

Vaurienne drank as well. "Your Majesty. As I said, this was a personal gift from my clan leader. It would be difficult to part with," she said.

"My dear Gala. You drive a hard bargain. I'll tell you what. I'll buy 150 blasters – but only if you give me the hummingbird – as a personal gift. That's my final offer," she said. Oshi finished her Euthanasia and firmly placed the empty glass, upside down, on the table.

Vaurienne drank and began to reply, "Your Majesty. I really don't think –"

"That was my final offer, Vaurienne," Oshi said stiffly, placing her hands 'palms-down' on the table – indicating she really was finished negotiating. At that point, Vaurienne had only two choices: take the offer or walk away.

The two stared at each other. Vaurienne finished her drink. Both glasses were empty, but no servants came to remove them. The mood was quiet and tense.

"If that is your final offer," Vaurienne began.

"It is," said Oshi flatly with both hands grasping the table now.

"Then I must accept," Vaurienne said as she bowed her head slightly. She slid back her chair and stood up. She returned the hummingbird to its the velvet bag and walked to Oshi. "Please accept this hummingbird as a personal gift from me in order to seal the deal." Oshi placed her hand on top of Gala's.

Oshi took the gift. She stood up and hugged Vaurienne. "I knew we could come to an agreement, Gala," she whispered in the messenger's ear. They let go of their embrace and continued holding hands facing each other. Servants came and took the final two empty glasses. One of them handed a small package to Oshi. "Oh yes, thank you," she said. Oshi, in turn, handed the package to Gala, adding "this is that item you requested. Although, for the life of me, I don't know why you want to keep doing this."

"Well it...it helps me... fit in," said Gala. "And thank you."

All over Minos, but especially in the Donja, fitting in was very important. Outsiders were rarely trusted and often persecuted (or worse).

They began to walk toward the great staircase. "I enjoyed doing business with you, as always," Oshi said. "Please give Gruun my regards."

"I will. And the pleasure is always mine when I get to visit you. Good night, your Majesty," Vaurienne said as they parted at the top of the stairs – tenderly pulling their hands apart, lingering for the tiniest moment with their fingertips barely touching... until their hands fell away from each other.

As Vaurienne arrived at her room, her stomach began to rumble. She clutched at it in some distress. "Ugghhh!" she said to herself. "Too much spiny worm poison." She shoved the door open and kicked off her heels as she ran toward the bathroom, yanking that dress over her head.

CHAPTER 3

The Donja

The next morning…as the suns rose, Gala was already at the stables (fully recovered). Per usual, she was the first in her party to be ready to go. While she waited for Yuni and Two-teeth, Vaurienne greeted Artax. "Good morning, big fella! How is my favorite friend in the whole world?" She hugged him closely – at least as high up as she could reach. Artax was more than eight feet tall, while Vaurienne capped out at just a little over five feet. As such, her arms only reached part way around the animal's massive neck.

She grabbed a brush and began to stroke his fur. "I hope you had a good night's sleep, sweetie. We've got several days' ride ahead of us," she said. Artax snorted through his lips. He bent down his thickly muscled neck and nuzzled Vaurienne. She knew what he wanted – and she dug into her pocket to bring out a few golden sugar cubes from dinner the night before. "I didn't forget you, buddy," she said softly as she held out her hand. Artax plucked both of the sugar cubes from her tiny hand with one swipe of his monstrous, wet, yellow tongue.

Vaurienne grabbed Artax by the loops of his horns, pulled his head down and looked him in the eyes. Her small face was dwarfed by his huge countenance. "I love you, big guy. Do you know that?" Artax responded by swiping that massive tongue across her face. "Eewww," she said. "I guess that means you love me, too." Vaurienne smiled – and her face dripped a little. She went over to the water trough and splashed her face. "Come over here, Artax. I want you to be sure to drink up for the trip back across the Donja." Her rammel shuffled over and lapped big, noisy mouthfuls of water. As the mammoth beast drank, Vaurienne stroked his side. Her fingers traced a scar in the shape of a large V on the side of his neck. "I'm sorry," she said softly, almost to herself.

Vaurienne heard footsteps. She patted Artax on his 'V' – absent-mindedly brushing his mane hair over the scar – and looked up. "Two-teeth, Yuni… About time you guys got here."

"You said suns-up," gritted Two-teeth through his half-closed mouth. He often talked that way in a feeble attempt to hide his remaining teeth – or to hide the space for the teeth he didn't have. It was kind of silly; everyone knew he only had two teeth. And anyway, that was his name! (Then again, thought Vaurienne, that probably wasn't his given name. She assumed that at some point in his life, he probably had more than two teeth – and he probably had a different name. Anyway, that's what everybody called him now.)

"Both suns have been up for over half an hour," Vaurienne replied. "Make sure your rammels are watered. Saddle up and let's get going."

"Do you think you're in charge of us?" Yuni asked.

"Look, we have a three-day ride through the Donja. I'm just doing my job," Vaurienne replied. "You do yours and we won't have any problems. Oh, and I got a new tent for you from Oshi." They mounted their beasts and began the journey into the desert back toward Glastalica, Gruun's home and the main (basically, the only) town in Hamada.

Two-teeth looked at Yuni as they followed behind Vaurienne. He sneered and made a slicing motion across his neck. Yuni smiled at him. Two-teeth tried to smile back, but having only two teeth, the result was unsettling at best; it really didn't have quite the effect a smile should have. They were only a few minutes into their trip when they came up on a pack of wild Caliga Boars, easily recognizable by their curly tails and piercing, glow-in-the-dark eyes. Vaurienne led a wide berth around the pack. Two-teeth looked back as they passed; "Why don't we kill a boar and roast it?" he asked aloud.

"We don't have time to fight a pack of Caligas," said Vaurienne. "We need to get Gruun's money back to him." Secretly, she thought some Minosian boar barbecue might taste pretty good – but she had to focus on the mission.

"Gala Vaurienne," sneered Yuni. "You're no fun."

They rode on for hours without saying another word. There was no love lost between the three. Yes, they were all members of the Jade Clan, and that connection forced them to work together because that's what Gruun expected. But beyond duty, there were significant differences. Two-teeth and Yuni were born into the clan. They were 'naturals.' Vaurienne had adopted the Jade Clan – or rather the clan adopted her. A 'spare' – someone who wasn't born into a clan – can join but must pledge loyalty to that clan. Joining a clan wasn't for the faint of heart. Even after being accepted into a clan, spares were usually thought of as 'less than.'

Rarely were spares fully accepted into a clan. Spares...as the name implies, weren't considered integral parts of the team. They were basically 'extra.' There were actually very few of them. Sometimes, they were only temporary. However, Gala's status seemed to have become more or less permanent. While they might be helpful in a pinch, there was always an air of suspicion around spares. Questions lingered... Did the spare leave his or her previous clan? Where was the spare from? Was the spare a spy? Of course, Vaurienne was also part spy in her job for Gruun, so she was good at that. Unfortunately, that fact just fueled more suspicion of her among some of the natural-born Jaders. Sometimes, part of her job required 'stretching' the truth – like when she told Oshi she only had one Hummingbird. She felt sorry that she had misled Oshi, but she was glad that she still had another Hummingbird. (She kept it safely hidden in her hair – just in case.)

Meanwhile, if her traveling companions didn't like her, she didn't much care for them either. Vaurienne did all the work; they were just there for show – supposedly for protection. It wasn't considered fitting for a messenger to arrive alone, plus it might look like a Council member couldn't afford to send more than one person on an assignment – and that would never do. On Minos, appearances always mattered. Perception was sometimes more important than reality.

Still, she tried to get along with them, but they didn't make it easy. Usually, they wouldn't talk to her – except about business or to complain. So she mostly kept quiet on their trips. Early on she tried to make conversation but after years of being rebuffed, laughed at, ignored, and just plain insulted, she decided silence was the better approach.

Both suns were at their zenith. It was approaching the hottest part of the day. From now 'til dusk, the temperature would continue to rise to an almost unbearable level. "We'll make camp here," Vaurienne said. After sundown, we can get a bite to eat and continue on when it cools down." The three unpacked their tents and hunkered down for the afternoon.

The tents were open on the ends to promote air circulation. But the green sand dust was ever-present in the Donja. On good days, the dust was light. On bad ones, the dust storms could be brutal. The worst storms have covered entire caravans in minutes. Today seemed like a good day. Vaurienne looked skyward and felt the hot sun on her face. It was always hot in the Donja. They ducked into their tents to get shelter from the powerful suns.

As the suns went down, Vaurienne was the first to step out of her tent (as usual). "Get yourselves some food! We head out in a few minutes!" she shouted to the others.

"Did you bring food for us?" Yuni asked.

"You were supposed to pack your own food from dinner last night," Vaurienne replied. (Yuni knew that, but she wanted to start trouble.)

"Well, we thought that since you had a fancy dinner with 'her Majesty,' that you might bring us poor naturals some table scraps," Two-teeth added.

Vaurienne knew they had packed their own food, but she wasn't that hungry and she was trying to get along. "I do have a couple of slices of clord pie if you'd like to share," she said as she opened her pack. Both Yuni and Two-teeth were more than glad to accept her offer. They grabbed the slices from Vaurienne's small, outstretched hands. (Neither bothered to say thank you.) "You're welcome," she said.

"Hmmmpphh," Yuni snorted.

"I hope you at least remembered to fill your water flasks," Vaurienne said.

"Of course we did. We're riding through the desert, you dumb spare," Two-teeth said under his breath (but loud enough for Gala to hear).

"Just trying to watch out for my team," Vaurienne said under her own breath.

As they were packing up, Two-teeth slunk around the other side of Artax and lifted Vaurienne's extra water-flask. Artax turned and saw Two-teeth skulking around. He lowered his head, bellowed, and gave Two-teeth a head butt knocking him backward about 10 feet into the sand.

"What the vamp is going on over here?" Vaurienne asked as she heard the commotion and saw Two-teeth lying back in the sand.

"Your crazy rammel knocked me over," said Two-teeth. "Well, you probably got too close to him and made him nervous. These are sensitive creatures, you shouldn't be sneaking around them," she replied.

"He needs to be put down," said Two-teeth. He drew his weapon, but remained sitting in the sand (to hide the fact that he was sitting on Gala's water-flask). Vaurienne stepped between Two-teeth and Artax.

"Put your weapon away," Vaurienne said. Two-teeth didn't move. He kept his blaster pointed at Artax (and Vaurienne), considering his options. Vaurienne drew her curved blades; in the blink of an eye she landed one right in front of him, inches away from the center of his outstretched legs. "The next one won't miss," she said.

"Let's just get going," Yuni said.

Two-teeth slowly holstered his weapon. He rolled over and quickly covered the water-flask with sand as he got up and swatted sand from his pants. Vaurienne looked back to Artax and then went to retrieve the cutta she had thrown. She and Two-teeth glared at each other.

"He's a stupid animal," Two-teeth said as he held his stomach and walked back to his own rammel.

Vaurienne climbed on Artax's back and rode back toward Two-teeth. Standing over him, she looked down and said, "Artax has saved my hide more than once. I'm pretty sure he's smarter than you. And besides, he's my friend." She glared at Two-teeth. "Don't threaten my friends."

Two-teeth ignored her. He rolled his eyes, looked back at Gala and tried to climb up onto his rammel, who stepped to the side just as he was trying to mount. Two-teeth fell again, but this time he went face-first into the sand. Yuni laughed. Vaurienne quietly smiled. Artax nodded.

He got up and cursed his rammel. He kicked it in the stomach. Then he walked over and whispered into the beast's ear, "If you ever do that again, I'll cut your throat and leave you as carrion for the rat vultures." Straightening his jacket and feeling somewhat redeemed with himself, Two-teeth – much more cautiously this time – carefully mounted his rammel. Yuni witnessed the entire episode but said nothing.

"Come on comrades, we need to get going," Vaurienne called.

Riding at night was much cooler than trying to make it through the intense, searing Donja heat with two high suns. But make no mistake, nighttime was still hot. The dark green sand absorbed heat during the day and radiated it back all night. Traveling at night was easy for rammels due to their natural navigational abilities. Even though tonight was a double-dark, and it was hard to see, the rammels navigated their way with ease. In contrast to the dense darkness on the ground, the stars in the sky seemed exceptionally bright. Vaurienne looked up and marveled at the uncountable number of twinkling stars against the blackened night sky. She sighed. Another day and night before they would arrive at Hamada Castle. Gruun would be pleased at the order she had gotten.

They continued on past daylight. Around mid-day on the second day, they stopped to camp again. They were Jaders; they were used to the desert. But the past couple of days had been particularly hot – and they had only one night to rest at the Gold Oko. It was a good thing they had brought plenty of water.

They camped the second day. When they awoke from their siestas, they ate some of the food they had left. None was especially hungry. The Donja did that to you. But they did drink plenty of water. Vaurienne drained her flask. But she wasn't worried, because she knew she had another, larger one filled for the rest of the trip. They packed up and started on another night leg of their journey.

The wind began to stir just after dawn the next morning. Even though the suns were out, the sky turned darker. They all knew a storm was coming. They had traveled light with little protection as this was not yet storm season. But, storm season or not, the breezes surely meant one was coming. They would have to make the best of it. Dust devils popped up here and there throughout the morning and swooped briefly along the dunes before dissipating. The swirly, little green vortexes were almost cute, but Gala knew they were harbingers of something much more ominous. The vortexes started to get more common in the heat of midday. The three comrades stopped to camp but it wasn't much use. So much green sand was blowing that they couldn't get any rest in their flimsy tents. And the storm was getting worse. Vaurienne knew what they had to do.

"Two-teeth, Yuni!" she called out. "Get up. We have to keep going. If we stay here, we're likely to get buried. Our only choice is to keep moving," she said.

Two-teeth was frustrated, but Yuni knew Vaurienne was making the right call. "You know she's right," Yuni said to Two-teeth.

"Yeah, but I don't like it."

The wind was whipping the dark, green sand around more fiercely now. They had to put additional coverings over their faces. They were all more than thankful for their eye-guards.

Before they got going again with their rammels, each took a drink of water. Except Vaurienne; when she went to the other side of Artax's saddle, her second water-flask was missing. She looked in the pouch in her saddle bag where it was supposed to be. But the pocket was swaying back and forth in the swirling winds, empty. She looked in another pouch. Nothing. She instinctively looked around on the ground. "Vamp," she said to herself. *The wind must have wrenched it free somehow*, she thought. The gusts were starting to howl louder now. Yuni and Two-teeth had already started out. She looked around on the ground, but saw nothing. "Hey, guys!" Vaurienne yelled. "Can I get a drink?" It was difficult to hear with the wind blowing harder than ever. Both Two-teeth and Yuni heard their comrade but glanced at one another and pretended they did not while they continued trudging forward into the sandstorm.

"Ugh," Vaurienne said to herself and she climbed up on Artax. She patted him on the neck. "Let's catch up to the others, Artax," she said. At least he heard her.

The storm continued to get worse. It was almost impossible to see anything – except for the occasional sunlight peeking through so that they at least thought they were going in the right direction. But the rammels knew where they were going. The creatures had a sort of homing sense about them. As natural-born desert creatures, their species had developed that innate navigational ability thanks to evolution and Levon's special gravity properties. Vaurienne trusted Artax to get her home – way more than she trusted either of her comrades. She leaned close and put her arms around his neck – at least as far as her little arms would go around that massive neck – and held on tightly.

The rammels plodded slowly, purposefully on through the afternoon and night. The riders fell asleep and would surely have fallen from their saddles if they hadn't been strapped in. When the suns were high in the sky, the rammels stopped as they were used to doing at that time of day. Vaurienne was the first to awake.

"Better get down guys," she said hoarsely. "Yuni, Two-teeth – we need to get under our tents." All of their faces were covered in green sand. That damn green sand was everywhere. It got underneath their clothes. It got into their shoes. It got impacted into their skin – even though they were shielded with protective clothing.

But now, the suns were bright and the sky was clear. They had to get shelter. Two-teeth and Yuni drank from their water flasks.

"Hey guys, mind if I have a drink?" Vaurienne asked.

"Sorry, we're all out," Yuni said, casting her eyes away.

"What?" Vaurienne asked?

"I guess we must have drank more than usual because of the storm."

"Yeah," said Two-teeth. He quickly put his second flask back in the saddle and picked up his first flask (now empty). He uncapped it and held it upside down to show Vaurienne – a single drop fell to the ground.

"No!" Vaurienne said.

"Oh, well, it can't be helped now," said Two-teeth. "We'll be home tomorrow. Just have to tough it out. We are Jaders, after all." Yuni half-smiled at Two-teeth as she walked by.

They crawled into their tents. Vaurienne's lips were parched and cracking; she touched them with her fingers. She collapsed to sleep.

Vaurienne was not the first one up after this day's nap. Her comrades awoke earlier and drank their fill. A few minutes later, Yuni kicked Vaurienne in the foot, but Vaurienne did not respond. So Yuni kicked her in the other foot. "Hey, spare, it's time to get moving. The suns are down. We need to leave. We can make it back to the castle tomorrow."

Vaurienne rolled over. She was dehydrated and beginning to cramp up. Somehow, for people without water, Yuni and Two-teeth didn't look nearly as bad as she felt. But she knew she needed water. "Guys, I really need water. Don't you have any left?"

"Sorry, we're all out," said Two-teeth. "You really should have brought extra." Vaurienne glared at him over her dry, cracked lips.

"Ummm, you do have a rammel," Yuni said. "You know, the desert angels, givers of life? Ring any bells?"

"I don't want to take water from Artax," Vaurienne replied flatly.

"That's what it's there for. He's got two mammoth ram horns. One of them could fill your flask several times over. Besides, we'll be home tomorrow," Yuni said. "He won't even notice; go ahead. You need to do this."

Vaurienne took a step and cramps seized her leg, dropping her to the ground. She hacked out several coughs. She didn't like the idea of taking water from her friend; she didn't even want to consider it as an option, but deep down, she knew Yuni was right. She struggled to her feet and got a short, hard, hollow, red tube from her pack. She walked around to the front of Artax. "Hey, boy," she said as she petted the side of his face. "I'm in a bad way. I really need some water. Do you think you could share some with me?" she asked, not knowing what kind of response she even expected. Artax swiped that huge tongue across her face. Then he stepped back and turned his head to the side, exposing the soft, pink place behind one of his big horns for Vaurienne. He was offering himself to her.

She carefully rubbed his neck and tried to put the tube in as gently as she could. It wouldn't go in. She tried pushing harder, but still no luck. "You have to jam it in, hard," Two-teeth said.

"I don't want to hurt him," Vaurienne replied.

"Well, we don't have all day. And we're all running out of water, so get on with it," Two-teeth replied. "Or don't; it'll just be your funeral."

"No major loss," Yuni said, only loud enough for Two-teeth to hear. He smiled his uncomfortable smile.

A tear rolled down Vaurienne's face. She pulled the tube back and jammed it into the back of Artax's horn – hard. She winced, but Artax was fine. Vaurienne put her mouth to the tube and drank. It was the best water she had ever tasted. It had a hint of sweetness and was oddly cool, even in the middle of the Donja heat. She drank some more. Then she filled her flask (halfway). She hugged Artax and rubbed the area where she had plunged the tube. It seemed to close up quickly enough. "Thank you, old friend. You're the best."

"Can we go now?" Yuni asked, already on her rammel.

Two-teeth climbed his rammel and said, "Come on Vaurienne." Vaurienne went to roll up her tent.

Maybe she saw something out of the corner of her eye...a shadow? She was focusing on her tent and it just didn't register at first. It was getting dark, so maybe that's why she didn't see it clearly. But when she turned around and took a step – there it was. Staring into her eyes, a camo mamba. This one must have been 10 feet long. Vaurienne froze. The snake was too close for her to get away. It rose up and looked her directly in the eye.

Yuni and Two-teeth stopped to watch, but didn't move to help. Vaurienne stepped gingerly to the left. The mamba followed her move. This was not a good sign. It had zeroed in on her and clearly wanted to engage. For someone as small as Vaurienne, the poison from a mamba that size would likely kill in seconds. The snake slithered closer. It rose higher and its head started swaying back and forth, indicating a strike was forthcoming. There was nothing she could do. The serpent could strike more quickly than she could get to her knives – especially as she happened to be holding a tent at that moment. But what else could she do? She had to risk it; she took a deep breath.

As she threw the tent at the snake and went for her cuttas, the snake dodged and reared back to strike. The mamba was faster than Vaurienne. She was going to lose this skirmish. Just then, a huge rammel foot stamped down on the mamba's head with a small puff of green dust. And then another huge rammel foot stomped on the other end. The snake was stretched end-to-end between Artax's huge hooves. Vaurienne went for her knives and made two quick cuts slicing that snake into three pieces – all with her eyes closed! The pieces of the reptile twitched in the sand. Artax squished the head deeper into the sand. He had saved her twice in the span of a few minutes. She hugged him again. "Artax, you are my savior." Then pulled his head down and kissed him on the forehead.

She took another deep breath, put her knives away, and climbed onto Artax. Two-teeth and Yuni were still looking at the scene they had just witnessed with their jaws dropped. "What, have you never seen a rammel and a messenger get the best of a camo mamba?" she said to her comrades. Vaurienne climbed on top of Artax and leaned over to whisper in his ear. "Thanks again, old friend." And off the team went with Vaurienne and Artax leading the way.

The next morning, they saw Glastalica and, in the distance, the walls surrounding Hamada Castle looming on the horizon. The castle towers were silhouetted against the two rising suns. Guards patrolled along the tops of the walls. Vaurienne and Artax were trailing behind the others.

STORYTRAX: *All Along the Watchtower* - Jimi Hendrix

ACT II ~ HOMESTEAD

CHAPTER 4

Opening Night

Twelve years earlier...on the continent of Botan.

The Clemens home at RB#4, Farmgrid 11 was rather unremarkable. The rural farmhouse had certainly seen better days. It looked as if the original paint color was yellow but that had faded and was now (mostly) covered over with a kind of whitewash. There was some grass but there were also more than a few bare patches of ground. Regardless of the mild shabbiness of the surroundings, there was love on the inside. Even though it was not obvious in the slightest, the beginnings of something remarkable were brewing in that very home.

****

Filled with the excitement of opening night, ten-year-old Ruby took the stage and introduced herself to a rapt, motionless audience.

"Good afternoon ladies and gentlemen. My name is Ruby G. Clemens and I will be your master of ceremonies this evening," she announced with a deep bow.

The audience, seated in mismatched chairs and on pillows, did not move a single muscle. Teddy, Dolly, Flopsy, Missy Lou, the Queen, Bubbles, Patch, Buddy, Furbie, and her brother's green tractor, plus a stuffed version of a bullparr that she called Bard (her favorite) were seated in a semi-circle encompassing Ruby's 'stage' (aka her bed).

Upon her right hand sat a noble knight; upon her left sat a fair maiden with golden hair.

"Sir Stephen of Kendrall, please meet Gwendolyn the Fair." Ruby helped the knight bow before the maiden; Gwendolyn (also aided by Ruby) responded with a curtsy.

Ruby reached high into the air with Gwendolyn, "Oh, save me kind sir knight; save me please! I have been imprisoned in this tall tower for more than a year. I miss my family. I am very sad. Can you help me?"

"What foul villain has plucked you from freedom and locked you away in such a barren, dank, and lonely place?" asked Sir Stephen of Kendrall. "It must be one with a soul as cold as ice."

"It was the evil Prince Trajan who kidnapped me and who has hidden me here. I am at your mercy," she said from high atop Ruby's hand.

"Fear not fair Gwendolyn, I will come to your rescue with my trusty sword and reliable rope!"

"You are my hero!" swooned Gwendolyn.

Sir Stephen grabbed his reliable rope (a skein of pink yarn) and tossed it up to Gwendolyn the Fair who caught it in her mouth and grasped the rope (Ruby quickly tied it to the top of her bedpost). Ruby sent Gwendolyn sliding zipline style down the rope to Sir Stephen.

The two kissed a puppet kiss and embraced (as much as their unbendable elbows would allow).

"The End," Ruby announced to her audience. Sir Stephen bowed deeply to Gwendolyn and then to Ruby. Gwendolyn bowed deeply to Sir Stephen and to Ruby. In turn, Ruby bowed deeply to each of her handheld pair. Finally, all three bowed to their audience and basked in the glow of imagined appreciation (and faintly audible cheers?) from their stuffed admirers.

"Ruby!" called her mother. "Why don't you go outside and play with your friends? They're asking for you!"

Ruby tossed Sir Stephen of Kendrall and Gwendolyn the Fair onto her bed. She climbed down from the stage and hopped to her bedroom door where she grabbed her left leg (which was plugged in to charge) and put it on. As she fit the leg into place, she punched a quick code on translucent buttons underneath the skin. The lighted buttons grew brighter for a moment then faded into the artificial skin.

Her electronic leg seemed to melt into her own skin. Ruby sprang to her feet and began to run out the door. Catching the door frame with her hand, she leaned forward and then pulled herself back. She walked resolutely to her bed and set Sir Stephen of Kendrall and Gwendolyn the Fair upright together. "Please forgive my haste and sudden departure," she apologized with another deep bow. "I must beg your leave. Until we meet again."

She continued bowing as an additional measure of respect while backing out the door. Then she turned and ran down the hall. Ruby was a precocious child with flashes of wisdom beyond her years. But sometimes, like all children, she just wanted to play with her friends.

CHAPTER 5

Kickball

In their rural environment, there weren't many children close by, so Ruby played with her brother and the same group of friends all the time. Ruby headed toward her brother, Baron, and those same six friends who were already playing kickball in the field by the pond.

"Come be on my team!" urged her friend Mae-Ellen. Ruby joined her out in the field. Soon eight children were playing, laughing, and screaming – as children do when they are filled with delight and having fun unburdened by cares of the world.

The score was tied; one each for Baron's team and Ruby's team. It was Ruby's turn to kick. She nonchalantly leaned over and scratched her leg as she got into position. The ball began rolling toward her; she eyed it steadily, watching it roll closer. Slow and smooth – her favorite pitch. *Wait for it...Wait...Patience...Just a bit more...Not yet...* she thought as she waited for the ball to come ever so close. "Now!" with a quick hop and one giant step, Ruby swung back and threw all of her tiny frame into the effort to kick the ball as hard as she possibly could – with an accompanying grunt for good measure.

The ball traveled upward and out across the field. It continued its angled, skyward trajectory. Almost in slow motion, the ball rose higher and higher as it started a long – and ever-lengthening trail – that extended past the orchard of blue ice cream bananas and on further still until it was out of sight. Ruby smiled a smug, little pirate smile and began trotting around the bases with her curly red hair bouncing in the late afternoon sunlight as she ran. Mae-Ellen cheered wildly.

"Hey!" yelled her brother Baron, "That's not fair. You cranked your leg up again!"

"Oh, did I? (She glanced over her shoulder at him as she rounded third base.) Sorry," replied Ruby with a broad, toothy grin framed by her shocking blue lips, as she turned back toward her brother on the pitcher's mound. She jumped on home plate and into the waiting arms of her teammates.

"We win! We win! We win!" they chanted. (*There goes another ball*, thought Baron as he shook his head and cracked a smile.)

The other team ran to home plate to join the fun. They ran and chased each other around; they laughed and began spinning around in circles – faster, faster – until they all fell into an exhausted heap on the soft green grass. Out of breath, sprawled out next to each other, they lay still and breathed deeply…catching their breath and staring up at the clouds.

The warm suns were just beginning to set. The long, darkening shadows were a stark contrast to the gentle, yellow rays of the suns. Ruby spoke up, "I see a pony in the clouds. I wonder where he's going." She was a highly observant child.

"Where who is going?" sighed Baron. (This wasn't his first rodeo.)

"The lost boy and his pony, obviously," responded Ruby flatly.

"I don't see the pony. Where is it?" asked her friend Marta.

Ruby pointed toward the setting suns, "Look there, Marta, near the Alpha Sun. Do you see it?"

"Oh, yes! I love ponies!" replied Marta.

"Look just a little farther over and you can see a gingerbread house. I bet they're lost and hungry."

"How do you always see such things?" asked Ho.

"Oh, I see much more than that." Ruby added. "I think that the boy became lost looking for his pony. Now that they've found each other, they don't know the way home. They're both lost – and hungry. Perhaps they will eat a little of the gingerbread house. But, of course, you know what that could mean – especially if an old witch lives there."

The evening shadows grew longer as the suns dipped lower in the sky. Baron looked toward the orchard – he knew something interesting that was attracted to blue ice cream bananas on hot summer evenings. He got up and walked away while the others squinted trying to see shapes in the clouds as the light slowly waned. Baron crouched down a few feet away – at the edge of the orchard – and then jumped up. He came running back with a dragon-flier he held by one leg. The insect let out a tiny puff of red and yellow flame.

The other children turned their attention from the disappearing clouds that were now almost impossible to see. Then they focused their attention on Baron and his dragon-flier. They oohed and aahed at the way he handled the tiny, fiery beast. It was as if he were a wild animal tamer. Another puff of flame. More oohs. More fire. More aahs. Baron held the flier high – it shot out a long flame (for such a small insect). The children applauded. He held it low and spun around while the insect projected more red fire. The light of day was all but gone and the fire-breather, under Baron's control, was making a mini-flame show in the twilight. Puff, puff.

Baron began to show off. He whirled around again as a thin trail of flame flowed from the dragon-flier encircling his head. Then Baron whipped the flier under his out-stretched leg trailing more fire.

"Ooowwwwww!" Baron shrieked. "Vamp!"

The dragon-flier flapped quickly away – through a few smoke rings – into the night air with nary a glance back toward his former captor. Baron was left holding his leg which now had a small scratch – not too deep, but evidently somewhat painful. Blood trickled down to his ankle.

"Eewwwwwww," several of the children cried.

Ruby turned away. She could not stand the sight of blood.

"Are you okay?" Ho asked.

Baron took a deep breath and grimaced as he grunted, "No problem," not wanting to let on as to his obvious pain.

"It's your own fault," Mae-Ellen said to him. "You know dragon-fliers will strike with their sharp tails if you hold them too long."

"Yeah, I know," said Baron. "I was just having fun; I thought I had another minute or two before it got angry. I'll be okay. Look, the bleeding's stopped already."

Ruby wouldn't look at her brother; she couldn't forgive him for getting cut and making her see it. (Not yet anyway.) She started walking away.

"Rubes," he said. "I'm fine. See, it's no big deal. Just a scratch."

"You know I can't see blood. I'm afraid it'll make me pass out. My stomach will get all twisty-turny, and I'll be really embarrassed in front of my friends. Besides," she lowered her voice, "if I pass out, my leg will re-set and then I'll be even more embarrassed." She looked up at her big brother with tears welling up in her eyes. She turned away again. "Why did you do that," she asked her brother facing away.

"Sometimes, you just gotta let go and dance Rubes!"

She turned and stared at him. Ruby seemed to be on the verge of forgiving her brother...

"Ruby, Baron! It's time to go!" called their mother.

STORYTRAX: *My Ruby Blue* (Inspired by *My Baby Blue* - Badfinger)

Dance the Night Away - Van Halen

CHAPTER 6

Going to the Storyteller

"But I don't want to hear the Storyteller!" Ruby complained.

Ruby's mother turned toward the freckle-faced 10-year-old (four years younger than her brother). "Honey, we've discussed this. It is the duty – and the privilege – of every 10-year-old to hear the story of Runyon Falls from the Storyteller himself. Baron heard the stories. I did, too; so did your father. Our parents heard the Storyteller, and so did their parents."

"Mom, I shouldn't have to do everything just because someone did it a thousand years ago. You're the one who told me that we shouldn't do something just because everyone else does."

"If all my friends jumped off the top of Runyon Falls, would I?" she added mockingly, "Of course not."

Her mother chuckled, "You're absolutely right. All the same, you *are* going to hear the Storyteller," mother said with a tone of finality.

Father walked up and handed the kids their screens. "I just finished with the security upgrades," he said.

Ruby took her screen and pivoted back toward her mother. Not one to give in easily, she continued in her attempts to avoid the Storyteller. Because logic didn't work, she tried for the emotional angle. "The truth is, I-I'm kind of afraid. I've heard that the Storyteller is very big and that he – he – he–" she looks up at the sky thinking intently – "… he *eats* children. Sometimes he even… burns them alive in his storyfire."

"That's only happened once, when a particular little girl wouldn't pay attention," Ruby's father chimed in.

Ruby looked worried for a moment, then her father and mother burst into laughter.

"That's not funny," she frowned.

"Ruby, it is the duty – and the privilege – of every 10-year-old to hear the story of—" her father began.

"of Runyon Falls from the Storyteller himself," Ruby mockingly finished, bobbing her head. She knew that line by heart. In the past year, she must have heard it at least a million times – and four years earlier when she heard it said to her brother as many times or more.

"Exactly," her mother said. "Besides, the Storyteller has a way about him. He actually makes you feel as though you are there – inside the story. I even remember feeling—"

"Dear!" Ruby's father interjected as he looked at her with a knowing smile.

"Oh, yes," Ruby's mother replied, smiling back at him.

Baron wouldn't be joining them. He went to hear the Storyteller four years ago.

Ruby, her mother, and her father piled into their yellow anti-grav transport. Ruby stared out the window as the trees and clouds whizzed by. "Did you know that Runyon Falls is known all over Levon for its healing waters?" Father asked. "Uh-huh," said Ruby, distracted.

After a time drifting through the sky, Ruby's mother looked into the back seat. "Ruby, aren't you excited? It's the duty – and the privilege – of every 10-year-old to hear the story of—"

Ruby takes over again, softly "...to hear the story of Runyon Falls from the Storyteller him—"

"Look, we're heeeeeere!" Ruby's father shouted.

Ruby looked down as they approached the edge of the greenstalk forest. It was very dark and the sky was full of stars. Ruby observed a yellow-orange glow emanating from behind the thick wall of greenstalks. They swooped by Runyon Falls and glided over a roaring fire to a hidden parkbay.

CHAPTER 7

The Story of Runyon Falls Begins

The sound of gently whirring motors dissipated into nothingness as vehicles lit with underglow floated gently down…pausing there, suspended inches from the ground. Parents hurried children out of their anti-grav travelers (aka 'floaters'), hopping out gull-wing doors and dropping to the ground. They headed up the hill and toward the trail into the woods, finally traipsing down the worn path to the fire circle.

Another girl stared at Ruby. "What's wrong with your lips?" she asked.

"Nothing's wrong. That's just the way they are," Ruby replied with a smile.

"She might be sick," the girl's mother said as she pulled her daughter back. "Probably best just to keep your distance from that one."

A boy walked by and stared at Ruby. He pointed at Ruby and snickered to his friends. "I think she must be drinking paint," one said. Another chimed in "Or that's the worst lipstick ever in the history of the world!" They laughed and ran down the path.

"Don't pay any attention to them," Ruby's mom said to her. "Your lips are perfect – and they're beautiful."

As they approached the bottom of the hill and began to climb upward toward the storyfire, Ruby's leg began to feel heavy. Each step was more difficult than the one before. Her leg began to feel heavier and more unresponsive. Her pace slowed considerably as she lagged behind her parents. "Hey guys, something's wrong with my leg," she said.

Her parents looked at each other sadly. "I thought you told her," said her father to her mother.

"I didn't want to. I thought we agreed you were going to tell her," her mother replied. "I thought there might be a chance...But, I guess we avoided that conversation a little too long."

"Guys, we've got a problem. My leg is dead. I thought it had a pretty good charge, but it seems like the battery is totally done. Oh well, I guess we'll have to go home," Ruby suggested.

"Actually, it's not really a problem," her father said. "We should have told you before –"

"We meant to," her mother interjected.

"Most electronics don't work in this place, sweetie," her father explained.

"Okaaaayyyy," Ruby said. "That's kind of an important thing to leave out for me, you know?"

"We're sorry Rubes," her mother said.

"I can carry you," her father added.

"Dad, I'm ten years old. I really don't think –"

But her father scooped Ruby up and sat her on his hip. They disconnected her leg – leaned it against a huge, towering Friend tree (with its huge outstretched 'arms' reaching around) – and trudged up the hill. Ruby started to complain but they were already on their way, and she surmised that her complaints probably wouldn't have been very effective anyway. Besides – even though she wouldn't admit it to her parents – she was actually getting a bit curious.

Everyone made their way toward the huge, blazing fire and took a seat in a semi-circle. The Storyteller was waiting there; he was almost glowing in his long white beard and flowing robes, lit by the alternating shadow and light of the dancing flames. The huge waterfall behind him magnificently contrasted against the backdrop of a million stars. Though some distance away, the roar of the falls could be clearly heard….and their powerful rumble, felt.

Most of the children were eager for their first visit to the Storyteller. Their eyes were wide with wonder; some giggled with delight; a few appeared frightened. Ruby's father let her slide from his hip and set her down. Ruby looked up at him as if to say *Don't leave me.* Her father patted her on the head and said, "Everything will be just fine," as he stepped back with the line of parents. Twenty-one children were settled around the fire. There were hugs and kisses and a few more pats on a few more little heads....then the parents quietly slipped away. The children looked anxiously around at each other, waiting...

The old man began to get somehow brighter. It was curious that the children hadn't noticed him so much before. He started to give off as much light as the fire. He had been floating close to the ground earlier, but now he had risen up until he was hovering high above the flames – which lit him from underneath in an eerie glow. He then looked down at the children seated in their half circle. "I am the Storyteller," the old man told the children gathered by the roaring, crackling fire. As he spoke, he seemed to be having a conversation with each child individually. "Listen closely and you will hear the story of Runyon Falls."

There was a loud popping crack from the flames. One of the children gasped loudly! The Storyteller glared at the small girl. He floated in her direction, leaned toward her, and his harsh gaze slowly softened. "Hush, child. It is only my storyfire. It won't hurt you." The girl looked up – her eyes wide. "Everything is fine. You are happy. You will be quiet and listen." She smiled and became entranced by his words as they pulled her in and settled her mind.

The Storyteller's voice was booming, and strikingly clear, despite the sizzling of the flames and the dim, persistent rumbling of the falls. He spoke with a mystical rhythm; his voice danced with enchantment – as if it could take a child on a journey simply by the power of its cadence and melody.

The Storyteller closed his eyes and took a deep breath. He paused for a moment, as if he were praying. Then he began:

"The village of Tansin was once a pleasant and peaceful farming community. The center of the town had two general stores, a blacksmith, a stable, a small hotel, several shops, and a post office, along with a few dozen rows of houses. Scores of farms spread out from the center and surrounded the hamlet. It was a wonderful place to live. Children, especially, loved the wide open spaces where they could run and play.

"Tansin had stood as the dividing line between the empires of Zakar and Geisl for more than a thousand years. It had become a safe zone where citizens of both countries could enter and not face the threat of death from the terrible conflict between the two giant kingdoms. Many came there to trade. There hadn't been an attack inside the walls of Tansin for almost six hundred years. This was because the former ruler of Tansin, Runyon, had negotiated a truce between the ruling families of Zakar and Geisl. Runyon was a gentle, but persuasive leader who believed in peace. Though there was peace, it was uneasy at best. Tensions remained high. Attacks were not uncommon, but at least they occurred outside of Tansin.

"As the reputation of Tansin as a place of peace grew, merchants and others made their way there to trade. As long as the peace lasted, Tansin flourished. And the peace had lasted for more than six hundred years.

CHAPTER 8

The Tale of the Sherable

Despite lying between two vast powers – or maybe because of that – and perhaps, also owing to its long history of peace, tiny Tansin had no army of its own. The town circle thought that having no army actually made Tansin safer. Generally, it was thought that no one would attack because everyone valued peace – at least enough to have a safe place to trade. Further, if it became absolutely necessary, the town could potentially ally with one (but never both) of the powerful countries on its borders.

Of course, Tansin did have its own Sherable to keep the peace and address disorderly conduct. Sherable Josiah was more than up to the task. At more than six feet and a half feet in height, his ripped, muscular physique made him an imposing figure indeed.

The sign on the door read 'Sherable Josiah Edmund.'

"Sherable, come quickly!" shouted Moravia, as she burst through his door. "They're at it again!"

"The Miller twins?" inquired Sherable Josiah with a chuckle.

"Yes," huffed the girl with the long, black hair and brightly colored dress. The Miller twins had been 15 years of nothing but trouble.

Sherable Josiah grabbed his hat and looked toward his weapon wall. Eschewing the crossbow and the mace, he grabbed his sword, a dagger, and a rope. Hopping toward the door, he slipped the dagger into his boot. Outside, he rounded the corner to see the Miller twins taunting a young girl in the middle of the street. The twins had enormous heads, hands, and feet relative to the size of their bodies. Twice her size, they were shoving the poor lass back and forth like a rag doll.

Josiah walked up and the boys stopped pushing the girl. "You ain't got no business here Sherable," barked Colin Miller.

"Hmmmmpphh! It appears to me that you're disturbing the peace and harassing this young lady," retorted the Sherable.

"We got rights too," piped up Jared Miller. "She smiled at both of us. And she won't tell us which one she was really looking at."

"Back away from the girl. Leave her alone and move along."

"We just want to know which one of us she was smiling at!"

"Just get along, now."

"I wasn't smiling at either of those beasts," the girl said.

Colin drew his small sword and attempted to flash it menacingly at Josiah. Although it was a sort of a real sword, the scene appeared almost comical as Colin swished his pint-sized weapon through the air.

"I wish you hadn't done that," said Sherable Josiah. He started to draw his own, huge sword, then – noticing the crowd – thought better of that approach. Instead, he decided to make a lasso out of his rope and then he approached the twins."

"Oh, looky! He's going to tie us up 'cause we've been bad," mocked Colin.

"Not if we cut that rope of his with our steel," offered Jared, as he unsheathed his own miniature blade. Those twins were bad news. It could have been a tense moment, but Josiah knew how to handle such moments. He was a natural at it.

Swinging the rope above his head, Sherable Josiah moved toward the twins. As he drew near, he stopped suddenly and let the lasso fall to the ground, immediately looking straight up behind the twins with his mouth gaping wide open. Everyone else looked up into the sky in the same direction, including the twins (of course).

Josiah seized the moment and quickly grabbed the rope. He swung it behind his back and lassoed the twins. Then the sherable jerked them to the ground, causing them to lose their grips on their 'sword-lets.' The crowd roared with laughter! "You'd think they might wise up sometime," muttered Josiah as he turned and threw the rope over his shoulder. He began dragging the twins down the dirt street to jail when their mother, Mrs. Miller, showed up with several boxes, carried behind her by a helper.

"What have they done now, Sherable?"

"They were taunting that young lady over there. And then they had the nerve to draw swords on me. They'll have to spend a night in the scooper."

"Oh, Sherable Josiah," Mrs. Miller pleaded. "You know what's right. You always protect our townsfolk. But isn't there a sinta we can find? Some way around this problem?"

"No problem." Josiah continued walking past her – with the twins whining in tow – toward the scooper. He knew Mrs. Miller could be very persuasive and he didn't want to stand around and talk to her.

But she followed the sherble and her boys down the street. As he drug them up to the threshold, Mrs. Miller moved in. "Dear sherable, I know my boys have been bad, but I promise, if you release them into my custody, I will make sure they are punished."

"And they'll promise never to do it again," she added. "Right boys?"

"We promise! We Promise!" they squealed in two whiny voices.

"Mrs. Miller, the answer is no. There is no sinta here. They acted improperly and they must be punished."

"Sherable, as I said, I will punish them. You have my word. What can I do to convince you?" she said slyly, stepping toward him with a wry smile.

"Nothing. Now please move along." He knew she was up to something; he just didn't know what.

"Josiah, I know that you're doing your job – and doing it very well," she said as she pulled a box from her pile. "I just happen to have made some fresh clord pies that I'm taking to market," she said enticingly as she was fully aware of his weakness for clord pies. I'd be happy to give you one if you could see your way clear to letting me handle their discipline.

"No. The answer is no. I've told you…. Wait, did you say 'fresh' clords?"

"Yes, I picked them myself, early this morning – you know that's when they have their peak flavor." She knew his weakness and exploited it again as she had many times before.

Most of the crowd had dispersed, but the few that remained began to shake their heads and turn away. Everyone else knew Josiah's weakness too.

"That's not fair. You know they should go to jail," he tried to resist. She opened one box and the warm aroma began to melt Josiah's will as it almost visibly wafted about his head.

(Not only could the children around the storyfire "see" the aroma of warm clord pies, they could actually smell those pies! They licked their lips and some even rubbed their tummies. More than one mouth watered.)

Josiah waivered; his face softened; his knees began to wobble. He looked from the pie to the twins tied up at his feet and back to the pies. He stared longingly at the pie – took a deep whiff – then looked back at the twins again. He was clearly on the ropes.

Sensing the timing was right, she pounced "You're such a big strong man, you probably need *two* pies," she said shrewdly as she pulled another from her stack. Josiah looked at the pies; his stomach rumbled loudly as he clutched at them.

"Well, okay," he said. "But you better not let me see them in town for a month." The twins, still tangled in rope, grinned at one another and tried to stand.

At that moment, Josiah yanked his rope off the twins and they fell to the ground again. He grabbed the pies and walked inside – slamming the door behind him with his foot. Mrs. Miller grabbed each twin by an ear and began to drag them away while screeching to them about the trouble they were in.

"But what about Runyon?" Ruby blurted out. "I thought you were supposed to tell us about Runyon Falls!"

The Storyteller spun in her direction with his robes trailing behind him, blowing in the heat rising up from the storyfire, and stared down at the child ominously. "It is forbidden to interrupt the Storyteller," he boomed – his words echoing off the greenstalks. The eyes of all the other children were as wide as saucers. Floating silently, pausing for emphasis, he said over his shoulder with half a smile, "But I shall let the infraction pass... this time."

"Yes, what about Runyon Falls..." he mused. "There is, of course, much more to be told." He leaned toward his audience – his face seemingly even larger and glowing brighter than before – and gazed into the eyes of each of his diminutive audience members. He took a deep breath as he pulled back a bit, then slowly exhaled.

"But, that is all for tonight," he added in a somewhat softer tone. The Storyteller looked weaker. His glow had begun to diminish. He was even floating lower now – closer to the ground.

"We will continue the story next time." He turned and began gliding away, disappearing along the dense greenstalk trunks.

The only sound now was the crackling fire burning low. A few embers floated skyward... The parents arrived and quietly collected their sleepy children.

CHAPTER 9

High Pitch

One week later.

One of Ruby's eyes opened slowly. Lying in bed on her side with red hair fluffier than her pillow, that one green eye peeked through a bevy of curls. She gazed at the rising suns outside her window. They shone warm and wonderful on her face, exaggerating her bright blue lips. She smiled. That one eye closed as she drifted back to slumberland.

Bam, bam, bam! Baron pounded on her door. "Come on, let's go play softball!"

She groaned softly, not wanting to move from her comfy sanctuary of warm bedclothes.

"You can pitch today!" Baron called. Both of her eyes flew open ALL THE WAY! She sat bolt upright, brushed back her hair and rubbed the sleep from her eyes. (Sir Stephen of Kendrall fell to the floor.) Her hands stretched her cheeks and then let go to reveal a huge smile, just before a whole bunch of hair fell right down across her face again.

Ruby hopped off the bed and across the floor. She grabbed her leg from the charging station and touched the translucent buttons, only glancing for a second to see the artificial skin dissolve into her own. She began to run out the door but screeched to a halt – and then ran back to grab her over-sized glove and ball cap. She stood in front of the mirror and pulled her hair back, trying to make that cap fit snugly over her curly red locks. (As if it could possibly fit onto her head any other way BUT snugly.) It never did seem to fit as well as her brother's. She always thought his hat looked way cool. Oh well, close enough!

She ran toward the field where her brother and friends were all waiting. Baron picked up the bat that Father had made for them and handed it to Mae-Ellen.

Ruby's smile shone through those bright blue lips. She walked sprightly to the edge of the field.

Ho tossed her the ball.

"Go on," urged Baron. "It's your turn to be the pitcher."

Ruby was thrilled that it was finally her turn to pitch again. Forgetting all about the previous incidents of overshooting, she strutted to the pitcher's mound and glanced around – basking in the limelight. After all, pitcher was the most important position on the team. Everyone knew that.

She began her wind-up – big, looping swings of her arm ending in an underhand release that virtually blasted from her hand. Mae-Ellen stood ready...watching the ball as it approached the plate – and then just watched it sail by – at least six feet over her head. Ho was behind her as catcher. It went over his head, too. He tried to jump up – and even stretched his glove as high as his arm could go, but it was no use.

Ruby had been working so hard to slow down her pitch and get it under control. But it *always* seemed to go high – usually really high. Ugh.

"Still going high, huh?" Mae-Ellen commented.

Ho went to get the ball. "Give it another shot," he suggested.

Ruby was ambidextrous, so she decided to try her other hand this time. She wound up and pitched once more. Again the ball sailed far over her intended target.

She tried yet again. Same result.

"Maybe if you try a little more softly," Baron recommended. She knew he was right. But she didn't want to pitch too softly because then everyone would hit the ball every time. Ugh. But they couldn't play at all if the ball always flew over everyone's heads. So Ruby pitched softly. The ball went right over the plate – and Mae-Ellen cracked it! The rest of the game went that way. Every one of Ruby's pitches was slow and every one of the opposing players walloped those pitches.

At the bottom of the last inning, Baron was up to bat. Ruby did not want him to crush the pitch, so she wound up good and fast and unleashed a rocket in his direction! It sailed *eight* feet over his head. Ho went to retrieve the ball.

"You can do it," he said. "Just focus."

Ruby doubled down. She took a deep breath and began her wind-up – a bit slower this time....more deliberate. As she sped up her windmill, she released the underhand pitch with power and grace. It began lower this time, but then rose and rose and rose to fly almost *ten* feet over Baron's head. Ho went to retrieve the ball. Frustrated, Ruby's last pitch was slow and utterly mashable. Predictably, Baron knocked it 'out of the park' for a home run. (Out of the park was past the edge of the big oak tree.) Trotting around the bases, he smiled at his little sister, "Maybe next time kiddo."

She smiled back at her brother. "Nice hit big brother. And you did it without electronic supplementation!"

"You can get those pitches down, Rubes," said Baron. "Just keep practicing. Why don't you try throwing at the wall outside of father's workshop?"

"Ruuuuuby, Baaaaaaron! It's time to go to town!" called their mother.

'Town' was a generous term for their little hamlet. It was small indeed; one main street lined with a few buildings on either side (probably smaller than Tansin). They were hours away – past the ternium mines – from the main capital city of Wedding-Shi.

"Are we taking the floater?" Ruby asked?

"How's your leg – got a good charge?" asked her mom.

Ruby pulled lifted her shorts and tapped her thigh twice. A watercolor red light appeared – looking something like a tattoo on her leg. It read '81%.' "Yeah, I'm good. I could go for hours," she said. The red numbers faded away.

"Good, it's a great day for a walk," her mother said.

They walked down the dirt road talking and laughing. Ruby's crazy hair bounced all over the place and her brother's cool cap almost flew off in the wind, so he turned it around and wore it backward. They walked by the edge of the greenstalk forest – a thousand acres of huge tree-like plants a hundred feet high. The greenstalks looked a little like trees but then again not. They were more like giant stalks of dark green celery.

A few minutes later they were at the edge of town. They went to the general store to pick up some snacks for their upcoming vacation. Ruby wanted clord snacks – she loved them! But her mother counseled against that decision, "You know how you always eat too many and your stomach doesn't like that. Let's get something healthy. Cheese and crackers!" she said with a wink and a smile. She was very pleased with herself.

Mothers are like that sometimes. They think they come up with a great idea and then they smile and wink at you. But they usually don't pick out the best snacks.

After the general store, Ruby asked, "Can we go to the thrift shop Mom? Pleeeeaaasseee?" That old second hand store was Ruby's favorite place in town. It was a treasure trove of surprises and valuable things that only the most intelligent and creative people could really appreciate – and that was definitely Ruby: creative and intelligent. She was also certain that she had an excellent sense of style. (She knew that because Ho told her so last week.)

"Okay," said her mom with a smile.

Baron, on the other hand, wasn't thrilled about looking at other people's old stuff, but he went along because he really didn't have anything better to do.

They went into the store and there were, according to Baron, piles and piles of crappy junk. But Ruby's perspective was far different. She saw hidden gems and potential finds waiting to be unearthed. Her eyes grew even bigger (if that were possible) to try to take it all in. Aisle after aisle, shelf after shelf, table after table of discarded riches, just waiting to be re-discovered and brought back to life! *What stories they could tell*, she thought.

Ruby held up a yellow shirt to her chest. She dropped that when she saw a red and white polka dot jacket that she just had to try on. She pulled it on and looked in the mirror, turning first to one side and then to the other. She thought it made her look sophisticated – even mysterious as she pulled the hood up – so what if it was about six sizes too large.

"That thing swallows you whole," laughed her mom.

"The coat that ate Ruby!" Baron said. "Let me get a video of that!"

But before he could get the shot, Ruby had ditched the jacket and moved on to the next aisle.

She looked back at her brother in his ball cap. "You do have a cool hat," Ruby said. "I think I want a cool hat, too." So she skipped over to the hat section. There were all kinds of colors and styles. What a joyous selection! She put on a cowboy hat and looked in the mirror, putting her fingers into her imaginary holsters. Then she tried on a fedora with a feather in the brim, while smoothing it and smirking in the mirror – raising one eyebrow. After that, she donned a pillbox hat – on her tiptoes – while she batted her eyelids. Next she pulled a yellow toboggan down over her ears – she couldn't get all of her hair stuffed inside so it spilled out all around – looking like her head was on fire. (At least that's what Baron said!)

"Sweetie, you two stay together," her mother said to them. "You can look at hats for a few minutes; I have to go call your father. I'll be right out front – in the rocking chairs across the street."

Ruby rummaged through the next stack, not finding just the right thing. She needed something that was more...her. Surely, it had to be here. She moved a few hats off the top of another stack – and there it was! A small knit hat – sort of a reddish color – brighter than magenta, maybe with a touch of purple? It wasn't really fuschia… *What color is that?* she thought. *Raspberry! Yes, a raspberry hat.* Ruby grabbed it and placed it on top of her bushy mane. She had to pull it down a bit and position it – a little more to the side. Yes! She loved it!

"A beret?" Baron said with a high-pitch in his voice as he walked up behind her.

"What's a beret?" Ruby asked.

"That's the kind of hat on your head," Baron responded.

"Oh," she said. "Yes, yes, a beret it is. I think it looks fabulous."

Baron thought the color clashed with Ruby's red hair and blue lips, but he knew there was no arguing with her. If Ruby said it was fabulous, that meant she had made up her mind. Anyway, what did he care about a girl's hat? And what did he care about colors for that matter? His color references consisted of about eight or so basics – and raspberry was definitely not one of them. He didn't think anyone needed more than eight colors.

"I'm going to buy this with my own money," Ruby said aloud – partly to Baron but not really to anyone in particular. She wore it proudly to the front of the store, beaming all the way to the checkout line. She handed the tag to the clerk and paid for the hat without even taking it off. Then she walked outside with her brother. When they got onto the wooden sidewalk, she asked Baron to take a picture of her. Ruby smiled big for the photo. "I'll take a video and post it on KikTalk. That way, Gram can see it," Baron said. Ruby was so happy with her purchase – and her sense of style!

They saw Mom across the street and she waved them over while she sat in a rocking chair talking on the phone to their father.

The two began to cross the street. Just then some older girls walked past in the opposite direction. They stared at Ruby and her new treasure. The tall one said to the short one, "Look at that ridiculous beret. She doesn't even know how badly it clashes with her hair – not to mention those odd blue lips." The short one laughed, "I know. It's just so...so gaudy!" They giggled together and continued walking past.

Ruby stopped short in the street. The smile fell away from her face. Her eyes lost their gleam. The rosiness in her cheeks went a little pale. Her ten-year-old heart tried to ignore those words but it seemed as if other people were looking at her and pointing and laughing as well. Ruby was no longer so pleased with her purchase.

She had loved her new hat so much only moments ago. But now....now she couldn't wear it. She felt she had been a fool. How could she not have realized? Why didn't Baron tell her?

Baron was walking right beside his sister. Upon hearing these words, he became angry and wanted to defend his little sister. With clenched fists, he turned to run after those insensitive girls and give them what for! Ruby instinctively put out her hand onto Baron's chest. "No," she said.

"But-but—" Baron stammered. "They can't do that."

"Just. Just stay here," Ruby said.

She took a deep breath to muster her courage (with a few short ones in between – but she was not going to cry) and turned around. She strode slowly back to that second-hand store with that raspberry beret clenched tightly in her hand. She walked in through the out door, out door. She went to the checkout counter. Ruby paused and looked at the faded treasure in her hand with a single tear rolling down her cheek. She laid it gently on the counter, turned and walked away.

Ruby crossed the street again toward her mother and Baron. Her mother finished her phone call and looked up. "What's wrong?" asked her mother. "Didn't you want to get a hat?"

Ruby fell into a deep hug with her mother and held on tightly burying her face; Mother hugged Ruby back with a big, arms-all-around-you-mom-hug that – at least for a few seconds – made Ruby feel a little bit better. (Another deep breath.)

"No, I changed my mind," Ruby said with a sigh.

"Oh, okay sweetie. Maybe you can find something you like next time," her mother added. "We have to hurry; it's almost time to go see the Storyteller again!"

CHAPTER **10**

Two Kingdoms

Just as before, the floaters descended from the sky and dropped toward the ground, stopping to suspend themselves inches from the ground. The families and children went up the hill and to the trail into the woods. At the circle, the fire was blazing as brightly as before and so strong that the heat kept the young ones from getting too close. The Storyteller was again waiting – and glowing. He hovered above the storyfire but the flames and the smoke just seemed to avoid him somehow. It was as if they bent around him.

Ruby had to be embarrassingly carried again. This time her father took her piggy-back style, so at least she didn't look like a little baby. She also wore long pants this visit, so her missing leg would be less noticeable.

The light of the fire surrounded the children as the flames frolicked to and fro; casting light and shadow in a hundred ever-changing directions. The low roar of the thunderous Runyon Falls in the background was ever-present.

The Storyteller descended toward the dancing flames – as he had done for centuries. His booming voice projected almost through each child. They could *feel* the vibrations from his words. He spoke powerfully, but also tenderly.

"Remember our tiny, peaceful village of Tansin, nestled between its two powerful and jealous neighbors? Tansin was the home of Sherable Josiah and the Miller twins."

"But the village Tansin was not to be peaceful for long. To the north, there was the kingdom of Zakar, ruled by Prince Trajan. To the south was Geisl, ruled by Empress Giselle. Trajan and Giselle were bitter enemies, as their families had been for a millenium. Still, the peace had held for centuries.

"Trajan and Giselle were discontented. Power often leads people to feel they deserve more – no matter how much they already have. They were no longer content to control only lands of the south or of the north. They were each too greedy to be bound by the shackles of peace sworn to by their fathers. Hopes for continued peace began to grow dimmer as clouds of war darkened the doorstep of tiny Tansin."

****

"The palace of Zakar has stood for a thousand years! None can oppose the powerful and wise, the handsome and clever, the noble and good, the honest and delightful, the sovereign, most high Prince Trajan!" spoke the crier. "Zakar is the most powerful kingdom in the land!" he continued. "His royal highness Prince Trajan – the one true ruler of Zakar and all the cities of the north, has announced that he will take a wife." "All honor and grace be to the King's choice; henceforth she will be known as Rhiannon XIII."

Trajan had a nasty habit of needing new wives, and he liked the name Rhiannon. Whenever he would tire of a queen, she would be sacrificed to Bale, the God of Fertility, and he would replace her with another, re-naming his new queen Rhiannon as well. Trajan had a massive and formidable army; he fed his soldiers well on the spoils of his plunder. They were free to massacre and pillage any city they conquered, as long as one fourth of the city's gold and ternium was brought to Trajan. Zakar's main fields were fertile indeed; they were the perfect place on Levon to grow Clords. The tangy fruits grew thick and sweet three times a year without fail – their oblong, burgundy-colored skins covered the ground like a blood-red snow.

****

To the south lay the kingdom of Geisl. Its main source of wealth was the bounty in its mountains. Several of them yielded prized ternium crystals. These crystals are found nowhere else on the planet of Levon. Ternium crystals come in two colors: yellow and white. When touched together, they create light. But they cannot be moved while generating light as the stones emit a strong current while in contact with each other. Empress Giselle paid her armies with the gold and ternium taken from under the mountains. She also bought goods and provisions from far and wide with her precious underground harvest.

The yellow metal and shiny gems bought things of beauty, but the mines were a dismal place to be. The miners were slaves to the empress, mostly prisoners from battles and conquered cities. But some were sent there as torture or as punishment – for crimes committed, or imagined.

Empress Giselle was enthralled with power; she reveled in it and nothing symbolized power to her more than gold. Her bed was made of it; she wore gold jewelry. She drank from golden goblets and ate from golden plates with golden utensils. Her walls were adorned with gold-etched wallpaper. Indeed, she was the only one allowed to wear gold inside the palace gates. Violating that edict has sent more than a few to the mines. In Geisl, Giselle was to be revered as a goddess, the divine ruler of the land.

To an outsider, Trajan of Zakar would have appeared to be more brutish, more savage… Meanwhile, Giselle of Geisl would have appeared more refined, with social graces befitting royalty. In reality, they were equally ambitious, equally vicious, and equally self-serving. Either would slit the throat of an enemy, a negotiator, or even a friend if it pleased him, or her.

****

"As has been observed, 'Absolute power corrupts absolutely.' Without guardrails or limits, power and ambition create their own justification for any behaviors so that, eventually, anything becomes acceptable.

The Storyteller's intense gaze into the eyes of the children with the backdrop of the brightly glowing embers made them feel the hotness of his point – just as they felt the heat of the fire. As he rose higher above the flames, he paused for effect and took a deep breath.

"But what about Runyon?" asked Ruby. "You still haven't told us anything about Runyon Falls!"

"Yes, Runyon Falls," echoed the Storyteller softly as her turned toward Ruby. "There is more to the story. But that is for another time."

He floated gently down toward the ground and his glow dimmed. This time, he almost walked – or glided very close to the ground, as opposed to floating high above it, and again disappeared into the forest.

The parents came to gather their children. Most were so sleepy, they had to be carried. Ruby wasn't the only one this time.

CHAPTER **11**

Ruby's Dream

Normally, Ruby's nights were restful and her dreams were pleasant. But some nights were not so pleasant; neither were some dreams. When that particular dream wormed its way into her head again, she became part of it. She had mostly forgotten what happened that terrible day – just pushed it from her brain. But in this dream, she remembered that say so clearly, so vividly; and felt it so deeply. It became more than a dream. The dream brought back the incident in agonizingly painful detail. This dream was coming less frequently now, but when it did come, it visited a vengeance upon the ten-year-old.

Five years earlier, Ruby was playing with her friends in the field by her house. It was a crisp, fall afternoon. They were playing kickball. Baron, Ho, Mae-Ellen, and the others were all there. Ruby wasn't very good at kickball then but she loved playing with her friends.

The sky was a clear, deep blue – just a few puffy, clouds with some orange streaks.

It began as a soft, shrill sound in the distance. Barely noticeable at first, but it began to get louder. Initially, the children continued playing their game.

The high-pitched whine got louder and faster as it moved closer. Baron dropped the ball. The sound had grown to a shrill screech from above. The children all stared skyward.

A flash of light and then the sky grew dark for a few seconds – until a bigger flash was followed by a cacophonous rumbling. The sunsilght shone again. The next second, chunks of flaming metal flew down all around them. The children began screaming and running in all directions.

One particularly malicious shard of metal seemed to track Ruby as she ran. It followed her steps and seemed to go right where she was running. It tore through her leg like jelly, knocking her to the ground.

She rolled down the hill shrieking in pain – and reaching for her leg. But her leg was gone. There were only grass and air where her leg should have been. And the blood. There was lots of blood. Her blood.

Ruby couldn't react. She was frozen – in pain, in shock, and in confusion. She was paralyzed on the ground, her leg severed at the knee. In the dream, she could see herself from above. She could see the terrible look on her face, frozen in anguish. Even in the dream, she had to look away. The sight of the blood was too much for her. Too much a reminder of the pain – what she had lost – the shock and fear. And the pain, terrible pain. Seconds afterward, in contrast to the shrill incoming whine, there was complete silence. No children yelling; no birds chirping. Just emptiness where there should have been sounds.

The sirens of the MedAlert team began a different, but just as piercing, sonic intervention into her dream as they arrived to help. Though they were sounds of aid, they were no less disturbing – connected as part of the same awful chain of events. Ruby was the only one injured that day.

Tossing and turning in her bed. Safe now, but for that awful dream. She cried out and clawed her way along the bed, reaching out, grasping for something, stretching forward, but finding only air, and then falling to the floor, covered in sweat. Her mother came in – by now used to this pattern. She sat on the floor and wrapped her arms around Ruby, holding her tightly. "It's okay sweetie. It's all over now. I'm here. You're safe. It's just a bad dream."

Ruby sobbed softly in her mother's arms.

Of course, Ruby now had an advanced electronic prosthetic leg. A complete replacement – by almost any measure, it was superior to the original. It was stronger, faster, better in almost every way. She even had partial feeling in the new leg – or she almost thought that she did – sometimes. It wasn't her original, biological leg, but it was now hers. The artificial limb (she hated that terminology) was even designed to grow with her by expanding itself in minute increments over time to approximate her own growth patterns – at least to a point. After all, it wasn't living tissue so it couldn't really grow. Anyway, it would be able to adjust for several years. Her father explained it all to her.

Once in a while – as she grew – her father had to re-calibrate it for the simulated growth so that she didn't walk lopsided. But other than that, she was pretty happy with her new leg. Her parents said she might need to get a replacement in the next few years or so because of the growth simulation limits. But, all in all, she was quite satisfied with the replacement. Of course, she would have preferred not to need a replacement in the first place, but this one was pretty cool.

The only lasting negative effects were the dreams – and the deep-down, in-the pit-of-her-stomach, complete revulsion to the sight of blood. But the dreams were becoming less frequent now. Ruby always tried to be positive, so, from that point of view, she actually felt quite lucky. (When she wasn't having nightmares.)

She had to get those memories out of her head. As it was already getting light outside, she grabbed her over-sized glove and a softball – and went to practice pitching (with both arms) at a target Baron had drawn on the side of Father's workshop.

CHAPTER **12**

Gravitational Forces & Amusements

The dreaded family vacation. Every summer, Ruby's family packed the floater up to its gills and piled in on an adventure off to who knows where. Her parents knew, but they always kept the destination secret until their arrival. They lived modestly, but Mother and Father always tried to be creative and resourceful enough to come up with something interesting for their summer vacations.

Lots of kids her age were beginning to chafe at the mere thought of a forced week together with their parents. But Ruby actually kind of liked the idea. Sure, she missed her friends. But she did enjoy the air of adventure and the mystique of a journey with an unknown destination. What surprises might they find? What strange people might they meet? What extraordinary experiences might they have?

Sometimes it wasn't all that adventurous. Take three years ago. Their trip to the lake ended up being somewhat less than a five-star experience. The roof leaked – in *her* room – but at least it was on the far side of the room. And it only rained two days, so it wasn't the worst experience ever. But a puddle formed under the leak. When Ruby dropped a candy wrapper, it fell onto that puddle and floated like a little boat. *It was strange*, she thought, *why some tiny moments remained etched in her memories.*

Anyway, the bottom of the lake was sort of mushy-muddy. Not the most pleasing experience between your toes. And, to be fair, she was still getting used to her new leg – trying to interpret her sensations. Getting her new leg stuck in the muck was not just a little embarrassing. The artificial leg was a great deal heavier than her other, 'real' leg. It's times like that when she was GLAD that it was just her family together on the vacation.

Last year they didn't actually go anywhere. Dad called it a 'staycation.' Money was always tight, but it seemed to be even more so last year. Mostly, they just hung out with their parents and played board games. But this was another year – a new year – time for another adventure. She and Baron had no idea where they were going. But they were told to pack for warm weather, so at least they could be optimistic.

They played virtual ping pong in the back seat for awhile – a slight violation of the technology restrictions. That is until Mom complained that they were distracting their father. He was very focused on the drivescreen – and actually got a little perturbed at them. Very unlike Father on a vacation. These trips were usually his time to shine. He enjoyed planning and getting away with the family probably more than any of them. The children devolved to looking at their screens.

After a while, Mom suggested that they download the newest safety tracker, Traxx. No child wanted to be tracked, so they said, "Maybe later" (at the same time). They smiled at each other on this jinx. But Mom insisted. So they started the downloads. But the grid in the floater wasn't the fastest, so it took a while. Eventually they drifted off to sleep.

"We're here!" shouted her father – much more like his usual vacation-self.

The sign – floating high above the ground – read "Gravitational Forces & Amusements." And in small letters underneath: Edutainment at its finest! "It could be worse," thought Ruby. (This was the first time in practically forever that their vacation involved something that actually cost money.)

Her father landed the floater in a spot at the far end of the parkbay. He glanced around to make sure no one could see and then pushed a small button underneath his seat; connections automatically did their thing – looking for all the world like a dozen snakes plugging into sockets, electrical outlets, and plumbing pipes. Then the floater transformed before them into a tiny two-bedroom, one-bath camper. Father had definitely flouted the technology restrictions with this one. They were ready to go experience the wonder of gravitation and other forces – and to be amused!

The Clemens family was pre-registered – on the list as 'special visitors' – so they were admitted through the short line. They strolled past the

Land of Newton and *Magneton Village*. Further on there was *Experimental Fusion Alley* – that's where kids could do all sorts of hands-on gravity and other scientific experiments.

Education – schmeducation. Baron and Ruby were there for the fun stuff – they had read all about GFA a few months ago. (Now they knew why their father had suggested that link!) They wanted the crazy-advanced, cutting-edge experiments and the wild (dangerous?) rides! They looked up 400 feet to the top of the *Velocity Drop* (stomach buster) and then stared in awe at the *Big Bounce* – where you could get inside a huge bouncing ball and bounce against 20 other kids inside similarly huge bouncing balls. How much better could life get?

All that stuff looked fun, but there were specific attractions that Baron and Ruby each wanted to experience. Ruby wanted to ride the *Galaxy G Force Accelerator*. It let any rider dial up g-forces as high as they wanted – but if you passed out and let go of the accelerator, gravity returned to normal. Some of Ruby's friends on KikTalk posted that it was a real rush! (KikTalk was a virtual community where the under-16 crowd shared their lives – sometimes too much sharing – with a heavy focus on pictures and videos with catchy captions. The logo was sort of tongue in cheek: it was a boot going into a mouth.) Baron's goal was to lift 100,000 pounds – on video – in the *Reverse Gravity Cloud Arena* (of course to be posted on KikTalk). The *Reverse Gravity Cloud Arena* was built around an unusual naturally-occurring site in which gravity is extremely weak (the scientific name was a gravity geyser). In fact, the whole GFA park was built around this major attraction. It was the only naturally occurring gravity geyser on dry land.

Anything inside this area – clearly marked with a huge bright red stripe painted all the way around the perimeter – weighed far less than it did outside the arena. Inside the reverse gravity cloud arena - or RGCA, a 10,000 pound metallic box might weigh only 10 pounds due to the gravity geyser. *Everything* was around a thousand times less heavy in there – depending on the substance. Dense, metallic items were affected more by the gravity geyser. Baron told Ruby that he heard one kid got injured in the RGCA a few years ago when he broke the rules by trying to sneak out a thousand-pound marble in his pocket. He was fine until he crossed the big red warning stripe – it broke both his ankle *and* his shin bone. It also ripped a wicked hole in his pants. (They don't have thousand-pound metal marbles inside the gravity geyser anymore.)

CHAPTER 13

Fun In The Park

Baron and Ruby were so excited! They couldn't wait to jump into the rides and the experiments – and the food. Oh yes, park food! It might not have been super healthy but it was a wondrous cornucopia of scrumptiousness! Candied clords. Clord juice – extra sweet. Fried concoctions of all sorts – with clord syrup for dipping. (Clord was the national fruit, after all – a delicacy grown only on Levon.) Cakes and pies (chocolate, vanilla, lemon, swirl, and, of course, clord). Toasted roast beef sandwiches – with clord jelly. Spuckers – a type of candy that made your face pucker up and caused you to talk funny for a minute or so.

A few kids walked past them just as one popped a spucker into his mouth. "Look at meeeee!" he squealed in a high-pitched voice. "I'm a big astronaut with a tiny voice!" His friends all roared with laughter as their gaggle continued past. More of them popped spuckers and talked in those hilariously high, tinny voices.

Ruby and Baron laughed too. They stopped at the first refreshment stand to pile their plates high. Mom and Dad strolled around the park as the children were old enough to be on their own for a while. Still, Ruby did notice that her parents were tracking them both – at the highest level on that security app. As Baron and Ruby stuffed themselves, Ruby also happened to notice that a man behind dark glasses seemed to be staring at them. She was used to people staring at her lips – although it always made her uncomfortable.

"Baron," she asked between bites – and with her mouth still half full, "Is that man staring at me?"

"What man?" Baron replied as he took a huge bite of clord pie.

"The one behind you at the high table, over beside that giant magnet," Ruby said just as she took a long sip of clord juice staring intently with almost-crossed eyes as the red juice wended its way through a crazy straw past her blue lips.

Baron turned around and looked at the man who suddenly turned away and looked off toward the rides. Baron stared in the man's direction for a moment while he chomped on his enormous mouthful of pie. After chewing a while, and staring a while longer in that direction, Baron swallowed and then turned back to Ruby. "I don't think he was looking at us. Besides, you can't even tell with those dark glasses. Anyway, did you catch those crazy green boots?"

They both laughed at the man's shiny, dark green boots – in such hot weather! – and continued eating. "And who wears a full-on wool suit on a hot day like this?" Baron asked. They laughed with each other while they discussed their plans for the grand afternoon. Baron couldn't wait to get into the Reverse Gravity Cloud Arena. He wanted a video of himself lifting huge amounts of weight – with one hand. Ruby was fascinated with the Galaxy G Force Accelerator. "I want to see how many G's I can take before I throw up!" she giggled excitedly.

They finished their snacks and headed off toward the rides. But Baron's attention was immediately diverted by a pretty girl – close to his age – walking toward *Experimental Fusion Alley*. From Baron's perspective, the suns shone directly on the young lady. Even though he thought the girl was about his age, Ruby was pretty sure that girl was several years older than Baron. Nonetheless, Baron wanted to head in that direction, so Ruby was obligated to follow along with him. (They had promised their parents that they would be on the buddy system. Parents are sometimes soooooo overprotective.)

They passed the first experimental station – *Crystal Combinations*. This was where park-goers could combine ternium crystals to create light shows. But there were way too many kids lined up for that one. (Besides, the girl Baron was following continued on.) The next station was called the *Insection Station*; it had something to do with bugs. Baron's new 'friend' glanced back in his direction so he pulled Ruby to the side pretending they were interested in Insection. Ruby was not.

The lady at the *Insection Station* was showing how one special insect could be squashed and apparently come back to life. These special insects in this experiment were called shaving leeches. The lady grabbed one of the shaving leeches (she had on a thick glove; it was pink with black lightning bolts all over it) and threw the leech onto the ground. Several of the children near the front screamed and jumped back. Shaving Leeches were not something you wanted to get too close to. They were nasty little critters that looked like shaving razors with legs. They had a reputation for being able to shave a man's face clean off!

The lady then walked up – looked up into the crowd – stretched out her leg – and stepped on the leech. Yellow blood spurted out the side under her shoe. There was a collective scream of 'Ewwwwwww' – along with a few squeals. Baron said, "Cool." Ruby turned away. The sight of blood always made her squeamish – and this yellow version definitely made her feel like she was going to be sick. (Although her nausea might also have had a little something to do with the jumbo bag of chocolate-swirled clord candy she'd devoured in the past 10 minutes.) The lady picked up her foot and the shaving leech slowly began to 'unsquish' itself – sort of like a tiny balloon being slowly inflated – as it sucked the blood back inside its body. After it was mostly re-inflated, it seemed to wander back and forth until it got its bearings. Then it started to scurry away, but the insect lady scooped it up with her huge, pink glove and put it back into a purple pouch marked "Dangerous."

"Does anyone know where Shaving Leeches live in the wild?" the lady asked.

Without really thinking, Baron blurted out, "Yeah, they live near flowing water – often in greenstalk forests, right?" he asked.

"That's right, young man!" the lady responded.

"But aren't they kinda dangerous to have here in an amusement park?" Baron asked.

"You are correct, young man. Shaving Leeches can be extremely dangerous. They attack in packs somewhat like Earth Piranha. That's how they do the most damage. If one attacks, the others can smell blood and, if enough of them get excited, they can vibrate together giving off a musical 'call' which can attract a lathered swarm. If that happens, they can devour a rammel in a matter of minutes. So, here at the park, we only let them out one at a time to ensure the safety of our guests."

While watching this entrancing demonstration, Baron had forgotten about his quarry. Suddenly, he remembered that he wasn't there to see insects. He looked up, but the object of his affections had disappeared from view. He looked to his left and to his right down the alley but to no avail.

"How on Levon did you know where Shaving Leeches live?" Ruby asked her brother.

"Gram told me. She knows all about bugs," he said. "Anyway, "I'm bored with these experiments. Let's go do some fun stuff.

Ruby was definitely up for that, "Absolutely!"

CHAPTER **14**

Clean and Jerk

They arrived at the Galaxy G-Force Accelerator – Ruby's number one favorite attraction that she had never done before and wanted to try more than anything else in the world. Ruby's stomach was still not happy with her – and she didn't feel much like getting squished like a pancake – or a shaving leech – right at that moment. "Here we are," Baron said.

Now was definitely not the time for her to ride anything that might make her stomach reaction more intense. Desperately wanting to avoid the G-Force Accelerator – and just about everything else – Ruby needed to change direction. "Didn't you want to go to that upside down gravity thing?" she asked her brother.

"You mean the Reverse Gravity Cloud Arena? Heck yeah!" Baron replied. "But, are you sure? I thought you wanted to see how many G's you could take first."

"Not now. Maybe later. You do want to go to that Gravity Cloud, don't you?" she asked.

"Oh yeah! Let's do iiiittttttttttt!" he hollered. He took off running down the path – with Ruby in hot pursuit (well, maybe lukewarm pursuit, with one hand on her stomach).

The line to get into the RGCA was pretty long. But Baron was so pumped up, he didn't mind waiting and Ruby was thankful for somewhat of a respite. While they were standing in line with Baron practicing his poses and giving Ruby instructions on the perfect angle for the videos he wanted posted on KikTalk, Ruby saw a glint of light off something green and shiny. But her view became obstructed by a bunch of kids walking by. After the kids passed, Ruby couldn't locate the green glint anymore. Maybe she was imagining things. She continued to look while Baron talked about how jealous his friends would be of his video.

The line moved up much quicker than Ruby had expected. "I think they let in 10 kids at a time," Baron said. "This is going to be awesome!"

Two of the park ambassadors – they always traveled in pairs – came up to the people behind Ruby and Baron in line. "How is your day?" they asked. "Would you like to answer a few questions about your day at the park? You could win a free clord pie!" The ambassadors were park workers that tried to get everyone to answer questions and get pies. They seemed to have permanent smiles and were way too cheerleaderish for Ruby. They wore obnoxiously large nametags with their names and "Have a Nice Day" printed on them. Every park employee had those same big, glittery nametags. Red and white striped shirts with black pants completed the uniform. They also had these kinds of floating halos over their heads – Ruby thought the floating halos were supposed to have something to do with anti-gravity. Anyway, the line was moving up again so Ruby and Baron escaped being cornered into the survey.

When they turned the corner, Ruby thought she caught sight of a green flash again. It seemed to be behind some bushes – or then again, maybe it wasn't. When she tried to focus, she couldn't really see anything green. She wanted to get out of line but it was no use. Baron continued talking about the best angles for his video. "Do you think I should let my hair fall down over my eyes? Should I use ONE hand or TWO…? Hmmm…." he asked out loud. Ruby didn't respond, but it didn't matter because he wasn't really asking. It was more like he was talking to himself. Baron was a great brother most of the time, but when he got absorbed into himself like this, he didn't pay attention to much else.

The line moved up again. They were so close now! "Next!" yelled the gatekeeper.

As they approached to the entrance, Ruby saw a man with dark glasses and the same shiny, emerald green shoes. Actually, that green wasn't really emerald, maybe jade? (To Baron, it would have been just green.) But it wasn't the same man from earlier. Again this man seemed to be staring intently at Ruby. It was hard to tell because of those dark glasses, but Ruby was pretty sure this man was staring at her, too.

"Hey Rubes," Baron called. "Are you coming?" She and the man were almost frozen staring at each other. Time seemed to stop for a moment.

"Hey, Ruby Blue! Come on! We're in!" Baron shouted excitedly. She followed her brother through the gates of the gravity cloud, leaving the man in the green/jade boots behind. There were safety signs and warnings all over the place. A CAUTION video aired in a loop on a monitor suspended from the ceiling and everyone had to watch before entering. The video explained about the gravity cloud and how it was a natural phenomenon.

The spokesperson on the monitor began, "The area in the Reverse Gravity Cloud Arena is encompassed by a 12-foot high wall marked with a big, yellow stripe at the top. For your further safety, there are rotating lights with rows of black X's down the sides. In addition, there is also a huge red stripe on the ground outside the entire perimeter to mark where the gravity geyser effects begin. This unique phenomenon reverses the effects of gravity on different materials to a greater or lesser degree. It affects everything to some extent, but there are exceptionally powerful impact on heavy, dense metals, like lead, gold, platinum, iridium, and burdenite. It is not safe to take any of these items outside of the red line." Burdenite was the least expensive and actually the heaviest, densest metal, so most of the 'toys' in the gravity cloud were made of burdenite – or concentrated burdenite, which is an artificially condensed version of the metal that made it even heavier and more dense.

As they entered, Ruby noticed how big and high the walls surrounding the gravity arena were. She guessed they were there to protect people (mostly boys) from 'accidentally' carrying one of the heavy 'toys' across the line and injuring themselves – or someone else.

Baron surveyed the arena. He looked over the collection of toys to decide what he wanted to lift for his video. He took a deep breath, puffed out his chest and stroked his chin as he contemplated. Of course, there was the big barbell; that's why he came. But there were also 10,000-pound boxes of solid gold and iridium satellites – some as big as a floater! *It would look pretty cool to lift something over his head that was so big*, he thought. There were at least a dozen zaffers strewn on the ground. Zaffers were 1,500-pound lead balls – kind of like overly dense cannon balls – but they only weighed a little over a pound each in the arena.

Ruby picked up a zaffer and tossed it to Baron underhand 'softball' style. "Hey, catch!" she yelled. It sailed over his head. They both laughed.

Baron looked around again; he had made his decision.

"Are you ready to take the video?" Baron asked back to Ruby with a smile. She held up her screen and waved it in his direction. "No," Baron said. "You have to use mine! Here you go." He tossed Ruby his screen and it floated slow-motion style as it tumbled ever-so-slowly in her direction. She dropped her screen into her pocket to try to catch his. She missed her pocket and bobbled Baron's screen with both hands, but finally secured it. "Nice catch Rubes!"

Baron smiled and turned toward his goal. He took another deep breath, and strode – no, more like strutted – to the heaviest toy in the arena. It was a barbell with two big balls of concentrated burdenite on the ends. It was marked 100,000 pounds. Of course, inside the gravity cloud, it weighed about a thousand times less. But a hundred pounds was still a hundred pounds; it's not like it was a feather. Still, Baron walked up to the barbell lying on the ground. He adjusted his feet and took yet another deep breath. He rubbed his hands together and bent down to grasp the bar.

Baron looked up at Ruby. His face was focused. He was mentally preparing for his lift. His eyes looked straight ahead. Honing in; centering himself as he prepared. He was concentrating completely on his goal.

"Do you need any help?" one of the attendants blurted out surprisingly from behind him. (It was a lady.) "What? No, I've got this," he told her. Then he re-focused on the challenge in front of him. He took a deep breath, bent over and grasped the bar, preparing for his lift.

"Are you sure you don't want any assistance?" the attendant asked once more. Once again distracted from his efforts, Baron straightened up and looked at the lady. He took another deep breath and let it out slowly. "No, thank you," he said. "I'm sure I can handle this one by myself." He smiled at the lady. She smiled back. It almost seemed like some sort of Minosian stand-off. The attendant was trying to help a guest and didn't want to do anything else at that moment. But Baron was having none of it. He wanted to lift that burdenite barbell by himself – and get it on video – without a middle-aged park attendant in his shot. They stood there. The attendant smiled at Baron. Baron smiled back at her. He nodded. She nodded.

The suns beat down on them. Baron was beginning to sweat. The attendant fanned herself, still smiling.

"Hey, that's mine! You took it!" came a small, shrill voice from across the arena. The attendant turned to look toward the voice. Seeing two children argue over a toy, she turned back to Baron and said, "Well, I guess you can handle this one by yourself. I have to go check on the young ones." She traipsed off to settle the dispute.

"Thanks for the help!" Baron said under his breath. He turned back to Ruby. "Are you ready, Rubes?" She nodded and smiled.

Baron squared up to the barbell. He rubbed his hands together. Then he took a deep breath and let it out. He then shook his hands and arms out to the sides. He stretched his neck by moving his head side to side. Finally, he turned to Ruby and winked. Then he bent over and curled his hands around the bar. "Light weight, light weight," he said to himself. "Nothin' but a peanut. Here we go."

Baron yanked the barbell upward and bent his knees to pull the weight onto his shoulders. Steadying himself, he bent his knees a bit more to get a good push and thrust the barbell straight up into a full arm extension. He stood straight up and held the lift. He had lifted 100,000 pounds! He looked over at Ruby with his eyes open wide as if to say, "Did you get it?" Ruby smiled and nodded to her big brother. He let the barbell fall to the ground. "Whoooooeeee!" he hollered.

Baron jumped up and pumped his fist in sheet excitement. But he hadn't counted on the fact that a low gravity environment would affect his jump quite so much. He soared almost 10 feet up...and kind of lost his balance as he was not expecting to be airborne for that long. His body rotated forward, of its own accord, and he began to fall. Although he fell more slowly than he would have in regular gravity, it was still a fall – as in going to the ground out of control. As such, Baron face-planted there in the gravity geyser. And yes, Ruby got the whole thing on video. Struggling mightily to hold back laughter, she slid the screen into her pocket and helped her brother up.

CHAPTER **15**

Cornered

The two left the Reverse Gravity Cloud Arena. Ruby's stomach was feeling mostly better now – and she was genuinely happy for her brother who was positively elated watching himself on video.

They walked along the midway. "Would you like a snack?" Baron asked. "I'm famished from lifting all that weight."

"No thanks, I'm good," Ruby responded. (She unconsciously rubbed her stomach. Maybe next time, she would only get the *medium-sized* bag of chocolate-swirled clord candy.)

Two men in dark green suits with dark green boots approached them. One was slender and tall with a black moustache that sat under his nose like an upside-down horseshoe; the other was a bit rounder with almost no hair and brown teeth! (Yuck!) "Hi kids," the more rotund gentleman said as they approached. "How are you enjoying the park?" Ruby noticed that the men were quite large up close; she recognized one of them as the man she saw at the snack stand earlier in the day.

"We're having a great time," Baron said as he tried to walk past. But the men blocked their path.

"Whoa there. Hold up. You're the Clemens kids, right? We're with park security. I'm sorry but you're going to have to come with us to the park office."

"Why? We didn't do anything wrong," said Baron.

"If you'll just come with us, we can settle everything in the office." Baron felt that something wasn't right with these two.

"What's wrong?" Ruby asked her big brother.

"Nothing," Baron said. "I think we need to get Mom and Dad."

"Kids, that's actually why we need to talk to you. Your parents are in the office already. They asked us to find you and bring you there. So if you'll just come with us." Mr. Moustache grabbed Baron by the arm.

"Why aren't Mom and Dad here?" asked Ruby.

Just then, two ambassadors walked up and said, "How is your day? Would you like to answer a few questions about your day at the park? You could win a free clord pie!" The ambassadors and their permagrins never took no for an answer. But this time, Ruby was so glad to see them!

As the ambassadors took out their clipboards, they asked "Where are you visiting from?" Ruby stared at their floating halos and their huge nametags.

"Does everyone who works at the park have those really big nametags?" she asked.

"Yes, that's park policy," they said in unison – with great big smiles. They looked at each other, smiled some more, and continued together, "We wear nametags so our guests can feel free more like our friends."

Ruby looked up at Baron and motioned her head toward the green-booted, dark-suited security guards in front of them. Baron – getting the clue – asked the security guards, "Hey, where are your nametags?"

"Ummmm. Security guards don't wear nametags. It helps us blend in," the taller one with the moustache said.

"You're not security guards," said the ambassadors – in unison again. "All park employees wear nametags." The ambassadors simultaneously broke into huge, blank smiles and turned their heads at opposing angles.

The green-booted duo looked at one another and each shoved an ambassador aside forcefully. The ambassadors got up and ran away. The men focused on Ruby and Baron – who took a step back.

"Rubes, does your leg itch?" Baron asked. He spun her to face him.

"Yeah," she said as she reached down to 'scratch' the side of her leg (turning it up) while she held onto her brother's shoulders. She kicked backward – HARD – catching Mr. Brown-teeth in the groin.

"Duck!" Baron yelled – and he pulled Ruby down on top of him just as Mr. Moustache lunged for her. The tall, thin man with the upside down horseshoe sailed over the children. "Run!" Baron yelled. He and Ruby took off running toward the front entrance.

A few seconds later, their parents ran up alongside them. "Mom, Dad!" Ruby started.

"We know," they said together. "We saw on the security monitor. Are you guys okay?"

"Yeah," Baron replied; Ruby nodded.

"Let's get out of here! Head for the floater. It's in the lot with the purple waah-waah sign," said Father. They ran for the exit. Ruby reached for her back as a twinge of pain shot up her spine, but she continued running.

The green-booted pair re-assembled and prepared to give chase. Mr. Moustache got up and tried to wipe the dirt off his suit. Mr. Brown-teeth was still partially bent over from Ruby's kick. "We have to get them," grunted Brown-teeth through a grimace looking up at Moustache.

Six real security guards – with big name badges – surrounded the green booted pair. Those two weren't going to chase anyone – not anytime soon.

CHAPTER **16**

Detour

Mom, Dad, Ruby, and Baron hopped into their yellow floater. Mom mashed the disconnect button and the floater transformed around them back to its familiar saucer shape for transportation mode. (They really didn't care about the technology restrictions at tht moment.) Dad punched the accelerator and they blasted forward – staying as low to the ground as he dared.

Everyone was pinned to their seats. (Ruby finally got a couple G's after all!)

Trees, bushes, buildings – all dissolved into a blur as the Clemens family careened onward as fast as their family-grade floater could manage.

Baron looked at the scope on the main dashboard. The red dot labeled 'home' was getting farther and farther away as the blue dot (their floater) was going in the opposite direction. "We're not going home?" he asked?

"Not right now," Father said quietly.

The floater rose a bit higher. "Can you get my new ternium reactor for me? It's under your seat." Father asked Mother.

She reached down underneath where she sat and pulled out a small silver box with connecting wires running under the dashboard. The simple box had two buttons – one red and one green. "Are you sure about this?" she asked. "I didn't think your testing was complete."

"It's a risk," Father responded, "but we don't have a plethora of options right now." HE reached over and pressed the green button.

The craft started to shake. A growling hum came from the rear engine as the craft slowed momentarily in mid-air and then lurched forward; it was a low, guttural sound at first, but it slowly got faster. The bass-like sound evolved into a baritone. Then the sound grew still louder as they picked up speed. Next, the growl morphed into a tenor. The modulation continued to rise into a higher pitch – converging into a soprano whine – and then a big pop!

Silence. But the little yellow family floater was now creating a streak of its own. The foursome was re-pinned back to their seats. Seat belts weren't necessary. None of the passengers could move a muscle. Ruby couldn't even lift her leg! (She was definitely getting those G's!) Stargazers on the ground would have seen only a yellow blur. Ruby and Baron looked toward each other – with great effort; their eyes first as big as saucers, then fluttering backward. They both passed out from the acceleration.

"Tanner, are we going…to…" Mom began. Her eyelids fluttered then closed. Her head did not move as it was already pinned against her seat back. "We're… going to be…" Father started to say. He tried to take a breath but it wouldn't come. He tried again, "We…" but it was no use. He passed out, too.

The floater raced across the night sky like a low-flying meteor. It disappeared into the night until the blurry, yellow streak faded into the darkness.

****

There was a tiny shell-roofed farmhouse – from the sky it looked to be not much larger than a child's clubhouse. It sat by a small pond. Two large trees provided shade and partially obscured the house. It stood silent and alone. Prairie land stretched for miles and miles to both sides of the house against a backdrop of the ocean. The only indication of life was a few dragon-fliers flitting close to the ground.

In the distance, an approaching high-pitched whining sound faded into a lower frequency that eventually matched the harmony of the dragon-fliers buzzing about. The little yellow floater slowed with a whirring bubble sound and drifted to a stop behind the tiny shell-roofed farmhouse. Again, all was quiet except for the dragon-fliers.

The moon was full and bright; the stars twinkled over the prairie, the tiny house, and the motionless yellow floater. One sun was was below the horizon and the other hung low as the day became dusk.

****

Ruby and Baron were in the back seat of the floater – alone. The front seats were unoccupied. The floater was no longer moving. Ruby awoke. She rubbed her eyes and pushed her floppy, curly red locks backward. She sat up and her hair fell in her face again. "Ugh," she muttered. She tapped her leg, pushing unseen buttons with three different fingers and grabbed an elastic band from a just-opened secret compartment. She pulled her hair back again – this time securing it back with the band.

"Baron," she whispered as she tapped her brother on the shoulder.

"Unnnhhhh," Baron groaned and turned away. Ruby looked at the front seats – only to find them empty.

She looked around and had no idea where she was. "Mom! Dad!" she called. No answer.

Turning back to her brother, she raised her voice, "Baron, are you awake?" No response. "Baron!" this time, she shouted.

"What?" he said as he popped straight up. Unfortunately, for him, his six-foot, two-inch frame was about eight inches taller than the inside height of the floater. Which meant, of course, that he banged his head on the ceiling. "Owwwwww," he cried. Baron's hands flew straight to the pain on the top of his head – but his hands also hit the ceiling – which made his hands hurt as well. "Owwwww!" he yelled louder this time. Then he fell to the floor and sat there holding his head and looking at Ruby.

"Good morning clumsy," she said. They both laughed at Baron's gangly antics. Baron sat back down and rubbed his head and then, in turn, each hand. When the laughter drifted off into the air, Ruby asked her brother, "Where are Mom and Dad?"

"I don't know," Baron replied. "And by the way, where the vamp are we?" Ruby just shook her head and shrugged her shoulders while peering out the windows.

Bam, bam, bam! There was a loud banging on the back of the floater. Ruby and Baron froze. Big brother put a finger to his lips. They waited without making a sound.

Bam, bam, bam! came the banging again. They heard a scratching noise on the outside. Someone was trying to open the door. Ruby hid behind Baron. The door unlocked and began to open slowly.

"Oh, you're up," Mom said as she peered in through the open door. I wanted to let you sleep but we do have things to do. Come on, let's get you guys some breakfast." Mom backed away from the door. Ruby jumped out and hugged her! Baron came over and hugged his mother, too – sort of a sideways hug because, you know, he was almost 16 years old.

"Come on inside," Mom said. "Would you like something to eat?" she asked as she opened the back door of the tiny farmhouse. The three of them walked inside.

CHAPTER 17

Explanation

Dad was making pancakes with warm clord syrup! Ruby's favorite. There was fresh goat milk and hot chocolate. (Ruby chose the goat milk.) And Mom made biscuits with scrapple. (Baron put his finger in his mouth and made a gagging sound.) Sunsflower honey and goat butter for the biscuits. Dad was also frying up fresh waah-waah eggs – which were plentiful (and free)!

It was truly a picture-perfect breakfast – worthy of a KikTalk moment. But Baron and Ruby were too hungry to think of taking pictures just then. They sat down and quickly served themselves – just as Dad brought another stack of pancakes to the table. The setting was idyllic – a family together in their farmhouse having a wonderful breakfast. Except – only hours earlier – they had run from mysterious green-booted men – who were trying to kidnap them. Of course, there was also the incident with the experimental ternium reactor – and everyone passing out – leaving the floater to fly itself to this tiny farmhouse. And by the way, this wasn't even their house! So...

"Thanks for the breakfast," Ruby began, "but… what's going on?"

"Yeah," Baron quickly added – between mouthfuls. "What – I mean, where are we? And what did Dad do to the floater?"

"And who were those guys in the dark suits and green boots at the gravity park?" Ruby asked.

"How did you guys know that we'd be running by?" Baron wondered aloud.

Ruby put her fork down. "Something's wrong," she observed – and popped a honey biscuit in her mouth. "Isn't it?"

"Yes," their father said. He grabbed Mom's hand. "We definitely owe you two an explanation."

"Your father is a scientist," Mother said. "He actually used to be sort of famous – in scientific circles, at least."

"I studied on Earth for several years," Father said.

"Wait, you've been to Earth?" an astonished Ruby asked. She and Baron stopped eating for a moment and stared at their father. This was important news. They didn't know anyone who had actually been to Earth. The trip took almost two years. How could they not have known that their father had been to Earth before now?

"At first I studied in a geographical area called the state of North Carolina at the merged NCSDAE (North Carolina State/Duke Advanced Engineering University); we called it 'Duke State.' My specialty was bio-engineering. The military paid for my education. Afterward, I went to work for them to continue my research. I invented several biological enhancements for the military back on Earth. But my work was being used for things that I didn't agree with. I guess I should have known that was a likelihood when I agreed to work for the Space Force and later the Interstellar Defense Corps.

"When I began, the work in advanced prosthetics was used for helping soldiers – and others – to recover from devastating injuries. Also, the military paid for my education so I had previously agreed to work for them for a period of time. My commitment was to work for the Space Force and later the IDC for six years. I had hoped that the groundbreaking work would eventually make its way to help many others," Father said. He looked at mother and then at his children.

"Unfortunately," said Mother, "The IDC began weaponizing your father's creations. Eventually, they didn't even wait for soldiers to lose limbs in battle. They just started cutting legs and arms off of healthy soldiers so they could be fitted with advanced prosthetics."

"They even made me build weapons into the prosthetics," Father said.

"Advanced prosthetics…. You mean – like my leg?" asked Ruby, with her head turned at an angle.

"Yes, Ruby, my dear," her mother answered. "Your father moved back to Levon to get away from the military and so we could start our family together."

"I really didn't have any money in those days – not much different from now," he chuckled. "But I was a scientist, a mechanic, and something of an inventor, so I figured I could find a way to provide for a family. Along with the house that Oliva's parents left us – this house – we decided we could make a nice life on Levon. It was safe. The air was clean, and the people were good. It was more rural than Earth – but that was fine with us. The tech restrictions meant that I really wouldn't be able to continue my research in any significant way, but I was content to be a mechanic – work on floaters, screens, and other simple machines."

"We had Baron, and then a lovely little girl with crazy, red, curly hair," her mother said. Ruby smiled. "You two made friends and life was just what we had hoped for."

"Not to interrupt, but that sounds like a bedtime story. Happily ever after. And really boring," said Baron.

"It really was pretty much like a story. We were definitely happy," said Mother.

"Then there was the incident when those things in the sky rained down on the farm. The day that shrapnel took your leg, my dearest," said Father.

"The doctors said they might be able to get a prosthetic for you. But we didn't have enough money for one that would work like a real leg," her mother said. "So we borrowed money to get the materials and tools to create something better. Your father worked day and night for six months to build the one you have now."

"But that one won't last much longer. You're still growing, so we needed something bigger. I don't want my daughter hobbling around like a mountain goat with one leg shorter than the other," her father said.

"And having back problems," added Mother.

"Is it so wrong to want your daughter to be able to walk?" he turned and asked Oliva. Father got up from the table and stared out the window. "I can build it," Father said.

"I borrowed more money – a lot more this time – to create a more advanced replacement leg. I wanted you to have one that would last a lifetime. The only problem was that I couldn't get another loan because we were still paying off the first one. I had to get the funds from somewhere else. So I ended up using – a sort of alternative lender," Father said.

"The Jade Clan," said Oliva, trailing off softly, with her eyes looking nowhere.

"What's the Jade Clan?" Ruby asked.

"It's a… ummmm… Well, let's call it an unofficial group. A-a-uhhh… a group that has money to lend," Oliva said.

"Organized crime," Tanner added as a matter-of-fact observation. "I shouldn't have gone to them."

"We didn't have any other choice," Oliva added. "Ternium is so expensive."

"So those guys in the green boots wanted money?" Baron asked.

"Yes, son. I think maybe they were going to hold you two for ransom," Father said.

"But we don't have anything like that amount of money," Oliva said.

"We put all of that money – and whatever else we could scrape together into your new leg," said Tanner.

Ruby's eyes got big. She took a deep breath. "I don't need a new leg. This one is great. It doesn't matter if I grow a little. I lean a little to the left anyway. Besides, mom's pretty short, so I'm not likely to grow much more." Ruby said. "You could just give those Jade men the new leg you're working on."

"It doesn't work that way, sweetheart," Tanner said, still staring out of the window. "They want twice as much for the payback."

"What are we going to do," asked Baron. "Live on the run? Cool. Can I get a laser blaster?" He faked shooting sounds while pointing with his fingers, then bit into another biscuit.

"No, sweetie, that won't be necessary; we're going to go home," Mother said.

"But won't those Jade men find us?" Ruby asked.

"Your father has a plan."

"The Jaders don't know where we live. They may have seen our floater, and it's possible that they could have gotten intel on our departure direction. But there's no way anyone could have kept up with us. Besides, we are going to transform our anti-grav traveler. I found some supplies in the basement. I think we'll be able to come up with a new paint job, fins, and some special tricks before we leave the farmhouse. And since home is at least two thousand clicks in the opposite direction, they still won't know where to look for us anyway," Father said.

"Baron, will you give me a hand son?" asked Father. The 'men' went out to 'pimp' their old floater.

Mom got up to clear the table. Ruby stared out the window wistfully, chewing scrapple deliberately (which is pretty much the only way to chew scrapple). *Was this all her fault? Was her family in danger because of her stupid leg?* she wondered to herself.

ACT III ~ CLAN GAMES

CHAPTER 18

Gruun

Present Day. Back on Minos...

Gruun, the leader of the Jade Clan, was a large, hairy man, with a low, gruff voice. He wasn't particularly tall – under five and a half feet – and a good portion of his bulk was in the middle. He had thick, bushy eyebrows and an unkempt full beard. Both were curly and slightly tinged with green, as was his exceedingly superfluous forearm hair. His reputation was one of avarice and he was sometimes regarded with revulsion. He was driven largely by greed, but also by power – and he had plenty of both. Another distinguishing feature of Gruun's was the triple hook he had in place of his right hand. He had lost it to a devil-shark while crossing the Great Ocean on a smuggling run many years ago – when travel between the continents was more common.

Gruun enjoyed flaunting his power and he wanted nothing more than to increase his control and influence over others. He tried to exert his clout over the Minosian Coalition with a modicum of success. He ruled Hamada which was the largest territory on Minos, but Jader territory was primarily desert and not very valuable. It was sadly ironic that the greediest of the clan leaders had the least – or could that have been the reason he was so greedy? However, his real goal was to take over the larger Botan to control its agricultural production and exports to other planets. Yeah, he wanted to rule the planet. For now, he ruled all the green sand area of Hamada with an iron fist (or hook, as it were).

Though the Donja Desert was a poor place compared to the coastal okos, Gruun lived like a king – or at least a poor man's version of one. While the fertile coastal okos could attract tourists and gamblers with their fabulous beaches and incredible vistas, the Donja was mostly arid – save for a small number of underground springs, including the largest, and most reliable one in Gruun's fortress compound at Hamada Castle. The castle was in Glastalica which was pretty much the only Jade Clan city of any size. The best-paying work by far in Hamada was working for Gruun which most everyone there did. Gruun's business was trading and he was good at it. He would trade anything but he specialized in 'hard-to-get' goods – usually items that couldn't be acquired legally because they had higher profit. Besides, the Council decided what was legal and what was not. In addition, enforcement was rare and, if necessary, easily bribed away.

The leaders of the coastal okos were greedy as well and though they were no slaves to laws or fairness, they were far less inclined to go to war and, more or less, they were content with their current state of affairs. They took pleasure in their palatial hotels and oceanfront estates along with their gambling revenue and small-time substance or weapons trafficking (for their own defense of course). They were fine being the biggest fish in their relatively small ponds. Familial hierarchy and loyalty kept Gruun, Oshi, Roden, and Nilo feeling comfortably secure in their positions as clan leaders.

But Gruun was different from the other clan leaders; he wanted more. He had been working on deals for more advanced weapons. There were rumors that he had acquired missiles which could be used in an assault on Botan. One of Gruun's most notable accomplishments was securing ocean access for his formerly landlocked Hamada. He won it in a bet with Nilo during a game of Poke & Roll. Nilo had been angry about it ever since. Gruun won a tiny strip of land with access to the sea; it was at the southern tip of the Blue Oko. It was reached via the Petrified Forest Pass. The location had come to be known as *Wager's Access* because that was how Gruun acquired it. There was no natural bay there but Gruun did have two ships, including his prized *Teach's Revenge*. Anyway, access to the sea was an achievement that no Jader ever thought possible, so Gruun wore it like a crown.

Gruun had one son, Cassius. He considered Cassius weak. Gruun sometimes even considered his chief messenger, Gala Vaurienne, to be something akin to a rebellious, adopted daughter even though their relationship was complicated. He trusted no one but respected Gala's cunning and resourcefulness more than what he saw as his son's mistakes, lack of initiative, and general disinterest in the family business. Gruun also disapproved of his son's tendencies in the area of personal romantic preferences. (Meanwhile, Cassius had a soft spot for Vaurienne as they had grown up together.)

As with the other Council leaders, Gruun had a preferred title: Your Eminems. He had heard it once and liked it, so he adopted it as his address of choice. Gala was pretty sure it was probably supposed to be Your Eminence, but once Gruun made a decision, there was no going back. And no one had the gall to tell him otherwise; or if they had the gall, they had the good sense not to showcase it.

Gruun also fancied himself a competitor. He made just about everything a competition. He competed with the other council leaders for the most power and the most money. (Not that either of them actually knew how much the others had. But Gruun was so into competing that sometimes he didn't care whether or not it was possible to know if he had won.)

He wanted to have the most land (check); he wanted to have the latest weapons (check); he wanted the best smuggling operation (check). He would challenge anyone at just about anything – especially if he thought he had an advantage – even past the point of absurdity. A few weeks earlier, he challenged a 14-year-old boy to an arm-wrestling match. Gruun weighed nearly 300 pounds and the lad would have been lucky to tip the scales at 125 pounds soaking wet. (Since this was the desert and there wasn't much water, we'll call him 120 pounds). Gruun had someone set up a table in the middle of the compound and made the boy arm-wrestle him –five times – with each arm. Of course, Gruun won all ten. (As a parting shot, he also broke the boy's wrist in the last match – for good measure.) Arm-wrestling the humongous Gruun with a that menacing triple hook was no one's idea of a fair fight.

But today he was happy with Vaurienne and her successful negotiation with Oshi. (Another win for Gruun.) He invited his Gala to the great hall and toasted her success with his lieutenants and a huge mugs of green beer. All of the Jade leaders gathered next to the long mead-hall style, rectangular table.

"Congratulations to Vaurienne for the sale to Oshi! 150 new blasters!" he toasted.

Cassius and most of the others raised their beers aloft. But a few Jaders were reluctant to raise their mugs for a spare.

Gruun stood up.

Louder and more forcefully this time, "I said congratulations to Gala Vaurienne on a successful business venture with Oshi of the Gold Oko," as he raised his mug high. He looked around – everyone slowly raised their mugs.

"Congratulations!" someone shouted. And then another, and then several more "Good jobs!" and "Here, here's!" They all drank.

Gruun's competitive streak had no limits. While it's true that he often looked for an advantage, he also had no qualms about creating his own advantage, however he could get it. His need to win seemed to be virtually unquenchable – even if the competition itself were meaningless.

After a few more rounds of green jade beers, Gruun demanded that someone try to outlift him in 'chairs.' This was one of Gruun's favorite competitions – a rather un-creative game. The chairs around the hall table were massive. They were thick, solid, wooden structures – strong enough to support rammels. Suffice it to say that they were extremely heavy. It's also important to understand that this competition was not just about strength. Chairlifting was also about balance and leverage. Gruun was definitely strong, but his mass and center of gravity were also particularly well-suited for an event of this type. Gruun picked up one chair over his head to start. "Who will challenge me?" he asked with a roar.

Everyone in the hall had been through this before. But Gruun needed a challenger. So they pushed a young buck to the front. His name was Lance. "You can do it, Lance!" a yell came from the back of the crowd, along with a chorus of laughter. Lance was rather slight but he gave it a try.

Unfortunately, try was all he could manage. He barely lifted one chair off the ground. He actually got three legs up but couldn't quite get the whole thing off the ground. After several minutes of grunting, he was dripping in sweat and gave up.

After an awkward silence, mercifully, Rogan shouted "Gruun wins!" And then others, "Gruun wins! Gruun wins! Yaaaayyyy!" came the yells.

"That was too easy. I need someone who can give me a run. Do I have no one who can even test me?" he asked with his crooked pirate smile. Gruun bent down and stuck his hairy arms (and trihook) under two huge chairs and then slowly rose to a standing position. "Who's next?" he asked.

No one stepped forward. (Part of the reason was that no one liked to lose, but beating Gruun wasn't always the healthiest option either.)

"Have we no strong Jade men in this entire castle?" he inquired aloud as he slurped another gulp of beer.

Finally, boosted by liquid courage, Evan stepped up to enjoin Gruun's competitive spirit. "I'll take a shot, your Eminems," he said slightly slurringly. Evan walked around the chairs, seeming to study them as he walked back and forth while guzzling more beer. "Aha," he said. Evan took another swallow and set his mug down on the table. He pulled out one chair from the table. He pulled out a second chair and placed it beside the first. Then he pulled out two more, placing them on top of the first two. "Oooohhh!" someone yelled.

"He's going for four chairs!" shouted another. Rarely had anyone (other than Gruun) lifted three of these massive chairs. And this was definitely a surprise (not to mention, a slight breach of etiquette) for the opening lift. But Evan had some size himself and he looked like he might be able to pull it off.

Evan stood behind the chairs and wrapped his long arms around them. With a great grunt, he strained to lift all three of the considerably heavy pieces of furniture. They didn't seem to move at first. Slowly, Evan began to stand. He paused for just a second on the way up, but let out another grunt and continued until he stood up straight. His face looked like an over-ripe clord. The shouting subsided. It had been a long time since anyone (other than Gruun) had lifted four chairs. Evan dropped them to the floor with a thunderous thud.

"Hurray!" someone shouted. "Well done," another hollered. There was a chorus of hooping and congratulating as well as clinking of mugs – and more drinking.

Gruun was not amused. This was his event. He took several gulps to finish his beer, with the excess spilling down his mouth and forearm hair, and slammed his mug down. He walked down the other side of the table and wiped his mouth with his forearm (the left one – the one without the hook). Gruun pulled out one chair. He pulled out a second and turned it upside down on top of the first. He pulled out a third massive chair and then a fourth, which he turned upside down on top of the third. Four huge, heavy chairs. He added one more chair on top. Gruun cracked his neck. He cracked his knuckles (on his real hand). He walked up and grabbed the twin stacks – five chairs – digging his tri-hook into the sides of the chairs. Gruun grunted and strained, but the chairs began to rise – slowly – until he had lifted them to a standing position. The hall fell silent; but Gruun wasn't finished. Then he heaved, yelled "Arrrrgggghhh!" – and raised all five chairs over his head.

The hall went wild with cheers! "Five chairs!" exclaimed one.

"Vamp! It's a new record!" shouted another.

"Gruun wins!" yelled someone else.

Soon, they were all chanting, "Gruun, Gruun, Gruun, Gruun!"

Gruun basked in the glory of his latest win. (Picking up dining chairs... It was enough for the moment.)

"Vaurienne, now that you're fresh off your latest business success, would you like to lift chairs against me?" Gruun asked, with sweat dripping down his face.

The place got quiet. (Now, in any other place, this would have seemed ludicrous. A slender, young woman being asked to lift heavy furniture to compete against a huge, older man. A man who had, only moments ago, bested others by lifting copious amounts of weight. But this was

Hamada, and these were Jaders. It didn't have to make sense; it was who they were.)

"No, Your Eminems," Vaurienne replied. "You are far stronger than I. It would be no contest. In fact, I believe you are the strongest Jader of all. Perhaps the strongest Jader ever," she responded.

More whooping and hollering with random shouts of "Gruun, Gruun, Gruun!" Jaders pounded the big table with their fists.

That response caught him off-guard. He smiled. She was sly, this Vaurienne. He was glad she was working for him. Still, Gruun didn't really like anyone being 'the winner' over him. He turned around and raised his mug to the Jaders – who cheered him on even more. Gruun thought about asking Gala to arm-wrestle; that might be fun. But by the time he turned back around, Vaurienne had made her way out of the dining hall. And Rogan handed Gruun another green beer.

CHAPTER 19

Red Dawn

Vaurienne went to the stable to check on Artax. "How are you, buddy?" she asked as she scratched his neck.

"He's been better," replied the stablekeeper. "One horn is nearly empty and it will take some time for his body to refill it. We'll give him plenty of water, but another concern is that ankle. It's really swollen and he's been limping. What happened to you guys out there?"

"Oh, no," Vaurienne gasped as she dropped to her knees to look at Artax's ankle. She tried to touch it but the rammel lifted that massive hoof gingerly away. "We were attacked by a camo mamba in the Donja. I thought we'd killed it before… I didn't know he'd been bitten. Will he be okay?"

"It's hard to tell," said the stablekeeper. "Rammels are so big that they can usually fight off mamba venom. But he'll need a lot of water to dilute the venom – which will be taxing on his system. Trouble is, his body's trying to replenish his horn water at the same time."

"Please take care of him," Vaurienne said. "He's my friend."

"I'll do my best," said the stablekeeper. I'd say he's got a good chance as long as we keep him out of the suns and give him plenty of water. The next couple of days will be crucial."

"I'm going to stay with him," she said.

"Suit yourself," said the stablekeeper.

The keeper filled Artax's water trough and tossed Vaurienne a blanket on his way out. Artax drank a lot of water. Then he settled down on the ground. Gala snuggled up against him for the night.

The next morning, Vaurienne received her new assignment from Gruun. She was to collect a debt from Roden of the Red Clan. She would have to go to the Red Oko. Gruun had smuggled some refined ternium – six buttloads – to Roden from the mines outside of Wedding-Shi in Botan. Now was the time designated for Roden to pay. The amount due was three million levs. Gruun assigned Mr. Moustache and Brown-teeth to accompany his messenger. They weren't her favorite escorts but they were tough – that would be good if there was any trouble. Besides, it wouldn't do any good to argue with Gruun about personnel decisions.

Roden may well have been the wealthiest of the Minosian Coalition leaders, but he was also the stingiest. His wealth was known across Minos but he was even more well known as a cheapskate. He never paid easily – and rarely on time. He was always looking for a better deal – even after the deal was done. Of course, this behavior annoyed everyone who dealt with him. But, as he was the richest man on the continent, and the leader of an Oko, as well as one of the members of the Minosian Council, traders – and others – still did business with Roden. They just had to know what they were in for.

"Gruun," Vaurienne said as she approached her leader. "I'm about to leave for Scarlet Beach, but Artax had a tough time in the Donja. I'll have to leave him here. Can we take the old floater?" she asked.

"Yes, it's charged; I'll have it supplied and brought to the gates directly," said Gruun. He had keenly observed Artax limping the day before when Vaurienne returned. "I already spoke to the stablekeeper."

"Please be sure they take care of Artax. I don't know what I'd do if anything happened to him," she said.

"Vaurienne, he's as good as healed. I'll take it as my personal responsibility to make sure he's attended to."

"Thank you, your Eminems."

"Good luck on your assignment, Gala," Gruun said as Vaurienne climbed into the floater with her escorts. "Bring me back my money. Just don't gamble it away in the casinos!" the hairy-forearmed clan leader laughed.

****

Gruun often made quick decisions – some would call them rash – but he considered them evidence of his quick mind and leadership capability. For example, when Gala Vaurienne returned from the Gold Oko, Gruun sensed an opportunity. Gruun had noticed the rammel's slight limp. So the Jade leader graciously offered to take care of the rammel for Gala while she was on her next assignment. Gala didn't like leaving Artax. He was probably her best friend in the clan – or anywhere else for that matter. But she left her rammel under Gruun's care (not that she realistically had much choice in the matter).

Gruun despised weakness, and he thought it was part of his responsibility as clan leader to get rid of it. After Vaurienne left on her next mission, he drained the horn water from Artax's second horn into a huge mug and drank it – for its purported carnal properties. He made a big deal of drinking that water so that all the ladies would see him. Then he ordered his 'worthless' son Cassius to take the rammel into the Donja to die.

Cassius protested. "Father, Gala will be most displeased. She does love this creature. It's like her pet," he said.

"I don't care. Do I need to remind you who's in charge around here?" Gruun responded.

"But there's no reason to waste the life of such a proud beast. He's still got a lot of good years left. Artax is strong, he could still be helpful to the clan," Cassius suggested.

"Son," Gruun countered, "You are weak. I told you to take this animal into the Donja and leave it for the rat vultures. If you don't take it right now, I'll blast its brains out here on the ground where it stands – and your next job will be to clean up the mess."

"But Gruun –" Cassius protested.

"Don't make me ask you again. It's time you man up."

Gruun turned and put his hairy forearms around two ladies as they walked toward the castle. "I'm really starting to feel that horn water!" he said loudly. His lady-friends giggled.

Rammels have a homing mechanism that is second to none. However, it works with the planet's magnetic and gravitational fields along with the water in their horns. Take away their horn water and they get lost in the desert like any other poor creature. Of course, their great horns also hold their reserve water supply. So, again, take away their horn water and they are doubly-defenseless in the Donja.

Cassius was not happy with his father's short-sighted and cruel decision. But it was useless trying to argue. So he slowly led the rammel away. "Come on Artax. I'm sorry, boy. I truly am," he said. Artax followed obediently.

****

Apart from being a shorter journey than her previous trip from Glastalica to the Gold Oko, the trip to the Red Oko was also decidedly faster because of the floater. It was unusual for Gruun to let anyone take a floater out – and also unusual for him to agree so quickly to let her use it, Gala thought. The Jade Clan had only a few of the vehicles and Gruun was quite protective of them. Not to mention, it was part of the Minosian psyche that they didn't need to rely on technology. (Even though they seemed to have no such concerns with advanced weaponry.) Gruun must have really wanted that money from Roden. It probably didn't hurt that this was the oldest floater he had. It was a dented, red job with a sawed-off top. As it happens, that color would fit in well with their destination. When the team arrived at the Scarlet Beach, it was late afternoon. They proceeded toward the grand entrance of Roden's abode. Even Vaurienne had to admit it was impressive. Although Roden was cheap, he was also simultaneously discriminating. He wanted the best of everything – he just didn't want to pay too much for it. The entrance to the Vermilion Hotel* and Casino Resort was pure ostentation. Huge gates and manicured gardens lined the avenue approaching the front entrance.

> *Unlike the residences of the other Council leaders, Roden did not have a personal palace. Instead, he created an expensive hotel – another way to increase

his income. Of course, he did reserve a rather substantial section of suites for his own, personal use.

There was also a vast and magnificent collection of gardens with a host of statues dedicated to the stories of the Red Clan on the side of the hotel opposite the ocean. The gardens contained dozens of flowers – all shades of red, of course. There were Minosian sunflowers – 10 feet tall with huge red blooms and yellow rings around the centers. In front of those were rows and rows of red zinnias – nearly three feet tall. There were also fields of bright crimson clover that covered huge swaths of the approach to the Vermilion – on both sides of the road right up to the walkway. On the other side of the hotel was the Scarlet Beach. A wide pathway was lined with mammoth tropical cannas. Their green-black leaves and huge, virbrant red blooms pointed the way toward a coast composed entirely of a pristine section of smooth, fine, red sand. It made an eerie complement to the blue sky – and the seemingly endless sea.

Roden was not there to greet them. (No surprise there. Vaurienne was certain he was in no hurry to pay the money he owed.) Red-hatted porters approached the floater and opened the door. "Welcome to the Vermilion at Scarlet Beach, home of his lordship, Roden of the Red Clan," said one of them. "Please proceed into the hotel for your rooms. His lordship has prepared the finest accommodations for your stay."

Vaurienne and her escorts entered the hotel. They were greeted by more red-hatted porters. "Thank you for coming to visit," another said. "His lordship has reserved two suites for you," another said. "Let me show you the way so that you can get settled."

"When may we see his lordship?" Vaurienne asked.

"He is quite busy at the moment, but he looks forward to seeing you in the morning," the porter replied.

"In the morning?" asked Vaurienne. "We are here on a matter of important business. We expected to see Roden tonight."

"I'm so sorry but that won't be possible. His lordship is unavailable today," said the porter.

"This is not what I was told. Roden was to meet with me, as Gruun's representative, today," Vaurienne said. She began to reach for her curved blades.

"That won't be necessary, Miss Vaurienne," said a woman walking quickly toward them. She recognized the woman as Roden's messenger, Neptunia. Gala holstered her cuttas.

"Hello Vaurienne," said Neptunia.

"Hello, Neptunia" Vaurienne replied.

The two messengers eyed each other and shook hands formally. "My comrades, Mr. Moustache and Brown-teeth." Mr. Moustache nodded and Brown-teeth smiled, exposing his uncomfortably colored chompers. (It was another ugly, unpleasant smile.)

"Vaurienne, I am so sorry. I know that you planned to meet with his lordship today but Roden had to attend to urgent business. He is expected back late tonight. We have put time in his schedule for you at sunrise tomorrow. By way of an apology, Roden has offered to pay for your rooms and give you full access to the resort, including the Bar Opulenza," Neptunia said.

"What about the Casino?" asked Mr. Moustache. (Vaurienne glared at him. Communicating with messengers and other Council leaders was the province of messengers. It was a faux pas of Mr. Moustache to ask this question.)

"Yes, of course. You have access to the entire property. His lordship has even graciously staked each of you with 100 levs at the fortune's wheel – and 100 levs of chips to use at any of the card tables – or the bar."

Vaurienne wanted to argue but she knew this was part of Roden's negotiating plan. "Thank his lordship for his generosity," she said. "We will see him in the morning."

They turned to walk toward their rooms.

"Vaurienne," Neptunia called. "I made sure that your room had a grand bath. It has four different showering fountains that pour into a basin inlaid with precious gems. I also stocked it with a variety of naturally scented soaps and oils." Neptunia smiled.

Vaurienne walked toward her room. She was not smiling. Everyone always seemed to want her to bathe. But she couldn't. It was a waste of perfectly good water. After all, it wasn't the Jader way – and it might even be 'unhealthy' for her to be so... exposed.

Vaurienne's room was truly extravagant. She threw her pack on the bed and looked around. This one room was almost half the size of the dining hall at Hamada castle. She stared at the ornate bath. She ran her fingers along the smooth coolness of the tub. *Perhaps*, she thought, *if things were different.* She looked out onto the red-sand beach and the Great Ocean. Then she went out to find the bar.

Opulenza read the sign atop the entrance. *This must be the place*, thought Vaurienne. She went inside and walked up to the bar. "Jade beer, please."

"I'm sorry," said the bartender, "but we don't have that on tap. Can I interest you in an amber stout?"

"Yeah, sure, whatever."

She took a long, slow drink and made a face indicating she was not a fan. She looked around at the collection of art in the bar. It was very bright for a bar, too nice. She could tell that most of the patrons had money. They were also very quiet and respectable and, well, boring.

Neptunia walked in and sat down.

"Hi Nia," Vaurienne said.

"Gala," Nia began, "This is a place for the high-end crowd. If you'd like to go somewhere a little more relaxed, I know just the place. And they have Jade beer. Besides, those 100 levs will be gone in a few minutes here, but at Mitch's Tavern, they'll last you all night."

"You had me at Jade beer. Let's go before I shoot someone out of boredom," Vaurienne said with a smile. "How far is it?" she asked?

"Well, we could walk – but in your floater, we can be there in no time," Nia suggested.

"Oh, all right," Gala responded. They went to the front of the Vermilion and one of those guys with the red hats brought the floater around.

STORYTRAX: *Crimson and Clover* - Joan Jett & the Blackhearts

CHAPTER 20

Finch

Mitch's Tavern. Definitely more Gala's kind of place. This was a bar! Big, wooden tables with lots of chairs and a bar that stretched all the way down the side wall. This was no crystal palace. It was dark enough so that everyone couldn't see everyone else's business, but there were candles on the tables so customers didn't bump into things. Gala could let her hair down here, figuratively speaking.

They found a spot at the end of a large table and sat down. Nia yelled over at the bartender, "Two Jade beers, Holland!" They looked around; customers were ambling in. The clientele here was decidedly different from the Opulenza. Much more of a working class feel. Gala liked this much better.

Nia was the closest thing that Gala had to a non-animal friend outside of the Jade Clan. (Or maybe even inside it.) They were about the same age and came into their roles as messengers at around the same time. They had formed a friendship when they decided to negotiate in a way that allowed both of them to win – and to make their bosses happy.

The bartender walked over to their table to deliver their drinks.

"Thanks, Holland," Nia said.

"Anything for my favorite messenger," Holland replied with a mock bow. He reached around and scratched Nia's shoulder. They shared a glance.

"Holland!" shouted a man from behind the counter.

"I've got to get back to work," he said to Nia. They smiled at each other.

"Friend of yours?" Gala asked.

"We've been pretty friendly for a few months now," Nia replied.

"He's cute," Gala observed. "So, this is your favorite place?"

"Yeah, I like the scenery." She took a drink while watching Holland hustle back to the bar. "And the service." They both laughed and clinked glasses.

"It's been a while since I've seen you, lady," Nia said.

"Well, Gruun's been keeping me busy," Gala replied. "He's got me going to all the okos. Deals, negotiations, buying, selling, collecting, and … well other things," she continued.

"That man is so lucky to have you. He ought to treat you better," Nia said. "Speaking of which," she took another drink, "How are things in that department?"

"I'm okay," Gala replied, "You know me, roll with the punches."

"Hmmmpphh. I hope those other things aren't anything that might get you killed unnecessarily," Nia said.

"Come on, Nia. In our line of work, that's pretty much a constant risk for all of us," Gala said.

"Yeah, I know. It's just that you seem to take more risks than most. I think it's your damn boss," Nia said.

Gala emptied her mug and slammed it down onto the table. "Two more Jade beers, Holland!" she yelled.

"First name basis, huh?" Nia asked.

"Well, your friends are my friends, right?" Gala responded with a wink.

"Wha--what...what the vamp is that?" Gala asked. "There's something hanging from the ceiling over in the corner. No, wait. It's-it's…. moving, I think. What's in this beer?" She looked at her glass and then back at the thing hanging/moving in the corner. It was bigger than a bread box or the head of a full-grown rammel – one-third the size of a barrel. It was shaped like a rectangular cube but more rounded, especially on the corners. But this thing had eyes! And a nose, but it was sort of smushed into its face.

"That's Finch," Nia said, "He's a bullpar."

"No way!" Gala said in surprise. "They have their own bullpar here? I've heard about them but I've never actually seen one in real life."

"I guess they're pretty rare," said Nia.

"Can I touch it?" asked Gala.

"Not unless you want to lose a finger, little lady," said a red guard sitting a few seats away. "Don't you know about bullpars?' he asked, as he slid a few seats closer to them.

"Bullpars are amazing animals," he began. "They float above the ground – usually about eye-level. Like some of the other creatures on Levon, they've somehow evolved to use the planet's gravity fields. Did you know that they never have to land? They can float – or fly – whatever it is that you call what they do, forever. They can hover in one place, and sometimes do, for months. Or they can fly – float faster than a bird."

"Glide," said Gala.

"What?" said the red guard.

"Glide," she repeated. "Bullpars glide. That's what they do."

"Yeah," said the guard.

"Rova!" said another red guard who just walked into the bar.

"Come on over, Dion," Rova said.

"Who are your new friends?" Dion asked as he sat down next to them.

"We've actually just met," Rova said.

"We haven't been formally introduced," said Nia. "My name is Neptunia, messenger for Roden." She pulled her cloak back to show her insignia. The two guards froze.

"I'm sorry, we didn't mean to be disrespectful," Rova said as he moved to sit a few chairs away. Dion followed.

"No problem Rova. It was nice meeting you," said Nia.

The girls smiled at each other. Dion walked back over to them. "Begging your pardon, but my name is Dion, what's yours?"

"My name is Gala Vaurienne, messenger to Gruun."

"Pleased to meet you, Miss Vaurienne," said Dion. He bowed partially and walked back to sit with his friend.

Holland approached with another round. "What was that all about, love?" he asked Nia.

"Nothing, sugar cheeks. Just some harmless fun. I was starting to tell Gala about Finch but we were...interrupted. You could probably tell her more than I could. How long has Finch been here?"

"He's been at Mitch's for at least a couple years. That's what the captain told me," Holland said.

"Who?" asked Nia.

"The captain. You know, that guy over there in the big hat. He's here almost every night. I'm pretty sure he's been here a lot longer than Finch – and maybe even longer than the owner."

"I'm very interested in bullpars – ever since I was a child. I've read a lot about them, but I've never seen one up close," Gala said.

"Well," Holland sat down. "Finch is the only one I've ever seen as well. But I think he pretty much fits all of the legends," he said. "You know the phrase, 'stubborn as a bullpar?' He fits it to a 'T.' If he doesn't want to move, twenty red guards couldn't pull him away."

"What does he eat?" asked Gala. "Pretty much whatever he wants. I didn't see him eat anything the first month I was here. They say that bullpars can go without food for much longer than that. Some of the customers like to feed him. Sometimes Finch will eat what they give him, but much of the time, he just ignores them. I have seen him eat off people's plates, but they usually think that's fabulous. You know, because bullpars are supposed to be such good luck."

"Do you think Finch is good luck?" asked Nia.

"Absolutely," said Holland. "I met you soon after I started working here and met Finch." He kissed Nia quickly. "And the owner loves him. Says Finch has brought him all kinds of business, so he definitely thinks Finch is good luck. Yeah, I'd say he's lucky for sure. Most folks think the same thing. If someone – or something – makes you *feel* lucky, do you suppose that's what luck really is? It's funny; sometimes customers even ask him for advice and things."

"Are you telling me he talks?" asked Gala.

"No, and most of those folks are probably just drunk. But a good listener can certainly get more information and stories than even the average bartender with Finch around. It's almost like he has some sort of magic power. People want to talk to him."

"What about water? I've read they don't like it." said Gala.

"Not at all. If he even sees me coming with a bucket, he glides to the other side of the bar," said Holland.

"Wait, you have to mop up?" Nia asked. "I thought you were the head bartender, now."

"Uhhhh....well. I'm more the head bartender's assistant. I help out while I'm learning – sort of like an internship. But that's just while I'm studying to be an engineer. I want to work for the IDC someday."

"I see," Nia said somewhat sarcastically.

"Holland!" yelled the head bartender.

"That's my number. Gotta go. See you later, Nia?" he asked.

"If you're lucky," she responded with a wink.

"I think he's wonderful," said Gala.

"Thanks, I'll keep him," said Nia. "I think I've found a pretty good one."

Gala laughed. "Oh, I'm sorry. I'm sure Holland is great. But I was actually talking about Finch."

"Girl, you are just a little bit weird. Maybe that's why I like you."
They clinked mugs and took two big chugs.

Two large, blue-hooded customers walked over to Finch; they were wobbly drunk. "Bullpars are supposed to be good luck," said the first one. He pulled back his hood and offered some food to Finch. Finch ignored it. "You need to eat from my hand so that I can get some of your good luck," he said. He placed the food right in front of Finch, who continued to ignore it. "Here, take it," he urged. Finch didn't move.

"Look, you stupid animal. Take the food. It's right in front of you. How dumb are you? All you have to do is take a bite!" he said loudly.

Gala had heard enough. She arose from her seat. "Hey blueboy, leave the bullpar alone. I don't think he's hungry," she said.

"Little girl, you should probably go away before someone cuts you into little pieces. Now stop interrupting me. I'm having a conversation– "

"–with an animal. It's not really a conversation if you're the only one talking. Give it a rest. Bullpars are proud and noble creatures. They should be respected, not bothered," she said.

Nia came to get Gala. "Hey girl, let's go sit down," Nia said. She added in a whisper, "I need to talk to you." They went to sit down at a table a bit farther away from the bullpar and his harassers.

"What are you doing?" Nia said. "Those guys are bad news. Blue guards in from Azuri Bluff. They're itching for a fight – and you don't need to be the one to give it to them. Remember, you're here on business. A black eye or a stab wound might detract from your negotiations tomorrow."

"I like bullpars. They're legendary creatures and no one should be treating such a majestic animal like that," Gala responded.

The blue guard who was trying to feed Finch was getting angrier. "Here! If you won't eat from my hand, then you can have it all over you!" he shouted and threw the food at Finch. Finch didn't move. In fact, he had remained motionless this entire time. Gala watched in disgust; instinctively, her hand moved slowly toward her knife. Nia put a hand on Gala's shoulder and shook her head.

"Interested in bullpars, are you lassie?" said a voice from behind the next booth. An old man with a big, faded, black hat and a long, red feather was facing the other way. He slowly poked his head around the booth. The hat (and the feather) had definitely seen better days. "Captain Ferrus, at your service, ladies. Mind if I join you?"

"Captain...What are you a captain of?" Gala asked.

"I used to be Captain of *The Emancipation*."

"Hey, I've actually heard of that ship. It was the most famous sailing freighter in Minos," Nia said.

The captain got up. "Yes, she was the fastest ship to ever make the intercontinental run. We were quite successful for years – that is until the legal intercontinental trade broke down. Now, *The Emancipation* is in dry dock at Pelican Point. I spend a lot of my time here. I sometimes think if I had enough money, I'd fix her up and take her out again." He paused and looked wistfully off in the distance. "But then I usually get another drink."

"I'm sorry," said Nia. "What did you want?"

"Your friend here was asking about bullpars. Am I right?" he said.

"Well, yes, but we really don't –" Nia started.

"I had a bullpar adopt me for about three years. Glorious part of my life. I can tell you all about 'em."

"Thanks," Nia started again, "But, as interesting as that is, we–"

"–would love for you to join us," Gala said – as she slid over.

The old captain quickly sat down. "Not only are bullpars stubborn, they are virtually indestructible. I saw one get hit by several blasters – not a scratch. They just bounced off of him. They're usually pretty docile. But they can turn into nasty, fierce creatures when provoked. This one here, this Finch, seems to be exceptionally patient."

Holland walked over. "Hey, are you guys doing okay? Is this old coot bothering you?"

The captain looked at Gala with a weak smile and his eyes opened wide. She smiled at Nia. "We're okay," Nia said. "But the ladies do need a few more drinks lad – you can make mine a Gemini whiskey please."

"Where was I? Oh yes. Did you know it's thought that bullpars can live for hundreds of years. The creatures are actually quite rare," he said.

"What did you mean when you said a bullpar adopted you?" Gala asked.

"Well, bullpars are proud creatures. They don't need people to take care of them. But sometimes – no one really knows why – they adopt people or places. Just like my friend, Shay, adopted me. Just like Finch here seems to have adopted Mitch's. They stay with a person or a place for as long as they want, then they move on."

"They may look soft and cuddly with their smushed noses and cute faces, but they have another side. If they feel threatened or are made sufficiently angry, they can turn vicious rather quickly. You don't see 'em on Finch right now, but bullpars have big, sharp teeth and they can rip the door off a floater. Once a bullpar clamps down, almost nothing can make it let go. They also have these claws that are like giant mountain eagle talons – they can slash a man to threads in a couple of passes."

"Is everything about them so violent?" Nia asked.

"Oh, no, sweetie. They only get mean and nasty if they need to," the captain continued. "Why, usually bullpars don't bother anybody. And I definitely believe they're good luck. If they like you, you can even pet 'em and hug 'em and such. Just don't go thinking that they're like a pet. Bullpars are probably smarter'n us folks. They do pretty much what they want, when they want. They're unpredictable. Ohh, another thing," Ferrus added. "They have an incredibly advanced sense of smell."

"Like a dog?" asked Nia.

"No, not like a dog, you loper," Ferrus said. "A bullpar's sense of smell is so advanced he can even tell if you're related – just by smelling you."

"Whatever," said Nia as she shook her head and took another sip of her green beer.

Meanwhile, the blue guards were still bothering Finch, who was still ignoring them. "You are just a stupid, worthless animal. You can't even eat," one of the blue guards shouted. He poured his drink right on top of Finch. When the mug was empty, they started laughing hysterically.

Finch remained steadfast, floating silently, and dripping softly. Gala started to intervene. Nia restrained her. "Again, not a good idea."

"Your friend's right, sweetie. Those two are bad news. Besides, I have no doubts that Finch can take care of himself," said Ferrus.

"Get over there!" yelled the bartender.

Holland walked over to Finch with a mop and a bucket. Finch gently floated a few feet backward. "Guys," he said. "Tell you what, if you leave the bullpar alone, the bartender has offered to buy you a round on the house."

"Come on, Kive," said the second blue guard (Mong). "We came here to drink. I like free." They walked to the bar. The bartender served them two beers. Kive 'accidentally' knocked one over. Sorry about that, I'm going to need another. The bartender reluctantly but quickly and quietly filled him a fresh mug. Mung thought that was funny, so he did the same thing.

Holland began mopping up around Finch. Gala was not happy. She ducked away from Nia and walked over to Holland, grabbing a towel from his shoulder. She began wiping Finch, patting him down.

"Whoa, don't do that," Holland said. "He might bite you."

"I'm just trying to help clean him up," Gala said. "People like that make me so angry. Bullpars are such wonderful, regal creatures. Why, I hear they're smarter than people," she glanced back toward the captain. "I can't believe anyone would treat him like that."

"His name is Finch," Holland said. "Hi Finch, allow me to introduce myself. I'm Gala Vaurienne," she said with a partial bow.

Nia walked over. "It's getting late, Gala. You have a meeting first thing in the morning, remember."

"Yeah, you're right," Gala replied.

The blue guards walked back over to Finch. "Hey stupid bullpar!" Kive said as he threw nuts at Finch.

"Don't do that to him," Gala said as she looked up from the guard's belly button; he was quite a bit larger than she had originally thought. He dropped some nuts on her head, too.

"Guys, I have to clean all of that up," Holland said. "We gave you free beers, what else do you want?"

Then Kive threw nuts at Holland, and a few more at Finch, too. For his part, the bullpar seemed oblivious to everything going on around him.

"I want satisfaction," Kive said. "I heard about this bullpar at the Vermilion and how interesting he was and how he's supposed to be good luck. Well, I haven't seen anything to make me think he's anything but a stupid, floating bag of shaka. And the rest of you aren't any better." With that, he raised his mug and poured it on Holland's head. "What a loper! That's the most fun I've had tonight, eh Mung?" They both laughed sloppily.

The captain intervened somewhat tentatively. "Ahem, you two blue gentlemen really should behave better. I highly recommend that you leave this bullpar, these ladies, and this lad alone."

"Ha ha. *You* highly recommend? Well, I highly recommend that you go back to your seat or I'll blast these ladies and this 'lad' right in front of your drunk old carcass. What do you think about that old man?" Kive said.

The captain shrugged at the ladies as if to say 'sorry, I tried' and then walked back and sat in his booth. He smiled sheepishly and took a drink of his whiskey. Then Mung stepped up to the still-dripping Holland and looked him up and down. Both Nia and Gala began to reach for their knives. Mung turned and kicked over Holland's bucket.

The blue guards thought that was the funniest thing ever. They laughed riotously. Finch slowly turned, as if on a spindle, to face the blue bullies.

"I think you guys are going to have to leave the bar now," Holland said.

Mung pushed Holland down onto the floor so hard that the assistant head bartender slid back several feet and crashed into a table. Holland got up; ready to fight. But the head bartender did not want trouble with the Blue Oko.

"Gentlemen, no need to fight. What say I buy you another round?"

"Wonderful idea," Kive said. "And these girls are going to join us for a drink."

The blue guards turned toward the ladies, towering over the smaller messengers. Kive grabbed Gala and Mung grabbed Nia. That was the beginning of a big mistake. Finch opened one eye wider than the other and focused that eye on this scene chameleon-style (only one eye moved as the blue guards pulled the messengers toward the bar).

Nia yelled, "Let go of me!" Mung laughed. Gala struggled, flailing, trying to get to her cuttas. Holland got up from under the table and stood alongside the head bartender.

"You need to let the ladies go," he said.

"Or what!?" asked Kive? The head bartender looked at Holland; they nodded at each other.

"Or we'll stop you." They both stepped forward, blocking the blue goons' path to the bar.

Meanwhile, both Gala and Nia were struggling mightily, landing ineffective blows on their much larger assailants. Mung and Kive, while still holding the messengers with one hand each, used their free hands to swipe Holland and the head bartender away with one stroke – sending the would-be defenders flying. The blue two then started dragging the messengers toward the bar. For their part, Gala and Nia were still struggling to reach their knives.

Finch was still observing, still statuesque.

The whole bar was now watching this scene play out. No one else seemed either motivated or brave enough to intervene further. The captain took a big swig of liquid courage and got up from his seat once again. The old man crossed in front of the blue guards and their struggling quarry.

"Get out of the way, old timer. Someone of your age is likely to get hurt in a bar fight," said Mung. Ferrus stood his ground. He wanted to do something courageous. He wanted to stop these bullies. All he could manage – and that took every fiber in his being – was to remain standing in that spot. Sweat poured down his face. His mouth slowly fell open and he began to shake.

Kive swung Gala around and struck Ferrus with the young lady's green boots. By now, everyone in the bar was focused on nothing but the blue goons. No one else dared to help. Finch rolled his one eye back to its normal position and closed it. He seemed to take a deep breath – which was more animation than he'd shown all night. Then he moved like lightning. His talon-like claws dug into Mung's back causing him to scream and relinquish his hold on Nia. In the blink of an eye, Finch moved on to Kive, biting his arm. Of course, Kive let go of Gala. She quickly stepped away. Of course, he also screamed loudly.

He shouted something like, "My arm!" But it sounded more like, "Maaaaaahhhhhhh!" Of course, Finch didn't let go. He had a good bite – and he was enjoying it.

Mong ran out of the bar, screaming and reaching in vain for his bloody back – now turned to jelly. Kive was still screaming and trying to run. But he couldn't take a single step. His feet were running in place on the wet floor. Finch had him in complete lockdown – anchored in suspended space. "My arm! My arm! Let go! Please leggo my arm!" he begged.

Holland ran to Nia and Gala.

"Are you all right?" he asked.

"We're fine," said Gala.

"What about you?" asked Nia. "I'm okay, just a little wet." he responded. "And my ego is a little bruised."

Kive was still yelling. "My arm! Let go of my arm! Aaaaahhhh! Aaaaahhh!" The captain's somewhat crooked smile had given way to laughter; he was enjoying himself immensely from his seated position on the floor.

Holland walked up to Finch and almost placed his hand on the bullpar's back, but thought better of that. "Finch, I think he's had enough. You can probably let go now."

Finch looked up at Holland with a roll of one eye and then back at Kive. The bullpar bit down harder – with a crunching crack. Only then did he reluctantly release his jaws and return to his normal resting state. The blue guard's arm was hanging as if bent from the middle of the forearm because Finch had bitten it clean through the bone. Kive began to bleed – in spurts! He was still screaming and grabbed a towel from the bar to wrap his wound as he ran out the door.

Nia, Holland, and Gala walked toward the exit. As they passed by the captain, he held up a toast and said, "Thanks for the show! Finch likes you, sweetie. By the way, did I tell you that bullpars love clords?" He took another sip of whiskey – and his smile got even bigger.

There was a bowl of fruit on the bar. There were a several clords in the bowl. Gala walked straight to the bowl and grabbed a clord. She presented it to Finch with a smile and a reverent bow. "Thank you, my hero," she said. Though the clord was the size of a footie, Finch reached out and consumed the entire clord in a single bite. Though Gala wasn't sure, he sort of seemed to smile.

"Ohhhh, I wish you hadn't done that," Holland said, flipping back up the small sign in front of the fruit bowl that said 'Do Not Feed to the Bullpar.'

"Why not? He deserved a reward," Gala said.

"He certainly did, but clords give him...a...a reaction," Holland said.

"What kind of reaction? Will he be okay?" Gala asked?

"Oh, he'll be fine. It's actually the rest of us that might have to worry," Holland said. "We found out a while back. Although we think that

Finch can eat just about anything, if he eats clords, he gets really …well, he has these… digestive reactions."

The three walked out of the bar and got into the floater. Gala drove; Nia was in the passenger seat and Holland was in the back. When they pulled away, they saw Finch silhouetted against the light of the open door. At that moment, they heard an extremely loud foghorn – *BERRRRRRMMP!* – it must've come from a ship in the bay. Some of the windows in the bar shattered. Holland was doubled over in the back seat, laughing hysterically. *BERRRRRRMMP!* The foghorn blasted again. But it was so loud; it sounded closer than Pelican Point. Holland continued laughing like a crazy person – slapping the seat with tears in his eyes.

Dozens of customers ran out of the bar holding their noses. Captain Ferrus strolled toward the door. He took the opportunity to reach behind the bar on his way out and pilfer a bottle of Gemini whiskey, hiding it under his long coat in a single motion. Customers leaving the bar scattered in all directions. Some of them fell on their knees as struggling to breathe.

"I tried to tell you," Holland said, between laughing breaths, "Clords give him wicked gas. Ha ha ha ha!"

The captain walked out of the bar with his bottle, smiling ear-to-ear. He tipped his hat to Gala. Yet another foghorn blast permeated the air – *BERRRRRRMMP!* – and broke the remaining windows in the bar. They all laughed as they drove back to the hotel.

The captain stood and looked at the stars. He took a drink of whiskey. And then he saw something he hadn't seen in more than two years, Finch gliding out of the bar.

CHAPTER 21

Odds On

The suns were shining through the window of her fabulous hotel room. Vaurienne admired the ocean view as she sat up in the comfy bed and stretched. It was glorious – especially seeing it unfiltered. She went to the balcony, opened the double doors, and listened to the quiet, soft rush of the waves as they crashed onto the shore. The sounds and the setting were serene; she could stay here for a while…Or even in the Gold Oko with Oshi. The okos were so different from Hamada. Sometimes she wondered, *What if things were different? What if....*

But the time for wondering was done. There was business to attend to. She grabbed her eye-guards and popped them in – it was always good to be prepared when traveling to the Donja. Eye-guards were essential gear, almost as important as water. But they were especially important when riding in an open-air floater. The sand could scratch one's eyeballs like thousands of tiny shards of glass. She'd seen an older Jader with scarred eyeballs when she was young.

She knew the negotiations would be tough today, even though the terms were already clear. Roden knew what he owed...and he would probably pay it. But then again, it was Roden. And the amount he owed was three million levs. That was not pocket change, even for Roden. Besides, he never met a debt he was content with paying. The negotiations never seemed to stop with him. You never really knew what you had in your pocket until you were through the door and well on your way out of the Red Oko.

She got ready and knocked on the door of Mr. Moustache and Brown-teeth. "Hey guys, let's go get some breakfast before the negotiations start," she yelled through the door.

Mr. Moustache opened the door a crack. "Brown-teeth is just getting up. We'll meet you downstairs."

Gala went down to the hotel's breakfast buffet. There was a smorgasbord of options, including mimosas and morning dews. She opted for just pancakes and warm clord syrup with some goat's milk. While she was eating, Nia showed up and said a quick hello as she walked past. (It wasn't considered good form to sit with a negotiator on the opposite side of the table right before a business deal.)

Gala smiled as she took a bite; it was nice to have a friend – even if the friend was in a different clan and even if they didn't get to see each other very often. Still, a friend was a friend, and she was glad to have this one.

As Vaurienne was finishing, Mr. Moustache and Brown-teeth arrived at breakfast. They each grabbed a stiff mahogany root lungo and a handful of pastries. Brown-teeth shoved about five into his mouth at one time and gulped down his drink, with crumbs falling hither and thither. Mr. Moustache meticulously ate a single pastry, one small bite at a time – three in a row – followed by a single sip of his hot beverage after each bite. They didn't bother to sit.

Neptunia approached the Jade crew. "Roden will see you now in the Tansin Grand Casino. Please follow me." Vaurienne got up, nodded toward Mr. Moustache and Brown-teeth, and they followed Neptunia. They walked down several hallways, each more ornate than the last. They had to pass through four more doorways guarded by the men in the small, red hats. Finally, they made their way into the Tansin Grand – the most opulent of several casinos at the Vermilion.

"Your Lordship, May I present Gala Vaurienne, messenger of Gruun," said Neptunia. "She is accompanied by Mr. Moustache and Brown-teeth." Brown-teeth and Mr. Moustache nervously sat at a table in the back. They didn't welcome the attention. Their job was to watch the door and basically give the appearance of 'muscle' in case anything went wrong. The reality was that two or three people in a sprawling complex controlled by an Oko leader with a virtual army at his disposal were little more than ceremonial window-dressing. But that's the way things were handled on Minos. Part culture, part ceremony, part family, part showin' off. (Although Gala's comrades *were* carrying the latest Browning blasters.)

Roden was, by far, the least height-gifted clan leader – even shorter than the trollish Gruum. He was a rotund man but with smallish features; even the triangle beard on his chin was under-sized. He had plump, reddish cheeks. Rare for a Minosian, he was bald.

The Red Clan leader was seated at the center of a long table. To his left and to his right were a dozen or so underlings, including Neptunia. Roden wore a large, red silk turban. It was wrapped around the middle with a wide golden-threaded band, and in the center of that band was a huge ruby. He rose to greet Vaurienne.

"Welcome to Scarlet Beach and the Vermilion, Vaurienne. It's so good to see you again," he said. "Please sit, be comfortable so we can talk."

She sat on the other side of the long table, in the lone center seat, facing Roden.

"Before we talk business, can I get you a drink? Have you had breakfast?" he asked.

"Thank you, my Lord," she said. "I've eaten."

"Good then. Would you like a drink? Perhaps some amber stout?" he offered.

"No, thank you, my Lord," she replied.

"Very well," Roden said. "Perhaps I could offer you a Jade beer…or a Blood & Sand?" he offered.

"That's very kind of you, my Lord. Nothing for me, thanks," she said.

"Oh, but perhaps some Gemini whiskey? Or what about a simple sand-apple cider?" he asked.

"My Lord, you are too generous, but I am quite quenched at the moment," Vaurienne said.

"Very well, then," Roden said.

Roden whispered to an attendant behind him who quickly scurried away. "I've just ordered you a few things – for later – in case you change your mind."

In a moment, a different attendant returned with a rolling cart. He proceeded to place in front of Vaurienne a variety of drinks – one by one – everything she had just declined, including an entire bottle of Gemini whiskey.

"Thank you, my Lord," Vaurienne said with a slight nod.

After the attendant left, Vaurienne inquired, "Lord Roden, might I trouble you for a tall glass of cold water?"

Roden smiled and chuckled a bit. "Certainly, Vaurienne, messenger of Gruun," he replied with a wave of his hand. A few seconds later, yet another attendant returned with a glass of water, which was placed in directly in front of her.

"Are you drinking, my Lord?" Vaurienne asked. "Oh, I never drink during negotiations," he said. "At least, not until we have a deal."

"Well, my Lord, perhaps we should open this whiskey right now. My understanding is that we already have a deal. You and Gruun agreed to terms nearly three months ago at the last Council meeting. We delivered the special grade of ternium you required last month. I'm just here now to collect the payment," said Vaurienne. "How would you like to make that payment, my Lord?"

It was a risky move, going straight to the payment request. It was a slight breach of etiquette and she knew Roden wouldn't like it, but she really didn't want to sit there all day to collect what was already agreed to be paid.

"Vaurienne, ever the shrewd negotiator. I like your fire. Right to the point. But, it will take some time to get that amount of money together," he said.

"My Lord, you did know I was coming to collect. Actually, the agreement was promised to be paid yesterday," Vaurienne said. "You do intend to pay, do you not?"

Calling Roden out, so directly, so early in the meeting – in front of his cadre – was definitely an aggressive move. Vaurienne was pushing the envelope. Mr. Moustache squirmed uncomfortably in a his seat.

"Of course, I will be happy to pay what I owe, my dear. You know that I always pay my debts," he said.

"Well then, is there a problem?" she continued to press the issue. "I was under the impression that you were the wealthiest of the Minosian leaders, so I would think that you certainly could pay your debt. Or am I wrong, my Lord?"

Roden was taken aback at her brazenness. Most of his aides were just as shocked. Neptunia glared at her. (She shook her head to Gala and mouthed, "What are you doing?") Vaurienne pushed her water aside; she looked directly at Roden, pausing for effect, and downed the Blood & Sand in a single gulp. Then she wiped her mouth with the back of her hand.

"There is no problem, Vaurienne. (He looked around.) As I said, I am more than happy to pay my debts. Trade among the clans is the lifeblood of our shared economies. We have to work together to survive. Now, I know that the Donja may not be as comfortable as the Okos, but we all have our homes. It's important that we continue the trade so that each of the clans can get what they need. Why, I've been trading with Gruun for more than 20 years."

"My Lord, I think you're trying to change the subject. Let me be direct: Are you going to pay or not? If not, I'll have to report you to the Council," said Vaurienne. "You've said twice that you'll be happy to pay, but I still don't see any money. Would you like me to have my comrades help your bankers pack it into our sacks?" She looked back at Mr. Moustache and Brown-teeth at the table behind her. They were shocked and glued to their seats; Brown-teeth's mouth was hanging open (showing his slightly sickening teeth – in their varying shades of brown). Mr. Moustache sat stone-faced and motionless. They had never witnessed such a break in protocol.

"Now see here, Vaurienne, messenger of Gruun," Roden said. "There are certain expectations of our business arrangement, certain conventions that I thought you were aware of."

"The only expectation I have right now is that you will pay Gruun the sum that you agreed to pay when we delivered your ternium: The sum of three million levs. So, I repeat, what is the problem, my Lord? Could it be that you don't have the money?" (Vaurienne was violating any number of customs, but she was loving it. Sure, there might be a penalty at some point, but not now; she was in the moment, letting loose as she had rarely done.)

"Of course I have the money. I am the richest leader on Levon. I could pay a 10 times that amount!" Roden stopped short. Vaurienne had knocked him off his game. He was searching for an emphatic ending to his statement but he couldn't find the right words. "Before breakfast!" he added forcefully, striking the table with his tiny fist, but his exclamation had somewhat less impact than he intended.

Several of Roden's underlings were trying to understand what he meant by that. Was it some sort of code? Vaurienne knew she had him on the ropes, so she decided to close in for the kill.

"So, Roden, have you had breakfast yet?"

"No, not yet," he said. "I was going to have it brought in during our discussions," he said.

"So, if, as you say, you can pay 10 times the amount you owe before breakfast, I guess – since you haven't had breakfast yet today – this is the perfect time to pay the much smaller amount of three million levs, right?" she asked.

Roden exasperatingly pushed his turban back on his head. He looked to the left and then to the right for support from his underlings. They offered none. He took a deep breath and let it out slowly.

Vaurienne was loving it. "My Lord, would you like to pay me now – and then have some breakfast? I'm sure it will make you feel better. And then we can crack open this bottle of whiskey. Does that work for you?"

"I-I-I..." Roden took a deep breath and blew it all out. "I guess so."

"Roden, my Lord, you drive a hard bargain," said Vaurienne slyly as she stood and raised her glass in his direction.

Roden whispered behind him to an attendant. Then he reached over and grabbed the bottle of whiskey. He opened it, ignore the glass in front him, and drank several huge gulps directly from the bottle. A moment later, six large bags were placed on the table in front of Vaurienne.

Roden motioned with his hand; then everyone got up and began to mingle. Roden took a moment and gathered himself; he approached Vaurienne. "You are a force of nature, my dear. I was not expecting that. You do realize that is not how I typically handle things."

"I apologize, my Lord, but I need to get back to my leader with the money."

"Speaking of your leader, I wonder if Gruun knows about the show you just put on here. I tell you what, if you will play me one hand of Poke & Roll, I won't have to share the embarrassment of this morning with him. Hmmmm?"

Vaurienne didn't want to play Poke & Roll with Roden. She really just wanted to get out of there with the money and her body intact. She had definitely surpassed anything she'd even heard of in a direct negotiation with a Council leader. Etiquette was out the door. But now, she was beginning to think that she might possibly have let her eagerness get the better of her. As she saw it now, there were two likely possibilities. On the one hand, if Roden told Gruun, she would probably feel some pain. But on the other hand, Roden might be too embarrassed to tell Gruun. On the other-other hand, she was now thinking that playing cards with Roden might be a good move to help smooth things over a little."

"Certainly, my Lord. But just one hand," she said. "Gruun is expecting me."

"Of course, Vaurienne," Roden said. He whispered to an attendant who was nearby. "Someone will get a dealer and set up a table for us so we can close out this business with a little fun. How does that sound?"

"That's great. It would be an honor to play with you, my Lord," Vaurienne replied obsequiously.

The attendant returned and whispered to Roden. "Our table is ready, Vaurienne. Shall we?" he pointed the way toward a table with a waiting dealer. Roden pulled out the chair for Vaurienne and she sat down. Mr. Moustache and Brown-teeth stood behind Vaurienne.

"This is not a good idea," whispered Mr. Moustache.

"I don't have much of a choice," Vaurienne whispered back.

Roden sat down. Three more assistants showed up and put the six bags of money on the table in front of Vaurienne. Mr. Moustache and Brown-teeth each took two bags and set them at their feet.

"My Lord, with your permission, we will begin," said the dealer.

"Absolutely," said Roden. "Vaurienne, do you know how to play? Perhaps Alvin should review the rules so that you feel more comfortable with your wager."

"I don't plan to bet much," Vaurienne said. "Just a friendly game, right, my Lord?"

"Of course, my dear Gala," said Roden with a smile.

Poke & Roll: A popular Minosian card and dice game that has four rounds of betting, as follows:

1. **Bet 1**
2. Lap 1: Each player gets three cards
3. **Bet 2**
4. Lap 2: Each player rolls a die and receives that many additional cards
5. **Bet 3**
6. Lap 3: Each player rolls a die and has the choice to a) receive that many more additional cards, or b) to 'poke' an opponent, by taking that many cards from an opponent
   a. If an opponent is 'poked,' he or she gets another roll as 'compensation'
7. **Bet 4**
8. Reveal

- A Minosian sunsdeck consists of 64 cards.
- There are 15 of each color (red, green, gold, and blue) – along with 4 black suns.
- Black suns cards are wild.
- The player with the most matches wins.

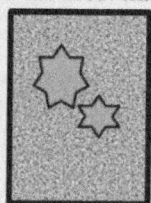

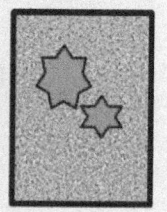

MASTER POKE: A hand with all four black suns automatically wins.

"The name of the game is Poke & Roll. We have a brand new

Minosian Sunsdeck and a regular six-sided die. We'll have the standard four rounds of betting and will play with table stakes. Only what is here at the table can be bet; no additional funds may be added without the full agreement of all parties. At the end of the hand, whoever has the most cards of a single color is the winner," Alvin said. "Do you both understand and agree?" he asked.

Vaurienne nodded. Roden nodded – and smiled again at Vaurienne.

Alvin placed the die in the middle of the table. He opened a new deck of cards and said, "Opening bets, please."

Roden deferred to Vaurienne. She pulled out the hundred levs that she had gotten the night before. Roden matched the bet. The dealer gave Vaurienne and Roden each three cards. Vaurienne snuck a peek at her cards. She had two red suns and a single blue. Roden didn't bother looking at his cards.

"The bet is to you, my Lord," Alvin said. Roden laid a gold bar on the table. "Uh oh," Vaurienne thought. The only money she had was about 150 levs. The gold bar was worth twenty times that." She pulled all the money from her pocket and looked at it in her hand. Roden looked at her and said, "That's fine, my dear. It's just a game – for fun, right? We'll call it even."

She put all her money on the table.

"My Lord, would you care to roll?" Alvin asked.

"Oh, no, please let our guest roll first," Roden said. Alvin placed the die in front of Vaurienne. She picked it up, shook it in her hand and rolled it across the table.

"One," said Alvin. He dealt her an additional card. Vaurienne looked at the card. It was a third red. "Not great, but not bad," she thought. The dealer placed the die in front of Roden. He picked it up, blew it, and rolled. "Five," said Alvin. He dealt Roden five more cards. Roden now had eight cards to Vaurienne's four.

"As you have the highest number of cards, the next bet is yours, my Lord."

Roden pulled out another gold bar and placed it on the table. Vaurienne had no more money.

"My Lord, I'm sorry but I have nothing else to wager," she said. "My dear, it would be exceedingly bad form to quit in the middle of a hand," Roden said. Vaurienne looked around. Unbeknownst to her, a sizable crowd had gathered and the subject of their interest was her game with Roden. "Surely, you must have something to wager so we can continue our game," Roden said.

Mr. Moustache leaned over and whispered in her ear, "I told you this was a bad idea. You're an inexperienced spare. You're screwing this up. Gruun should never have put you in this role. If you quit now – in front all these witnesses – it would be considered a slap in the face to the Red Clan. Add that to the spectacle you put on earlier and you're on the verge of creating a clan-clash. Gruun will have your hide for this. And I, for one, will be happy to watch him skin it off you. You had better find something else to bet."

Vaurienne was more nervous than she had been in a long time. She looked around – at nothing. She had nothing else to wager. Then she saw the bags on the table. Bags full of money. But that was Gruun's money. She couldn't. But if she didn't, she would likely create an incident that could lead to a clan-clash. The thought occurred to her that this might have been Roden's plan all along. And she had fallen for it!

Then she remembered. Her hummingbird. She loved that blaster. It was so small, and cute, and powerful. She did not want to lose it. But she had little choice. She pulled it out and laid it on the table.

"What is that, a toy?" asked Roden.

"No, my Lord. It is an advanced blaster. A prototype concealed-size derringer model. One of the IDC's newest weapons."

He picked it up and examined it. "Is this really a weapon?" he asked.

"Yes, my Lord. It is small but quite powerful," she replied.

Roden picked up the hummingbird and inspected it. He aimed it at a huge chandelier in the center of the room and fired. The blast shattered the light and blew it off the ceiling. It rained a thousand tiny lights inside the casino. Everyone shielded their eyes as bits of glass fell to the floor. What remained of the magnificent feature hung, swinging precariously for a moment, until it fell to the ground with a thud.

"Very well, I accept this as the wager." Roden set the weapon on the table. Vaurienne let out a deep sigh.

"Your roll, my Lord," Alvin said as he placed the die in front of Roden. "No, I'll defer to our lovely guest from the Jade Clan again," Roden said. Alvin moved the die to Vaurienne. She rolled. The die rolled almost to the edge of the table, then rocked backward. "Two," Alvin said.

"I'll take 'em," Vaurienne said.

Alvin slid her two more cards. She leaned down and looked under the slightly upturned cards. Two more reds. She has six cards now, but five reds. At least she had a fighting chance. A longshot perhaps, but at least a chance.

Roden grabbed the die, blew it again, and rolled.

"Six," said Alvin.

Roden smiled. I think I'll poke this Jader. The crowd "oooohhhed." Alvin slid all of Vaurienne's cards over to Roden. She had no cards at all now. But she was due a final roll as 'compensation.' She picked up the die, shook it – and blew it this time – as she had seen Roden do, then rolled.

"Five," said Alvin. He dealt her five final cards. She didn't look at them this time. "What did it matter?" she thought. She only had five cards – total. Roden now had 14. Even if all hers matched – and there was a slim chance of that – the best she could do was a tie. The minimum number of matches Roden could have would be five – because he now had her five red cards. And that was the best possible outcome! What was far more likely, was that Vaurienne was going to lose. All of her money would be gone – along with her only remaining Hummingbird. She felt foolish.

"Final bets," said Alvin.

Roden looked at his cards. He looked at Vaurienne. "I'm sorry my dear, but a man must play his best hand," he said. He took the turban off his head. He placed it – along with that huge ruby – on the table. The crowd watching went silent for a few seconds. Then the murmurs started. Though she had tried to maintain a poker face up to this point, her mouth began to hang open and her eyes grew wider. She had forgotten about the final bets.

"My Lord, the bet is too much, I have nothing else to wager," she said and hung her head.

Roden reached over and gently lifted Vaurienne's chin. My dear, you have plenty of money to match my bet." He nodded toward the two bags of money still on the table.

"But, my Lord, I cannot," she said. "That is not my money. It belongs to Gruun. You know what that would mean."

"I'm sorry, Vaurienne, but you did agree to table stakes. And those bags are on the table," Roden said. "Alvin, is that correct?" he asked, rather loudly. Roden smiled at her.

"Yes, the rules say that bets must come from what is at or on the table at the beginning of the game. You both agreed to the rules," said the dealer. She knew she was in trouble. Mr. Moustache leaned over. Vaurienne hoped he had something helpful to say. "I'm going to make sure Gruun knows exactly how you failed," he sneered.

Well, she thought, *that wasn't particularly helpful.*

Her only good idea was to try going on the offensive. After all, it had worked pretty well earlier. "That's ridiculous. I'm not betting my leader's money," she said. "I'm going to fold and take the bags back to Gruun. You win, Roden."

She stood up and grabbed the bags. About two dozen red guards closed ranks around the table. She didn't have her blaster. The Jade party of three was extremely outnumbered. She looked to her comrades. No help there.

Vaurienne slowly turned and placed the bags back on the table.

"Wise decision, my dear," Roden said. "I will accept the one million levs in these bags as a match to my ruby. Please sit and let's finish the game. She sat down hesitatingly. She was going to lose Gruun's money. There was no way around it. She would certainly lose her position as messenger. Gruun would probably throw her back in that awful cage. That was enough money that he might even kill her. She'd seen him kill for less. And the worst part was that she had walked right into Roden's trap. She had been over-confident – and it was going to cost her.

"Time to show your cards. My Lord, you have the highest number of cards, so you reveal first," Alvin prompted.

Roden turned over a pair of blue cards. Then he turned over three gold cards. Then he turned over four red cards. He still had five remaining cards, face down. "What is he doing?" thought Vaurienne. "He's playing with me, in front of all his clansmen."

"Payback is a vamp," Roden whispered. He turned over his remaining five cards – they were all red. He had nine red matches. There were cheers from the crowd of red clansmen.

"Please reveal your cards, Vaurienne," Roden said. He was clearly enjoying this.

"What's the point?" she asked softly.

"The point? The point my dear, is that we must finish the game. We must follow the rules. You see, you really didn't follow the rules this morning, but now we will follow them to the letter – as it should be," said Roden, smiling confidently.

"You know what he's going to do to me," she said quietly.

"That, my dear, is something you should have thought about before you shot your mouth off earlier," he whispered back.

"Vaurienne," he said much louder (for everyone to hear), please show us your cards. You do still have a chance to win," he said with a smirk. "Albeit an incredibly small and highly unlikely chance," he added in a whisper.

Everyone was looking at her. She felt sick to her stomach. Perhaps if she waited; if she didn't turn her cards over, she could delay the inevitable. She could surely hold off turning those cards over for a few more minutes – or even longer. Maybe a few days? She was thinking that a year or two might be good.

"We do need to see your cards to finish the hand," said Alvin.

This was it, Vaurienne thought. *She had tried to fit in. Tried to be a Jader – not that it was something that she really ever wanted in the first place. But this was her life now. And today, that life was going to end.*

She reached up to the table and turned over one card. She didn't even look at it; she stared straight at Roden. She wanted to see his face. Was he going to gloat, smile? Did he care in the slightest that he was serving her up like a waah-waah on a platter to Gruun?

"One black," said Alvin.

"What!?" said Vaurienne.

She looked at Alvin. He had half a smile. She turned over her second card. Afraid to look at the card again, she stared straight at Alvin this time.

"A second black," he said. The crowd noise was getting louder now. People were straining to see. Brown-teeth unclipped his blaster. Vaurienne was almost more nervous now than before. She put her hand on the third card; she hesitated. The tension was incredible. Her hand was actually sweating. She pulled her hand back and wiped it on her shirt. She reached out to put her hand on the third card again and slowly turned it over. "A third black," said Alvin. The crowd grew completely silent.

She took a deep breath – that almost sounded like thunder amid the stark lack of sound – and turned the fourth card. "One gold," said Alvin. Roden exhaled a sign of relief.

"His lordship, Roden, has nine red matches. Vaurienne, messenger of Gruun, has one gold and...." She turned over her last card. "Four blacks," Alvin said. "A master poke. Vaurienne wins."

Everyone was stunned. Vaurienne most of all. Part of her was relieved. Another part of her wanted to celebrate. Yet another part of her wanted to throw up. But all of her parts wanted to get out of that casino – fast.

Alvin pushed the bets from the middle of the table right in front of Vaurienne. She scooped the money from the table into her pocket. She dropped the gold bars into one of the bags. She picked up the turban and examined it. She looked at Roden. She pried the big ruby from the turban with one of her cuttas. She threw it up and caught it. Thanks for the game," Vaurienne said. She then slid the turban back to Roden. "I can't take your hat," she said, "my Lord." She turned and smiled to herself. Then she took a deep breath and let it out slowly. "We're leaving now. Get the bags," she said to Mr. Moustache and Brown-teeth as she strolled past. Roden was still sitting at the table with a shocked look on his face.

They packed the bags into the floater and quickly left the Vermilion and the fields of crimson clover. On the way out, she thought she saw Finch on the front steps. But there were a lot of people around him – if it was him. Anyway, she was solely focused on getting the floater and her winnings back to Hamada. On the way out of town, they passed Captain Ferrus.

Vaurienne slowed the floater.

"What are you doing?" said Mr. Moustache. "We need to get out of the Red Oko and back to Hamada."

"Yeah," added Brown-teeth.

"I just need to take care of something," she said. "Hi Captain!" The floater pulled close to him. Vaurienne reached into her bag – pulling out the gold bars and the big ruby. "Maybe this is enough to get your ship back in the water," she said as she tossed all three in his direction. "Good luck!"

"Thank you, young lady!" the captain yelled after her. He looked toward the coast and *The Emancipation* at Pelican Point. That old, griseled face broke into a wide grin. The suns shone on him. The blue sky was at his back; the wind blew his long beard and even longer hair. Life was going to be good again. He took a drink from his Gemini whiskey bottle. Or rather, he tried to take a drink. The bottle was empty. He turned it upside down. "But I sure am thirsty," he said to himself. He looked back in the direction of the tavern. Then he turned again toward the coast. He couldn't decide which way to go. He was pretty sure the bars and that big ruby would give him enough money to fix up his ship. *Maybe*, he thought, *I could get a drink first*. He looked toward the tavern and then back toward Pelican Point. He wavered. In the end, the captain turned and walked toward Mitch's Tavern.

ACT IV ~ EVOLUTION

CHAPTER 22
Pillow Talk

Twelve years earlier...

After disguising the floater and cleaning up around the farmhouse, they had used up the better part of the day. Evening was approaching with the two suns setting together; it would be a very dark night. Baron and Ruby settled in on the twin couches; Mom and Dad tucked them in. Oliva walked toward the bedroom door…she looked back at Tanner. "Tuck me in?" she asked as she removed her shirt.

"Good night kids," Tanner said as he hopped up and tripped over Baron's shoes. He closed the bedroom door behind him. Husband and wife kissed passionately – and stumbled into bed. Oliva snuggled close to her husband. She lay her head on his chest and he stroked her hair.

"Tanner, how did they find us?" Oliva asked.

"I don't know, Liv," he responded. "I tried to be so careful."

"I feel like I've been hiding for a lifetime. First the two-year trip from Earth to get away from the IDC, then the past 20 years here on Levon – and now the Jade Clan. We built a home and made a family. What was I thinking?" he asked aloud and rubbed his hair backward with both hands.

"What's done is done, my man. You did what you thought best for our little girl – for all of us. And I agreed," Oliva said as she turned to face him on her side.

"I know honey, but we can't let them find us again. Our family could be in real danger. These guys are seriously bad news," Tanner said. "It might not go as well next time."

She caressed his face. "We just have to make sure there isn't a next time," said Liv.

"I just need to think this out. They obviously don't know where we live—," he began.

"—Or they'd have been to our house by now," she finished.

"Right," he responded as he sat up. "The only thing I can think of is that they somehow tracked us through the gravity park. That's where they were – they seemed to be waiting for us. Those quatchees must have known we were coming."

"Maybe the kids put something up on that KikTalk thing they use," Liv suggested. "We have three layers of security and anonymization on their screens, not to mention our home security efence, but maybe some small clue slipped through out onto the grid."

Tanner rolled out of bed and started pacing, stroking his chin. "I guess that's possible," he said. "I've been turning this over and over in my mind; You know, I still think it had something to do with the park. When we won the tickets, I was careful to have them picked up at 'will call' and not actually sent to us."

"That's my scientist," Liv said. "Analyzing and thinking over and over. That's one of the reasons I love you. But, however the Jaders found us, we just need to be sure it doesn't happen again."

"Absolutely. Well, there's no way they could track us after we used the ternium reactor to high-tail it to your parents' old farmhouse. I'm just concerned because they've never gotten this close before," he said.

"Me, too, but I trust you with all my heart, Tan," she said.

He looked out through the window at about a million shining stars. Levon's low light pollution (one of the benefits of technology controls), along with tonight's double-dark, made the stars appear exceptionally bright. "I don't think I've ever seen so many stars," he said.

Liv turned on her back and looked up through the huge skylight ceiling and marveled at the uncountable number of twinkling stars against the black night sky. She sighed. The sight was positively mesmerizing.

"By the way, I should tell you something," he started to say. "When we engaged the ternium reactor to boost our speed—"

"—It gave us all wicked headaches," Liv said, lying back with a smile and gently rubbing her temples in small circles. "Yeah, we pretty much figured that out."

"Well, yes, that," Tanner agreed. "But the trip that took us half an hour to get here will take ten times as long on the way back home. To get that extra boost with the ternium reactor technology, it actually burned up the ternium… and basically fried the reactor. Which means that, on the way home, we'll be flying at regular speed."

"No complaints here," said Liv, rubbing her forehead.

Tanner went back to bed. He pulled a huge blanket over the two of them. "Maybe," he suggested, "the Jaders somehow found out he would be at the Gravity Park because of the ternium." He continued to think about how they were almost found while his wife cuddled up to him. He kissed her head. They spooned; drifting off into a welcome night's sleep.

The next morning, the family was in the floater on their way home (albeit at a much lower speed than their previous adventure.)

Ruby and Baron were strapped in their back seats, still drowsy from their early departure. They dozed as the floater rose and headed toward home. Liv looked back at her children then turned to look at her husband. She put her hand on his shoulder, rubbed his neck a little, and smiled.

Later, when the kids woke up, Baron asked Ruby to play some of her old music. "Can you play some of those ancient Earth tunes?"

"What do you want to hear?" she asked.

"Maybe something fun. We'll be stuck in the floater for hours and hours. If we could at least pretend we were moving – or dancing, that might make the trip go a little faster," he suggested.

Ruby picked a song called *99 Red Balloons* by Nena. Father pushed a button on the control panel, connecting her screen audio to the floater speakers, and turned up the volume. (He loved those 'ancient Earth songs' just as much as Ruby did; he had heard a lot of them in his favorite bar during his time on Earth. He would go there every weekend with his old buddy Jalen and listen to those songs for hours.)

Father couldn't get up and dance (because he was driving) so he did the next best thing: Finger dancing! He claimed it was his own invention. While he sat in the driver's seat with both hands on the wheel, he would move his fingers to the beat. He moved them up and down and all around. Sometimes both hands in unison, sometimes alternating. He thought it was so much fun – and beyond cool.

Mother, on the other hand, thought it was rather embarrassing. "Hon, please don't do that," she begged. But Father was having so much fun, he continued finger dancing anyway. Oliva shook her. Baron and Ruby thought the entire thing was hilarious. They pretended to do their own version of highly exaggerated finger dancing in the back seat – partly to the music and partly mocking Father. Oliva laughed with the kids. But Father didn't care. His family was safe, they were together, listening to music, having fun, finger dancing, and they were on their way home.

STORYTRAX: *99 Red Balloons* - Nena

CHAPTER 23

Waah-Waahs

Three weeks later, the Clemens family was safe at home...

Ruby seemed to have finished her final growth spurt. At the age of 10 and a half, she now stood five feet, three inches tall. Her left leg (the artificial one) was a little over an inch shorter than it should be. She loved that leg even if having one leg shorter than the other was causing her to walk a little funny. It usually didn't bother her too much, but her back did hurt sometimes. Nonetheless, Ruby was not one for complaining. Besides, she knew her father was working on a new leg for her. She would just have to tough it out until the replacement was ready.

"Mom, whatcha' doin'?" she asked as she strolled unevenly into the kitchen.

"Working on your screens – I want to be sure the newest security upgrades are functioning properly," mom said.

"Oh," Ruby responded as she absent-mindedly twirled her already impossibly curly hair.

"Perhaps you would like to read a book?" her mother offered. "The latest upgrade gives you cloaked access to the libraries of all four planets – and several space stations."

"No thanks. I read a book yesterday – and two the day before that," Ruby replied. "And I've already done my geometric physics homework for the whole summer. I'm tired of angles and hypotenuses and arcs and velocities and acceleration and range and trajectories. I'm just bored. I want to go and DO something."

"That's great sweetie. Geometric physics can be very helpful in lots of ways."

Ruby glared at her mother and then rolled her eyes.

"Anyway, your brother and your friends are playing outside. You could join them."

"Yeah.... I guess I could. It's just that my back hurts when I run a lot," Ruby said.

"I have an idea," Mom suggested. "Why don't you get some chillato from the outdoor freezer? Get some for your friends, too."

"That's probably a pretty good idea. It is kind of hot outside," Ruby responded with a big smile. (Once in a while, moms actually did have good snack ideas.)

"Oh, and today is the first day of the Waah-waah migration. You might get lucky and see a show," Mom said.

"Yeah, that IS a pretty good idea!" Ruby shouted. She ran out the back door toward the freezer.

A few minutes later, Ruby rounded the corner of the house with an armload of chillato cups – the kind with the old-fashioned wooden spoons stuck to the lids. As she came into view, she yelled "Anybody want chillato?" She brought sand apple cream, cinilla crunch, blue banana, and, of course, clord.

Baron and all of her friends rushed toward her shouting "Me, me, me!"

They dove in with gusto as the cool sweetness and luxurious creaminess hit their tongues. The smooth yumminess slid down their throats and washed away some of the afternoon heat.

"Mom said the Waah-waahs might start their migration today," Ruby suggested.

"That's cool," said Ho. "We could lie down in the grass on the hill behind the pond and watch them."

"Chillato and a show," Baron said. "That's what summer is all about – Life is good." (Of course, that didn't really make a whole lot of sense. But that was Baron. He often said things like that, to try to sound cool.) They took their treats and found a comfy place on the hill to relax and wait for the Waah-waahs.

****

Waah-waahs are migratory birds on Levon. There were once so many of them that huge flocks could blot out the sun for an hour. When the human population grew and others settled here, the Waah-waahs began to die off. There are still lots of them but they don't own the skies anymore.

They were large birds – bigger than wild turkeys or even condors. Sometimes their wingspans were up to 12 feet across. They had speckled feathers and calls that sounded something like a baby crying. That's where they got their name "Waah, waah." They also laid lots of eggs – big ones. They laid so many eggs that they sometimes forgot where they laid them. The parents flew off in these huge flocks – if the eggs had hatched, the hatchlings came with them. But a lot of the eggs don't ever hatch. People like to collect them and eat them for breakfast. Each egg is about as big as a softball, so one is plenty for a person to eat.

The ones that don't get found eventually go rotten. The smell of a broken, rotten waah-waah egg is intense. It is worse than an Earth skunk. The putrid aroma can literally make one's eyes burn. You can always tell when they are rotten because the shells turn from their fresh-looking, light brown color to a dark yellow with a black swirl pattern that looks like it was painted on. Not only do the rotten ones smell terrible, they also become dangerously acidic. You definitely don't want to eat those!

Several years ago, before Ruby lost her leg, Baron was helping mother gather some waah-waah eggs to eat for breakfast the next day. He was only about six years old and didn't know about the rotten eggs. He found three eggs and brought them to the house. As he climbed up the steps to the front porch, he dropped a rotten-yellow one. It crashed to the steps and began to stink horribly. The acidic egg even ate a hole right through the step! Father had to wear a face mask when he replaced the step. Even after it was replaced and the whole area painted, mom swore she could still smell that odor on the hottest summer days for years afterward.

People loved to watch the flocks of waah-waahs migrate. These elegant birds really put on a show. If you catch them at the right point, their migration turns the entire flock into something like a kaleidoscopic sky-dance. They make what appear to be highly choreographed movements. (There are videos on KikTalk of these flowing, intricate migratory air-dances. Kids often try to put them to music that matches the motions of the birds. Of course, they usually have to edit the videos to match the music, so the visuals end up being kind of choppy.) Some have reported that the birds actually respond to amplified music.

****

"Thanks for the chillato Ruby," Ho said with a smile – tapping her hand with the back of his while holding the chillato cup. "You're a great friend."

"Oh yeah, thanks," echoed Mae-Ellen.

Baron stood and bowed. "Why thank you so much my dearest sister. You are ever-so-kind and most considerate to bring us these cooling treats on a hot summer day," mused Baron.

Ruby rolled her eyes. She knew he was teasing her about Ho. (It was pretty much an open secret that Ho had a crush on Ruby. Ruby kind of liked him too, but at the age of 10, she figured she had more than enough time to worry about boys.)

Ruby pulled out her screen and scrolled to her music. She had that special folder she labeled "Ancient Earth Tunes." Baron usually made fun of her for listening to music that was hundreds of years old, but she liked it. She was looking for one song in particular. She hoped it would be something that might flow well with the waah-waahs – if they were lucky enough to see an air dance. "There it is," she said softly to herself. The screen read: "You Make Me Feel Like Dancing" (not the original by Leo Sayer, but the funky remake with bouncier bass) by Adam Levine & Franki Valli.

She hit play. The music started.

"Not that ancient stuff again," Baron bellowed. "Ugh."

"I think Ruby's got great taste in music," Ho retorted.

"You know, it is kind of cool," Mae-Ellen added.

"Ugh," said Baron. Seeing that he was outvoted, he quit complaining.

Ruby cranked the volume.

About that time, as if on cue, two waah-waahs flew right over them – announced by their characteristic "waah, waah" cries. The two birds looped each other and then flew in a circle. The pair were joined by a few more who flew into view – along with more cries of "waah, waah." Soon there were more than a dozen birds flying in figure eights. The cries silenced as the flock became absorbed into the music; Ruby turned it up again. A moment later, there were several groups of waah-waahs doing their own figure eights. And their movements seemed to be following Ruby's ancient Earth song. More and more birds joined the air dance. There must have been a thousand of them performing in the sky! It was a surprising but captivating show.

"Hey!" shouted Ruby. Baron had grabbed her screen.

"Let's see what else you have here. Are there any ancient Earth tunes that aren't lame? How about something with some energy and power!?" He scrolled through Ruby's list. "What's this? "What I Like About You" by The Romantics. Baron hit play, turned up the volume yet again and aimed the screen skyward.

The Waah-waahs responded. Their spirographic antics converged to the music. The children watched the incredible show. Birds flew and danced all across the sky. Up and down, round and round. In and out, responding to the music. It was as if a thousand birds had planned and choreographed this dance to this particular piece of music. Music they had almost certainly never heard because it was hundreds of years old – not to mention, from another planet. Unbelievable. Yet it was a truly magical visual display of coordination and rhythm. Ruby even felt that she was floating and swooping along with the waah-waahs. Did she actually float a few inches above the—?

"Hey!" Baron screamed as Mae-Ellen took the screen from his outstretched hand.

"What else do we have from the older-than-dirt sounds from a thousand light years away?" she asked. Mae-Ellen scrolled through the list and it stopped on something she didn't understand – but the picture on this piece of music looked interesting. Mae-Ellen couldn't even read the language, but she hit play anyway. "What the heck, right?" The screen showed: Eine kleine Nachtmusik by Wolfgang A. Mozart.

The waah-waahs began to respond. They appeared to descend into chaos for a brief moment when the music changed, but quickly re-organized yet again to follow the melodies and rhythms from Ruby's screen. The living shapes they created, and their harmonic motions, were fluid and beautiful. The birds flew impossible routes, together and separately. Thousands of years of practice ingrained into their collective consciousness along with Levon's unusual gravity allowed them to put on a real concert. They seemed to sense the music and sense each other, responding to both with grace and style. Swooping and gliding. Fast then slow. Whatever the music called for, the waah-waahs delivered.

Strangely, the entire flock was completely silent during their spinning, pirouetting, acrobatic performance. Minutes upon minutes of soaring here, diving there, and putting on a show for the ages. They seemed to defy gravity and the basic laws of physics as they moved in impossible combinations. How could a flock of birds create such art – and all perfectly coordinated with the music!?

Ho grabbed the screen – and switched to a cacophonous current tune that was popular with the older kids – "Contra Stand" by Slimba PRTY. Deep bass and strong percussion permeated the air. "This is my favorite song!" he yelled. But the song lacked melody. The birds began to separate. It was as if – without the coordinated rhythm – they could not feel each other or perform together. At once, a thousand birds seemed to lose their connection. They separated and flew in different directions; some up and others down, finally re-organizing into a traditional V shape – albeit a massive one – and continued off on their journey.

Ho had stood up and started dancing by himself with his eyes closed. He didn't see the waah-waahs fly away. He also didn't see the other children glaring at him for ending their sky show. They looked at each other and all threw their chillato cups at him. He opened his eyes – a bit embarrassed because everyone was staring at him – and his awkward gyrations. He froze for a second. "What?" he asked. Everyone laughed. Ruby rolled her eyes. Ho's song was still playing. He started dancing again. So the others shrugged their shoulders, then they all got up and danced like crazy people along with him.

STORYTRAX: *You Make Me Feel Like Dancing* - Adam Levine

What I Like About You - The Romantics

Eine Kleine Nachtmusik - Wolfgang Mozart

Contra Stand - Slimba PRTY

CHAPTER **24**

Soul Vessels

It was time for another visit to the Storyteller. The Clemens family piled into their 'new' floater and set out for Runyon Falls.

"Where's that cool silver speed box that blasted us away from the gravity park? That thing was awesome!" said Baron.

"It's in my workshop," answered Father. "Fried out I'm afraid. It can only work once; the circuits are burned out and the ternium is spent."

"Oh, so no more super-speed trips, huh?" said Baron.

"Not for a while," said Father.

"I'm okay with that," added Mother, subconsciously rubbing one temple.

They zoomed across the treetops until the trees became giant greenstalks. Then Father looped around and descended into an open spot.

"Dad, I wish there was a way I could walk up the hill. It's kind of embarrassing without my leg," said Ruby.

"I know sweetie. But electronics just don't work here," said Mother.

Mother turned to Father and whispered, "Tanner, isn't there something we can do? I know she doesn't want to be carried like a child."

"I do have an idea, but it's not very sophisticated," Father whispered back. "Let's see what she thinks."

"Ruby, I built you a pair of crutches if you'd like to use them instead. I wasn't sure how you might feel about them. They're in the back," Father offered.

"Sure," Ruby said. "Anything is better than being carried up there like a baby in front of all the other kids."

They all climbed out of the floater and Father handed Ruby the pair of silver-grey crutches – with little red feet! Ruby tried them out and adjusted the height – her father had built them an X-style spring mechanism. "I think I'll disconnect my leg and leave it in the floater, instead of against a tree," Ruby suggested.

"That's my girl," said Mom. "Always thinking two steps ahead."

They could hear lots of chatter coming down from the storyfire – almost like the cacophony before an orchestral performance. After hiking up the hill with crutches, Ruby was (of course) the last one to be seated. Her parents (and Baron) made their way back down the hill, leaving the 10-year-olds with the Storyteller.

The Storyteller rose high above the fire – and swept around the circle with his robes flowing behind him. He made eye contact with each child along the way. As he returned to the center, he glowed even brighter while the darkness around him seemed to grow even darker in comparison. An aura of light surrounded him as he spoke in his powerful tones that pulsed through the children's bodies. They could literally feel his words beating in their chests.

"The powerful demon Caligula was in his lair, right on these very grounds. He had sown seeds that he hoped would lead to generations of evil for him to enjoy.

The rulers of Levon's three kingdoms met once a year around the huge suns dial. Years before, they had decided it was best to have an annual three-day meeting on neutral ground to avoid any misunderstandings.

Zakar, in the north, was ruled by Prince Trajan. Geisl, to the south, was under the control of Empress Giselle. In the center, the republic of Pavirlo (and its capital, Tansin) were represented by Judge Paxton.

Caligula arrived at the summit of the three leaders on the third day. He strode to the middle of the suns dial. He apologized for interrupting their meeting but said that he had come to offer the great leaders a token of respect, tribute for their prudent leadership. He had come bearing rare gifts for each of them.

Caligula was a horrid creature. He was red and black with huge fangs and massive, streaked bull horns atop his oversized head. His body was a combination of a giant man and what looked like part wolf though he stood upright – all 20 feet of him! This was a powerful demon who would stop at nothing to bring more evil to the world; he thrived on the misery and pain of others. His angled eyebrows curled down between his eyes and continued backward joining the spartan hair on his temples.

As you might imagine, the three leaders were suspicious of his offering. Trajan moved his hand to his sword.

"What do you want in exchange for this supposed tribute?" asked Trajan.

"We're not in the habit of conducting state business with demons," said Giselle.

"I ask nothing in return. I merely want to give to you great leaders something that will help you govern better and longer for your people. It may be difficult for you to understand, but demons are not always bad. You see, I also desire a certain continuity – it helps promote peace and stability. After all, I do live here, too. The beast took out three bundles from his pack. Each was wrapped in an exquisite, miniature blanket delicately embroidered with gold and tied with a red ribbon. He placed one at the feet of each leader, along with a deep bow.

"I know who you are and I don't trust you," Paxton said. "We should be wary of anything this demon offers," he said to the others.

"I assure you my reputation is a bit ... exaggerated," Caligula said. "Please hear me out. I want only to offer you the power to extend your reigns so that you may continue to make wise decisions for your countries. I humbly ask that you do me the honor of unwrapping your gifts."

The three leaders looked at each other. They did not move.

"What if these aren't gifts at all?" Giselle wondered aloud.

"These bundles might contain poison or deadly snakes," Trajan speculated.

"No, no," Caligula replied. "Please. I'm trying to do something good – good for each of you, good for your people and for your countries."

The leaders were not convinced.

The demon prostrated himself before Paxton and slowly, gently unwrapped the gift in front of the judge. He held it up high – golden goblet with a crystal neck and bejeweled base. An ancient language was inscribed in a circle around the center. The three leaders stood transfixed – staring at the beautiful gift held aloft in the hand of the ugly beast.

Paxton gasped, "That can't be… a Tenso Baka."

"Yes, these are indeed soul vessels, my learned judge," declared Caligula. "They are the rarest of the rare."

"And you have a triumvirate?" asked Giselle slyly.

"I believe the last three remaining on Levon are here before you now. And I'm offering them to you."

The power in these talismans was great. Tenso Baka granted the users long life – at least a thousand years – or more! But they could do more than just extend the soul of the user in his or her own body. A soul vessel can also switch souls between bodies. They were known to exist in groups of three – called a triumvirate.

Each of the leaders knew the awesome magic of the gifts that lay before them. They had heard the legends of transferring souls. Leaders, even good ones, enjoy power. Caligula could not have chosen a more tempting gift for these three.

"You use the power of the soul vessels in this way," he explained. "First, strike the rim so that the goblet vibrates, then merely drink holy water from the vessel while it still resonates. They can grant you near immortality. The only requirement to accept the gift is that you drink from it willingly, voluntarily. Think of the wonders you could accomplish with an extra thousand years? How much could you grow? How much could you learn? What could you do as a leader with centuries to get wiser and lead better? How much could you help your people?"

"But to begin, for the magic to work, the triumvirate must be initiated together in this place. This act will forever link the three users together with this place.

To prove that I want nothing in return, I will leave these precious vessels for you now. Do with them as you wish; they are yours to keep," said the beast. "I trust you will use them wisely. I bid you farewell." Caligula, with smoke rings coming from his nose, bowed deeply and walked off into the night.

Around the storyfire, the children sniffed an aroma of smoke hanging in the air. Several saw fading smoke rings rising upward; many felt the need to wave that smoke away from their faces. (But the smoke could just be from the storyfire itself, right?)

CHAPTER 25

Sinister Succession

Prince Trajan and Empress Giselle decided immediately that they should call upon the magic of the soul vessels. Paxton was more reluctant. "We should think about the consequences of our actions tonight. If we proceed, we will not be able to turn back the clock," he warned.

"We can live longer. We can take better care of our people," said Giselle. "Don't be unreasonable Paxton," she pleaded.

They walked toward the center of the suns dial.

"Why would we want to turn back the clock?" asked Trajan. "Paxton, you're being shortsighted. Think of the good we can do. It won't hurt anyone else if we live longer."

"We can't waste this opportunity. These gifts are too valuable," observed Giselle.

"You know she's right Paxton," Trajan added.

"I'm just… I'm concerned that we're not thinking this through. Power like this can have tremendous consequences," warned Paxton.

"We need to do this together," Giselle said.

"Paxton, we need you. This is the right thing to do. I have some holy water with me here," said Trajan as he pulled some vials from his pack. He poured some into Giselle's cup and then his own.

Paxton was reluctant to hold out his cup. He was looking down. "I'm not sure," Paxton began.

Trajan pulled Paxton's forearm up so that his goblet could be filled. "Let's drink a toast," Trajan raised his goblet. "To long life!" he said. Giselle raised her goblet alongside Trajan's and said, "For our people!" Paxton looked at the other two and slowly raised his goblet as well.

Trajan clanged his goblet into the other two. They began to resonate and hum. The three leaders, without fully appreciating what they were about to do, lifted the vessels to their lips. Paxton looked back and forth between Giselle and Trajan….and then the three drank.

****

Eighty years later, the three leaders returned for their annual meeting at the suns dial. They barely looked a day older. Their spouses and compatriots had passed away. It was clear that they would live a very long time…thanks to the Tenso Baka.

Another twenty more years had passed. At this annual meeting, Giselle did not arrive for the first day of the meeting. On the second day, a woman that might have been Giselle's granddaughter arrived. "I am Giselle II," she announced. "I will be representing Geisl from now on."

Trajan and Paxton were worried – about their own lives! "What happened to Giselle?" asked Trajan. "Is she dead? The soul vessel was supposed to extend our lives."

"It did," said Giselle flatly. She smiled. Paxton walked up to her. He put his hands on the young lady's shoulders and looked deeply into her eyes. He drew back aghast. "Please, oh please, tell me you did not use the Tenso Baka in that way," he pleaded. He realized what Giselle had done.

"What in the name of Caligula is going on here!?" Trajan asked.

"Yes," Giselle said. "Our dear friend Caligula. He made it possible for us to live forever, but our bodies continued to age, even if very slowly. But did you not remember that he also gave us the power to move our souls to younger bodies so that we could not only live longer, but enjoy that fountain of youth to the fullest? I simply took advantage of that option."

****

As deplorable as that was, Giselle did not just steal a body, she created a spectacle of her misdeed, a sheer celebration of succession. She announced to the people of Geisl that she did not want a monarchy that passed down by birth. Instead, she, Giselle, wanted to choose a young, innocent soul to prepare to lead the kingdom. She explained to the people that this plan would share the leadership and ensure that many could bring their ideas, perspectives, and compassions to rule. This would be a practice that would continue as tradition from that point forward.

It was actually quite simple. Giselle would choose a young maiden – usually one very beautiful – then invite her into the palace to live as her heir. Giselle would teach the youth about good governance, and how to negotiate, and organize armies – the important things that leaders do. Then when the time came – usually the maiden's twenty-first birthday – there would be an elaborate ceremony in which Giselle introduced her new heir to the people. The country held a grand ball in honor of the occasion – which she dubbed 'The Succession.'

There was music and dancing and feasting. Fancy gowns and jewelry adorned many a party-goer. Near the end of the ball, Giselle would make a pronouncement that she was giving up the throne that very night. She would announce that she was letting a new leader take her place. She would bring the maiden up on stage in front of the hundreds attending in the palace ballroom and introduce her as the next empress.

Giselle told those assembled that she would take the maiden whom she had trained to be the new ruler of Geisl into her royal anteroom behind the ballroom. She would sign her official abdication naming the child the new leader – the next Giselle. Then, she announced to the crowd, that she, Giselle would willingly commit suicide so that the new leader would be free to rule as she wished. She claimed it was a selfless act for the good of the country.

Upon entering the royal anteroom, Giselle took a key from around her neck and unlocked a massive wooden cabinet. She removed the two goblets from an ornate box. First was the golden Tenso Baka with its crystal stem and bejeweled base. In it, she poured holy water. Second, was a smaller silver goblet into which she poured the poison for herself.

"Let us drink to you, the new leader of Geisl," she said to the girl. Giselle struck the soul vessel with her ring and it began to hum. She raised the golden goblet to her mouth and drank. She then struck the goblet again and handed it to the maiden, who also drank as it hummed. Thet held hands across the table. The maiden could barely contain her excitement. Her face was glowing with anticipation!

The awful magic of the vessel switched their souls. The crafty old leader was now in the body of the young maiden. Moving souls is not an easy process and proved disorienting – but less so to Giselle who knew what was coming. Alas, the young maiden (now in Giselle's old body) fell to the floor and awoke confused and unsettled – she had no idea what was happening to her.

But Giselle (now in the maiden's young, vibrant body) was quick to help her up and comfort her, handing her a silver goblet to drink from. When the old body succumbed to the poison, the new Giselle signed the letter of abdication (she never signed the document prior to disposing of her 'predecessor') and went back to the ballroom to announce that she had accepted the mantle as the new ruler of Geisl.

This unholy ceremony of succession would be repeated time and again, whenever Giselle decided that she needed to feel younger.

****

Trajan was intrigued with this idea though he definitely wanted to keep his family at the helm of Zakar. Then and there, the evil prince devised his own ghastly plan for doing just that.

He had no shortage of wives (Rhiannons). Many of them bore him sons. Why couldn't he just pick one of his sons that he didn't like particularly well and ….

So that's what he decided to do. Unfortunately, the first time was much more difficult than he could possibly have imagined.

Trajan determined that he was to have the body of his eldest son. This son, Hugo (from the previous Rhiannon), was tall and strong; a great fighter. So Trajan intentionally distanced himself from Hugo. He didn't talk to him much and sent him out to fight campaigns, to lead his armies. Trajan dismissed this son. He usually left a room soon after his Hugo entered. Trajan decided it would be easier to transition if he didn't have a deep relationship with that son.

On the contrary, another son, who was just nineteen years old, was Trajan's favorite. Aidan (from his current Rhiannon) was a great conversationalist. Trajan joked with him and hunted with him. They got along as well as any father and son. Aidan told fabulous stories – and Trajan could listen to this son for hours on end. They developed a great bond. Trajan decided that he was going to give Aidan a place of honor and take care of him for the rest of his life.

Hugo was jealous of the relationship that his father had with Aidan. But it seemed that nothing Hugo did was good enough to earn praise from Trajan. Hugo tried everything to get his father's attention. He attacked the armies of Geisl many times. He stole land from Pavirlo to increase Zakar's domain. But, Trajan continued to keep this son at arm's length.

Trajan was getting older and decided that he would trade souls with Hugo as soon as Hugo returned from the next battle. He hosted a feast in honor of Aidan and the entire castle ate and celebrated and drank and danced.

A messenger arrived from the battle – the poor soldier was beaten and tattered. He bore tragic news: Hugo was killed by a cadre of enemy archers. He fought bravely; it took seven arrows to bring him down. And the enemy burned his body.

Trajan was heartbroken by this terrible news. But not because he had lost his eldest son. Trajan was saddened because he was about to lose his favorite son. That very night, Trajan switched souls with Aidan. It was easy getting Aidan drunk as the young man had no idea what his father was up to. After the switch, Trajan threw his favorite son (now in his old body) out a castle window. Now Trajan had a new, young, vibrant body.

In later years, the transitions became easier. If he could take the body of his beloved, he could certainly do it with any that he cared less about. Nonetheless, Trajan made it a point not to get too close to any of his sons from that point forward, lest he be put into the same situation. In this way, he conveniently avoided any future emotional entanglements.

CHAPTER 26

Gram

Ruby awoke in her own bed with her leg charging in the corner. She did not remember her parents bringing her home from Runyon Falls the night before. Her arm held Bard close. She nuzzled his belly with her nose. She couldn't exactly tell why, but she felt sad.

Ruby rolled over and stared at her ceiling. She looked around her room. It was cozy and warm and she couldn't imagine a better place to be. She tried to put that awful history out of her mind. How could Giselle kill those girls? And Trajan...his own sons. Unforgivable. She wanted to forget.

It was just a story. But it felt so real. It got inside her somehow. And there was nothing she could do about it. She felt as if she could cry. If that was her history, she wasn't sure that she wanted to be Botanian.

Ruby heard rumblings and a commotion coming from the kitchen. Oh well, the suns had been up for a while, so she figured she should probably get out of bed. Besides, she had to see what was going on. Ruby threw her right leg over the side of the bed and jumped up. She almost lost her balance as she winced from the pain in her back (because of the fact she'd been wearing her artificial leg – even though it was a bit shorter than it should have been). She found herself hopping back and forth on one leg trying not to fall. She was making a lot of noise herself. Slamming into her nightstand. Hopping some more. She reflexively put her arms out to steady herself. Leaning and shifting her weight the best that she could, she almost regained her balance – but only for a second.

Slowly, she tilted just a little to one side – and then leaned a little more – causing her to hop again to try to stabilize herself. First it was only one hop, then another, and another. They came in quick succession afterward; she was losing the battle with gravity. Ruby made one last-ditch lunge toward her prosthetic leg. She covered more distance than she thought possible – for a moment she almost seemed to fly toward her goal – but ultimately slammed onto the hard floor with a crash. "Vamp!" she shouted (a bit muffled as her face was on the floor).

Ruby had landed on her knee. She was so embarrassed – and quickly looked around to confirm that no one else had witnessed her partially acrobatic falling with virtually no style. *Whew*, she puffed. Pride damaged but still in one piece, she pulled herself up to sit leaning against her dresser and rubbed her sore knee.

Her bedroom door opened with a slow creaking. Standing there was a short, attractive woman with black hair (save for a few streaks of grey) pulled into a pony tail. The woman wore an apron and had flour on her hands. She also had the cutest glasses sitting right at the edge of her nose. This woman was the best – at just about everything – and Ruby loved her dearly. "Gram!" Ruby yelled.

Ruby flung her arms wide open. Gram came and hugged her. Then they both sat leaning against the dresser. "I love you! When did you get here?" Ruby asked.

"This morning," said Gram. "I thought I'd get here early and make some breakfast."

"I fell," said Ruby.

"I heard," said Gram.

"Oh," said Ruby.

"I think everyone else in the house heard, too," said Gram.

"I hurt my knee."

"I'm sorry sweetie," said Gram. "Do you want me to kiss it and make it all better?"

"No thanks," said Ruby, chuckling. "I don't know if that really works. But could you just sit with me for a minute down here?"

Gram put her arm around her red-haired bunny hopper. Ruby rested her head on Gram's shoulder. Gram stroked Ruby's crazy, curly, red hair.

****

After breakfast, it started to rain. Gram said it was "comin' up a cloud." And she was right. The sky darkened and the wind began to howl. Soon enough, it was coming down in buckets!

"Here you go, Gram," said Baron as they walked into the living room. Baron had just downloaded KikTalk onto Gram's screen. "Now you can see my cool videos. The app will recognize my name and give you a notification when I post something. Just click on it and you can see me."

"Why thank you dear. I always want to see my grandson," she said with a smile. Ruby walked up behind them. "Gram doesn't want to see your dumb videos," she said. Ruby grabbed Gram's phone and added her name to the notifications. Just then, a bolt of lightning lit up the darkened morning sky – followed by a huge boom of thunder.

Even though they were safe inside, Ruby didn't much care for storms – except for when Gram was around, because that usually meant story time! Gram and Ruby would snuggle on the big, comfy couch. Baron would join them on the couch – but not snuggling. (He made that clear.) Mom and Dad usually sat in their chairs and listened.

Gram was an amazing storyteller. When she spun up a tale, it was better than watching a movie. It was probably better than being there – wherever there was – for that particular story. Yes, the Storyteller at Runyon Falls was incredible, but Gram was pretty good, herself.

"What story are you going to tell us?" Ruby asked.

"What story would you like to hear?" Gram asked.

"How about the one with the two rockets racing from Earth to Levon?" Baron suggested.

"Or the one about your favorite son?" Dad offered.

"Ummm…No. Not that you're not a fabulous son – and dad – but we actually want to hear something interesting," Ruby said.

Everyone laughed.

"Gram," Ruby said. "Can you tell us a story about you? A real story, something that truly happened? I love all of your stories but I recently decided that I want to know more about my family. We just learned that dad studied on Earth! Did you do fascinating things when you were young?"

"Oh, now that I'm old, you're suggesting that I'm no longer interesting. Is that it?" Gram joked.

"No, you're the best!" said Ruby.

"Yeah, Gram, I like Ruby's idea. Tell us about something that happened to you when you were young," Baron said.

"Well, children, I'm afraid my real life isn't all that interesting. My mother moved to Levon from Earth; my father was a native of Levon. I grew up here. I went to school and studied my insects – I met your grandfather in school. Then we had your father. We just lived a regular life. I'm sorry but there's nothing very special about me."

Ruby sat straight up. "Yes, there is! You're more special than anyone. We love you more than anything!" Ruby said.

"Thank you, sweetie and Gram loves you all very much as well. I didn't mean to imply that I haven't had a wonderful life – I definitely have. I just meant that it wasn't too exciting." Gram looked off into the distance.

"I don't even care if it's exciting. Your stories are always the best. Tell any story you want," said Baron.

Gram paused. She took a deep breath. "There actually was one pretty special thing that happened to me when I was about your age, Ruby. I haven't told many people. Your grandfather knew, and of course, my parents. It's not really a story, per se, but it's something I've thought about many times over the years." She looked across to Tanner. "I haven't even told you about it, son."

"Sounds to me like this is the one," said Father. Ruby smiled eagerly and snuggled up to her grandmother.

"Well, you all know the Storyteller of Runyon Falls?" asked Gram.

"Of course. It is the duty –" Ruby began

– and then everyone joined in, "and the privilege – of every 10-year-old to hear the story of Runyon Falls from the Storyteller, himself." They all smiled.

"Don't tell me you dated that old dude," Baron said. They all laughed again.

"Oh my, no. He's far older than I am. In fact, I heard the stories from him when I was 10 years old, just the same as you all did."

"Does anyone actually know how old the Storyteller is?" asked mom.

They all looked at Father – he often knew about random things like that. "I certainly don't," said Father.

"Neither do I," said Gram, "but he was already ancient when I was a child, so now he must be very old indeed."

"Anyway, even before I went to the Storyteller to hear the story of Runyon Falls," said Gram.

"From the Storyteller, himself," said Ruby.

"Yes, from the old Storyteller, himself," smiled Gram. "Even before that, I loved *hearing* stories. I didn't realize how much I loved *telling* stories until after I visited Runyon Falls.

"Hey, I have a question," asked Ruby. "Does that guy ever get around to talking about Runyon Falls – about the falls – about that place?"

"Rubes, it's not polite to interrupt when someone's telling a story," Mom said.

"Yeah, I get that. The Storyteller doesn't like it when I comment during his stories, either," she shared.

"You actually interrupted the Storyteller – himself?" asked Father.

"I was too scared to interrupt him," said Mother, "That big, booming voice went right through me."

"And floating over the fire. That's still kinda scary to me even now that I'm almost grown," said Baron.

"Let's get back to Gram's story," said Dad.

"We're sorry, Gram," said Mom.

"No problem at all, my little ones," said Gram. "So, I loved stories very much. Everyone didn't have their own personal screens when I was a child. We read books and told stories. We even watched movies in huge theaters with lots of other people."

"I felt the stories at Runyon Falls deeply. I think the Storyteller somehow sensed that. I caught him looking at me several times – or at least I thought he was looking at me."

"When I got home, I would repeat his stories to anyone who would listen. To my parents, to my sister, to my friends – as long as they were older than 10. I just wanted to share the tales of the Sherable and the Two Kingdoms, and the others. They became real to me. That's when my friends started telling me how good a storyteller I was.

"After the final story, my parents were late coming to pick me up. I was waiting and the Storyteller started talking to me. I guess he was just being nice because we were the only ones left and he didn't want me to be scared – even though he was sometimes what scared me most. But when he talked to just me as a child – just as one person, not an audience – his voice wasn't so loud and he didn't seem quite so intimidating. When my parents finally came to pick me up, they told me that the Storyteller wanted to talk to me more. He wanted to show me where he lived."

"Did you see where he lives?" asked Ruby incredulously.

"I didn't know anyone ever got to see his home," said Father.

"Well, I did," said Gram. "I took the invitation and went to visit the Storyteller in his cave. He said that he could see how I felt his stories very deeply. He told me that my parents had shared with him how I liked telling stories and how they thought I was gifted. He agreed that I had the makings of a great storyteller."

"I didn't really understand what he was saying to me. After all, I was only 10," said Gram. "He told me about how he shared the stories of our ancestors in this place, in the shadow of Runyon Falls. He talked about the responsibility he felt for helping to educate the youth of Levon. At first, I had no idea why he was telling me all these things. But he was asking me something very special – something I didn't fully appreciate at the time. He was asking me to become his apprentice – in essence to become the next storyteller."

"What did you say?" asked Ruby.

"Sweetie, I said 'no,' of course," said Gram. "I was 10 years old. I wasn't going to live with an old man and his long beard and flowing robes – in a cave, no less." She sat up straight. "That would have been ridiculous. All the same, it was nice to be asked."

"He said that he couldn't be the Storyteller forever. He told me that he had only made that offer once before." He seemed so old. I did love the stories, but I really didn't want to live in a damp cave. Anyway, it seemed so odd that he would ask me, a little girl, to take over being the storyteller. I thanked him, of course. It was the polite thing to do. And then, I said goodbye."

"Mom, that's fantastic," said Father. "My mom could be the Storyteller of Runyon Falls! I can't believe it."

"Well, If I had accepted, you wouldn't be here. I said no to that offer. And I've had a fabulous life, a career in entomology, and a wonderful family. I wouldn't change my decision for the world," said Gram as she pulled her two grandchildren close to her. Baron rolled his eyes, but reluctantly accepted the hug.

"Besides, I get to tell my stories to you two," she said with a big smile. She hugged her grandchildren. "Although there is a tiny part of me that sometimes wonders, what if...." Then Gram looked off wistfully.

CHAPTER 27

Upgrade

Father's workshop was a sight to behold. From the outside, it looked like an ordinary, rather plain building. It was light brown with two windows in the front and two in the back – both usually had the shades pulled down. One of the front windows was even boarded up. (It seems that someone had broken it with repeated softball pitching practice sessions.) But on the inside, it was not so ordinary; indeed, it had a significant high tech feel. There was a big working table in the middle with a single chair and a light directed at the center.

Lining the walls were shelves and storage compartments with components and tools and all sorts of gadgets in various states of repair. This was where Father fixed just about everything that folks in town needed fixing. He fixed simple things as well as complex machines. He was a whiz with vehicles, especially floaters. But he also fixed toasters and screens. Father could repair just about anything.

But he didn't just fix things, he also made new things. Father was an inventor. He created Ruby's leg (even though she had pretty much outgrown it now). In fact, there were still parts of other legs hanging from the ceiling. (He made it a point to continue his work on advanced prosthetics when he had the time or when he could get supplies – neither of which seemed to happen often.)

Levon had self-selected long ago to be a low tech zone. Significant technology transfer controls were put into place. Advanced gadgetry was rare on Levon. That meant that Father's workshop was special. (Or, put another way, it was not necessarily in full compliance with the planet's various technology restrictions.) Indeed, Ruby's own leg was not common knowledge. Outside of her family and close friends, no one else knew about Ruby's advanced leg. And Ruby had to trust they would keep her secret.

Of course, almost everyone had a personal screen. And floaters were not uncommon. There was the grid – which connected virtually everything. It wasn't like they were in the days of stone tablets or anything. There was plenty of technology around, just not the highly advanced stuff. Certainly not out in the open. Most of the folks on Levon liked it that way; supposedly it made them feel closer to nature. So, things that Father was working on were generally best kept behind the closed doors of his workshop.

On the working table was the fried shell of a small silver box with two buttons and some dangling wires. The silver box was burnt with streaks of black across the top and it was partially split open. It was the remains of the ternium boost reactor that accelerated the Clemens family from the gravity park to the tiny farmhouse. The little silver box did its job; it saved the family.

Father often spent many hours in his workshop, sometimes late into the night. He always seemed to be tinkering with an electronic component, fixing a neighbor's floater, or making something for the kids – or Mom – when he wasn't working on one of his special projects. Now he was working on something very special: a new leg for Ruby.

With his limited consulting job at the Gravity Park, he had finally gotten enough raw materials to finish his new, nano-grid ternium reactor. He was now working on connecting it to a new leg for Ruby.

This was going to be a major upgrade. After all, he was fairly certain she had reached her full height, so it would be her 'forever-leg.' He so wanted to have it completed before now, but the development took a lot longer than he had hoped – not to mention, he had to scrape together the money for the materials.

The ternium reactor was more challenging than he had anticipated. The kind that he'd used in the floater was relatively easy. The problem with that version was that it quickly burned through the ternium – along with most of the other components. He needed an approach that could tap into that energy but still be able to control it, channel it, throttle it back, and use it to power the leg – without blowing up. That's when he hit on the idea to create an elastic compression algorithm to control the magnetic containment field. And Voila!: The nano-fiber ternium reactor.

This little breakthrough meant that Ruby might never have to charge her leg. The power source should theoretically last for multiple decades until it might need outside juice. She still might want to take it off for comfort. But this one was much lighter, with a skeleton of silicon-infused composite carbon fiber. Even though this leg was lighter, it was twice as strong. *Ruby could kick a hole in a brick wall with this leg*, Father thought. *Heck, she could probably knock down a building, but that might burn out the reactor.*

The artificial skin was made of microscale ceramic particles that were cross-layered to optimize strength and to give it a more natural appearance and feel. The skin was self-lubricating (with moisture from the air) which was important to help maintain flexibility, but it was also waterproof so Ruby could actually go for a swim with both legs!

Father had been working on this version for almost three years. He had known for a long time that Ruby was going to need a new leg eventually. But some of the components were particularly expensive. And they lived on a shoestring budget as it was. That's why he needed to take the extra consulting work at the gravity park. That gig paid pretty well for such a short engagement – and the park was willing to pay part of his compensation in ternium. (Even though, in retrospect, he realized that might have been a far greater risk than he initially thought.)

Father opened a compartment on the back of the leg, up at the middle of the thigh. Next he went to his shelves and pulled open a drawer to reveal a small pouch, delicately embroidered with silver and tied at the top with a blue string. He opened the pouch and dumped a small silver box into his hand. There were two wires sticking out of the bottom. He grabbed a sonic welding tool and carefully installed the new ternium reactor into his new creation.

He closed the leg and it powered on. There was a slight humming sound on start-up that soon dissipated into silence. Was something wrong? Father tickled the bottom of the foot to see if it would react. The foot pulled away quickly. He chuckled, surprised at how effective the tactile interpreter was on this thing – not to mention the silencing shields. The sensitivity was even more heightened than he had dared hope. He tapped the side three times in quick succession – a small holographic keypad appeared. Tapping a few keys in the proper sequence, he turned off the leg. It was finally ready.

Father looked at his huge, black and silver Space Force watch. Engraved with his name, it was the only thing he still had from his old life. There was still time tonight! He picked up the prosthetic and began to walk out. But he stopped at the door, turned around, and laid the leg on a nearby shelf.

He turned back and scanned the workshop. "Where is it?" he asked aloud to no one. "I know I put it in here." He opened one drawer and then shut it quickly. He bent down to look under some electronic components on another shelf. "Not there…" Father stood up, looked around the workshop – scanning first to the left, then to the right – while stroking his chin.

A smile slowly appeared on his scruffy face. He walked to his desk and opened up the lower left drawer. "Eureka," he said to himself. Father reached in and pulled out a big red bow. He then walked over to the leg and stuck the bow right on the foot. He stepped back and smiled at his wrapping job. (Well, at least he tried.) Then he picked up the present, switched off the light over the table, and headed toward the house.

As Father neared the back door of their home, he heard Oliva and Ruby talking. He looked (and listened), crouched by the side window.

Ruby hopped across the room and flopped on the couch. "Mom, my back is hurting again." She snuggled Bard and held him tight. "I love that I have a super-advanced artificial leg, but I might have to switch to the crutches for a while." Mom sat down with Ruby and pushed those curly locks out of her face to see a few tears on those freckled cheeks. "If you think that's best, then you're probably right. I don't want you hurting your back permanently," Mom said.

"Do you think that we could buy me a new leg?" Ruby asked. "I know we don't have a lot of money, but… It's just that I really like being able to walk around like everyone else. I can do more when I use both hands instead of having to hold onto my crutches. She paused for a moment and took a deep breath. "You know what? Never mind. I'll be okay," she said. "Other people are much worse off than I am. I have my family and my home."

Mother hugged Ruby.

Father's heart was breaking. He couldn't wait any longer. He threw open the door and yelled "Surprise!"

Ruby looked at her father with that goofy grin on his face and that big red bow on the foot of a prosthetic leg. "Is that for me?" she asked softly.

"Yes it is, my dear. A brand new leg. This is the upgrade you've been waiting for!" Father said.

She jumped up to run and hug her father. But she forgot that she didn't have her (old) leg on. She took one step and then – air. Ruby fell face first onto the chair beside the couch. "Ummmphhhh!"

Father chuckled. It was one of those moments where it probably wasn't appropriate to laugh, but it really was kind of funny.

Ruby looked up. She wasn't very happy – and she was embarrassed. (Not a great combination for a pre-adolescent.) "Dad! That's not funny! Come over here and give me my new leg!" Ruby shouted sternly, pointing toward the floor.

Father, a little ashamed at his laughter, and feeling sorry for his daughter, dutifully walked over.

"Help me put it on!" Ruby said. "Please?" she added much more softly.

Father bent down and put the upgrade right up against Ruby's residual leg. He tapped the side three times and the holographic keypad appeared. "Here is your keypad, sweetie," he said. This green button turns on your leg and the red button will put it in sleep mode. If you want to de-activate it completely, you push the green button and then your security code. I set a code for you: It's 4-2-1 – the number of days in a (Levonian) year." The new leg hummed to life and melded with her skin.

"It's perfect," she said.

"And it's the right height!" Mom said. "So your back should get better soon." Ruby turned and stared at her mother. "Heeeyyyyyyy… Did you know about this, mom?" Ruby asked.

"Yes, sweetie. Your father has been working on this for quite a while now. But he swore me to secrecy. He wanted it so much for you. We both did," said Mom.

"It has quite a few upgrades," said Father. "I can show you how they work."

"Umm, Dad. I've had an advanced prosthetic leg for years. I'm pretty much an expert. I think I can figure it out," Ruby said positively. She stood up. "The height is perfect!" She wiggled her shoulders up and down. Then she stepped back and forth. "It looks wonderful! It even feels good, too!" She hopped on it a few times – and then jogged in place for a few seconds. "Oh, Daddy, thank you so much!" She wobbled as she took her first steps forward and fell into a hug with her father. She buried her face in his chest. Her curly mop partially covered his face. He hugged her back. They hugged for a long time. Ruby smiled and didn't want to let go. Father had to blow some of that red hair out of his face to breathe. "Oh, sorry," she said as she pulled away, beaming, pushing some of that voluminous red hair out of her own eyes.

"Let me show you some of the new features on this model," Father began.

"I got this," Ruby said. She stood up and stepped away from her father – but still holding his hand (just in case). She was a little wobbly in her first steps.

"It will take some getting used to. It's not exactly the same as the old one," Father said. Ruby took a few more steps. She seemed to be getting the hang of it. "It never needs charging – and you never even have to take it off," said Father.

"Watch this," she said. Ruby leaned down and jumped six feet into the air – flying over the couch and landing on the other side – with a couple hops… and a wobble, but she threw her arms out to her sides and quickly steadied herself. She could tell this leg was lighter and had much more power. "Wow," she said, turning back to look at her parents.

Oliva hugged Tanner. "I love you," she said. "Thank you for being so brilliant and taking care of our daughter."

"I bet I can jump across the whole room," said Ruby.

"Honey," Father said. "I haven't shown you all the features yet. This leg is quite a bit more powerful than you're used to. You might want to take it easy until you become accustomed to what it can do."

"No problem dad, watch me!" Ruby said as she tried to jump across the whole room. She did jump across the whole room – and then some. She jumped a little too far. She only needed to jump about 20 feet to get over the blue-and-green flowered couch, but she could have gone further – 30 feet or more. That is, she could have leapt that far if the wall on the other side of the couch hadn't stopped her in mid-flight."

Ruby crashed into the wall with a thud – her face pressed sideways against the wall – and sort of slid down to the floor. "Owww. Vamp," she said (a bit muffled because of her face still being against the wall).

"Oh my gosh, sweetie, are you all right?" her mom asked as she ran toward Ruby, now sitting on the floor holding the bump on her forehead.

"Yeah, I'm okay," she sighed. "Just probably need to get used to the new leg before I do anything, you know, crazy."

"That's a great idea," Father said. He pulled out his screen and swiped in Ruby's direction, zapping the documentation to her. "I just sent you the specs and a sort of user manual I wrote up. Some bedtime reading to bring you up to speed. It really does have some important enhancements that I think you'll like. You probably do need to learn about them so you don't hurt yourself."

"Gotcha," she said with a wink. "That's probably a good idea."

"Rubes, I do need to tell you something important. This leg is a highly advanced piece of machinery. One of the major enhancements on this upgrade is a 'crisis mode.' It's a warning that will notify you if there might be irreparable damage to the leg. It will alert you so that you can take action or avoid a situation where the leg might be permanently compromised," Father told her. "In addition, it has an override feature. Now, I pray that you will never have to use this, but…" He looked his daughter in the eyes, knelt on the floor in front of her and put both hands on her shoulders. "If you find yourself in a dilemma where you need more power – something of a life or death nature – that you can't avoid, you can override the crisis mode."

"The override will give you all the power you'll need – and then some. But that extra power will come at a cost. Please understand sweetie, the override is a 'one and done.' If you override, there's no turning back. Using that feature could possibly save your life in an emergency, but it will fricassee the leg just like the silver box from the floater. There's a good chance it would explode so I wouldn't want to be anywhere near it when the override melts down. This is not a toy, sweetie. If you absolutely have no other choice, hit the red button three times and enter your code, then press the green button."

"Okay. That's pretty serious, Father," said Ruby all stern.

Father realized he was being a bit dramatic, so he added. "Did I mention that you don't have to take this on off if you don't want to?"

"Never?" Ruby asked. "Not if you don't want to," Father replied. "Cool…" said Ruby admiring her new upgrade.

"I think it's time someone went to bed," Mom said. Ruby, her mom, and her father walked arm-in-arm down the hall. (Baron was playing video games in his room.)

CHAPTER 28

Spin Doctor

The hill on the other side of the pond was a great place to sit and watch the clouds – or Waah-Waahs for example. But it was also good for other things.

The kids had an old barrel from Father's workshop that he had ceded to them last year. It was a great coup that Baron had 'negotiated.' Usually, Father was extremely disciplined with everything from his workshop. He managed the inventory like a man possessed – partly because they were always short on money and he needed those supplies for his work, but also partly because he was just so darned persnickety when it came to scientific things. Of course, he also didn't want to get caught violating the technology restrictions.

****

Several times the kids had tried to get boxes or other leftovers from Father's workshop to play with. No matter how many times they asked, the answer was always a firm, but polite, "No." But there was this one thing: a barrel. Baron knew just what he could do with it. He had to have it.

Of course, he started by asking as soon as he saw it in the workshop – although children were usually not even allowed inside the actual workshop. But Baron saw the barrel through an open door. Predictably, the answer again was a firm, but polite, "No." At least five or six times in this case.

So Baron had to start formulating a plan. He began laying the groundwork almost immediately. Sometimes his mind worked that way – very quickly. He was like Father in that way – meticulous in his planning and steady in his execution. Baron commented that he really liked that barrel. Father said it wasn't a child's plaything.

But Baron had other ideas. A child's plaything. That's exactly what he wanted to do with it: play! It came almost up to Baron's shoulders. He figured he could fit inside it if he scrunched over a bit and held his knees to his chest.

Later that day, Baron mentioned to mom that he wanted to build something for himself and for Ruby. "I think I can invent a toy that Ruby and I would love to play with for hours. Do you think I should work on it?" he asked his mother. "Or I could just do some KikTalk videos, I guess."

Mom didn't like him making silly videos all the time. She thought it was a waste of time and energy. So she definitely wanted to encourage something else. "Baron, you know, I think your idea about inventing a new toy is a great idea," she said. "Tell me about it."

"Well," he replied. "I don't know. Maybe I should forget it. For this idea, I'd need an old barrel and we don't have one of those. And I know we can't afford to buy one..." he said slyly. "I thought I might try to invent something – you know – like Dad does? But maybe he's the only inventor around here. Never mind. I'll just go make a video or something." He went to his room.

Mom started to thinking. Where could she get a barrel for her inventor son? She thought she had seen one somewhere. But where? It wasn't in the house, that's for sure. Maybe the garage?

She went outside to the garage. "Nope, not here," she thought. "Just Tanner's exercise equipment and the floater. I know I saw a white barrel somewhere." "Tanner! Tanner!" she yelled as she walked outside.

"Yes, dear?" Father called from behind his workshop door. "What do you need?" he asked. Oliva knocked on the workshop door (Father expected everyone to knock before entering – and the whole family indulged him...even if they did think it was a bit silly). Then she went in. "Dear, Baron wants to try to work on a project for Ruby and himself. I really think we should encourage him, don't you? I'd rather he do something productive instead of making those ridiculous videos all the time."

"Of course, dear," Father responded, somewhat absent-mindedly as he was focused on repairing a neighbor's groupscreen. "We just need to get him some materials," Mother suggested. Father put his sonic drill down and looked up – paying more attention now. "But not from my workshop, right?" he asked.

"No, not anything you're using. And certainly not anything dangerous, sweetheart," she said as she walked around the workshop toward the white barrel. "What exactly did you have in mind?" Father asked. "Oh, I don't know," Mother said as she looked around while backing toward the barrel.

"Oops," said Mother as she bumped into the barrel. It almost fell over but she quickly caught it. "You're not using this barrel, are you?" she asked. Father, who had already figured out the gig, decided to play along. "I was actually going to use it in an experiment," he said. "It's an important experiment to determine the safety of waterfall travel."

"Oh," said Oliva. "I didn't know you were studying waterfall travel."

"I wasn't going to but the idea just came to me. I was thinking perhaps that we could put the kids in it and push it over Runyon Falls. If they live, then it's probably safe."

"Tanner! What are you talking about? You can't send my babies over a waterfall in a barrel!" she started, but soon realized from the grin on his face that he was teasing. "Did Baron already ask you about this barrel?" she inquired.

"Yes, about an hour ago," Tanner said. "I guess he can have it. But tell him he has to clean it out thoroughly and paint it before he uses it."

****

That's how Baron got the barrel. But then he and Ruby had to invent their new toy. They went into the workshop to get it (after knocking, of course) and rolled it out slowly. Father watched them. "Mom said it was all right," Baron said sheepishly.

Father just smiled and nodded. Then he shook his head and chuckled as he went back to his work.

Outside, the kids sprayed the barrel down with the hose and then washed it inside and out. With as much soap as they used and the water they sprayed everywhere, they might as well have taken baths outside. They were soaked! Baron told Ruby that he was going to make a great toy for them. "I'm going to call it the *Baronator*!

"Stand back, Ruby. This could be dangerous." He got a huge hammer and tried to knock out the closed end of the barrel. He pounded and pounded. Nothing happened.

"What are you doing?" Ruby asked.

Baron looked at her but didn't answer. He pounded some more. Then he turned the barrel over and pounded some more. He was starting to sweat and breathe heavily.

He took a deep breath and had to switch hands to continue pounding.

"Can I help?" Ruby asked.

"I've got this," he said. "You're not big enough to swing this hammer."

He continued pounding. The noise seemed to get louder. But the barrel wasn't budging. The end was stuck just as tightly as it was when he began. He walked around his nemesis several times. He inspected it inside and out. After nearly 10 minutes of pounding, he hadn't done much damage – save for a number of tiny dents. This barrel wasn't going to give in easily.

"Are you sure I can't help?" asked Ruby again.

Baron looked at his sister and said, "I don't need any help right now." He wiped his brow and then walked over near the end of the barrel, positioned his feet, swung the hammer back and pounded on the end some more. He was sweating more profusely now. The end of the barrel silently mocked him.

Baron fell back and sat scowling at the unforgiving barrel. He pulled his shirt up to wipe the sweat from his face. He had to think. He looked up at Ruby, standing there.

"Hey Rubes?" he suggested. "Would you mind cranking up your leg and – you know?"

"You know, what?" Ruby asked. (She knew exactly what he wanted but she wanted to hear him say it, especially as he had been ignoring her offers of assistance.)

"You know… Can you do your thing?" Baron asked.

"What thing is that, exactly?" Ruby asked. "I didn't think you needed any help. I'm too little anyway. I couldn't possibly lift that big old hammer," she teased.

Ruby was stubborn, but so was Baron.

"Come on," he said. "Can't you just do your thing?"

Ruby was having none of it, so she decided to milk it a little. "I'm just a little girl. You don't need me; besides, you clearly have it under control. I think I'll go inside and get a snack. There may be one last piece of clord pie."

"Unnhhh." Realizing he had been shortsighted, Baron swallowed his pride. "You're right, Ruby. I'm sorry I didn't pay attention to you. I wanted to do it myself." She stared at him. "Could we do this together?" he implored

"Make a *Baronator*?" she inquired. "I don't know if I'm into that." She walked around and began to look off toward the pond.

"What if – what if we called it something else?" he asked.

"I don't know. What did you have in mind?" she inquired.

"Well…let me think. What if we called it the *Rubaronator*?" They looked at each other and both shook their heads. "Maybe something like… *Steamroller*?"

"I don't think so… Maybe *Upside Down Cake*?" Ruby asked.

They both shook their heads again and laughed.

"Hey, how about…the *Spin Doctor*?" Baron suggested.

"*The Spin Doctor*," she said thoughtfully. I like it." She smiled at her brother and waltzed over to the barrel. They both dragged it between two trees, then backed up and looked it over. Seeing that the placement was good, Ruby reached down to scratch her leg. She got a bit of a running start and kicked the heck out of that barrel. It made a kind of sick crunching sound. Then all was quiet. A few seconds later, the end fell to the ground with a long, gentle creaking sound – and then it rolled around a few times until it came to rest.

Baron was right there with some tape, yellow paint, and two brushes. Together they painted the Spin Doctor. When they finished, Ruby hand-lettered the name on the side in black: *Spin Doctor*.

That's how Baron – and Ruby – got their new toy.

CHAPTER **29**

Barrel Roll & the Bard

The hill on the other side of the pond was definitely good for lots of things. Ruby and Baron – and their friends – often found themselves at the top (or the bottom) of that hill – doing one thing or another.

One particular game they enjoyed was going for rides in the *Spin Doctor*. That big, yellow-striped barrel was the perfect size for a kid – even a fairly big one like Baron. Starting at the top of the hill, one of them would serve as the launcher, holding the *Spin Doctor* steady, while another (the rider) would crawl inside.

The way it worked was that the rider had to say "Okay!" and stick his or her 'thumbs up' out of the side of the barrel before it was released – or pushed. (They came up with this approach after a few mishaps, including a broken finger ~ Mae-Ellen, a sprained neck ~ Ho, and several instances of more than mild annoyance regarding premature launches ~ all of them – not to mention a broken screen ~ Baron).

Anyway, once the all-clear was given, the launcher pushed the barrel and it began to roll down the hill. It usually started slowly (depending on who was at the top and whether or not he or she felt like giving the *Spin Doctor* a really hard shove) and then accelerated, building speed on the way down the hill. It should probably go without saying, but there was no steering to speak of. Likewise, there were also no brakes. When a ride began, it pretty much went wherever it wanted and as long as it wanted. Riders had to hold on and enjoy the trip!

And enjoy they did. Roll after roll. The hill never failed them. Every time they got in, the *Spin Doctor* rolled them down – and got them tipsy – over and over and over. The feeling was exciting – if somewhat uneasy. The rider inevitably emerged somewhat shaken and slightly wobbly. The others enjoyed watching the rider try to take his or her first few steps at the bottom of the hill. Of course, those steps were never in a straight line. The initial strides often varied greatly in length and speed – usually changing directions like a zig-zag and often with a hesitation here or there.

Baron actually held the record for the longest ride. (Home court advantage and such. Anyway, it didn't hurt that when Baron was riding, Ruby was often pushing – and a little extra leg power at the start was certainly not holding him back.) For the record, he rolled almost all the way down to the huge, old oak tree – just barely into the shade cast by the giant tree's canopy. Father told them that his grandfather had planted acorns there (from Earth!) more than a hundred years ago – around the same time he started the ice cream banana orchard.

The ice cream bananas were originally from Earth as well. But they were now extinct on Earth due to the changed climate. However, Levon was the perfect environment for these tasty blue fruits. The soil, the climate – just about everything made Levon and the ice cream bananas a perfect match. Even the dragon-fliers were especially attracted to ice cream bananas. And the little fire-breathers made the perfect pollinators for the unusual blue treats.

Everyone wanted to ride! They couldn't get enough. Four of them taking turns was just about perfect timing – as it usually took more than a minute for each rider to re-establish equilibrium.

Ho's stomach felt queasier for longer than usual after his seventh (or eighth?) roll down the hill. He wasn't quite over that feeling when it was his turn again. But he climbed in with all the enthusiasm he could manage. He swallowed hard and took a few deep breaths. "Okay," he half-yelled. There was an unexpected pause. "Are you okay?" Ruby asked. Ho extended his arm out the side of the barrel – and his thumb went slowly up.

"Bonsai!" Baron yelled and gave the *Spin Doctor* a great running start. Ho thought that Baron meant to say 'Banzai' but he quickly forgot about that as his entire world began to spin uncontrollably. It felt like the rolling would never stop. He so wished that he had a brake. But no such luck. The *Spin Doctor* set a new distance record with Ho as the rider! He actually went past the old oak. But Ho didn't notice. His eyes were closed and he was pushing against the inside walls of the barrel as hard as he could – just to hold himself together. When the barrel stopped – waaaayyyy down the hill, Mae-Ellen screamed, "That's a new record!" Ruby and Baron whooped with excitement as they ran down the hill.

The barrel sat motionless. They expected Ho to jump out and whoop it up with them on his great achievement. But Ho didn't come out of the barrel very quickly. Everyone wondered if he had passed out. Inside the barrel, it felt much hotter than before to Ho. He was sweating. He finally released his tense, almost-rigid muscles and sort of fell half-in, half-out of the *Spin Doctor*. Ho rolled over, shook his head and slowly crawled out. He tried to stand up, but took several awkward steps to the side and fell on his butt in the grass. He slowly got up again and tried to steady himself against the barrel – which rolled away leaving Ho leaning perilously to one side. Not unpredictably – after a long, slow, ever-increasing lean – he fell to the ground again.

The others had run down the hill whooping as they came toward Ho. But they were quiet now, watching him. This time, Ho got up to his knees. His stomach was not happy with him. It seemed to want revenge for the repeated, extreme circumvolution. Ho put his hand to his mouth, but it was too late. Vengeance came. It was a nasty, nauseating vengeance. Everyone backed away to give Ho some room. Aside from some mild embarrassment, he actually felt better afterward. Baron snickered; a few seconds later, they were all laughing.

They decided that they'd probably had enough rotational fun for one afternoon. They trudged up the hill and plopped themselves down in the soft grass. Lying on the hill, still half-dizzy, they looked at the blue sky streaked with orange and dotted with puffy clouds.

"What are those orange streaks?" asked Mae-Ellen.

"I think I've seen those somewhere before," said Ruby. But she couldn't quite remember.

"I've read about these," Baron said. The budding scientist explained further. My astronomy book said they were only visible at night – anyway, these streaks are caused by meteor showers from the dust belt caught in the field between our two suns. They can create impressive light shows." None of them had heard this before, but Baron's description made sense – and they didn't have the energy to question his assertion. They had certainly never seen orange meteors during the day – that was unexpected, but they did like the streaming effect. The clouds even seemed to spin a little (more for some of them....)

"Isn't the sky beautiful?" asked Mae-Ellen.

"I'd like it better if it stayed still," commented Ho as he rubbed his eyes. Ruby chuckled softly; she put her hand on his shoulder.

"Sorry about the extra strong push, Ho," Baron said. "But look at the bright side. You did set a new record for the longest ride in the *Spin Doctor*!" They slapped hands – or they tried to. It was somewhat awkward trying to do that while lying on a hill in the grass – especially because they were both still a little off-balance. So they missed. But they just chuckled and looked at each other as if to say, *let it slide*. It was too much effort to try again.

They all caught their breath and enjoyed the momentary respite. After a few moments of silence, Ruby asked (no one in particular), "Do you ever think about what it might be like to fly? I do," she said. "I imagine that Bard is a real, live bullpar. He's with me and he's teaching me to glide like bullpars do."

"Who's Bard?" asked Mae-Ellen.

"He's my bullpar," said Ruby.

"Her stuffed animal," added Baron.

Ruby ignored Baron and continued, "Bullpars don't show just anyone how their magic works, you know. But he really likes me. I'm his favorite. You know how bullpars adopt people sometimes? Well, Bard adopted me. He's my good luck friend forever.

"Bard's not like they say bullpars can be – you know – nasty or dangerous. He's not foul-tempered at all. He loves me. He lets me hug him. Anyway, we're walking down this very hill and I say, 'I wish I could fly like you Bard.' He turns around in mid-air and looks at me, as if to say, 'Sure, I can show you how to glide.'"

Mae-Ellen, Baron, and Ho, were tired. As they lay there, breathing softly on the grass, they were content just to listen to the soothing sound of Ruby's voice – with her latest story – as they gently floated along on her words.

Ruby continued, "So I was walking down the hill. Bard usually floated about as high as my shoulder. But as I walked down the hill, he continued floating at the same level. By the time I got to the bottom of the hill, Bard was almost 15 feet up in the air – way over my head. I was jealous. I looked up at him. I kept walking and he maintained pace with me, gliding along. Ever so slowly, he drifted downward until – by the time we got to the orchard, Bard was back to his usual elevation – eye level.

Even though bullpars are can be be mean and irritable, Bard loved me. I could hug him and kiss him and he let me snuggle with him. Of course, bullpars are very strong – also smart and independent – so he could have stopped me at any time, but he didn't; we had a special relationship.

"While we were talking together, I took a risk and asked him again if he could show me how to glide. He stopped in mid-air, motionless. As I had continued walking, I was several feet ahead of Bard before I realized he was no longer beside me. When I noticed, I walked back to where he had stopped. He leaned his head a little to the left and then flew around me, stopping right in front of me, face-to-face. I reached out to pet him – of course he let me.

"Then Bard flew around me slowly, again and then a third time. He stopped behind me and nudged me back in the direction of the pond and the hill. I didn't know what he was up to, but I went along anyway. We walked out of the orchard, across the field, and up to the top of the hill. He kept guiding me in the direction he wanted me to go.

"Bard flew up under my arm. I thought he wanted me to scratch his back – or his tummy. He likes that. His feet have sharp claws which would be great for scratching, but his legs are so short that he can't reach much of his torso. So he likes it when I scratch him. Just me. Most people are afraid to touch a bullpar. And they're probably smart to be wary.

"But when I tried to scratch him this time, he pulled away – floating backward along an unseen plane – almost like a level pendulum. He came back toward me and nuzzled up under my other arm. So, I tried to scratch him with my other hand. That was obviously not what he wanted, because he backed away again. Next, he floated up to my face and then down to my feet. He circled me around and around, several times, rising higher with each pass. When he got to the top of my head, he floated away up toward the sky and slowly drifted.

"Ohhhhh," Ruby said. "I wish I could fly, too. When he heard me say that again, Bard spun around and flew straight back to me. To be clear, when I say he flew, I mean that he glided or floated or whatever it is that bullpars do. He doesn't have wings and it doesn't really look like he should be able to fly. Except the thing is that he floats in the air as if hanging by invisible strings – and he moves whichever way he wants to. So I guess you could call that flying. He circled again and nuzzled under my arm again. What a strange creature. I could not understand what he was trying to tell – Wait! Was he actually going to help me learn to fly?

"I slowly wrapped my arms around him as if I were going to hug him. Bard slowly pulled away, upward. He pulled away from my arms. I released my grip. Maybe I was wrong. Of course he couldn't teach me to fly. I'm a person, not a bullpar. Besides, my leg was probably too heavy anyway.

"But then Bard came back again and nuzzled my arm. I got the idea that maybe he wanted me to hold on again, but tighter. Now I knew Bard loved me – and that I was the only one he even let touch him. But my mother had warned me to be careful, because bullpars can be dangerous. So, the idea of holding onto Bard tightly enough so that he couldn't get away – with the hope that he was going to try to lift me off the ground.... Well, that was a little scary... But also exciting..." Ruby smiled.

"You know how it is when your mother warns you not to do something and to be careful – and you know she's right, so you agree completely? But then later, you find yourself in a situation where you're actually considering doing that something that you know you shouldn't. And you're absolutely certain that this is what mother was talking about. While I was pondering this situation, Bard rose up again and stared deeply into my green eyes. He floated very close. Face to face, we could feel each other's breath. He stayed right there, barely inches from my face, for what seemed like several minutes. Then he floated around me and again nuzzled under my arm.

"Was he trying to say, 'trust me?'" *What the heck*, I thought. "So I put both arms around my friend and held on as tightly as I dared. He slowly lifted me upward. We rose together. Off the ground. And then some. My feet were dangling. I was focused on Bard – and holding on.

But I could tell we were going up. After all, I could see the top of Father's workshop – something I couldn't normally do from my regular height. The breeze blew through my unruly hair, but we started to move and the rushing air soon began to push backward, blowing the hair out of my face.

"I took that opportunity to look down. 'Wow!' I said aloud to myself. "We were nearly thirty feet up. I was flying! I was actually flying! I closed my eyes for a second – and buried my face into Bard's soft, furry underside. Slowly, I gathered my courage and looked all around. The view from above was different. I liked it! I could see much farther – our whole farm: Father's workshop, the house, the pond, the orchard, the fields – all the way to the end of the path down to the road.

The other kids imagined themselves floating along with Ruby and Bard. A breeze blew through Mae-Ellen's and Ho's hair as well. (Baron's close-cropped hair wouldn't move in a hurricane.)

"Can we go higher?" I whispered in Bard's ear. "At least, I think that was his ear. It's hard to tell with bullpars. I mean, I'm sure they *have* ears, but it's not at all clear where they are." Bard understood what I wanted. He took me higher. It didn't seem to be any trouble for him. Soon, we had floated over the treetops. I bet we were even as high as some of the tallest greenstalks!

"Flying was exhilarating. I wish I could do it by myself. But being with Bard was wonderful! My arms were beginning to get tired. My hands were interlocked tightly so I couldn't let go, but my fingers began to get numb. I didn't care. I didn't want our adventure to end!

"I guess because my fingers were losing feeling – or maybe partly because I was paying more attention to everything else, my hold began to slip. And it didn't happen slowly. Once it started, it went straight from a little slipping to a lot of falling. 'Aaaaaahhhhhhh!' I screamed. Without Bard, I was a fish out of water – or a bird out of air. No, that doesn't sound right either. Anyway, I was …. still falling!

"We must have flown over 100 feet high. Of course, it was lower now that I was falling. This was not going to end well. I'd probably break something. Maybe several somethings. I hope not my new leg. I'm thinking there will definitely be some serious pain involved.

"I continued to plummet toward the ground. My mind was going faster than I was falling! I struggled to spin around – perhaps I might be falling toward the pond! That might be the only thing that could save me from this height. I straightened out like a skydiver with my stomach down and head up so I could see better.

"But no. The pond was way over there. That was my last chance at avoiding total calamity. I was falling toward a patch of dry, hard ground. I had no idea where Bard was. I closed my eyes tightly.

"I took a deep breath and realized that was the sound of the air whipping by my ears. What else could I do but listen – and fall? After a few more seconds, I opened one eye. Bard! There he was! Face to face with me. Falling with me. I felt better just seeing him.

"But I was still falling! My arms were flailing around like a flame dancing on a candle in a thunderstorm. I couldn't grab onto Bard! The falling felt like it would never stop. Only I was more okay with the falling than the pending unwelcome stop that would surely interrupt my descent. I closed my eyes again.

"There was pressure on my stomach and it began to feel tight. Then I began to feel like I was being kicked in the gut – and the force was increasing. I was probably going to be sick. Great. I was going to get sick while falling to my death. I'll probably throw up — like Ho did in the *Spin Doctor*. With my luck, I'd pass it on the way down and then it would catch up to me. They'll find my crumpled, broken body with *that* having fallen on top of me. Yucckkk!

"Everything happened in an instant. My eyes closed even more tightly. I couldn't open them if I tried – not that I wanted to. The pushing feeling in my stomach began to hurt more. It was as if my stomach was going to be forced out – all the way through my back!

"Mae-Ellen and Baron rubbed at their stomachs.

"The sound of the wind-tunnel air rushing past my ears became softer. The world seemed to slow down. I've heard of things like that. I'm only 10 but I've read about how your life passes before your eyes when you're about to die – or how people sometimes see very fast things happen in slow motion. Brains are funny things. Something like that was definitely happening to me.

"Baron's hands clutched at the grass.

"It's kind of amazing that the mind can take a real-time event – like falling from 100 feet high –moving at an incredible rate of speed – and almost control time. My mind did that. It actually slowed time. Although I'm not sure why. These were not things I wanted to prolong: falling, fear, dying. Yet my mind slowed things even more. The sound of the wind in my ears became even quieter now – barely a summer breeze. I should have hit the ground by now.

"How could my final seconds go ever-so-slowly? I just wanted this deathfall to end.

"Everything seemed to be happening – in my mind at least – slower than I would have thought possible. The world was virtually stopped – as in – extreme slow motion. My crazy brain must be more powerful than I thought. I wondered, 'Is this how it feels right before you die?'

"As if falling from the sky weren't enough, this particular free-fall was taking forever! It was only dragging out the inevitable.

"Ho's hands clutched at the grass.

"The suspense was overwhelming. I just couldn't take it anymore. When was I going to be a pancake on that dry patch of dirt below? My heart was beating so fast, I could feel it throbbing in my throat. I could barely breathe. I let out what was likely to be my final scream, 'Aaaaaaaaahhhhhhhhh!' I ran out of breath. But I still hadn't hit the ground. So I inhaled and let out another scream. 'Aaaaaaaaahhhhhhhh!'

"The pain in my stomach had begun to subside somewhat. At least I wasn't going to throw up on myself. I suppose I could be thankful for that. Although I still felt this huge lump pushing against my abdomen. It almost felt like my body was wrapping around an invisible something.

"How could my brain do this to me? Was my mind playing a cruel joke? I felt as if I had stopped in mid-air.

"Without conscious effort, my hands shot out in front of me – but then something strange and unexpected happened. My hand touched something. This was it: the beginning of hitting the ground hard – even if it was in slow motion, it would still hurt. The result would still be squish city. Nothing could change my future – or lack thereof.

"But then my other hand touched something. It felt like dirt. Through my heightened sense of awareness, I noticed that the sound of rushing air had stopped. I heard another sound now. It was a bit muffled. But it sounded familiar. I knew I'd heard that sound before. Bard? Bard!

"I opened my eyes. I was stopped two feet from the ground. Suspended and definitely not still falling. Bard was holding me up at my mid-section. I was sort of folded over him – in an upside down V. He made another muffled growl-y, sort of purring sound – even though he was actually more like a dog than a cat – and squirmed out from under me. Then Bard floated gently back up to his normal hovering height. He looked the same as he always did. Meanwhile, I was drenched in sweat and totally freaked out, not to mention confused.

"Oh yes, without Bard's support, I also fell the last two feet to the ground – face first, of course. It took me a moment to process. I rolled over and spit out dirt. I lay there looking up at the sky. Then I sat up and brushed my hair back. Bard had flown underneath me and slowed my fall to save my life. Whoever said that bullpars were good luck, certainly knew what they were talking about.

STORYTRAX: *Flight of the Valkyries* - Richard Wagner (London Symphony)

CHAPTER **30**

The Demon's Dinner

The next evening, it was time for another visit to the Storyteller. Back at Runyon Falls, Ruby dropped her x-crutches to the ground and took a seat by the storyfire as before. The Storyteller rose from the darkness to a spot high above the flames. He began:

Caligula was pleased with himself. The seed he had planted a millennium before was bearing more fruit than he could possibly have imagined. He enjoyed the evil he had wrought. Trajan and Giselle used the Tenso Baka – the soul vessels – to extend their lives at the expense of innocents. They grew more powerful and more ruthless with each passing generation. Their unchecked desires fueled their corruption. They did as they pleased and enjoyed their dominance. Every successive transition further dulled their senses to the abominable acts they were committing.

Meanwhile, Judge Paxton was sick with himself. Although he had not committed the same horrible atrocities as Giselle and Trajan, he was witness to those acts. Indeed, he was part of setting that chain of events into motion. He participated in calling up the magic of the triumvirate. He had allowed the unchecked violence and abuses of power to continue. And even as he benefited from the gift of long life, he did nothing to protect his Pavirlo which continually lost land to Zakar and Geisl. He felt like an observer in his own life, paralyzed by guilt. He was ashamed of his inaction.

As Trajan and Giselle ruled with whims and punished with abandon, their power grew – as did their hate for each other. They also both pitied and despised Paxton for his weakness. All the same, they were mostly content to let him stay out of their way. Regardless, they were inextricably bound through the triumvirate.

Paxton was repeatedly elected to lead Pavirlo for his patience and kindness to others – and also out of respect for his age and wisdom. The citizens of Pavirlo thought that his relationships with the leaders of

Zakar and Geisl protected them from being overrun entirely by the two vast powers that surrounded them.

For more than 900 years, Paxton had not married. He felt he was not worthy of a relationship or a family because of what he had done. But when he met Magdela, she melted his heart and they wed. She bore him a son, whom they named Shiloh. One day, Magdela wanted to visit her ailing mother. Paxton did not want her to go because – now that Zakar had taken more land from Pavirlo – her mother's home was located outside of Pavirlo's boundaries. But Magdela insisted, and traveled despite his objections. His beloved was killed on the journey.

Paxton was more despondent than ever. He realized that he could not let this horrible path continue. It was too late for his Magdela, but at least he could try to do something for everyone else. He left Shiloh with a servant and sent word for Giselle and Trajan to meet him at the sunsdial in the greenstalk forest. He told them they must bring their soul vessels.

They arrived – none too happy at being summoned by the insignificant person they were bound to through the triumvirate.

"What do you mean by calling us here outside of the regular meeting time, Paxton?" bellowed a young, powerful Trajan. "Is there some emergency?"

Paxton, now older and beginning to grey, walked slowly into the ring of the sunsdial. "I cannot allow this to continue," he said simply and directly.

"You can't allow what to continue?" asked (another new) Giselle in her decorative robes trimmed with gold and silver.

"This evil that has permeated our land. It has gone on far too long," said Paxton. "I was part of it from the beginning and I did nothing. I am ashamed. You two have become what the demon Caligula must have wanted from the beginning."

"Paxton, you're old and you're not thinking straight. Besides, no one has seen Caligula for a thousand years. Why don't you let me help you back to your wagon?" suggested Trajan as he looked at Giselle. He put out his hand to Paxton. When he got close to Paxton, Trajan stabbed him in the side, then stepped back and let the old man fall to the ground.

"It had to be done," said Giselle, matter-of-factly, looking at her nails. "He might've done something crazy. Now, let's talk about dividing up what's left of Pavirlo." The two negotiated while Paxton lay bleeding on the ground.

Behind Giselle and Trajan, Paxton arose. "I may be have aged somewhat but I still have the power of the soul vessel. I cannot die any more than either of you while we are linked," he said. "But there is one thing I can do." Paxton took out his soul vessel. He raised it high and then smashed on the stone floor of the sunsdial. The crystal base and neck cracked and broke into five pieces.

"Nooooo!," shouted Trajan.

"You crazy old fool, do you know what you've done?" Giselle screamed. She reached for her face. It began to age in seconds. "I don't feel right," she said softly.

"What's happening to me!" Trajan stumbled; he had to hold onto the sunsdial to avoid falling. The power of the triumvirate was fading. The spell (curse) was broken.

They both grew older, slowly at first, but then noticeably faster. Giselle's skin began to stretch and fall off. She tried to push it back, but to no avail. Trajan tried to speak but only gasps came out. He lunged toward Paxton. "You did this!" he screamed as he fell short of Paxton. Giselle fell to the ground as well. Trajan and Giselle experienced the effects faster because their souls were not in their own bodies. They succumbed and withered away to bone, and then to ash, and finally, to dust, swept away by an opportune breeze.

The end was surely coming soon for Paxton too, but he welcomed it. He didn't feel that he deserved to live. And now that he had broken the spell and ended the cycle of evil, he was no longer needed.

Paxton stumbled into the entrance of Caligula's cave leaning on his cart for balance. This underground cathedral of elegance had once been Caligula's home. But no one had seen the terrible demon since he had made gifts of the soul vessels a thousand years ago. If I'm going to die anyway, I might as well see this place. And what an awesome place Caligula's cave was – his cavernous lair was inside a mountain containing an enormous waterfall. There were towers of rock and stalagmites and the cave walls were dotted with sparkling ternium crystals, generating more than enough light to brighten the cave.

Chambers and passageways were carved right out of the rock. Paxton walked into a huge room and virtually collapsed onto a stone chair with a sick, cracking sound. His old, crumpled body was racked in pain as it continued to age. As he let out a long sigh, his eyes closed.

Heavy breathing and a hissing sound awoke Paxton. His head jerked back when he saw a huge, wretched beast staring at him. "What are you doing in my home, old man?" Caligula shouted. "I should kill you right now. But I do want to thank you for helping create a thousand years of torture and bedevilment. It was so ... exhilarating. When your kind fight and die and kill and maim, I win," said the demon and he laughed a low, long, laugh to himself while his lips curled into a wry smile – if one could really call something that ugly a smile. "You and Trajan and Giselle have played your parts so well."

"Not anymore demon," said Paxton as he sat up a bit. "I've put an end to that. You'll get no more satisfaction from us."

"You're tired and weak, old man. Why don't you just give in? Think about it, Paxton. Wouldn't you like to have a younger body? You could enjoy life much more. Trajan and Giselle have the power and they aren't afraid to use it. You could join them."

"They are gone, demon. I've smashed my Tenso Baka," said Paxton.

"What!? You idiot!" yelled Caligula – breathing fire! He moved his head slowly due to the incredible weight of those enormous horns. It was as if his neck carried the weight of a huge mass of evil as his constant burden. In his fury, he punched through two huge stone columns...chucks of rock fell from the ceiling.

"Yes, demon. It's over. You've lost," Paxton said and slowly leaned back in the chair. He knew his time was short now.

"Aaaaaaaaaaaaaaagggggghhhhh!" Caligula leaned backward and roared.

A few jars tumbled from the back of Paxton's cart and crashed onto the cave floor, getting Caligula's attention. He stomped toward the wagon and saw a small child partially hidden under a tarp – and a few jars of jellied clords that had crashed onto the floor. He grabbed the child by the leg and held him upside down breathing his smoky breath on the youngling. Then Caligula took a few thunderous strides toward Paxton. "What do we have here?"

"No! My son!" Paxton said wearily. "Caligula, Shiloh is only three years old; he is an innocent. Please let him go," pleaded Paxton.

"Your kind is so weak," said Caligula. The demon licked the child from head to toe with a slimy, flittering, forked tongue. Paxton shuddered and a tear rolled down his old cheek; he shook his head slowly back and forth, slowly mouthing the word, "No." He reached out a hand but it fell limp against his body – and then dangled over the arm of the chair.

Caligula switched the child to his other hand and held Shiloh by the collar of his shirt. Then he glared at the now-motionless Paxton and muttered, "Stupid old fool." The awful demon tossed Paxton's body aside and shifted his attention back to the child. "At least you brought me lunch." Then he tilted his head back and opened wide as he placed the youngling into his mouth; Shiloh began to whimper. Caligula raised the child up again over those awful fangs. A huge drop of the demon's saliva dropped from the child's legs back onto Caligula's cheek. "I'm going to enjoy this."

The demon lowered the boy into his mouth once more. In a single chomp, the horrid monster bit off both of the child's legs while his searing-hot lips burned the ends. He severed the boy's bones with his powerful teeth, and crunched and chewed, then he swallowed. Licking his lips with that dreadful, slimy tongue, he said aloud (for Paxton to hear) "Children are quite tasty. Could use a little pepper."

Without warning, Ruby blurted out "Oh, that poor little baby! I wish I could just pick him up and give him a hug and protect him from that terrible demon." The Storyteller stopped and glared at her – as did most of the other children. Along with the Storyteller's gaze, part of his glow seemed to shine directly on Ruby as if his eyes provided a spotlight. She shrank back, sat down, and quietly said (mostly to herself) "Well, I do."

The Storyteller continued, "Paxton tried to get up and screamed "Nooooo!" His life waning, he fell back onto the stone chair and said, "My poor Shiloh, I'm so sorry. May God have mercy on us all and bless you my son." Paxton was spent. His head fell to the side and his last breath drained from his now still body. Caligula ripped a huge stalactite off the cave ceiling and crushed Paxton's lifeless form.

CHAPTER 31

Heartburn

The children around the storyfire were still mesmerized. Despite Ruby's momentary interruption, their eyes were once again fixed on the Storyteller. Many had their mouths agape. He continued.

"But the demon was still not finished," the Storyteller added as the falls continued their low, relentless rumbling.

He laid down the child Shiloh near a fire beside a large black kettle and walked away. Shiloh was in shock, afraid, and bewildered. His dirty, little face perspired and the sweat streamed soot away from his ruddy cheeks in squiggly lines. The child's eyelids fluttered while he drifted in and out of consciousness with what was left of his scorched legs.

Caligula jumped down to a lower level in the cave and began to turn redder. Smoke and flames came from his nostrils and his huge mouth. He began to change shape. He stretched and twisted his limbs in impossibly unnatural ways, popping and clicking. Caligula was returning to his true form – a dragon. His stubby tail grew longer. Scales sprouted all over his skin. He dropped to all fours as wings sprouted from his back. His entire body almost tripled in size. When the transformation was complete, he lifted his awesome head back and spewed flames a hundred feet high, charring the ceiling with burnt, black streaks.

Mighty and fierce, this demon was satisfied with his work for the moment. The next thing on his mind was to finish his meal. He flew back up to the main level where Shiloh was passed out by the kettle. Landing and feeling the space a bit confined, he bumped into the walls several times before he began to shrink back to his smaller but still-sizable, bi-pedal form to deal with the boy. Caligula slowly morphed back to his ugly upright self. His monstrous cow-like head with that big nose and those huge, sharp horns came into shape once again.

The beast reached for Shiloh, but then stopped. Caligula walked over to a shelf; grabbed one jar and raked the remaining contents of the shelf to the cave floor. He walked back toward Shiloh with huge, ground-shaking footsteps. When he reached the boy, Caligula poured purple pepper flakes all over the small child. Bits of pepper were silhouetted against the smoke from the demon's nostrils as they caught flashes of light from the crystals in the ceiling and floated down onto Shiloh. The child sneezed. Caligula smiled his terrible, twisted smile.

Yet again the monster reached out toward his dinner. But something wasn't right. His arm began to stiffen; then it stopped working altogether, refusing to respond. Caligula shuddered. The beast grabbed at his stomach – with his working hand. He began to wretch. He groaned a loud, unsettling sound that echoed against the cave walls. Caligula stumbled. The demon's stomach began to glow and throb. It also started to smoke as it pulsed larger and then smaller and then larger again. His mid-section expanded and contracted with each pulse of light.

Caligula dropped to his knees and began clawing at his stomach. It continued to pulsate. Green bile poured from the creature's mouth onto the cave floor and puddled there. The sounds coming from deep inside him were painful to hear. It sounded something like a combination of a cry, a roar, and gurgling boil. He rolled toward the wall and tried to claw himself up to a standing position.

Facing the child, he said, "You cannot do this to me! I am Caligula. I have taken a thousand souls and brought your kind to evil again and again. I am Caligula – Dealer of Death, Caligula – Warrior for the Wicked, Caligula…" He breathed heavily. The words became more difficult for him. "I am… No mere child can— " The monster doubled over in pain and fell to the floor.

Dragging himself up against the wall yet again, he struggled to speak. "Your pathetic little body is nothing. I will consume you to feed my anger and — " The demon seemed to be wrestling with something he couldn't control. Sweat poured down his grotesque face. He forced himself to stand upright – although his stomach was larger than ever now – and pulsing, stretching and contorting into odd shapes. It was glowing like fire trying to escape the confines of his body. His stomach was making sounds on its own.

Caligula tumbled back down to the lower level and let out a guttural roar. Then he screamed, "Aaaaaaahhhhhhh!" Shiloh awakened to this horrible sight and, despite being nearly blinded by pain, deathly afraid, and extremely disoriented, he dragged his tiny body behind one of the remaining columns. The demon looked down at his own belly, still pulsing, still contorting, and still growing. The ominous, low rumbling sound emanating from his gut was becoming louder and faster; it rolled in deafening waves. Little Shiloh covered his ears. The monster began to wretch with his stomach convulsing; he threw up a foot.

The beast screamed again – arms outstretched toward the ceiling – and then froze in silence... Time seemed to stand still for a few seconds...

The demon's stomach exploded! A thunderous explosion rocked the cave. The entire, horrible beast erupted into streams of flame that shot out in all directions. Pieces of the evil creature were cast as fireballs across the cave. The main force of the explosion ripped the top and side of the cave apart, collapsing it and exposing the falls to the open air. Much of the remainder of the cave collapsed in on itself. Inside what was left of Caligula's abode, those massive horns hurtled directly toward Shiloh.

They barely missed the child as they blasted themselves into the wall a few feet above him. There they were embedded into the stone, projecting outward like some sort of grotesque trophy.

Back at Runyon Falls, the children at the storyfire were spellbound. The storyfire itself seemed to grow in intensity as the Storyteller described the demon's demise. The flames in front of them surged in height and power when the demon Caligula erupted. The children wiped sweat from their brows. Ruby shook her head. She couldn't believe what she had just experienced. She needed time – time to process this story. What did it mean?

The Storyteller, himself, was now spent. His glow wasn't as bright as it was when the evening began – and he floated lower, closer to the ground. He glided slowly away. The fire, which had burned brightly before, had burned itself down to embers in just the last few moments. The air was quiet and the night was still. There was only the sound of the falls.

Parents arrived to pick up their children. Ruby looked up with droopy eyelids to see Father reaching out with her crutches. "Would you mind carrying me down tonight?" she asked with her eyes half closed.
Father smiled at Ruby and then at Mother – who took the crutches. Father picked up the little girl with the big red hair and impossibly blue lips and carried her down the hill in his arms.

CHAPTER **32**

Pocket Fail

A few days later, the weather turned colder. After breakfast, Father asked Baron and Ruby to help him plant some trees. Ruby declined, "I have to practice my pitching."

"Okay, I guess the Bear and I can manage without you," said Father.

The guys grabbed a couple of shovels from Father's workshop and headed down toward the big, old oak tree.

Their task was to dig a round hole, roughly the size of a toddler's swimming pool. "The hole should be six feet across and at least a foot deep," said Father. He looked up and Baron had his hands in his pockets. "Son, you should probably get your hands out of your pockets."

"Why?"

"For one thing, because I asked you," said Father.

"But it's kind of cold out here," replied Baron.

"Another reason you shouldn't walk around with your hands in your pockets is – if you trip, you're likely to fall on your face or on your rear end. Your hands would be stuck inside your pockets."

"I'm not going to fall," said Baron. Tanner looked at his son.

Deciding it would be better if he changed the subject, Father said, "Your grandfather dug a hole just like this – nearly a hundred years ago to plant the acorns that grew into this massive oak tree. We're going to do the same thing to try to grow a few more. We'll dig three holes and then gather acorns to plant in the middle of each one."

"So why do we need such big holes for such tiny acorns?" Baron asked. "The large holes help collect the water and that gives the trees a better chance of survival. Oaks are not native to this planet and often have a hard time getting adjusted. Haven't you ever noticed, we only have the one?"

"So why do we need three of these big holes?" inquired Baron.

"Your grandfather tried several times but this is the only one that he ever got to grow. I figured if we tried more holes, we might have a better chance at getting one to take root," said Father.

Bam! came the sound from across the field. A slight pause and then again, *Bam*! Ruby was throwing softballs against the side of Father's workshop.

"Why do you let Ruby throw balls against your workshop?" Baron asked. *Bam! Bam!* came another round in quick succession. She was throwing two balls at the same time – ambidextrously now. "I know you don't like it," he added.

"Well, son. Sometimes you put up with things that you don't like for various reasons," said Father. "For example, I don't think you should hang out with your hands in your pockets, but I've told you and you'll just have to learn for yourself."

"Dad, I'm not going to fall down. I think I can walk and chew clord candy at the same time," said Baron.

"I know, but it's just not the smartest thing to do," said Father. "You'll have to trust me on this. Besides, it looks sort of lazy."

Baron slowly took his hands out of his pockets and grabbed the shovel at his feet. He began to dig a hole by himself – several feet away from his father's hole. "See Father? I'm not lazy," said Baron.

"I know son. And I appreciate your helping me today."

Baron jumped on his shovel to force it deeper into the ground. "But," Baron asked, "Why do you let Ruby pitch against the side of your workshop? Are you trying to let her learn something?"

"Not exactly. I guess I just want to encourage her to teach herself. She seems to be really dedicated and I think we should support her in the effort."

"Whatever," said Baron, "She could probably practice all year and I don't think it would make much difference."

Bam! Bam! He was just finishing his hole in the soft, fertile earth.

They started working on the third hole together. They would dig up shovelfuls of fertile Botanian dirt and throw them into a depression in the ground at the bottom of a small hill. It wasn't very far – and it was mostly downhill but the dirt still flew into quite a dispersion pattern.

"Father, I was thinking that I might like to get a cool nickname," Baron said casually.

"Is that so?" said Father, as he stepped onto the shovel, driving it into the ground.

"Yeah," Baron responded. *Bam!*

"What kind of nickname?" Father asked. "Something like 'bear' instead of Baron?"

"No. I mean something cool. Like a super-hero name. But different; it just can't be too obvious, you know?" Baron offered. "So, it works like this. You take a word that is cool or tough and then put a twist on it. Ho told me about it."

"Do tell," said Father.

"For example, if I start with 'warrior' – which is pretty cool – I could change the first letter to a 'b.' That would be 'borrier.' But I don't want to bore everybody."

"Good point," observed Father. "Besides, if you had to write that down, it might come across as 'barrier.'"

"Yeah, see what I mean? I've been thinking about a lot of these. And it's way harder than I thought. There always seems to be some sort of unexpected problem. Like you just said," explained Baron.

"So what else have you got?" Father asked.

"Do you really want to hear?" asked Baron as he tossed another shovelful of dirt.

"Sure," said Father. "If my son's going to get a new name, I'd like to be in the know pretty early on." *Bam-Bam!* (Another two-hander.)

"I thought about starting with 'Claw.'"

"That sounds pretty tough," said Father.

"I know, right?" said Baron, pausing for a moment to lean on his shovel. "But the first thing I came up with was 'Flaw,' and that's not a name I would want.

"I see what you mean," said Father.

"Yeah, then I thought of 'Slaw,' but that doesn't work either."

Father chuckled. "So, you said you thought of several of these?" Father asked.

"Yeah, so I moved on to 'Eagle' and then changed it to 'Beagle,' but that's not very cool or tough."

"Uh-uh," said Father, shaking his head, trying to hide a grin.

"Then I thought I could make it more than just one word. So I thought of 'Baron von Tough.' But when I changed that to 'Baron von Snuff,' or 'Baron von Stuff' – or even 'Baron von Puff,' – none of those sounded cool either."

"You certainly have a challenge there," said Father, heaving a shovel of dirt.

"See what I mean? This stuff isn't easy. But if I'm going to have a tough nickname, I've got to keep trying,' said Baron.

Father was beginning to smile and was having trouble hiding it. He was proud of his son for trying and for his dedication, but he did find the process somewhat amusing. Still, he wanted to encourage Baron. "So do you have any other ideas?" he asked

"Sort of. But they're not working out all that well either," said Baron.

"Tell me some more; sometimes saying them out loud can help you think of other ideas," suggested Father.

"Well, I thought 'Scandal' was kind of cool as a starting point, but all I could come up with was 'sandal.' "I don't think one shoe is going to scare anyone."

"Then I thought I could start with 'Avenger.' But I ended up with 'scavenger.' I don't want my cool nickname to make people think of a rat vulture," said Baron.

"Good point," said Father, as he lofted another shovelful of dirt down the hill. They had finished the third hole. Father walked a few feet away to start on the fourth, but Baron was fully engaged in his nickname search. He dropped his shovel while continuing to brainstorm.

"Maybe I could try 'Legend,' Baron was now thinking aloud. "Legend, begend, crevend, reverend...Ugh! This is not working."

"When I was on Earth, there was a character they referred to as the 'Man of Steel,' suggested Father. He added with a smile, "What if your nickname was 'Man of Teal'?"

"Is that cool," asked Baron? Baron had no idea what teal was.

Father explained that teal is a color – sort of a mixture of green and a little blue.

"Thanks, but I don't think blue-green is very tough," Baron responded with a roll of his eyes.

Father felt for his son's plight but he couldn't resist having a little fun. "What if you started with 'Strong Man,' could you make that into 'Wrong Man'?" Father asked. He chuckled a little, but tried to hide his amusement from Baron.

Bam! Having stopped even pretending to dig now, Baron was getting chilled and put his hands back into his pockets.

"What if you started with 'Blaster,'? Then your name might be 'Caster' or 'Zaster,' Father suggested.

"Caster," Baron said aloud. That's interesting. Is that a word?" he asked.

"Actually, yes," said Father. "It's a small wheel on a piece of furniture that allows it to roll in any direction."

"I'm not sure you really understand how this is supposed to work," Baron said.

"Maybe you could turn 'Power' into 'Flower' or 'Shower'?" Father added. He couldn't hide his chuckles any more.

"Okay, I see what's going on here," said Baron and he turned away from his father. There was yet another *Bam!* but this one was followed by a crash that sounded like breaking glass!

"What was that?" asked Father, looking up from the last hole.

"I think it was Ruby," said Baron.

"Well, since you don't seem to want to dig anymore, would you mind going to check on your sister?" asked Father.

Baron rolled his eyes again – and took a deep breath that he let out fully before responding. "I guess so," he said as he looked back at Father and turned to go toward the workshop. But he stepped right into the first hole.

Because his hands were in his pockets, he couldn't get them out to break his descent. As a result, Baron fell face-first into the freshly dug hole.

For a moment, he stayed there with his face in the dirt. The words – his words, "I'm not going to fall," kept repeating in his ears.

Father looked up. Choking back laughter, he took a breath and steadied his voice. "Are you okay, son?" he asked with all the compassion he could muster.

Baron wriggled his hands out of his pockets and pushed himself up into a sitting position, spitting out a little dirt. "I'm fine," he said. Father looked at him and smiled. Baron smiled back. "Maybe I should be more careful about walking around holes with my hands in my pockets…"

Father nodded, "You may have a point."

Just then, there was the echo of another *Bam!* followed almost immediately by another sound of breaking glass. Father drove his shovel into the ground and left it standing there while he reached down to help his son stand up.

Baron dusted himself off. "Maybe we should go check on Ruby," he suggested.

"That's a really good idea, son," said Father.

They grabbed their shovels and headed up toward the workshop.

CHAPTER **33**

The Offer

Three weeks later. In the floater on the way to Runyon Falls.

"This is your final visit to the Storyteller," said Mom. "What do you think about that?"

"I don't know," said Ruby. "At first, I didn't want to go at all. But now, I'm sorry that this is my last visit. The way he floats and the way his voice gets inside you. It's kind of amazing." Mom was smiling at Ruby. Almost too much of a smile. Dad, too. "Hmmmm...," she thought; "What's up, Mom?" Ruby asked.

"Nothing, sweetie. I'm just so proud of you."

"I'm proud of you as well," said her father, practically beaming.

Ruby looked around for the hidden camera. "Uhhhh... thanks guys. It's always nice to be appreciated." Mom continued smiling at Ruby while Father drove.

"Okay, what is it?" Ruby asked. "Why are you guys acting so weird?"

"We're not acting weird. There's nothing wrong with parents being proud of their children."

Mom finally turned around to face the front. Ruby took a deep breath; she wasn't buying it. Something was up. But it didn't seem like they were going to tell her just yet. *Oh, well,* she thought. *Parents....What are you gonna do with them?* She pulled out her screen and began scrolling...looking for music.

When they arrived at the parkbay, it was night – just as it had been every other time she had visited the Storyteller. But something was definitely different this time. Theirs was the only floater in the parkbay. As they got out, and Father got Ruby her crutches, her parents were still all smiles, but not saying very much. Ruby wasn't usually thrilled about surprises, but this was especially odd for her. Her only consolation was that – if her parents were smiling – then at least *they* thought it was a good surprise. It could be lame to a 10-year-old girl, but she'd just try to smile and make the best of it – whatever 'it' was.

When they got to the top of the path, the storyfire was burning as usual. But there was no one else around. Not even the Storyteller.

"Go ahead and sit down, honey," said Father. Ruby sat in her usual spot.

"We'll be back in a minute, sweetie," said Mom. Her parents both leaned down and hugged her.

"Where are you going? Where is everyone else?" Ruby asked.

"This is a special night, just for you," said her father. "Just wait here. We'll be right back," he said as they walked off into the woods.

"Wait, you're not just going to leave me here...alone.. in the …" She looked around. They had, indeed, left her alone in the dark. It's a good thing she was 10 years old now and not too afraid of being alone in the dark. "Well, there is a nice fire… and I do have the stars," she said to no one in particular.

"Okay," she said to herself, looking around a little nervously. "If I'm going to be alone next to a storyfire, maybe I should try to come up with a story." For probably the first time in her life, she couldn't think of a story. Her mind was a complete blank. That was so unlike her. Finally, one idea popped into her head. It was the story that Gram had told them a few weeks ago...about the Storyteller.

Ruby heard a twig snap. She turned around with a jolt – her parents were talking to the Storyteller. They nodded and looked in Ruby's direction. All three were waling toward her. Actually, her parents walked; the Storyteller did his gliding thing in her direction. Mom knelt down and asked Ruby if she would like to see the Storyteller's house. Ruby jumped up, balancing on one foot, and screamed, "Oh yes!" Then she accidentally hop-stepped on a rock and fell down because she hadn't grabbed her crutches.

She looked up and saw the Storyteller's disapproving scowl, then she gathered herself and asked, "Are you sure it's all right?" Mother nodded and smiled. Ruby got up – this time with her crutches – and said, "Let's go." She started off, following the Storyteller. But her mom didn't move; neither did her father. "Aren't you guys coming?" Ruby asked.

"No, dear, I'm afraid the invitation is just for you – and it's a very special one," said Father.

"It's okay; we'll be back in about an hour," said Mom.

Ruby followed the Storyteller across the plateau. She looked back and her parents were waving. She continued on the trail with the old man. A few minutes later, she and the Storyteller went down into what appeared to be not much more than a hole under a massive old tree close to the falls. It was his cave!

At first, it was very cave-like. Dank and cool. But as they made their way deeper in, it became drier, and warmer – and, surprisingly, brighter. Ruby noticed the brightly-glowing ternium crystals all along the way through the tunnel embedded in the walls and the ceiling. When they turned a corner, it opened up into a huge room. Despite its stone walls, the room was actually comforting.

There were maps on the wall – Paxton's maps of Zakar and Geisl and Pavirlo. There were other interesting things – artifacts Ruby thought she recognized from some of the stories – as well as other unusual items. Ruby was pretty sure there was probably a story to go along with every one.

They walked a little further to a sort of sitting area. The Storyteller motioned for Ruby to sit in one huge, cushy chair; he sat in another right beside her. He offered her a drink; and began to tell her of his role of telling stories and how he has done it for so very long… "I consider it a true honor and indeed, even a blessing, that I have been able to share the stories of our people with the children of Levon. I believe I have been entrusted with a meaningful task that influences our young." Ruby noticed that the Storyteller's voice was different. It was not so powerful now, not so big and booming. It was still deep and strong, but softer, gentler. She liked it.

"But now," said the Storyteller with a sigh. "Now, I am beginning to grow tired. I need to know that someone can carry on the storytelling after I am gone. It is important for our whole culture to have a good storyteller." He told Ruby that he had tried to find another storyteller twice before. "The first was too afraid; the second did not accept," he said. Ruby guessed that the second offer might have been her Gram. The Storyteller looked at her. His eyes were old but kind. He waited patiently for her. Ruby slowly realized that the Storyteller was making the offer a third time – to her! She did not know what to say!

Ruby was dumbfounded. She was literally speechless. It took her a moment to compose herself. She had to catch her breath. "Are you asking me to be the next Storyteller?" she asked.

"Yes, my child. I am indeed," said the Storyteller. "I've spoken to your parents – and they approve – but they said it was all up to you. I know you come from good stock. And I have it on good authority that you're already quite the little narrator. My child, do you feel my voice when I'm telling stories by the storyfire?" he asked.

"Yes. Yes, we all feel it when you talk. Your voice – it- it's almost magical. Sometimes I think I could float away on your words. When you talk about food, I get hungry. If you tell us about a flower, I can smell it," she said.

"I believe that the best storytellers are ones who can feel the stories of others," he said. "In the same way that you can feel my words, I can also feel your emotions. I know that you would make an excellent storyteller yourself."

"I don't know," said Ruby. "I mean, it's really an honor to be asked, but I'm only 10 years old," she added. "I do think what you do is wonderful and magical. But I'm not sure if that's something I'd want to do for the rest of my life."

"What do you want to do with the rest of your life, Ruby?" asked the Storyteller.

"Well. I - I - I'm not sure. I - I might want to be an inventor or a scientist like my father, but I think I'll need time to figure that out. "Besides," she said. "As much as I do love storytelling – and story listening – I'm not sure I would enjoy telling the same stories over and over again. Wouldn't that be kind of like being in a play that never ends?"

"You are quite perceptive, my child," said the Storyteller. "Yes, sometimes it can feel somewhat repetitive for me, but when I see the wide eyes of a new crop of 10-year-olds, I feel energized – every time. Oh, and you should know, the stories I have told you are only a fraction of Levon's tales."

"But I thought that you told all the 10-year-olds the same stories," said Ruby. "Not exactly," said the Storyteller. "Sure, most of them hear the same basic stories about our land, but there are many more stories to be shared. Lots of adventures, and thrills, and some sorrow, too. And I could tell you all of them," he added. Ruby sat up straighter and leaned in eagerly anticipating a story. "But all of those stories are for another time," said the Storyteller. "For now, I'd like you to think about my offer. Ruby, this will be a big decision for you. And it could have a profound effect, on your life, but also on the lives of children for generations to come."

"Wow," she said. "No pressure there… I did mention that I'm 10, right?" she added.

"I know my dear. Why don't you think about it? And you can tell your grandmother I said hello."

"Okay, I will. I'll tell her – and I'll think about it," Ruby said, in a bit of a daze. "You know, you have quite a cave here. Do you live here all by yourself?" she asked.

"Yes, I do. But I wouldn't mind having company more often than I do," said the Storyteller.

"Huh, well, I could come back. Maybe when I come back, you could tell me some more stories," she suggested.

"I'd like that, Ruby," the Storyteller said.

"And, you could also show me around your cave – errr – house," she said.

"I think that could be arranged," said the Storyteller.

Ruby got up on her crutches and began to look around. "Hey," she said, "Is all this stuff real?"

"Yes, I suppose everything in this place is real," he said.

"I mean, like this," Ruby said. "This looks like a rope. The little sign below it says 'Sherable Josiah.' Are you telling me that this is the rope that Sherable Josiah used on the twins?"

"Indeed," said the Storyteller.

She walked over to a shelf. "And I suppose you're going to tell me that this is like an actual soul vessel," she said.

"Yes," he replied. "That is a genuine Tenso Baka. I believe there are only three – I mean two – now left on Levon."

Ruby stared at him. "Are you telling the truth?" she asked quite directly.

"My child, I have no reason to speak anything other than truth."

"Hmmmm… Okay," she said. "I'll think about it, but before I go, I have some more questions. How do you fly everywhere? I never see you touch the ground. Do you have some special kind of powers?"

"If you become the next Storyteller, you will learn all of my secrets, but there are some things I cannot reveal just yet," he said.

"Well, then, can you tell me how old you are?" she asked.

"Alas, that is something else I'd prefer not to disclose at this time."

"You know, you're really full of information," Ruby said. "Look, thanks for the visit. It's getting late and I'm kinda tired. I probably need to get going; I'm sure my parents will be back soon," she said.

"Very well, my child. I will escort you back to the fire pit," said the Storyteller.

"That's okay, I got this," Ruby said.

"Please do consider my offer," he said as he arose to bid her goodbye.

"I'll think about it, but I really am just 10 years old, you know. I know I act smart already, but I probably want to finish school and stuff before I start a job that's probably gonna last a thousand years. Anyway, you take care of yourself, Mr." Ruby realized she didn't know his name. She tried again, "Mister…" After an awkward silence, where the Storyteller didn't offer any assistance, Ruby decided not to ask. "Mr. Storyteller. Goodbye."

Ruby struggled a little with her crutches as she half-walked, half-climbed out of the hole-door that was the entrance to the Storyteller's home. She made her way down the trail and back to the fire pit. The fire was burning low but gave off enough of a glow to see. Her parents weren't there yet, so she sat down to rest. Walking with crutches took a lot out of her!

She took a deep breath and let it out slowly. *This is crazy*, she thought. *There's no way that I could be the next Storyteller. Could I? Is that even something that I want to do? Do Storytellers get vacations?* Ruby found herself yawning. She stretched out by the embers of the storyfire. Her eyes began to close. It was nice and cozy next to the warm coals. She was beginning to drift off. Did she hear her parents' footsteps approaching? She really did have a wonderful life…

ACT V ~ PERSPECTIVE

CHAPTER 34

Landing

Present Day...

Back on Botan, orange streaks appeared against the backdrop of an otherwise clear, blue sky. Moments later, the Interstellar Defense Corp ship from Earth approached the Botanian Guard's Paxton Base. It landed on the inland sand dunes just outside the capital of Wedding-Shi sending up a cloud of dust. As the Botanians had no space-going vessels, this was the closest thing they had to a landing pad. The ship was greeted by a representative of the Botanian Assembly and a small entourage.

"General Salinger, I presume," said Ambassador Kimea Imahori.

"Hello, Ambassador," said the general.

"I'll dispense with the pleasantries. As I'm sure you know by now, the attacks have increased," said Imahori.

"Yes, I received an updated brief en route."

"This way," Imahori pointed the general and his lieutenants to the assembly building.

"Cartney, post four guards at the entrance to the ship. I want four more with me. Everyone else stays on board until I get back," said Salinger. The Botanians and their visitors went into the building.

They were all seated around a large table. "We expected a larger force, general. How do you intend to address this threat with such a small contingent?" asked Imahori.

"Ambassador Imahori, I assure you, the IDC is fully prepared to support the Botanians as needed. The team I have brought with me is more than 150 soldiers. My ship carries a significant complement of weaponry. We can join your Botanian Guard and I have confidence we can address any threats to your safety," said Salinger.

Salinger was a dichotomous character. At once, he seemed both old and young; tough but diplomatic; focused but also disinterested; confident yet wary; comforting as well as slightly dangerous. Salinger walked with a mild limp. He was on Levon because the Botanian Assembly had invoked a clause in the Ternium Treaty which called for Earth (in the form of the IDC in this case) to help defend it from attacks.

"We noticed on the way in that several missiles shot over your capital city. What's the situation?" the general asked.

"No injuries. But the missiles did hit an old science-based amusement park," said Imahori. "Other than this attack, and the three previous incidents –"

"Four, ma'am," an assistant leaned in and whispered.

"Yes, other than the four previous incidents, the rest of the attacks appear to be mostly simulated – or off-target – like this one today," she added.

"Ambassador, my report only mentioned three previous incidents. Today's would make four, but what's this about an additional attack?" asked Salinger.

"It was a long time ago. Almost 17 years, we think. That was actually the very first event. It wasn't initially included in your report because we didn't connect the incidents until recently. But we now believe they are all related. And all from the same source: Minos," said Imahori.

"I guess we're here because negotiations haven't yielded any results," said Salinger.

"Exactly," said Imahori. "As you know, we have strict technology limits on Levon, so missiles of this kind shouldn't exist at all on this planet. Almost 300 people have been killed along with scores of injured. It's happened somewhat slowly, mostly over the past few years. Other than that first incident almost 17 years ago, most of the attacks have been simulations – little more than duds creating orange streaks in the sky before falling to the ground, with little damage."

"Two years ago was the first attack that resulted in fatalities. That's when we contacted you. In the past year, there were two more substantial attacks – each larger than the previous one. The latest – three months ago – killed almost two hundred people. Our intelligence sources indicate that the Minosians may be planning a much larger attack very soon," said the ambassador. "We have no defenses against weapons like this. Our best guess is that the Minosians, we think likely the Jade Clan, smuggled the missiles to Levon. But we found fragments of one of the missiles intact. I wanted you to see it." She turned to an aide, "Have the fragment brought in for the general."

Two techs in white uniforms brought in a large plastic box and put it on the table in front of the general. They opened it and retrieved an object about a foot wide wrapped in white cloth. They placed it in front of the general. Salinger looked up at Imahori. "Please take a closer look," she suggested.

Salinger unwrapped the cloth. A partial logo was visible on the fragment. " I - D – C," he read aloud. "This is ours?" he asked incredulously. "Surely, you don't think we would fire on a friend."

"No, we don't. Though we did have our doubts at first. We believe both of us may be the victims of the Minosian clans – in different ways. However, I think you can appreciate the gravity of the situation. You see, it is our lives and property that are at immediate risk. However, it is the reputation and capability of the IDC, not to mention, Earth, that could also be called into question."

"Understood, ambassador. I'm assigning a tracking team to work with your guard. We'll identify possible targets and establish a pulse radar protocol – one that won't violate your technology restrictions. I'll also have an offensive plan put together – just in case. And how are the negotiations going with the Minosians?" asked Salinger.

"Talks have broken off, again," said Imahori. "The Minosians have no interest in talking. Frankly, general, I believe we are on the brink of something bad."

"We'll get to work immediately," said the general.

He stood and left the room with his team. Arriving back at his ship, the *Vasco da Gama*, he told his lieutenants to make arrangements for both defensive and offensive action. "I want a status update at 0700," he said. Lieutenant Cartney, you have command. I have an important meeting west of here. I'm taking the shuttle."

The general boarded the shuttle and flew due east until he came across an orchard of blue ice cream bananas. He landed next to a small pond. The general looked at the farmhouse. He took a deep breath – held it for a count – and then let it out slowly. *Maybe*, he thought, *Maybe I shouldn't have come.*

CHAPTER 35

Visit

There was a knock on the front door.

"Baron, can you get that please?" asked Mom. "I'm working on something."

Baron opened the door. "Hi, are you – are you Baron?" asked the man at the door.

"Yeah, who are you?" asked Baron. "My name is Jalen Salinger. I've come to see your father."

"Hold on a minute," Baron said to the general. "Mom, some army guy is at the door for dad!"

Mom went to the door. "May I help you?" she asked the man.

"Yes, my name is Jalen Salinger with the IDC. I'm looking for Tanner Clemens."

"What do you want with him?" Mom asked.

"Well, we're kind of old friends – from back on Earth. I was in the neighborhood, so…"

"I don't recall him mentioning your name," Mom said.

"Well, it's been a long time, ma'am" said Salinger, with a little disappointment in his eyes.

"Okay, he's in the back. In his workshop. We can walk around," Mom said, letting the screen door close behind her. Oliva walked quickly. Salinger had to hustle to keep up. (It usually took him a step or two to get going with his limp.)

"How did you say you knew Tanner?" Mom asked.

"We started out in the Space Force. We were roommates, actually. We used to get into a lot of crazy things. Then Tanner got into his research and I was assigned to a lunar patrol. We haven't seen each other in more than 20 years," said the general. They continued walking. "As a matter of fact, one of the last times I saw him, he gave me this new leg."

Oliva turned to face Salinger. "You do know he doesn't want anything to do with the military, right?"

"Yes, ma'am. I'm pretty clear on that," he replied.

They arrived at the workshop. Mom knocked on the door and yelled "Tanner! You have a visitor - from Earth."

Tanner looked up. The general walked into the workshop.

"Tanner," the general said.

"Jalen," Tanner said. "Jalen, this is my wife, Oliva," said Tanner.

"Nice to meet you Mrs. Clemens," said Salinger. After a brief awkward silence, Oliva piped up, "Well, I'll leave you guys to it, then." She pushed the door closed and walked back to the house.

"What are you doing on Levon, Jalen?" asked Tanner with concern in his voice.

"I came to see my old friend," Salinger replied. "That is, if we're still friends."

Tanner put down his tools. He walked over to the general. "I... I... ," he began, then turned away. Suddenly, he spun back toward the general with a roundhouse punch, landing square on the general's jaw – knocking him back several steps. All was quiet. "I can't believe you came here. To my home, Jalen, my home! You know what I've sacrificed to get away. Why did you come here?"

Jalen recovered himself. He straightened up slowly and rubbed his jaw. Then he flexed his face muscles, opening and closing his mouth a few times. "I guess I deserved that. Man, you always did pack a mean punch, Tanner. But I'm really not here for you. Our presence was requested by the Botanian Assembly," said Jalen. "The orange streaks in the sky. It seems your idyllic little agricultural, technology-restricted backwater may be on the verge of a civil war," he added.

"The Minosians?" Tanner asked. "I should have known."

"Yeah, and I thought that since I was here, I might take a chance and see if an old friend might allow me to say hello and maybe... to apologize."

"So, you're really not here to take me back?" asked Tanner.

"No, I really just came to say hello," said Jalen. "Your name's still on a list somewhere. Desertion doesn't have a statute of limitations. And I'm sure that there are some folks that would still want to put you back to work for the IDC – or in the brig. But I'm not one of those people," Jalen said.

"You think I'm a deserter?" Tanner asked.

"No, I don't think you're anything of the sort. But that was the charge they leveled against you after you resigned."

"Look, if you don't want to see me... I just thought that maybe..." Tanner stared at Jalen. "Okay, I see this was a bad idea. I'm sorry. I'll just go," said Jalen.

"No, wait," said Tanner. "I – ummm – had a lot of anger when I left the IDC." "Oh, is that so," said Jalen, rubbing his jaw.

"Anyway, it's not like you helped me."

"I know, man. I'm sorry," said Jalen. "We were friends once. I'd like to see if we can be again." He extended his hand. Tanner looked at his old friend's hand. He stared at that hand and then looked into Salinger's eyes. Jalen's hand was still outstretched, waiting. Finally, Tanner reached out as well, and shook it. The men hugged.

"I see you're still wearing your Space Force watch," Salinger said. "I thought you wanted to get away."

"I did," said Tanner. "Still wearing yours as well, huh? This is the only thing I've kept from that part of my life. We earned these together."

"For meritorious service, above and beyond the call of duty," said Jalen. "I'm pretty sure we're still the only cadets ever to receive these."

"Some things, you never want to forget," added Tanner.

****

Tanner Clemens and Jalen Salinger met in the Space Force. They were cadets together. They were roommates in their second and third years and became close friends. Tanner even spent a few holidays with Jalen's family in Monroe, North Carolina. (At the time, the four-year roundtrip meant he couldn't realistically travel back to Levon on break).

Of course they had many late-night adventures that – more often than not – usually ended up back at their apartment playing some intoxicated version of "What will my future look like?" One would tell how he would be rich. The other would necessarily end up richer. One would conquer a country; the other, a planet. One night when they were particularly bored, and particularly drunk, they started talking about having their own families. Jalen didn't want children. But Tanner did; a boy and a girl. He already had the boy's name picked out: Baron.

"That's kind of a silly name," Jalen said. "It's not a silly name," responded Tanner. "That's the name of my future son. If I have a daughter, I might call her Anna."

"Yeah, your wife might have something to say about that," said Jalen. (For years afterward, whenever Jalen would catch up with Tanner, he'd always ask if he had his 'Baron' yet.)

After their six-year enlistment was up, they transferred to the Interstellar Defense Corps together. Tanner's path was to further his bio-medical research into artificial limbs and Jalen's path was to make a career in the military. Though they took different paths, they remained close friends.

A few years later, when Tanner was ready to test his latest prosthetic leg, he had a surprise volunteer. Jalen had been injured on a classified mission. Tanner was able to do his best to help his friend with a new leg.

When Tanner became disillusioned with his work – because of the things the military was doing (i.e. intentionally cutting off limbs of soldiers to get them 'super' replacements), he resigned his commission and quit the IDC. The problem was that the IDC didn't want him to leave. They kept delaying his departure. It was subtle at first: a paperwork delay here, an urgent request to stay another month there. Eventually, his superiors told him that he was too valuable; they couldn't let him leave.

Needless to say, Tanner was not happy. He tried everything but was blocked through all channels. So he called on his old friend, who had recently been promoted to Lieutenant Colonel. But Jalen was no help; his advice was to stay put because the IDC needed men like him.

Tanner tried repeatedly for another six months to resign his commission – following all of the necessary IDC rules to the letter in addition to the seemingly endless random obstacles they kept throwing in his way. Finally, in desperation, Tanner escaped by disguising himself as a farmer going to help increase production on Levon. When he got back home to Levon, he figured that his best employment option on a largely agricultural planet would probably be to actually become a farmer. He did his best to stay off the radar. He knew the IDC might want him back but it had been 20 years. Surely they had other capable scientists and newer technologies all these years later. He couldn't be that important to them now, could he?

****

"It's been a long time, my friend," said Tanner. "There's a lot to catch up on. Are you thirsty?"

"Thought you'd never ask," said Salinger.

Tanner more formally introduced his old friend to Oliva and Baron. They sat and talked at the kitchen table for hours. Jalen updated Tanner on his career – still no family. Jalen had worked his way up to general. He was now both the military and diplomatic representative of the IDC on this mission to support Levon.

"So life's been good, huh?" asked Tanner.

"Yeah, I can't complain. Other than my leg's been starting to give me trouble once in a while – the one you gave me. I think it may have been the space travel. You know, repeated blast-offs and re-entries."

Tanner caught Jalen up on his life as a Levonian farmer – and part-time tinkerer. He danced around the topic of his beloved Ruby.

"It's wonderful to meet your family. I'm happy for you, man. You really have it all," said Jalen.

Tanner began to cry. Oliva put her hand on his shoulder. "You might as well tell him, honey," she said. "Jalen," she said, "it was nice meeting you." She went off to bed. Jalen stood as Oliva exited the room.

He turned toward his friend, "Tell me what, Tan?"

"This life that I've told you about. I haven't exactly told you the whole story," Tanner began.

"How so?" asked Jalen, returning to his seat.

"My daughter, Ruby."

"You have a daughter? Where is she? I'd like to meet her, too," Jalen said.

"You can't. She's gone. And it was my fault," said Tanner.

"What happened?" asked Jalen incredulously.

"Ruby lost her leg and I had to borrow money to get the resources to build her a new one," Tanner said.

"Always the creative genius," said Jalen. "I still have the one you made for me." He patted his thigh.

"Except I didn't know anyone who had that much money. So I used an –uhhh –an... alternative form of lending," said Tanner.

"Sharks?" asked Jalen.

"Yeah. It was okay at first, but they kept demanding more and more interest. I couldn't pay, but I'd managed to keep my identity and our location secret so I thought we were safe. I was wrong," said Tanner. They sat in silence. "I think they took my daughter." More silence.

"Who took your daughter?" asked Jalen. "

"I don't know. I think maybe the people I borrowed money from – a great deal of money – took her. The Jaders," said Tanner. "Either they took her – or she's dead. Is it wrong to actually hope that your daughter was kidnapped? They didn't ask for ransom, so maybe… I just don't know."

"Wait, Jaders… Is that the Jade Clan?" asked Jalen.

"Yes, do you know who they are?" asked Tanner. "I didn't realize you were so well-informed on Levonian politics."

"Actually, I'm not. This Jade Clan is likely the reason I'm here on Levon in the first place. The Jaders, you called them – they're suspected of bombing Botan from Minos."

"Bombing?" asked Tanner.

"You haven't seen the orange streaks in the sky?" asked Jalen. "That's the trail of their missiles."

"Orange streaks, you mentioned those earlier. Yes, we've seen them, but I had no idea they were missiles. We thought they were meteors. I haven't heard about any attacks," said Tanner.

"Well, your government's been trying to keep them quiet. My understanding is that most of the missiles were duds...likely tests. But a few of them have been live. Evidently there were three recently that have caused a fair amount of damage – and then another one a long time ago," said Jalen.

"That's terrible," said Tanner. "I can't believe we didn't…" Tanner began but stopped short. He suddenly stood bolt upright. "A long time ago… How long ago? Was that 17 years ago?" he asked.

"Yeah, I think it was. Seventeen – that's what the minister said. I thought you said you didn't know about the attacks. How did you know it was 17 years ago?" Jalen asked.

Tanner's grip tightened until the glass shattered in his hand, cutting his hand on the shards. "That was the year Ruby lost her leg – on a summer day with a clear blue sky and orange streaks," said Tanner.

"Oh, man. I'm so sorry."

Tanner took a deep breath. "That was a long time ago. For now, it's probably best to focus on what we can control." He picked a few glass pieces from his bloody hand. "Let me clean up this mess and then we can take a look at that leg of yours."

"Really? Thanks, I'd appreciate it," said Jalen. "And then, if you're sure you're up to it, maybe I can give you a tour of the ship. She's a beauty."

CHAPTER 36

Hamada Castle

Minos.

Vaurienne, Mr. Moustache, and Brown-teeth returned to Hamada Castle with the three million levs from Roden. Vaurienne drove the floater right up to the front of the castle. Gruun walked out of the front door. "How did it go, Vaurienne?" he asked.

She put the six bags of money at Gruun's feet. "No problem. Here is the money, your Eminems," she said with half a bow.

"I'm surprised Roden paid so quickly. I thought it might take…days. It's never easy with him," said Gruun.

"I was able to put a rush on it, just for you," she said.

Gruun smiled. "That's why I like you Vaurienne. No nonsense. No games. Just results." Mr. Moustache glared at Vaurienne but said nothing.

"Moustache, will you put the floater away?" she asked. "I have to go check on a friend."

Vaurienne went to the stable but Artax's stall was empty. She yelled for the stablemaster, "Where's Artax? Where's my rammel?"

The stable master appeared, looking somber. "I'm sorry but he didn't make it, Vaurienne," he said, with his eyes toward the ground.

"No. That can't be right. You said he had a good chance," she said.

"I'm sorry, there was nothing else I could do."

"No, that's not possible. He was big and strong. He was…" her voice trailed off; she forced her lips tightly together.

Gala couldn't talk. She found her words stuck in her throat. She swallowed hard. "What happened to him? Was it the mamba?" she managed to choke out.

"No," said the stablemaster. "I think he would have recovered from that. I just – I think... It was all too much for him. The loss of his horn water, the stress... and maybe the mamba. I'm really sorry."

Gala could feel the tears pushing up behind her eyes. But she would not let them come.

She turned and walked slowly away with a blank look on her face. One of the stable boys caught up to her and began to talk as they walked. "I know what happened to your rammel," he said.

"Yeah," Vaurienne replied. "He died."

"But he didn't have to die," said the stable boy.

She stopped walking. "What do you mean?"

"I probably shouldn't be telling you this, but you've always been kind to me," he said. The stable boy looked around. There are too many people around. "Never mind," he said. "I have to get back."

He turned and began to walk away quickly. "Wait, you can't just leave me like this. What happened to Artax?" she asked.

"Nothing," the stable boy said loudly. "He just died. That's all." In a much lower voice, he added, "Meet me behind the stable tonight if you want to know more."

Vaurienne definitely wanted to know more. She was sad; upset; confused; and beginning to add angry to the list. Did someone hurt Artax? What else could have happened to him? She loved Artax. She was going to find out what had happened to her friend.

In the meantime, she went to visit one of the only Jaders that she actually liked: Cassius. He lived in Hamada Castle. She decided not to say anything to anyone about Artax until she had more information. She walked up the stairs to Cass's room and tapped on the open door; it creaked open. "Hi Cass. How are you?" she asked.

"Hey Gala, welcome back girl!" said Cassius and he hopped up to hug her. "Was your assignment successful? Did you see Nia?"

"Yeah, I had a good time with Nia," she replied distractedly. "Things got a little hairy with Roden but they turned out fine in the end," she said. "Although I don't think I want to play cards for a while." She walked to the window and looked out – down toward the stable. "But I did have a very interesting experience with Nia last night. We went to this bar and I saw a bullpar," she said.

"Really? I've heard about them. I saw one once when I was a kid," said Cass. "They're cool but they can be pretty dangerous, right?"

"Well, this one was dangerous to a couple of blue guards that were causing trouble. But Finch was actually kind of cool for everyone else," she said.

"Finch? You know his name?" asked Cass.

"Yeah," she replied with a slight chuckle. "We met this guy – Captain Ferrus. He told us all about bullpars. I guess one adopted him a long time ago," she said. "But it's not with him now. The captain had a ship. But he doesn't have that anymore either."

"Anyway, Finch gave these blue guards a vamp of a time. You should've been there. It was great. Then today I had to play Poke & Roll with Roden for a million levs of your father's money, so there's that," she said.

"What? You gambled a million levs of Gruun's money? Why would you do that?" he asked.

"Well, it's a long story. I pushed Roden to get the money faster, but then he kind of tricked me into gambling with it. I tried not to, but there were about 40 red guards that had other ideas. Anyway, I won, so your dad has his money. It's all good," she said, with a forced smile.

"Okay, sounds like you did have quite the adventure," Cass said.

"So what have you been doing?" she asked. "Well, you know me. I've been trying to keep out of trouble," he said.

"How's that working for you?" Gala asked.

"Hit or miss," he said with a smile.

"You need to just do you. Don't get discouraged," said Gala.

"You know my father doesn't like any of my friends. And he makes me live most of my life underground. I feel like a spy in my own home. Maybe I should be a messenger, like you, sweetie," he suggested. "I do get tired of sneaking around, but I gotta be me, you know? It's just that there are two competing sides to me. My father is the leader of the Jade Clan and I guess I could be in the running to be the next leader. But I want to do things differently. I want to be kinder, gentler. I'd like to open up the Council, change some things, and maybe get rid of some old customs."

"I suppose one of the old customs you might like to change is the one that dictates who you should date, right?" she asked.

"Oh yes, that would definitely be the first one, but I have loads of ideas about other things to change," he said. "But to make any changes, I'd kind of have to act the way a clan leader is expected to act first. And I'm just not sure I'm willing to do that."

"Well, Cass. I trust you to do the right thing," Gala said. She realized it was getting dark.

"I have to go take care of something," she said. "I had better go for now."

"Oh, before you leave, there is something I need to tell you," he started "it's something impor–"

"Vaurienne!" thundered Gruun. He was stomping up the stairs. "I need to talk with you," he said as he burst into Cass' room. Mr. Moustache lingered just outside the doorway.

"Vamp," said Vaurienne gently to herself. She stood up. "Yes, your Eminems." Gruun looked at Cassius.

"My office, Vaurienne. Now." He turned and strode out the door.

"I guess I had better go," she said to Cass.

"Okay, but we need to catch up soon. Bye now," he said, as she quickly left to catch up to Gruun.

Gruun was angry when Vaurienne got to his office. He was sitting in his big chair waiting for her. She had always thought that chair was too big for a man of Gruun's size; he looked devilishly childish sitting in it with his feet not touching the ground. Mr. Moustache was lurking against the back wall. (That seemed to be one of his better talents.) "You gambled one million levs of my money!? Have you lost your mind?"

"Your Eminems," she began –

"I don't want to hear it, Vaurienne," Gruun shouted. "Moustache told me about your gambling exploits – and Brown-teeth backed him up."

"Did they tell you I won? You have all your money," she said.

"Yes, and that's probably the only reason your head is not on a plate at my feet," he said. "And this business about violating Roden's expectations. You know he always wants to negotiate. You have to play the game with him. Follow the clan ways. Vaurienne, that's why I send you. I trust you to get the job done," Gruun added.

"Your Eminems, I was just trying to get your money for you. Wasn't that why you sent me?" she said.

"As I said, that's why you're still alive," he replied, more calmly. "But I will now have to fix this. Do you understand?" he asked.

"Yes, your Eminems. I'm sorry. I got carried away," she said.

"You cannot get carried away. I – we – are on the verge of some very big changes. Alliances are critical. I won't have you ruining my plans. You had better get yourself straight or there will be serious consequences," he said. "Follow me." He walked out the door. Vaurienne followed him to the lower level.

He continued to talk as he went down the stairs, "When I spent that summer on Botan all those years ago, I learned all I could about those people. The way they behaved, the way they thought. They are different from us. They think themselves so superior. And that storyteller idiot, oh how I hate him. I have met the enemy and I will win this battle.

Gruun opened a door to a small room containing a cage. Vaurienne shuddered. Gruun lifted her chin with his tri-hook. "Do you remember this?" he asked. Vaurienne nodded. "I should hope so. Do I need to put you back here?" he asked. "I also heard about your offer from Oshi. You're not planning on leaving me, are you, my little one?" Gruun asked.

"No, your Eminems. I turned her down. I told her I was loyal to you," Vaurienne responded.

"When you joined our clan, I told you what would happen if you crossed me. Do you remember what will happen?" he asked.

"Yes, your Eminems," she said.

"Perhaps a reminder is what you need. Hmmm?" he suggested. "I still have the same leverage," he added.

"No, I remember," said Vaurienne coldly.

"Good. I just wanted to make sure we still understood each other," Gruun said. "I've tried to take care of you. Treat you like you belonged to the Jade Clan. Don't make me regret that decision." He grabbed her by the ears and kissed her forehead.

"You know, I'll give you another chance. You've been a good messenger. But you will have to learn. You will not sit at my side as my deputy during the next Council meeting." Vaurienne had just earned that place of honor for the first time at the last Council meeting. "Instead, I'll have Cassius in that seat. You will still attend, but you'll sit with the senior guards at the back table."

Gala had no idea how she was supposed to feel. There were definitely mixed signals going on in her emotions department. She was glad that she had accomplished her mission; she felt lucky that she won the bet from Roden; she was devastated from the loss of Artax. She was also shaken by Gruun's threats; not to mention angry at Moustache; as well as disappointed by her apparent demotion. But she was actually a little relieved that this might be her only punishment. Her emotions were twisted up into a big tight, spinning knot. It was all she could do to contain them. She just stared at Gruun.

"Vaurienne, I'm glad we had this little chat. I feel much better. Don't you?" Gruun said as he walked out and left her standing in that awful room, alone.

Vaurienne just stood there for a moment. Then she wiped her forehead with her sleeve and hurried upstairs. She immediately made her way to the back of the stable. There was no one there. She was alone, again. Just then, a thin sliver of light slowly appeared and grew larger as the stable boy peeked out the back door. He saw her silhouetted against the castle fires. "I-I-uhh shouldn't be telling you this, but...." he began.

"What happened to Artax?" she asked firmly.

"Right after you left," the stable boy looked around nervously in the dark. "After you left, Gruun came to the stable."

"I know. He said he would look after Artax for me," she said.

"No," the boy shook his head. "When Gruun got here, he took Artax out to the courtyard and drained his other horn into a mug. Then he drank it down in front of everyone. Then he grabbed two women and went into the castle."

Vaurienne couldn't believe what she was hearing. "Artax needed that water," was all she could say. She stood stock still. "But that wouldn't have killed him, right? So where is he now?" she asked.

"Gruun made Cassius take him out into the Donja and leave him there," the stable boy said.

"No, that can't be true," she said, shaking her head slowly. "He wouldn't."

"Cassius protested. He didn't want to do it. But you know how Gruun is. He said that if Cassius didn't take Artax, he'd blow the animal's brains out right there in the courtyard. I have to go back inside," said the stable boy. "I'm sorry Vaurienne."

Gruun's chief messenger stood alone as the crack of light from inside the stable thinned back into a sliver and then disappeared entirely with the closing door.

CHAPTER 37

The Summit

The Summit was a meeting of all the Minosian clan-heads – held four times each year. Each clan leader hosted the rotating meeting in turn. This meeting was to be hosted by Gruun at Hamada Castle. The other clan leaders hated this location. They would much rather be in one of their more luxurious coastal estates. They all thought that Gruun was beneath them – and unanimously despised the Hamada Territory. They considered the Jade leader uncouth and the least intelligent clan leader. But he was a clan leader and controlled the majority of the land on Minos, as well as the majority of the trade and smuggling. Of course, he was also their weapons supplier. So they had plenty of reasons to keep dealing with him – even outside of the all-important tradition.

The Summit meetings usually lasted a full day and – with festivities – well into the evening. The obligatory dinner and entertainment were considered essential components of the quarterly events. As the host, Gruun was responsible for the agenda. Today they would address several items on trade and taxes, as well as a special item that Gruun had added. He called it: Opportunity.

He had his lieutenants line up beside him to greet his guests. As Gruun looked down the line, he noticed an empty space. With all the intensity he could muster, he shouted "Cassius!" His booming voice echoed off the walls of Hamada castle.

Cassius came out of the stable in a hurry, stuffing something into his pants. "Sorry I'm late, your Emimems," he said quickly.

"Don't be late again or I might change my mind about my deputy," Gruun said to his son.

Oshi arrived in a splendid gold dress along with ten guards, her deputy (Faron), and her messenger. Similarly, Nilo showed up with his complement of guards, his deputy (Cyrus) and messenger. Roden also arrived in his traditional red turban (and a new ruby!) – in six floaters – with ten guards, his deputy, and his messenger, Neptunia. As per tradition, Gruun and his host delegation stood outside the castle to greet everyone. Nia smiled at Gala as she walked by. Gruun had strategically positioned a single missile, pointing up toward the sky, near the entrance. Every visitor walked past the gleaming silver cylinder.

The back wall was bare, save for a single portait of Gruun's dead sister Imaelka. In the center of the room, four tables were arranged in a square, facing each other. Each leader and deputy sat at a single table. This is where the meeting happened. Guards and others sat at tables behind their leaders, keeping with their clans. According to custom, each visiting clan leader and deputy were given a small gift for attending. After everyone was seated, Gruun motioned to the servers to bring the gifts. The small boxes were ornately wrapped in dark green foil with light green bows.

Gruun wanted to make as much of a show about the gifts as he could. It was also expected that the host would welcome everyone and bring the meeting to order. Gruun, however, was not much of a public speaker. He had no problem ordering anyone to do anything or commanding a group – or showing off when he was well oiled. But this was different. He was speaking to people who were at the very least his equals. He felt somewhat nervous, threatened even, and began to perspire. He stood up and cleared his throat – and then mopped the sweat running down his generous brow and into his unkempt beard. "Ahem, welcome to my fellow clan leaders and guests. Thank you for attending this Summit meeting of the Minosian Council. Today, before we begin, I want to introduce you to my new deputy, my son, Cassius."

Those in attendance greeted the news with a smattering of applause.

"As is our custom, I am pleased to honor you with tokens of appreciation for joining me here in Hamada for our Summit. Please see the very special gifts in front of you. I invite you to open them now. As you can see, you have before you the very latest in concealed weapons. These are not toys, my friends. These are prototype IDC derringer-style Browning blasters. They are small, but they pack a punch. Each one is a powerful weapon. Oh, and please don't shoot yourselves in the foot. Ha ha," he said. His attempt at humor left his guests looking at each other awkwardly, not sure if they should laugh or....

"Thank you for this opening gift, Gruun," said Oshi, breaking the awkward silence. The others offer their thanks as well.

"I officially call this Summit to order," said Gruun. He slammed the table with a hammer (not a gavel, but an actual sledge hammer). He liked that much better than speaking; it gave him a feeling of control that he found especially satisfying. Then he sat down, relieved, and took several large gulps of green beer.

Roden, as the senior member, usually conducted the meetings. The council conducted its business throughout the day. Near the end of the day, the last agenda item, Opportunity, was up for discussion. "This is your new item, right Gruun? You're up. So, what is this opportunity?" Roden asked.

Roden was pretty sure he knew what it was – as did the other clan leaders. Gruun had been pushing for years to get the council to consider attacking Botan. But the other leaders were not inclined to go to war; as they were fairly comfortable with their current situations.

Gruun stood. His enthusiasm overcame his discomfort with public speaking. "I am proposing an opportunity for the Minosian Council to become... more. We can become more than what we are. I look to the future. In that future, I see us as leaders not just of Minos but as leaders of all Levon. We don't have to be content with only our continent – that is mostly colored sand. We are smarter and much more powerful than our weaker neighbors on Botan. This, my fellow leaders... This is our time."

Just as Gruun was starting to get going, there was a loud banging on the huge, timbered doors of Hamada Castle. *Thud, thud, thud,* echoed through the hall. Again came the knocking, even louder this time *Boom, boom, boom!* Gruun had to stop speaking because he had lost everyone's attention; they had turned toward the loud knocking at the end of the great hall. Two Jade guards opened the huge doors slowly, replete with a requisite amount of creaking.

All eyes were focused on the doorway. In glided a real, live bullpar. Everyone in the great hall was fascinated and stared silently. Of course, they were all aware of bullpars. They'd heard about them as children, seen them in books, even, though few had ever seen one in person. But why would a bullpar show up here, in the middle of a Minosian Council Summit in Hamada?

The bullpar silently floated forward into the room. It made no sound. It slowly, but steadily flew (if you could call it flying) to the center of the great hall. Then it stopped. It seemed the surprise visitor had left everyone speechless.

After a brief pause – and slow spin around an imaginary axis – the bullpar was on the move again. He glided toward Vaurienne's table with the other Jade underlings – and circled it once. Then the bullpar stopped, floating in mid-air less than one foot behind Vaurienne's curly black hair. And there it stayed. Never had a silent entrance been felt so intensely by so many.

Everyone looked at Vaurienne. The stares devolved into glares. She could feel the weight of their combined attention bearing down on her. Gruun, especially, had daggers in his eyes. After all, it was clear to him that she, Vaurienne, was interrupting his 'Opportunity.' This was his big speech, his chance to reach out, an opportunity for his clan and his people – all the clans – to be stronger. But she was ruining it. *He should have left her in that cage*, he thought.

For her part, Vaurienne was practically frozen. She did not want to turn around. She could clearly sense the presence behind her. And it wasn't as if she could ignore everyone in the room looking at her. No one said a word. Vaurienne sat as stiff as a board; she felt the blood rush to her face. She did not want to be in that room, in that seat, at that moment. Yet, all she could do was sit there. She wanted to leave – to run actually. But she sat there, rigid like a silent statue.

After what seemed like a brief eternity, Gruun cleared his throat. "Ahem," he said. "Ahem!" he said a second time, much louder. He slammed his sledgehammer on the table to get eyes focused back on him. The slamming jolted everyone out of their stupor. Attention shifted back to Gruun. (Albeit with an occasional glance toward the now-motionless bullpar.)

"As I was saying, the clans of Minos are in the best position ever to be able to extend our reach to Botan. Today, I am announcing that we have already started. The Jade Clan has launched multiple rounds of missiles over the past several years targeting the Botanians. Most of the attendees looked confused. Meanwhile, Nilo could barely hide a grin. There was a great deal of muttering about Gruun's claim.

"You've done what?" asked Oshi.

"I thought that might get your attention," replied Gruun. He smiled broadly. "Allow me to explain. At first, they were just tests," he continued. We wanted to see if the missiles could navigate the gravity challenges and get to their destinations. It took us a while to learn how to manage the technology. As we learned, we became bolder, and we began to use live explosives. We started out small, but a few months ago, we attacked a Botanian military site and our sources indicated a direct hit that killed more than 200 soldiers."

"Gruun, are you serious?" asked Roden. "Or just a complete idiot? This could plunge us into war. You have no idea what you're doing."

"Oh, but I do," said Gruun. We are gearing up for another, more massive strike in the coming days."

"You're a fool, Gruun. I won't be a part of this," said Oshi.

"But, my fellow clan leaders, you all are part of it already. The missiles came from Minos. I'm pretty sure the Botanians know at least that much, so you see, we are all part of this."

Nilo was suspiciously silent on this topic. Faron took it upon himself to call out the leader of the blues. "What does the Blue Clan have to say on this matter?

"The Blue Clan has decided to take a wait and see approach on this matter," Nilo said. Vaurienne and Neptunia suspected that Nilo at least knew about Gruun's efforts, and was possibly involved.

"Gruun," said Roden. "I am very concerned that you may be in over your head. And it seems that you might be taking the rest of the clans down with you. An attack is not something that Botan will take lying down. You do know the Botanians have a treaty with the Interstellar Defense Corps."

"Of course, I know that. In fact, I'm counting on it. Those gifts you have in front of you came from the IDC, as did the FirstStrike missiles I have – errr, *we* have been using. Of course, their leaders don't know about that. But I have a – business arrangement with a certain officer in the IDC who allows me to purchase, shall we say, surplus weapons. As a matter of fact, the IDC is already here on Levon. Our sources say they landed on Botan a few days ago."

"The Botanians will enforce their treaty and we will be at the mercy of the IDC. We are no match for them," said Roden's deputy.

"Relax, I have that under control. I've sent a team to 'welcome' the IDC – and to get some more weapons," said Gruun. "I'll have an update for the Council in a few days."

"Gruun, I'm not happy about these attacks. But you said there was something of an opportunity in this mess," said Roden. "Tell me more."

"Roden, once we control Botan, we will control the ternium mines, and one of the largest agricultural outputs of any planet. We can set prices and reap all the benefits of those natural resources. My best estimate is that we should rake in more than a billion levs per month, which the clans would share, naturally. Maybe their old Storyteller will want to add this chapter to the history of his stupid continent!" Gruun roared with laughter – and the hall rang out with cheers as virtually everyone guffawed along with him. There was little respect for the Botanian tradition of storytelling on Minos.

After a moment, the laughter died down a bit. "Are you proposing we take a vote on this?" Oshi asked.

"Oh, no vote is needed," said Gruun. "I've already taken the required actions for Minos. The rest of you will just have to help me share in the profits."

Nilo stood and held a drink aloft, "In my opinion, you've done a great service for all of Minos," he said.

"Yes, and the Blue Clan stands ready to support you in this effort," said Cyrus (Nilo's deputy and head guard).

"With that update, I declare this Summit of the Minosian Council adjourned," said Gruun. He slammed the table with his sledgehammer, breaking off the corner of the table. "Dinner and entertainment will begin in two hours at this location."

Everyone got up and began to disperse. All the scuttlebutt was about the missiles and the coming war – well, also about the bullpar. A green-booted guard approached Gruun. "There is a message, your Emimems, from Botan," he said, handing gruun a piece of paper. Gruun opened the paper; the message read:

```
To the Minosian
Summit and Leaders of
Minos:

The Botan Assembly
accuses you of
unprovoked attacks on
Botan. We have
notified the IDC and
expect arrival
imminently. We
implore you to return
to the negotiations
if there is any hope
to avoid war.

Ambassador Kimea
Imahori
```

Gruun crumpled the message in his hand and used his hook to light the corner from the fireplace. An underling brought Gruun a green beer. Gruun tossed the message into the fire with his hook and grabbed the beer with his hand.

After many of the attendees had departed to prepare for dinner, Gruun walked over to Vaurienne.

"Your Eminems..." she acknowledged.

"That incident in the middle of my presentation was unacceptable. I want you to take your bullpar out of this hall immediately," he said.

"But your Eminems, it's not *my* bullpar," protested Vaurienne. "I can't – I mean it doesn't do what I tell it –" she began.

"Get it out, now. I'll deal with you later," he said as he strode off in a huff, directly toward a grinning Nilo.

Nilo and Gruun walked alone to the corner and had a conversation. They were pointing back toward the middle of the room and gesturing toward Vaurienne, or was it Finch? In any event, their discussion was evidently somewhat heated. But they ended it fairly quickly with a handshake.

Gala looked at Finch. "Hi, Finch. I can't believe you're here. But you have to go. Gruun is madder than a rat vulture caught by the tail," she said. Finch didn't move. "We have to go," she said to the bullpar. Gala thought of trying to push him out, but then thought it might be better not to try to force a bullpar to do anything. So she tried to walk out to see if Finch would follow her. She got up from her chair and walked toward the door. Finch remained where he had parked himself almost an hour earlier. Gala turned back and looked at him. "Please," she said. Finch opened one eye wider than the other and slowly turned around – as if rotating on an unseen pole – and floated gently, but steadily out behind Gala. They went to Gala's room – and she begged Finch to stay there. Then she returned for the dinner.

Dinner was a lavish spread. Each clan leader always tried to outdo the other at the Council meeting dinners. All four delegations were there and Gruun, as host, also invited another dozen or so guests. In addition to dinner, there was, of course, lots to drink. Gala could think of several other places she would rather be. But, she didn't want to break any more traditions or cause another stir. There was just too much going on right now. She definitely didn't need to be in any worse trouble with Gruun.

Well, if she were going to be there, she was going to drink. She got herself two Blood & Sands and sat at a table by herself. Luckily Finch didn't feel the need to return and join her for dinner. She actually loved the idea that a bullpar had apparently adopted her, but his timing could have been better. And besides, as cool as she thought it was, she had no idea what she was supposed to do with him. Not that she couldn't use a little luck, although that didn't actually seem to be panning out so far. She took a long drink.

Nia came and sat next to Gala. "So, that was interesting," she said.

"Yeah, I guess we're going to war," said Gala.

"And you have a bullpar," said Nia. "I can't believe he followed you all the way from the Scarlet Beach. How long has he been here?" she asked.

"I guess he just arrived. You saw him the same time I did."

"Gruun wasn't too happy about it, huh?" said Nia with a smile.

"You could say that," said Gala as she took a gulp.

Cassius came by with a new friend of his. "Hi Gala, this is Sampson," said Cassius. Sampson had gorgeous, long, blonde, wavy hair. They sat down. "And hello Nia," he said.

"Sampson, this is Neptunia, messenger for Roden," Gala said. She didn't want to sit with Cassius. She was practically seething at him.

"Call me Nia," said Nia, reaching her hand out to Sampson.

"And this is Maresh," Cassius added.

"Hi Cassius," said Nia, "It's good to see you again. Oh – and congratulations on being named deputy,"

Gala glared at Nia.

"Ummm – Thanks!" Cassius said quickly. Cassius leaned close to Gala. "I've been wanting to talk to you," he said.

"Sorry, I don't have time," said Gala. She downed her second drink in a huge gulp. "I have to go," she said as she got up.

"Good night."

"But Gala," Cass started as Gruun's messenger was walking away. Vaurienne continued walking.

"Hi – Maresh was it?" Nia asked.

Maresh was staring at Vaurienne walking out the door. Cass bumped him with a hip. "What?" he said as he returned his attention to the group. "I'm sorry. Pleasure to meet you Neptunia," Maresh said.

"Call me Nia," she responded. "Forgive me, but you seem somewhat distracted – does it have something to do with my friend Vaurienne? Do you know her well?" she asked.

Maresh froze. "Ummm. Me? No, I – I – I really don't. I mean, I–" his voice trailed off as he glanced toward where Vaurienne had been a moment ago.

"I think our friend Maresh has a thing for Vaurienne," Cassius said with a smile as he reached out to hold Sampson's hand.

"No, that's not... I mean... Well, you have to admit she is rather captivating. And she's exciting and... Well, after all, she is Gala Vaurienne," Maresh said with admiration.

Gala was out in the courtyard now. Her mind was all mixed up. She thought Cassius was her friend. Maybe he was more like his maniacal father than she had thought. A figure came up behind her from the shadows.

Someone grabbed her shoulder. She spun around – with both cuttas drawn. It was Faron of the Gold Clan. "You're not going to stab me, are you, Vaurienne?" he asked.

"Sorry," she said as she holstered her knives. "Just a little jumpy, I guess."

"Good," said Faron with virtually no emotion. "In that case, I have a message for you. Her Majesty, Oshi, would like for you to join her in her room," he said.

"Why not?" Gala said. *What else could happen today?* she thought. They walked toward Oshi's chambers.

"Gala," Oshi said.

"Please come in." Gala came in and sat down. "I'll get right to the point. I want you to have this locket," said Oshi.

"Thank you. But, what's a locket?" Gala asked.

"Well, you wear it on this chain, around your neck."

"Thanks, your Majesty, but isn't that kinda big to wear around my neck?"

"It would be an offense to refuse a personal gift from one of the Council members. Besides, you'll get used to it. It is my hope that it might serve as a form of protection."

Gala knew it was useless to argue, so she said, "Yes, your Majesty."

The locket was built into the shape of the northern half of the Gilt Cove. Oshi wore another that was built into the shape of the southern half. "We each have half." The pieces connected into a replica of the Gilt Cove. Oshi demonstrated by leaning in closely and holding the two pieces together. "Allow me?" she asked.

Gala lifted her long, curly, black hair. Oshi stepped behind Gala and fastened the chain around her neck. Then the gold leader started to rub Gala's shoulders. "Would you like to stay here tonight?" she asked Gruun's messenger. Gala was surprised and not at all sure how to respond; without thinking, she stood up.

"Oshi, thanks for the gift. It's wonderful, really it is. But I can't stay tonight." Oshi kissed Gala on the cheek and said, "Maybe next time."

Gala hurried out the door.

CHAPTER 38

Adders in the Sand

Back on Botan.

Tanner rode back to see the *Vasco da Gama* with his old friend. Even though his military days were well behind him, he was still a scientist at heart so the offer of a tour to see the latest IDC batttle cruiser up close (with loads of new tech) was something he didn't want to pass up. Besides, he thought he might get some ideas for his research.

The *Vasco* was a new-generation battle cruiser, part of the Comet class. It carried a complement of 150 soldiers and its new ternium-powered arc engines could make the Earth-to-Levon journey in only 11 months (13 months faster than the older class of ships). The ship contained electronics and engineering components that Tanner would probably never see on technology-restricted Levon. He was excited to check out the latest advances. When Tanner and Salinger arrived at the ship, they were greeted by two Lieutenants.

"Report, Mr. Cartney," ordered General Salinger.

"Inspections were completed last night. All systems are within parameters. The crew is in good condition. The investigation of the missiles from Minos is ongoing," said Cartney.

"Thank you, Cartney. I'd like to introduce you to an old friend of mine. This is Tanner Clemens. Tanner, these are Lieutenants Cartney and Noffler," he said.

Cartney reached out his hand, "Pleasure to meet you, Mr. Clemens."

"Likewise, Lieutenant Cartney," said Tanner.

When Tanner shook his hand, Cartney immediately noticed his watch. "Space Force, sir?" he asked.

"Yes, but that was a long time ago. You're quite perceptive," Tanner said.

"Well, those watches usually mean something special. I understand they're custom made. Engraved with your name and birthdate. You don't see them very often. In fact, the only other person I know with one is the general," Cartney said.

"Lieutenant Noffler?" Tanner greeted the other officer. They shook hands as well.

"Nice to meet you sir." Noffler was definitely the quieter of the two.

"Clemens... That name sounds familiar. Have we met sir? Did you teach at the academy?" Cartney asked.

Tanner was now wondering if perhaps he had been a little too eager to see his friend's ship. But he replied rather non-chalantly, "No, I'm from Levon, born and raised. Some people think about your Mark Twain when they hear my name. The author's real name was Samuel Clemens."

"Oh, maybe that's it," said Cartney.

"Carry on gentlemen. I'm going to give Tanner a tour of the *Vasco*. Noffler, you're from Levon as well, aren't you?" said the general.

"Yessir," she said. "But I haven't been back here for more than 12 years."

"Are you going to visit family while you're here?" asked Tanner.

"No sir, I really don't have anyone left on Levon. The IDC is my family now."

"Very well. Carry on Lieutenants, I'm going to give Mr. Clemens the nickel tour."

"The *Vasco* is powered by twin ternium fusion drives. Of course, that ternium comes from right here on Levon. They are structured in a pair so that the energy can arc between the two; that's why they're called arc engines. You probably know a thing or two about that," said Salinger.

"I've done a little research of my own in the area of ternium powered drives," said Tanner.

"The *Vasco* is currently outfitted to transport 150 soldiers and about 10 additional crew. The ship has 10 decks with full sleeping, eating, and training facilities on board. She can carry enough supplies for a 48-month deployment. The ship is currently configured for multiple engagements. We've already been to the four known life-supporting planets: Earth, Payenne, and Zhasa, in addition to Levon. We've even been to a few outposts that don't support life naturally," he said.

"Impressive."

For defensive capabilities, we're equipped with FirstStrike missiles and Sonic Wave Cannons. Our pulse radar can find a target over ten thousand miles away. And every soldier onboard also has one of the latest Browning Vel-T blasters."

"This is amazing. The crew's quarters are much nicer than what we had 20 years ago," said Tanner.

"Yeah, they don't know how good they have it," said Salinger.

"So why are you here on Levon?"

"We're looking into the missiles from Minos,"

"Jalen, are you worried about the Minosians?"

"Tanner, it's always important to respect any enemy. So we're trying to be as prepared as possible. But frankly, any of your Minosian clans would be crazy to attack with this state of the art vessel sitting here in Botan. I don't think there's too much to worry about."

Lieutenant Noffer approached. "Sir, the men have asked if they can set up camp outside. Eleven months onboard has them climbing the walls. And they are amazed at the number of stars they can see here – way more than on earth," she said. "I thought it was a great idea, so I told them to start setting up an hour ago, but I did want to make sure you were aware," she added.

"Okay Noffler, just check the perimeter first and have guards take four-hour shifts on watch. You never can be too careful," said Salinger.

"Yes sir, understood. Would you like to come out and address the men, sir?" Noffler asked. "It would be great if we could all get together and actually see each other at the same time. Especially since there isn't a room big enough on the ship for that," she added.

"Sure, I'll be along in a few minutes," said Salinger.

"Sir, if you could come now...I mean everyone's already out there," said Noffler.

"Noffler, I have a guest. I'll be out in a few minutes."

"Yes sir," said Noffler and she left.

"What'd I tell you, Tanner? We really are the superior force on this planet," said the general.

"Jalen, are you sure you're only on Levon because of the treaty request?

"Absolutely, Tanner. If you're still worried about me trying to take you back, forget about it."

"Okay, I just... You know, it's been a long time and I have to worry about my family here."

Seconds later, sounds of blaster fire and men yelling filled the air.

"We're under attack!" shouted Lt. Cartney.

Salinger ran to the command center with Tanner on his heels. "Status report!" he barked.

"It appears we have as many as two hundred combatants, sir. They came on us with no warning. They just seemed to rise up out of the sand. Heavy fire. We have men down," said Corporal Aronda. "Sir, our guys were out there setting up tents, most of them don't have their weapons. They're getting slaughtered."

"Send Squad A out to cover. We need to get our men back to the safety of the ship," said Salinger.

"Sir, Squads A, B, and C are all outside," said Cartney.

"Dammit," said Salinger. "Get the next Squad up out there with weapons. We need to protect our men." Tanner slipped out behind Cartney and lined up to get a weapon.

"Hold up, you're not IDC," said Cartney.

"Your men are getting massacred out there; you need all the help you can get. Give me a weapon," said Tanner.

Tanner ran to the open door and started blasting with the squad. They took out several of the enemy and started to make some headway, but then got pinned behind a rock. Back in the command center, Salinger was looking for better ways to fight back. "Can we use the missiles?" he asked.

"No sir, we can't launch them while we're on the ground." "Then fire up the cannons!" he said.

"We have a line of the enemy coming in right now at three o'clock," said Corporal Aronda.

"Fire when ready!" said Salinger. The corporal pushed the fire button. But nothing happened. He pushed again, still nothing.

"Fire!" ordered Salinger. The corporal tried again – and again.

"Cannons are unresponsive, sir."

Jalen's screen started flashing. He picked it up. "Tanner, kinda busy here," said Salinger. "Someone get those cannons working!" he yelled.

"From that command, I gather the cannons are offline. Look, we're sitting ducks out here. We've got massive casualties and we're about to get overrun. That means they'll be at your front door in 2 minutes," Tanner said.

"Does anybody have any ideas?" asked Salinger.

"I do," screamed Tanner above the sound of blaster fire.

"I'm listening," said Salinger.

"Well, it's a bit risky but considering the situation…" Tanner started.

"Tanner, don't do this to me. You still talk too much around the idea. Just say it and say it fast," Salinger shouted.

"The engine exhaust. It's facing toward the attackers. If you emit a charge, it could send out a force wave strong enough..."

"Strong enough to level an army," said Salinger.

"Yeah," said Tanner. "I'm guessing it would push the ship backward a bit with only minimal damage."

Salinger shouted to Lt. Cartney, "Did you hear that? Make it happen. You've got thirty seconds."

"On it, sir," shouted Cartney.

"And where the hell is Noffler?" asked Salinger.

"Sir," said Aronda. "If we send out that blast, what happens to our men?" he asked. Tanner heard that question.

"Jalen, the blast should travel at least a foot or two above the ground. Anything below that deck will be safe. But anything above that height will get pummeled."

"Aronda, put me on encrypted comms for everyone out there, the entire team," ordered Salinger.

"Yes sir," he said.

"Attention IDC forces, this is General Salinger. You must get on the ground immediately. Dig in if possible. There will be a force wave coming over you in less than thirty seconds. Get down now. You must be under two feet. Your life depends on it."

"Is that pulse ready?" Salinger asked.

"Almost, sir," said Cartney. "Powering up now. We'll be fully charged in about 10 seconds."

"The enemy is about to break through the line, sir," said Aronda.

"IDC forces, hit the dirt! Get on the ground, now!" shouted the general. "Engage!"

A long, deep, slow-motion sound emanated from the *Vasca da Gama's* engines. Then a pulse of light shot from the exhausts. The light was followed by a distortion force wave that destroyed nearly everything from about two feet to 20 feet high for nearly a mile. Every enemy soldier. Every rock. Every tree. Everything for thousands of yards was flattened. The attackers were blasted backward and crushed by the awesome power of the wave. Many of their torsos were sheared off. Then there was silence. In stark contrast to the intense, overwhelming sound of the engine pulse, the sheer lack of sound was momentarily other-wordly.

Radio static broke the eerie silence. "Squad leaders, report," said Salinger.

"Squad D survived the blast sir."

"Squad E got down just in time." The rest of the squads reported in.

"Squad J leader here, sir. We suffered casualties from enemy fire, but the force wave seemed to take out all of the attackers."

"Tanner? Report," said Salinger.

"Our little group is okay. I'm here with what's left of Squad E. Your leader was killed earlier. But it looks like that pulse did the trick. The attackers were Jaders. I can tell by their boots – and their characteristic footprints." He stared at all of those Jader footprints – and at some empty boots on the ground. "Some of the fighters were knocked right out of those dark, green boots."

The attack was put down, but the casualties were severe. Almost eighty IDC soldiers were killed; another 20 injured. Two-thirds of the ship's complement was out of commission. Salinger was angry – at himself. They should have been better prepared.

"What the vamp happened?" asked Salinger.

"The biggest gap was the pulse radar, sir. It's possible the attackers arrived in a wooden sailing ship that didn't show up on our scopes," said Lt. Noffler "but that could be what we see on the long range scanner now."

"Why didn't the men on watch report anything? We're going to have to re-think how we fight an enemy that is both advanced and retro at the same time," said Salinger.

"Sir, they also have the new blasters," said Cartney as he handed one to the general.

"What? They have the Browning Vel-T's? We got those right before we shipped out," said Salinger incredulously.

"We also have another problem, sir. They hit one of the twin ternium drives in exactly the right place – or exactly the wrong place for us. It was a thousand-to-one shot, but they landed a blast on the modulation thruster, so the engines won't be able to arc. Any trip back to Earth would be challenging at best – and a helluva lot slower. Although we will have maneuverability on-planet in the lower atmosphere."

"Put a team on it. We'll need to get that engine fixed," said the general. "And let me know how the wounded are doing."

"Tanner, thanks for the help. We could use a man like you just now. As you can see, we're short-handed. Would you consider staying?" the general asked.

"Jalen, I'm glad you're okay, but I don't know. I have to think of my family – and what might be coming next," he said.

"I understand, brother," Jalen said. "But if we can't hold them off, your entire planet's gonna have bigger problems."

A soldier knocked on the general's door. "General Salinger, sir. There's a floater approaching. Appears to be a single pilot," said the soldier. "We are preparing to fire on it."

Tanner's screen vibrated. It was Oliva, coming to pick him up.

"Jalen, it's Oliva. That's no pilot, soldier, that's my wife. She was coming to take me home."

"Stand down, Aronda," said Salinger.

"Go to your family, Tanner. We got this," he said.

"Are you sure?" Tanner asked as he looked around.

"I'm not saying we couldn't use you, but this is your home. You've got your own problems." They shook hands. Tanner went to meet Oliva.

"Honey, the Jade Clan attacked. It's dangerous here. You should go," Tanner told his wife.

"Aren't you coming?" she asked, already sensing the answer.

"You know our history with the Jaders. This time, I can help fight back," he said.

"You don't know that. And we still have our son," Oliva said, looking straight ahead to avoid facing her husband directly.

"There's something you don't know, babe," he said. "The orange streaks we've been seeing in the sky? They weren't meteors. Those were tracers for missiles, courtesy of the Jade Clan. They've already attacked Botan – before today," Tanner said.

"I haven't heard anything about that," Oliva said.

"The government's been keeping it quiet. They called the IDC for reinforcements since we really don't have much of an army. But now, Jalen's lost more than half his soldiers."

"Are you sure? This is a lot to throw on a girl in a few seconds. But we thought the orange streaks were daytime meteors. The – the kids watched them like they were a show. Are you saying – oh my God – the same orange streaks when our home was hit, when Ruby lost her...." she said as her voice trailed off.

"Yeah, those same ones. Only they have more now," he said. "And they're not gonna stop coming. Oliva, I think they want to take over all of Botan. They would probably either kill us or make us work for them. I hid from the IDC, but we can't hide from this. I have to stay and help Jalen – or we might not have a home to go to."

Oliva knew her husband was right. But that didn't mean she had to like it – not one bit.

"I need you to do something for me, hon," Tanner said.

"Really?" she said. "You're going to stay here and fight and probably die. But you want me to do something for you?"

"Yeah," he said. "I want you to get my mother and take her to our house. Then you, mom, and Baron will be together. You can hide in the bunker underneath my workshop – if it comes to that. I just need to know that you're safe. Can you do that for me, please?"

Oliva thought about what her husband was asking her to do. She thought about the attack – only then did she notice the scores of flattened bodies – and green boots – on the ground ahead of her. She thought about the orange streaks. She thought about Baron and Gram. None of this was on her to-do list today. She just sat and shook her head. It was just – overwhelming.

"Liv, I need you. Can you do this for me?" he asked.

Oliva shook her head to clear her senses. Tanner put his hand on his wife's shoulder. "Look at me. I love you and our kids. Nothing can change that. But, as of this minute, nothing else is the same. Sweetie, our world is not what it was before today. We need to change the way we look at everything – and fast. What we do, how we react, our priorities – all have to take this war into account. And it could get a whole lot worse. We have to prepare for some tough times and even tougher choices." Tanner grabbed his wife and kissed her.

She kissed him back – and hugged him hard. They separated and Oliva nodded her head. "I got you. I'll get Gram and go to the house. Call me and let me know what's going on," she said.

"I love you," he said.

"I love you, too. You're such a badass," she said with a smile. Oliva pulled away in the floater and sped off.

While Tanner was out talking to his wife, Lt. Cartney pulled the general aside. Sir, I don't mean to question your judgment…"

"Well then don't," interrupted Salinger. The lieutenant froze. The general stared at him for a moment. "Okay, son, what's on your mind?" he asked.

"Well, sir," began Cartney. He then held up his tablet showing a photo of Tanner with a big, red "WANTED" label across the top. "I thought the name sounded familiar, so I did a little digging. That's definitely the same guy, Tanner Clemens. He even has the watch. You served together in the Space Force, didn't you sir?" asked Cartney.

"Yes, we did. But that was a long time ago," said Salinger.

"I have to ask, 'How well do you know this guy General?' I know he just helped save the entire mission, but… Sir, we are obligated to bring him back to Earth."

"I agree, Lieutenant. I really didn't know him that well, Cartney. Anyway, that doesn't matter at the moment; we have a bigger problem. We have to focus on the mission; there is no room for deviation," said Salinger. "We'll address the deserter in due time, but our priority right now is devising a battle plan to deal with this Jade Clan outfit. They are evidently much more resourceful and better equipped than we were led to believe."

"Yes sir," said Lt. Cartney.

"And get those damn cannons fixed!" the general barked.

STORYTRAX: *Adders in the Sand (*Inspired by *Riders on the Storm* - The Doors)

CHAPTER 39

Giant Sapphires

Minos. Hamada. Glastalica. Morning.

There was a knock on Vaurienne's door.

"Gruun has an assignment for us," said Mr. Moustache.

"Let's go," said Vaurienne, tossing an old, red physics book onto her bed. She'd been up for hours, trying to think. She was confused. She had lots of questions, but few answers. Her life was not right. She definitely knew that; she'd known it for a long time. Trying to fit in; fear sneaking in. Her trademark cool confidence was beginning to waver.

The only thing she knew for sure, at that moment, was that she had some more thinking to do. Gala decided her best move right now was to do what Gruun said. Take her next assignment – and complete it – as she always did. Maybe work would give her something to focus on. They were going to see Gruun in his office. As Vaurienne strode out past him, Moustache glanced inside her room noticing the ornately carved bed posts before he pulled the door closed.

"Good morning Vaurienne," said Gruun. "You have caused me some trouble lately, haven't you? First, you consider an offer to go to the Gold Clan. Then you treat Roden, shall we say, unprofessionally. Of course, then you gamble with one million levs of my money. And yesterday, that was the icing on the cake. You embarrassed me and interrupted my speech to the Summit and the other clan leaders. I am trying to build a future for all Minosians. What do you think I should do about this?" he asked.

"Your Eminems, I'm sorry," said Vaurienne. "I didn't mean to offend you. You know I didn't take that job with Oshi. And I had nothing to do with that bullpar. You know I've always delivered for you. Please, let me show you. What is my next assignment?" she asked.

"That's my Vaurienne. Always focused. No nonsense. That, I do like about you. Yes, it's true that you've never failed to accomplish any assignment I've given you. You have lied and spied and negotiated for me. That's why I value you – that's why I appreciate you so much. So I've decided to give you another chance," said Gruun, with a crooked smile. He looked at Gala, as if he were expecting some obsequious show of gratitude. Not getting what he was looking for, after a prolonged pause, he began again. "I want you to go to the Blue Oko. Meet with Nilo at his cliffside estate on Azuri Bluff. I've already talked to him. He's prepared to trade for five giant sapphires. He has them and I want them. Your job is to handle the negotiations and close the deal. Do you think you can make that happen?"

"Yes, your Eminems," she said.

"Good, that's what I like to hear," said Gruun. "I'm sending Mr. Moustache, Maresh, and Chandani with you. Leave immediately. I'll let you take the floater again – along with a trailer to bring back the sapphires. And Vaurienne, I want those sapphires. Don't come back without them."

Vaurienne left. Moustache followed behind – with a quick glance – and a nod – toward Gruun.

The four Jaders were in the old floater headed toward the Blue Oko. But they were not alone – behind them was a trailer – and a little further behind that – just out of sight – was a bullpar named Finch. The Jaders couldn't see Finch because he was hidden behind the cloud of green dust from the Donja sand kicked up by the floater.

They traveled without saying a word across the desolate green terrain. The landscape was barren and seemingly endless. There was, in such a desert environment, a raw and penetrating beauty – even against that powerful starkness. They continued onward. The only sounds were only the whirr of the floater's engine and the rush of the wind – plus the occasional clink of the trailer against the hitch.

As they passed through the mountains, the sand began to change color – from the dark green of the Donja to the royal shades of the Blue Oko. They began the climb upward. All three of the Okos were on the ocean, but while the Red Oko and the Gold Oko had expansive beaches, the Blue Oko was dominated by towering cliffs. And the tallest one was Azuri Bluff, home of Nilo, leader of the Blue Clan.

The floater headed toward Azuri Bluff. The approach was on a coastal cliffside highway. The views were absolutely stunning. The range of blues nearly overwhelmed their eyes. The blue sand, the darker blue mountains, the deep blue ocean, and the light blue sky were almost mesmerizing in concert. It was difficult to tell where one began and the other finished. In the distance, Nilo's enormous Cobalt Chateau at the top of the mountain seemed to rise to meet the clouds.

Nilo's home was truly impressive. But Vaurienne had to remain focused on her goal: Get the giant sapphires. She prayed she wouldn't see Kive and Mung – or if she did, she hoped they wouldn't recognize her. Vaurienne pulled the floater up to the entrance and the Jaders piled out to announce their arrival to Nilo's men. There were four guards at the front door.

"I am Vaurienne, messenger for Gruun. I have come with my comrades to meet with Nilo," she said.

"Wait here," one of the guards said. He disappeared through a large door.

A few moments later, Cyrus, head of the Blue Guards and Nilo's Deputy, came to the door to officially accept the Jade Clan's emissaries. "Welcome Vaurienne. Welcome Mr. Moustache. The Jade Clan is granted permission to enter and visit with Nilo," he said.

Vaurienne thought it odd that Mr. Moustache was being officially acknowledged, but she didn't want to make waves during a ceremonial act – at least not so soon after Finch's grand entrance back at Hamada. She shot Moustache a look, but said nothing to keep a low profile.

"Please come in and get yourselves settled. Nilo has prepared rooms for each of you – overlooking the ocean, of course," said Cyrus.

"Thank you Cyrus," said Vaurienne. "I'm eager to discuss the trade. When can we meet with Nilo?" she asked.

"Nilo is finishing up some other business. He is looking forward to speaking with the Jade representatives as well. He has invited you to dinner. But that won't be for a few hours. I suggest you get settled and rested from your journey. Dinner will be formal," said Cyrus.

"Excuse me," said Vaurienne. "What exactly do you mean by 'formal'?" she asked.

"Nilo has decided to have a formal dining experience this evening, so you are all expected to dress appropriately," Cyrus said. He leaned to whisper in Vaurienne's ear, "I think he wants to top Gruun's spread at the Summit."

"That's most gracious," said Vaurienne. She looked at her black and green leather-trimmed garments then looked at her comrades, dressed similarly to her. "But I'm afraid these are the only clothes we brought."

"Not a problem," said Cyrus.

"Gruun provided us with your measurements when we were in Hamada. Suitable attire has been tailored for each of you. You will find the garments in your rooms. One other thing, Nilo does not like eye-guards. He has asked that you remove them before coming to dinner. He likes to look his guests directly in their eyes."

"Is that really necessary?" asked Vaurienne, clearly uncomfortable.

"It is Sire's preference. Is that going to be a problem?" Cyrus asked.

Vaurienne didn't respond.

The silence only lasted for a few seconds, but it was palpable.

"No problem at all, Cyrus," Mr. Moustache intervened. "In the Donja, we never take 'em off. So we get used to leaving them in all the time. But this will be a great chance to let our eyes rest – and to enjoy the magnificent views from Azuri Bluff."

"Wonderful," Cyrus said, adding "I've often found that a different perspective can be… illuminating. Sometimes you can look at something you've seen a thousand times with just a slight change, and you see it in a completely different light."

They arrived in their rooms. Mr. Moustache and Maresh were given black tuxedos – with green boutonnieres and green ties. Chandani and Vaurienne were given elegant dresses – seafoam green, with royal blue pearls. Vaurienne was not happy with this development. She wanted to wear her own clothes. And she definitely didn't want to be seen without her eye-guards. Perhaps she could think of a way around that inconvenience.

Anyway, as she was alone in her room, she decided to take out her eye-guards – for a bit anyway – to let her eyes adjust to the light. She opened the curtains and gazed over the soaring cliffs and on down to the sea. The water was such a deep blue that she felt it might swallow her up. *A person could get lost in that blue,* she thought. *Lost and never seen again.* She walked out to the balcony and leaned over the edge. It would solve all her problems. No more Gruun, no more fear, no more stress. She stared out into the water...and leaned well forward, over the railing... At first on her toes, and then her feet lifted off the ground.

A knock at the door startled her. She jumped back down and spun around. Again the knock. She walked toward the door, then stopped. She retrieved her eye-guards and put them in before answering the door. The knocking came again. "Keep your pants on," she said as she opened the door. It was Cyrus. "What do you want? It can't be time for dinner yet," she said.

"Good evening, Vaurienne," he said as he bowed slightly. "I apologize for interrupting your rest, but Nilo would like to see you before dinner."

"Okay, give me a sec and I'll come down with you," she said.

"No need. Sire is here," Cyrus said. Nilo walked into view.

"Please forgive the unannounced visit, but may I intrude for just a moment? I'd like to talk to you before dinner," he said.

"Surely Sire," she said.

Nilo started to walk into her room, but Vaurienne had other ideas. She walked out while he was trying to walk in and bumped past him. She hadn't realized how large a man he was. Just like the blue guards back at the tavern in the Red Oko. "Could you show me the sapphires, Sire? I'd like to know what I'm dealing with," she suggested.

He was a little taken aback, but he said, "That's a wonderful idea, Vaurienne. It will give us a chance to talk."

Nilo held out his hand, gesturing down the hall. Vaurienne walked out. They were followed by Cyrus and several other guards. "Have you ever seen a giant sapphire, Vaurienne?" Nilo asked.

"No, Sire," she said. "But I've heard they are beautiful gems."

"Yes, they are quite special."

Their walk took them through two locked doors and about another dozen guards. Finally, they came to a massive door with a heavy iron lock. Nilo nodded at a blue guard holding an over-sized key ring. The guard jingled his keys and opened the huge lock – which was about as big as Vaurienne's head.

"The sapphires are quite valuable. That's why I need to have appropriate security," said Nilo.

"You can never have too much," said Vaurienne.

The guard pulled open the door. There was a tiny window at the top of the room. That small window let in a sliver of light. These few rays of sunlight shone down into one of the giant sapphires. That gem split the light and sent it across the room, bouncing off the other gems. They split the light many more times and criss-crossed it back and forth with rays upon rays bisecting still more rays of blue radiance. Together, the five giant sapphires amplified the light to fill the room with a maze of hazy, shimmering blue. It was as if glitter-water were floating in the air.

Vaurienne gasped in spite of herself. "Those are ... incredible," she said.

Each giant sapphire was taller than Vaurienne and twice as wide. She guessed each one weighed more than Gruun. She actually wondered if the floater could carry all five of them back in one trip.

"Wow," she said.

"These are what your boss wants," Nilo said. "I've agreed to sell them to him – for the right price."

"And I can tell you that you have come at a good time. Gruun's plans could greatly expand our influence. And I just completed a deal with Roden that I think will be very profitable indeed. In fact, I'm in such a good mood that our negotiations might go easy for you tomorrow. How about that for a surprise? Ha! Ha!" he said.

"I'm glad you're in a happy place, Sire," Vaurienne said with a slight nod.

"As long as nothing gets me too upset before tomorrow, your job might turn out to be rather easy indeed," Nilo said. "I'd better take you back to your room now. I'm sure you'll need some time to get ready," he said.

"About this formal dinner..." Vaurienne started.

"Yes, I know it may be a bit presumptuous, but it is important to me," Nilo said. "And I appreciate you and your comrades for humoring me."

"Uhhhh. Yeah, okay," she said.

"I have one more request, Vaurienne," said Nilo as they walked to her room.

"What's that," she asked warily.

"I would like you to bathe and wash that black out of your hair." Vaurienne was somewhere between shocked, insulted, and confused. She wasn't sure what to react to first. She was getting tired of non-Jaders telling her to bathe. But her hair. How could he know? She briefly thought of reaching for her knives, but quickly decided that would not be especially productive.

"Jaders aren't too fond of bathing in water," she said. "You know, it's the lack of water in the Donja. It's become sort of a tradition – and kind of violates our sensibilities. You understand, right?" she said, hoping to persuade him otherwise.

"Vaurienne, those are my requests. You do want to keep me in a good mood for tomorrow, don't you?" he suggested. She breathed deeply, considering her options. She had few.

"Yes, Sire, of course" she said. "But I'm afraid I don't know what you mean about my hair," she said. "All Jaders have black hair."

They had arrived at her door. "Yes, but I know you weren't born a Jader. You're a spare. Gruun told me about your...history. I know your hair isn't really black. So, my expectation is that you'll wash the black out of your hair in time for dinner. I look forward to seeing you soon," said Nilo as he left Vaurienne standing at her door. "Oh, and remember, no eyeguards, either," he called back.

Nilo, Cyrus, and their complement of blue guards disappeared down the hall.

Vaurienne stood alone in the hallway facing her door. She felt the blood drain from her face. Her knees went weak. She slumped against the door. Then she pounded the door. She hit it again and again. She regained her composure, opened her door and slammed it shut. "Shaka. No eyeguards; no black hair. What the vamp was going on here?" she asked herself. She had tried so hard to fit in; to belong to her clan. That's what Gruun had told her to do. What could he have been thinking by telling Nilo?"

CHAPTER 40

Exposed

As the leader of the Blue Clan, Nilo enjoyed certain privileges. Probably more than any other clan leader, Nilo made it a practice to enjoy the benefits of leadership and the spoils of his power. Sure, he was wealthy, as were the other clan leaders. He also had a fabulous residence, similar to the other clan leaders. Of course, he had his clan guards and spread his patronage around liberally to keep everyone in line. But Nilo went further than most of the other leaders.

For example, he had a personal harem of nearly 30 women. Some were officially wives while others were concubines. They lived in a designated wing of the Cobalt Chateau called the Bevy, and they were certain to be on conspicuous display at the formal dinner. Like the other clan leaders, Nilo had a preferred title. He wanted to be addressed as 'Sire.' Unlike the other clan leaders, he was much more insistent that the title be used as frequently as possible.

In her years working with Gruun, Vaurienne had less contact with Nilo than the other leaders. While she had fairly good working relationships with all of the clan leaders, her relationship with Nilo was certainly the least developed. She wasn't sure what was driving him. But at least he did seem to like her; she'd definitely gotten that impression before. This formal dinner and his insistence on special clothes, not to mention the washing – these requests were highly unusual. She definitely didn't like these expectations. She wondered, *Was Nilo setting these rules just to throw her off her game for the upcoming negotiations?* Clan leaders rarely make a move without an angle of some sort. And why did Gruun tell him about her hair? She shook her head; she had to focus on her assignment.

"Sire," Mr. Moustache said as he entered the cavernous formal dining room.

"Moustache," Nilo acknowledged.

There was a long table set for what appeared to be forty or so guests. Moustache guessed that the seats were for Nilo, Cyrus, the entire harem, the Jade visitors, and perhaps a few special invitees. The other Jaders nodded respectfully and each said, "Sire" as they passed Nilo. He acknowledged them with a wave of his hand.

Nilo's wives were busy helping serve and bringing hors d'oeuvres to the guests. Several even walked by and fed Nilo grapes and diced clords, trying to curry favor with their husband. Moustache wasn't completely sure, but it appeared that the wives enjoyed higher status than the concubines. He considered the harem and guessed that the group's social hierarchy might be quite interesting. He thought he might like to investigate that.

Nilo sat at the head of the table with Cyrus at his right. On his left was a seat reserved for Gruun's messenger. On either side were some of Nilo's wives. Next, the other Jaders were separated by more wives and guards. Neither Moustache, Maresh, nor Chandani sat beside each other. Nilo felt this encouraged communication between his visitors and the Blue Clan, as well as minimized the chance for the Jade Clan to talk to each other, or hide any conversations.

"Where is your messenger, Moustache?" asked Cyrus.

"I'm sure she will be along in a moment, Sire," he replied.

"May I get you a drink?" a wife (or was she a concubine?) asked Moustache.

He tugged at the collar of his shirt. He was not used to anything being so close around his neck. It felt like he was going to be hung. "Yes, please," Moustache said as he tried to relax. "A Minosian Double Sunset?"

Maresh and Chandani both asked for Jade beers.

Everyone was seated. All of the diners, both Blue and Jade, had their drinks. There remained one empty seat. The chair on Nilos' left was unoccupied. Dinner was about to formally begin, but the Jade Messenger had not yet joined the party.

Up in her room, Vaurienne had reluctantly done as she had been asked. Her eye-guards lay on the nightstand. She had bathed fully (for the first time months, and definitely the first time ever outside of Hamada). She even got rid of the black in her hair – well, mostly (a few streaks were pretty stubborn). She was uncomfortable for anyone to see her this way. Gruun and Cassius were probably the only ones on Minos who knew what she really looked like – although Oshi must've had some idea. She had hidden her appearance so carefully. Vaurienne struggled getting into her close-fitting dress. She found the clasps at the back to be awkward. And the shoes. They were horrible. The high heels were virtually impossible to walk in – like some sort of ancient Zakarian instrument of torture. On top of it all, she knew she was late.

She didn't want to go to dinner like this. She really didn't want to go to dinner at all. Maybe she could say she was sick. That really wouldn't be far from the truth. The way she felt at that moment, she could easily be sicker than if she had been drinking all night. She had spent years trying to fit in – to be accepted into the Jade Clan. At this dinner tonight, there was a good chance that her efforts could be undone. How could she ever go back? She decided to leave her hair down. Vaurienne grabbed her black lipcoat. She had used that faithfully for years. Every day, twice a day (or more); it protected her in the harsh Donja – in more ways than one. Then she put it down. *What the hell*, she thought. If this were to be a coming out, she might as well be all in. She stood and looked at herself in the mirror. Though she was nervous and apprehensive, she did think that she looked, well...pretty vamping amazing!

Nilo was perturbed that his guest of honor had not shown up. But it was getting late, so he motioned to the servers to bring out dinner. As it was being brought out, he whispered something to Cyrus. Then he stood, "I want to thank everyone for joining us here this evening. I'd like to extend a special welcome to our visitors from Hamada. Let's all raise our glasses to a productive meeting tomorrow. This negotiation will be an important one for...."

Several gasps filled the room. Nilo stopped mid-sentence. Gala Vaurienne had entered the room. But she looked different. Not just a little different, but like a completely different person. And she was drop-dead gorgeous. Nilo only half appreciated the sight in front of him. Most of the others had no idea who this strange-looking person was. Gone was the black hair. Gone were the eye-guards. Gone were the bulky, black, leather-trimmed clothes. Gone were the jade boots. In their place were flaming red hair, green eyes, an elegant dress, high heels – and shocking blue lips!

She entered the room slowly (she had to be careful in those high heels, though she did handle them flawlessly). All eyes were focused on her. The women were jealous. The men were either captured by her stunning beauty or confused by the presence of this unknown – and unusual looking – person – or both! When Vaurienne stopped at the seat beside Nilo, he pulled out the chair for her. When she sat, a few of the diners wondered why this person was sitting in the seat that was supposed to be saved for Gruun's messenger.

Mr. Moustache slowly began to recognize his fellow Jader. It had been more than a decade since he had seen those same blue lips on a little girl in an amusement park. He whispered under his breath, "Vaurienne." Maresh and Chandani looked at Moustache. They were more than a little confused.

At the head of the table, Nilo regained his composure and started to speak again. "Now that everyone has arrived, we can officially begin our formal dinner. Welcome again to my Jade Clan representatives, and especially to Gala Vaurienne, messenger of Gruun."

Maresh's mouth hung wide open in unabated astonishment. Chandani almost understood who she was looking at, but had trouble reconciling the two contrasting images of someone she thought she knew. She shook her head slowly – still confounded.

"Tomorrow's negotiations will be important for all of the clans. They will be a beginning for a larger Minos. I share Gruun's vision that expands our reach and increases our power. I raise my glass to all of you here tonight and to the future of Minos and all of Levon.

Vaurienne grabbed the Blood & Sand in front of her, brought the glass to her striking light blue lips, and drank.

"Vaurienne," Nilo began, as he sat beside her. "You are so much more beautiful than I could have imagined. Gruun told me; yes, he did. But I hardly believed a transformation so complete was possible."

"Thank you for the compliment, Sire," she said. Virtually everyone at the table continued to talk – about Vaurienne. The comments were in hushed tones, but the looks were clear. She was the only topic of conversation.

It was unlikely that anyone present had seen hair or lips like that. Virtually all Minosians had black eyes. Almost all clan members had dark hair. The Gold Clan members were the exception with brown hair and brown eyes.

Yes, flaming curly red hair, green eyes, and striking blue lips clearly indicated Vaurienne was not from Minos.

After dinner was cleared from the table, Nilo had sweet blue moon rum served for his guests. The Dessert was chocolate chess pie with blue whipped cream.

"Vaurienne, it has been a pleasure dining with you," Nilo said.

"Thank you, Sire," said Vaurienne.

"I'm so glad I got to see you like this," he said.

"Well, I am very much looking forward to our trade talks tomorrow. Let's see if we can get Gruun those sapphires, what do you say?" she said.

Nilo switched from the syrupy, fake diplomatic tone he had been using all night and spoke in a decidedly different tone. He spoke almost earnestly. "Vaurienne, I will lay my kingdom at your feet. You can have all the sapphires you wish," said Nilo.

Cyrus whispered something to Nilo, and his tone changed quickly back. "Until tomorrow, Gala, my sweet," he said. Gala found that exchange both odd and a little disturbing. Nilo and Cyrus made their exit.

Vaurienne tried to leave dinner quietly but everyone was still staring at the center of attention. Mr. Moustache approached Gala and grabbed her by the arm. "Well, aren't we full of surprises. I had no idea," he said.

"Well, of course you didn't," said Vaurienne wryly, as she jerked her arm free and strolled past him.

STORYTRAX: *My Girl* - Chilliwack

CHAPTER **41**

Sunsburn

Gala walked deliberately toward her room. She had to restrain herself from breaking into a run; she knew she still had to keep up appearances. She didn't want to lose face before the negotiations. Nilo was clearly pulling out all the stops to get her off her game. Anyway, if she really had tried to run in those heels, she would have likely broken an ankle. She was tired...and angry...and confused....but mostly – at that moment – she felt an overwhelming sense of exhaustion. She tore off her garments and threw herself onto the big bed and sunk deep into that luxurious mattress. She couldn't get comfortable at first. She tossed and turned, pulled the sheet up over her head and then kicked it off entirely. Gala screamed into her pillow. She rolled over and lay there, sweating, staring at the ceiling in the low light. She couldn't sleep; so she sat up and looked out the window. *Good grief*, she thought. *Even the moon is blue here.* She flopped backward into the cushiness, surrounded by pillows. Eventually, her eyelids became heavy and she drifted off.

Gruun's messenger awoke to find herself in the Donja many years earlier – when she was barely a teen. She had just gotten Artax. He was a ramlet and not yet fully grown, though he was still easily three or four times her small stature. Even then she had fallen in love with that cute, little, rambunctious – if still a little wobbly – rammel. She rubbed her eyelids; the eyeguards irritated the insides of her lids in the hot Donja suns. "Ugh...I hate these things," she said aloud to no one. She gazed up at the hot suns, shielded her eyes, and then applied another layer of protective black lipcoat. Both suns were in full force that day and she could feel their penetrating rays. Still, she preferred the heat.

She had walked Artax into the Donja as far as she dared. Although she could have relied on his keen, innate sense of direction, she was trying to learn her way around the Donja herself. And he was still not much more than a ramlet. Technically, he was old enough for someone as small as her to start riding. Gruun told her to hop on his back, but she liked walking beside him instead. It didn't feel right to her to ride a creature that young – especially in his somewhat gangly state. *Soon*, she thought as she stroked his ear while they walked. Gruun had also told her that she needed to mark her rammel, but Gala resisted.

They stopped for a break. She gave Artax a big hug – she could still reach her arms around his neck at this point, albeit on her tiptoes. They approached a huge, light brown and grey boulder; it stood in stark contrast to the green sand around it. She let loose of Artax's reins. Gala punched the boulder – and drew her hand back in pain. She shook it to try to shake the pain away. More angry now, she kicked that huge rock, breaking off a chunk of it and sending it flying. She quickly looked around to make sure no one saw. Satisfied, she took a deep breath and climbed up on top of the big rock.

While Gala sat on a boulder and drank from her water flask, Artax wandered over to a meager stand of wild saltgrass to graze. Gala just wanted to soak in the rays of the suns. She laid back and stretched her body across that massive rock. It was still early but the boulder was already soaking in the heat. In a few hours, she was sure that rock would be hot enough to fry a waah-waah egg.

After a few minutes of enjoying a bit of peace in the Donja, Ruby rolled over and sat up. She pulled her knees to her chest and gazed out into the endless, rolling green dunes. Even though she knew the Donja was a desolate desert, she still thought she could see rolling grassy valleys through the haze.

She was frustrated. Not only was Gruun trying to get her to ride Artax, he also told her she had to mark her rammel. That's not something she wanted to do in the slightest. She had to think of something else. She lay back again and allowed her mind to drift.

She saw a flash of herself inside a cage. The bars of the cage were being raked by the clank-clank-clank of a triple hook. How she hated that sound. She put her hands over her ears.

"Aren't you just Daddy's little girl?" Gruun said as he opened the door and reached for the scared, skinny, little red-haired girl.

She cowered at the back of the cage. "Noooo!" she whimpered.

"You will have to change to fit in here," said Gruun. He pulled her by the ankle to the door of the cage. Then he started glopping black ooze on her hair and rubbing it in.

"Aaaaahh!" she screamed, struggling.

After he had finished, Gruun said, "We'll have to let that sink in for a while. I'll be back tomorrow." He threw an old rag into the cage, slammed the gate shut, and walked away. Some of that black ooze had gotten on her face during the struggle. A bit even dripped into her mouth. The taste was horrendous. Gala started spitting. She kept spitting and trying to get that horrible taste out of her mouth. She wretched so hard, she awoke from her daydream. She sat up on the rock again.

But it was so warm, she soon drifted back into an uneasy slumber. This time, she remembered Gruun setting up a game of sorts. There was a board – not unlike a chess board – with black and green man-shaped pieces all of the same height. But there was a single red piece that was a head taller than all the rest.

There was a sideways boom of sorts that was designed to pass just over the tops of all the green and black pieces but the boom would continue swinging back and forth until it knocked the head off of the red piece (because it stuck out). Gruun moved the pieces around the board and Cass and Gala could choose where to put the red piece. But it mattered not where the red piece was placed. The boom would swing back and forth and, eventually, it would always knock the head off of the piece that stuck up too high: the red piece. The point of the game was to teach Jader children that they should not stand out from the crowd. They were taught that it was better and safer to fit in and not to be different. Ruby sometimes felt that the red piece was her. She could see that boom swinging toward her head. Here it came – swoosh…swoosh – faster and faster – closer and closer! She closed her eyes and heard the awful whack. That sound jolted her back to the hot rock. She sat up, drowsy, but not wanting to fall asleep again.

She had been through so much. Even then, she realized she would probably never see her family again. She pulled her knees back up to her chest. Somehow that made her feel a little safer. She rubbed her legs with both hands. She could almost feel the sensation in both legs.

She straightened her legs out and exposed part of her left leg. She began playing with the overload feature on her leg…flirting with suicide. *Maybe I can't go home*, (her leg started to beep/countdown) *but I could sure get the vamp out of here forever*, she thought. Gala pushed the red button three times. The translucent keyboard illuminated. She entered her code: 4 - 2 - 1. She looked at the timer as the warnings sounded. *What if I just let it go? This could all be over. I could get away – and I wouldn't hurt Artax. Gruun would never touch me again.*

"Gala!" came the sound of someone calling her name. "Gala!" shouted Cassius. "What are you doing up on that rock?" he asked as he approached.

Caught by surprise, she quickly tapped the red button a few times (shutting off the overload feature) and pulled her pant leg down before he got close enough to see (or hear, so she thought). "What was that beeping noise?" Cass asked.

"What noise?" she asked. Before he could answer, she added, "What are you doing out here, Cass?"

"Oh, sorry, did I encroach on your personal space or interrupt your alone time? I've heard girls need such things," he said.

"No, I'm always glad to see you," Gala said.

"Say, why is your face is pink?" Cassius asked when he got close enough to see her.

"It's called sunsburn," she said.

"Oh yes," he said. "I've heard of that; I guess it can happen to those who weren't raised in the desert. You've always been a little chalky anyway; a little color wouldn't hurt," he said with a smile.

"Way to boost my confidence about fitting in… Anyway, it's probably gonna hurt later," she said.

"You'll get used to the sunslight eventually," Cassius said. My father said all Levonians can adjust – because our kind has had two suns since the beginning.

The young Jader hopped down off his rammel and climbed up onto the rock beside Gala. His rammel, Alydar, wandered over in the direction of Artax and began grazing on the saltgrass shoots as well. "I see why you like it up here," he said as he stood beside Gala. Cassius sat down. They both gazed across the Donja. "So," he picked up a small stone and threw it out onto the lake of green sand. "Have you thought about marking your rammel?"

Gala did not immediately respond. She just continued starting off toward the horizon. Eventually she looked at Cass and then over toward Artax. She took a deep breath...and let it out slowly. More of a sigh than a breath really. Finally, she answered Gruun's son. "I have thought about it; I can't do that to him," she said. "It would hurt him. I won't do it."

A moment of silence. "I understand how you feel, Gala. But this is our way. And you know that Dad says you have to fit in." Gala did not respond. "You know I like you, right?" Cassius said. "I know that my father did not treat you well when you first came to Hamada. ...And I'm truly sorry for that. But I would never lie to you. This is something you need to do. Besides, he has been much nicer to you recently. I mean, you don't have to stay in that cage anymore. He lets you go where you please. And he even gave you your own rammel. That's something, isn't it?"

Gala liked Cass, too. He had a kind soul, she thought. "I know you're trying to help, Cass. But you really have no idea what I've been through. I wish I could tell you, but...." her voice trailed off. She was on the verge of accepting her new reality after four years on Minos. But Cass had little concept of the torture she'd experienced at the hands of the man he called his father.

Cass looked at her. He gently brushed a strand of her hair away from her eyes. "That looks better," he said. Cass sensed that Gala was troubled but he didn't know how to communicate with this person who was like an adopted sister to him. He didn't know what to say, or perhaps he was afraid to delve more deeply. He stared at her now-pink face and tried to speak, but no words came. Instead, he just sat beside his friend and put his arm around her shoulder.

The pain, the torture...being ripped from her family, caged like an animal...and...other things. Things she had forced herself to forget on those long, unbearably hot Donja nights. She had tried to escape at least 30 times before she lost count. But there was no place to go. The Donja seemed to go on forever. Even if she could cross the desert, she had a vague idea that she was still lifetimes away from the farmhouse or Runyon Falls. Sometimes, it was all too much. She turned away from Cassius and wiped a single tear from her cheek.

"Is something wrong," he asked?

"Just got some of that stupid green sand in my eye," she managed to cough out.

"Once you get used to your eye-guards, that should stop happening," he offered.

Gala was listening, but only in the most vague sense of the word. Cass's voice seemed to be a long distance away. She shook her head and stood up. She jumped down from the boulder. When she landed, she shook her head again, more ferociously this time – in a desperate attempt to rid the bad thoughts and memories from her consciousness. Of course, it didn't really work as she might have hoped. She got more dizzy than anything else. Ironically, she actually appreciated the distraction.

"Look," Cass started. He jumped down from the boulder as well. "I know you don't want to mark Artax but you have to. My father said that he would take Artax away if you don't mark him as yours – and he means it."

"No! Don't let him take Artax from me," Gala said, spinning to face Cass. "He's my friend. I can't explain it, but it's like we were meant to be together,"

"I know, Gala. The stablekeeper told me the same thing about you two. He said he could tell when a rider and a rammel were made for each other. Gala, I promise it won't hurt him." Cass pulled his rammel's reins to turn her head. "See?" he asked. "I marked Alydar – and it didn't seem to bother her at all."

"I know I need to fit in, but I can't cut Artax," she said.

"Gala, this really is best – for both you and Artax. Besides, you can use your new name. What was it – Variance?"

"No," she chuckled. "Vaurienne, Gala Vaurienne will be my name from now on. I guess I'll be 100% Jade Clan."

"So you're going to officially adopt the Jade Clan?" Cass asked?

"Well, I don't think I'll be going home anytime soon, if ever. So I guess I should really try to make the best of this situation," she said.

"Oh, Gala, I'm so happy. I know you didn't choose this life, but now that you're going to join the clan, we'll be more like brother and sister than ever!" Cass hugged her.

That caught her completely off guard. But it felt good to feel a genuine hug of affection. She couldn't remember when she'd last had one. Slowly, she returned his embrace. Cass let go of his pseudo-sister. "Are you ready to mark Artax?" he asked.

"I - I'm not sure. I get that it's important to fit in around here. But still, cutting a poor, defenseless creature. I don't think I can do it," she said.

"Gala, it's really not that bad. I can help you. Besides, it would also protect Artax. No one else could try to claim him, because he would be marked as yours. You would be free to take care of him as you see fit."

Cass led Artax up to Gala. She was standing as if frozen to the ground. "Get out a cutta," Cass suggested. Gala slowly drew a knife from its sheath against her hip. Her hand was shaking. She looked at Artax, with his huge brown eyes staring into her soul. She couldn't cut him.

She turned and ran toward a huge Trucca just a few paces away. Then Ruby drew her other cutta. She slashed across the thick, dense trunk of the cactus-like tree with one hand. Then she slashed across the other way with her opposite hand. She began cutting – first quickly, then more slowly at the trunk of the cactus tree. She attacked the Trucca as if possessed. She kept cutting and slicing. It was as if her blades were part of her hands. She worked that plant with her knives as if she were an artist painting a canvas. Cass watched in amazement as a shape began to appear. In just a few moments, Gala had carved a dimensional image of Artax into the trunk of the Trucca.

"If you're warmed up now," Cass asked as he opened up a flask of clord rum. He grabbed Gala's hand and pulled her back toward Artax. Then he gently lifted her wrist and poured a bit of clord rum onto the blade in Gala's hand.

"What's that," she asked.

"Let's call it an antiseptic," he responded. Cass turned and brushed back Artax's mane hair. "This is the spot," he said, pointing to the rammel's leather-like neck. I'll just hold him while you mark him with your V.

Gala faced Artax. She gently pulled his face toward hers and nuzzled him. "I'm sorry, big fella. I hope this doesn't hurt too much." Then she pulled his head down and kissed him on the forehead.

"Gala, come on, right here," urged Cassius, pointing at the spot.

Gala Vaurienne raised her cutta and put the blade to Artax's neck. She wasn't sure she could do this. She hesitated... She lowered her blade.

"Gala, if you don't do this, someone else likely will. Then you may never see him again. And I've seen the way some Jaders treat their rammels. This is the only way you can protect him."

Gala looked into Cass's eyes. Deep down, she knew he was right.

She patted Artax on his big, thick neck. She took a deep breath and raised her knife again. She lifted her cutta to the side of his neck and barely touched his thick hide with the blade, then paused again. She let out her breath – along with some of her resolve. But she gathered herself and focused with another deep breath and plunged the knife into his hide. Her tiny frame couldn't actually push the knife in too deeply but she tried and raked it down. Artax flinched a little. Then she moved a few inches over and did the same thing again, making the lines meet. Thankfully there was no blood. Gala let out the breath she had been holding.

"Now the rest," said Cassius.

"What?" she cried, almost in exasperation. "What rest?" she inquired.

"Well, you've got a great start, but a single slice isn't really a mark. You have to do it again so that you get the top layer of hide to peel off. That will leave the mark more permanently."

Gala held her stomach and choked back a dry heave. She looked at Artax. He did seem relatively unfazed; he was still chewing on some salt grass.

She steeled herself again. She made an identical set of cuts beside the first pair and then connected them. This made a bold "V."

"Now strip it," said Cass. She shook her head gently. "Come on; you're almost finished. You can't stop now."

Gala put her knife away and pulled at the top layer of hide from Artax's neck. He groaned a little. She yanked it off but closed her eyes as the V started to bleed. Gala dropped the pieces of skin in her hands. She turned and fell to her knees to throw up.

"You did it, Gala. I mean, Gala Vaurienne," said Cass. He poured some clord rum onto the wound and patted it with a rag. Artax moaned a little. "All good. Good boy, Artax. It's all over now. You and Gala will be together forever." He patted the rammel on the side.

Gala wiped her mouth with the back of her hand and pulled herself together. She approached Artax. "I'm so sorry, big guy." She went to hug him but accidentally touched the freshly cut V; Artax stepped back with a wince. He turned and retreated toward the salt grass. Gala stood there. She watched him walk away. All she could do was to whisper, "I'm sorry."

"Ouch," said Cass. "You might want to be careful with that cut for a while," he added. "Go ahead, approach him again. You did this for him."

"I don't think he wants to see me, right now," she said.

"Remember, you two were made to be together. Go ahead."

Gala glared sideways at Cass. But eventually, she walked over to Artax and gently rubbed his side – carefully avoiding the cut she had inflicted upon him. She whispered into his ear. "I'm sorry, boy. I promise I'll never hurt you again, no matter what." He turned his big head and looked into Gala's eyes. "Can you forgive me," she asked? Artax licked Gala's face with a huge yellow tongue. She threw her arms around him and hugged him – carefully.

Back on the soft mattress in her room at the Cobalt Chateau. Vaurienne hugged a huge pillow.

STORYTRAX: *Some Like It Hot* - The Power Station

CHAPTER **42**

Tough Negotiations

The following morning...

Mr. Moustache, Chandani, and Maresh met in the hallway at the appointed time. A moment later, Vaurienne came out of her room and walked down the hall with her flaming red hair – all wild and curly. Her eye-guards were back – and she had re-applied her black lipcoat.

"Good morning, comrades," said Vaurienne.

"Nice hair," said Maresh.

"I think I'll keep the look," said Vaurienne, "It works for me." She turned ahead and strode on between them; barely letting a small grin appear quickly across her mouth.

"Who are you?" asked Chandani.

Gala turned to Chandani. "My name is Ruby Gala Vaurienne, but you can still call me Vaurienne. Get ready. Gruun wants these giant sapphires and I'm going to get them for him. Be on your toes. Something feels funny about this negotiation. I know Gruun and Nilo already have some kind of agreement in place, but I don't trust Nilo. My guess is that he's going to try something," she said.

"Just what are you planning to do?" asked Mr. Moustache.

"I have no idea; be ready for anything. You know, expect the unexpected. Something seems – I don't know – somehow off. I can't put my finger on it; just a feeling. Anyway, consider yourself on high alert."

They walked into the room reserved for the negotiations. There was a familiar set-up. Two long tables facing each other. Nilo and Cyrus sat at one table. There were two seats at the opposite table – with labels:

Gala Vaurienne and Mr. Moustache. "What the –?" Vaurienne turned to Mr. Moustache. "Why did Nilo set a spot for you?"

"His house, his rules. I suggest we follow his lead."

Gala paused for a moment and then said, "Agreed."

Gala instinctively scanned the room – eight guards inside plus the two outside the door. She recognized the two at the door as Kive and Mung (from Mitch's Tavern). Kive's arm was still in a sling. She smiled to herself. (They didn't recognize her – probably because of her new 'look' – or maybe they didn't remember much from that night other than Finch – and possibly a couple of wicked hangovers.)

She also saw that the five giant sapphires had been brought into the room on a large cart. They were just as stunning in the morning sunlight – even more so – as this room had several large windows letting in tons of natural light. The blue light filtered through the magnificent stones and danced everywhere.

"Good morning, Sire," Gala said, with a partial nod of her head.

"Good morning, Sire," echoed Mr. Moustache.

"Cyrus, how are you?" Gala added.

"Good morning, Vaurienne, Moustache," said Cyrus.

"So good to see you, Gala – may I call you Gala?" asked Nilo.

"Your pleasure, Sire," she replied.

"Before we begin, would you like something to eat or drink?" Cyrus asked.

"Just water for me," said Vaurienne.

"Water is fine," said Moustache.

Someone came with their waters and also placed a tray of sweet rolls on the table in front of them.

"What would you like for your conclusion drink?" asked Cyrus.

"Blood & Sand," said Vaurienne.

"Perhaps a Jade beer?" requested Mr. Moustache cautiously. The libations arrived on trays within moments.

"These giant sapphires really are extraordinary," said Nilo. "Did you know that gems of this size and color have been found only on Levon? No other planet. And even here, they are rare," he said. "Do you know why Gruun wants them?" he asked.

"No," said Vaurienne, "but Gruun sometimes takes a liking to things. Usually, its weapons. But the sapphires? Who knows? Maybe he wants to hang them from the ceiling in Hamada Castle?"

"A giant sapphire chandelier?" Moustache said softly (mostly to himself).

"If that's the case, then he would have the most expensive ceiling decoration in all of Minos," said Cyrus.

"Yes," said Nilo. "Though these stones are valuable as gems, they are also useful in other ways. For example, they are used to control and convert high amounts of energy for interstellar drives. We've traded several to the IDC – indirectly of course," he continued.

"Interesting," said Vaurienne.

"Look, I really don't care. Let's just get this deal done. I'll offer you half a million levs each."

"That's 2.5 million levs. Do you even have that much?" asked Cyrus.

"I offered it, didn't I?" she replied. She patted her hips absent-mindedly. (The money was concealed in her belt.)

Cyrus looked at Nilo. Nilo pretended to consider it and then shook his head.

"Unacceptable," said Cyrus.

"Really? That's how this is going to go all day?" asked Vaurienne. "Nilo can't conduct his own negotiations?"

"I assure you the leader of the Blue Clan is a more than capable negotiator," said Cyrus. "But until your offer is more realistic, he has instructed me to speak for him."

Vaurienne rolled her eyes. Nilo smiled.

"Okay, I'll add a million levs. That's 3.5 million for all five sapphires. But only if your men load them up," she said with a grin. Cyrus looked at Nilo. Nilo pretended to consider this offer as well but then shook his head again.

"You're gonna play hardball, huh? All right. Four million levs for the sapphires. Would that work?" Vaurienne proposed.

"Well, you are getting closer," Cyrus responded.

"What, you're not going to look at Nilo and wait for the fake consideration and the pre-planned head shake before responding?" she asked.

"You are amusing, Vaurienne," Cyrus said. "But that offer is still not acceptable."

Vaurienne took a drink of water. She stared at Nilo. It was probably only for about a minute, but it seemed like an eternity as silence filled the room. "Sire, I've made several offers. You have seen fit to respond directly to none of them. You and Gruun already discussed the exchange. I was just sent to close the deal. Let's not play games. Please, tell me, what would you like for the gems?"

Nilo looked at Vaurienne. He smiled at her again. At first it was a Mona Lisa smile but it evolved into something genuinely creepy. It made her skin crawl. She shifted in her seat. She couldn't wait to close this deal and get the vamp out of there.

"Gala, for starters, I'll need at least five million levs," he said.

Chandani coughed from the back of the room.

"For starters?" Vaurienne asked.

"Yes," said Cyrus. "For a transaction such as this, I will require more than just a simple exchange of currency."

"*You* will require?" asked Vaurienne.

Vaurienne got up. She walked to the window and looked out at the ocean. Then she walked around the sapphires – those enormous gems shooting rays of sunslight in a thousand different directions. They really were extraordinary; miking little rainbows all over the walls. "I'll be completely candid with you, Nilo," she said as she stared into one of the sapphires. Gruun has authorized me to go up to a maximum of five million levs. So I can agree to that price," she said from her stance near the gems. "But no more."

"So, we are agreed on the five million?" Cyrus said.

"Yes," said Vaurienne.

"Can we drink to the closing now?" she asked, reaching for her Blood & Sand .

"Well, that is the monetary portion," said Cyrus.

"But there is still the matter of the ... additional compensation."

"Hmmmph," she scoffed. "What else could you possibly want besides money?" she asked, as she returned to her seat.

"I originally asked for Gruun to give me back *Wager's Access*, the connection to the sea from Hamada through the Petrified Forest Pass. You know, he really does want these sapphires. But he wouldn't budge on that. Your rotund green leader thinks that getting access to the ocean is the most important thing he's ever done. How I do hate Poke & Roll. Although he did tell me that taking over Botan would eclipse even winning that pitiful excuse for a port from me. Alas, I'm pretty sure he wouldn't give up *Wager's Access* for anything," said Nilo. "So I told him something else that I wanted – something I've had my eye on for years."

Maintaining her focus on the negotiation at hand, Gala tried to steer Nilo back.

"That's a very interesting story, Sire. But I'm still waiting for what else you want to close this deal."

"Ah yes, well that is somewhat delicate," said Cyrus.

"Mr. Moustache, how do you suggest we proceed?"

"Hey, genius," Vaurienne said. "Over here. Don't talk to him; you're dealing with me. I'm the messenger; do you understand?"

Cyrus chuckled. "Yes, Miss Vaurienne. I do understand, but unfortunately, you are the one who does not. It's probably best that you just close those pretty blue lips while the men talk." He leaned over and whispered something to Nilo.

Vaurienne almost lost her shit. She stood immediately. Her hands shot to her cuttas. "Have you lost your mind? Nobody talks to me like that!"

"Miss Vaurienne!" said Cyrus, standing as well. "This is a formal trade discussion with the leader of the Blue Clan. Unless you want to be the cause of a clan-clash.... And unless you are prepared to die at the hands of a dozen blue guards, I suggest you sit down and hold your tongue."

"Vaurienne, sit down," said Mr. Moustache softly through the side of his mouth. Vaurienne was furious. The color of her face was beginning to match the color of her 'new' hair. She looked around. She was pretty sure she could kill half of the guards in the room without too much trouble. But there were also the ones outside, not to mention the army in the entire complex. Then she thought about what Cyrus had said.

The ignorant blue deputy was probably right. That stupid, little sycophant was right. And she hated him for it. He shouldn't talk to her that way. But, in the end, she surmised that the best decision – for the moment – was to stand down. She slowly returned to her seat. As she sat, she whispered to Moustache, "I only count 10 guards…be ready in case we need to attack." Moustache didn't react.

"That's a good little girl," said Cyrus. Vaurienne's eyes shot a thousand daggers through Cyrus' heart. If only those daggers were real. "Mr. Moustache, before we were so rudely interrupted, I asked you a question. I'll ask it again, so we are clear. How do you think we should proceed?"

Mr. Moustache cleared his throat. "Cyrus, Sire, I believe it would be best for you to tell her directly."

"Really? Just like that?" asked Cyrus.

"Yes, I believe that would be the best approach," said Moustache, looking down and swirling his glass of water. He looked around the room. "I think we're all ready." Moustache nodded at Nilo.

"Tell me what?" she asked.

Nilo stood. "Gala, I think you will grow to love this idea as much as I do. I know you've been a successful messenger for Gruun, but this could be one of the best trade talks you've ever had. The additional compensation that I've asked for, and that Gruun has already agreed to pay, my dear, is you." Nilo raised his glass in her direction. "You can join my harem tonight. Another successful negotiation for the great Gala Vaurienne.

Vaurienne was dumbfounded. She was speechless. "You may have your closing drink now," said Cyrus. "The deal is done." Cyrus drank. Nilo drank. Moustache picked up his beer.

"Yeah, you might want to put that drink down because that's not gonna happen," said Vaurienne. "I don't know what you're trying to pull, but Gruun would never agree to that. And even if he did, *I* would never, ever agree to that deal. So, if you think this is funny, it's not. If you think this is going to be a successful negotiation tactic, let me assure you that it will not end as well as you might hope."

"It's not a tactic, Vaurienne. It's a done deal," said Mr. Moustache. He picked up his jade beer and drank a big gulp. Then he stood and stepped away from the table.

She had been shanghaied! Vaurienne jumped to her feet. Four blue guards closed in surrounding her.

"Take those knives out and place them on the table...slowly," said Cyrus. Gala was surrounded. She had been set up. She was double-crossed by her own, adopted clan. A tear ran down her cheek.

"That's so sad," said Mr. Moustache, mockingly. Cyrus laughed. Gala slowly grasped her cuttas. She looked at Mr. Moustache; he backed away another step. No help was coming. She was defeated before she had a chance to fight.

But no. She wouldn't give up that easily. There was no way Gala Vaurienne was going down without a fight. She lunged a surprising distance toward Moustache; her first cut was down that Jader's left cheek. She sliced off a big part of that stupid upside-down horseshoe moustache of his. (She quickly turned away from the sight of his blood.) He screamed and put his hand on his face, dropping his mug of green beer to the floor. Next, she disabled the two blue guards closest to her with ambidextrous outward thrusts, cutting across their throats as she leapt and spun between them. As the first two fell, the next two moved in. Gala ran toward them and dropped to her knees. She cut swiftly upward right between their legs as she slid between them. She coasted to a stop just past them, leaned back on her knees, then reached down and simultaneously sliced an Achilles tendon on each of them without looking back. The second pair also fell to the ground. *Four down*, she thought.

The four remaining guards spread out to face Vaurienne. "So you're next, huh? You do realize that you're going to end up like your buddies there on the floor," she said confidently. She liked fighting better than negotiating. The blue guards raised their spears. Vaurienne raised her cuttas. Even though the blue guards were far larger than Ruby Gala Vaurienne, she was brimming with confidence. She looked up at them and asked "Are you scared?" She waved her knives and held them up, ready to engage.

Mr. Moustache grabbed one arm from behind while Chandani grabbed Vaurienne's other arm. They twisted the knives from her hands and handed her over to the blue guards. Maresh watched the door.

"That was quite impressive, Vaurienne," said Cyrus.

"Bravo!" said Nilo. He clapped softly to no one. "I expected nothing less. I like a woman with fire! That hair, those lips! This is the best deal I've made in years," he laughed and rubbed his hands together in anticipation of consummating the deal later.

"So you're actually going to marry this hellcat?" said Mr. Moustache.

"Who said anything about marriage?" asked Nilo. They both laughed.

Vaurienne tried to fight to free herself. She pulled mightily. She jumped up and tried to kick. But it was no use. The guards restrained her hands and tied her ankles together.

"Oh," said Mr. Moustache, "You might want to fish that derringer out of her mass of hair."

"Moustache," she yelled. "Traitor!" One of the guards found the derringer in her curls and gave it to Cyrus.

"Thanks for that valuable intelligence, Moustache," he said. Then another guard gagged her.

"What a mess," said Cyrus. "Sire, we ought to charge Gruun more just for the inconvenience," he said.

"What are a few guards between clan leaders?" said Nilo with a chuckle. "I still think I got the better part of this bargain."

"Sire, thank you for the deal. We really should be getting back to Gruun. He's waiting for us at the Petrified Forest Pass. Do we have your permission to take the sapphires?" Mr. Moustache asked.

"Of course. But there is still the small matter of the monetary payment," said Nilo.

"The money is in Vaurienne's belt," Moustache said.

"Splendid. I guess you can be on your way. Oh, and do tell Gruun good luck with his exploits for me," said Nilo.

Mr. Moustache and Chandani rolled the sapphires out of the room and down the hall to be loaded onto the trailer. Maresh held the door. As it closed behind him, Cyrus and Nilo approached Vaurienne, still tied up on the floor, surrounded and subdued by the remaining four blue guards.

"Take her to the Bevy, but keep her tied up until she becomes more... submissive," said Cyrus.

Before they dragged her away, Nilo approached his new acquisition and leaned down toward Vaurienne. "My dear, you are so going to enjoy this. And even if you don't, I certainly will." He caressed her cheek with the back of his hand; she jerked her head away. He smiled, and then he laughed that sniveling little laugh again.

As Maresh re-entered the room from the back with his weapon drawn, a large object crashed through the huge picture window. Glass flew everywhere. The cool ocean breeze and sound of the surf rolled into the room – along with something else. Everyone instinctively shielded their eyes from the flying glass. When they removed their arms from their faces, through the bright susnlight, they saw a real, live bullpar.

Finch was not in his normal, cuddly, awkwardly cute form. Rather, he was positively scary looking. His teeth were bared. He growled low and long, with the guttural sound vibrating off the walls until it merged with the echo of the surf below. His talons extended slowly. Finch made short work of the four remaining guards. He threw two out the window – chomp and toss. The other two hurled spears at his tough bullpar hide. Direct hits. But the spears merely bounced off Finch. Undeterred, the guards attacked him with large knives, which also had no effect. But the buffoons kept stabbing at him, which only made him angrier. So he ripped off one guard's arm, then he bit another's leg clean off at the knee. Gala turned her head with a gasp.

Vaurienne rolled over on the floor and cut the bonds around her legs with shard of glass stuck in the floor. Maresh rushed over and cut the ropes on her hands.

"Why?" she asked, removing her gag.

"Cassius is a friend. He thought you might need some help, so he suggested to his father that I come along." He handed Vaurienne her knives. "But how did you?" he began.

Just then, Kive and Mung entered. "What is all this noise?" asked Kive.

"Get that girl," said Nilo. In a flash, Vaurienne leapt 20 feet toward Cyrus. Cyrus aimed the derringer at her while she flew at him as if in slow motion.

Maresh swung downward hard – right across Cyrus' arm knocking his shot off target and the weapon from his grasp.

"Thanks!" said Vaurienne. She landed on the floor and cut four fingers from Cyrus' hand in one slice while she stared directly into his beady eyes. Maresh smashed an iron flower vase on his head, knocking him silly, then Vaurienne kicked him hard – sending Nilo's deputy flying into the wall. Gala stood up and walked over to Nilo. "What would the men like to talk about now?" she asked.

Just then Kive punched her in the back – with his one good arm – knocking the curved knives out of her hands. She crumpled to her knees in front of Nilo.

"Vaurienne, you're only making this harder," said Nilo. "There really is no escape, my dear."

Vaurienne fell to the floor, face down. She reached out as she fell and grabbed the derringer from Cyrus' severed fingers; then she rolled over and shot Kive in the head – all in a single motion.

"My friend," shouted the enormous Mung. You kill my friend!" He ran toward her.

"Get her, Mung!" shouted Nilo.

Even as Mung ran toward the red-haired jader, Finch slowly glided between Mung and Vaurienne.

"Stupid bullpar," said Mung. "Last time, you surprise Mung. But this time, Mung ready. This time, Mung will...."

In a flash, Finch raked his talons from Mung's open mouth down through his throat and midsection, dropping his bowels onto the floor. They were soon followed by the rest of the huge blue guard in a grotesque pile of Mung – spurting blood. Gala held her stomach's contents in their proper place with some obvious effort, including a hand over her mouth, and shut her eyes tightly as she turned her head.

Maresh, Finch, and Vaurienne were now alone with Nilo. Gala stood and steadied herself. Then she approached Nilo. "I'll ask you again, what is it that the men would like to talk about?" asked Vaurienne again, mockingly.

"You haven't thought this through, have you, my dear? There's no way you can escape," said Nilo.

Vaurienne walked right up to Nilo and kicked him in the face, whacking out a couple teeth, and knocking him out cold.

"Finch, you're a lifesaver. Literally," she said.

Without thinking, she hugged him full on. During her hug, Finch relaxed back to his mildly cute, if somewhat awkward form. She looked at his big eyes. He looked back at her. "You're the best, Bard" she said. Finch opened one eye wider than the other. Gala realized her mistake. "I'm sorry; I meant Finch," she added. The bullpar seemed to wink at her – and then he did his slow glide thing out through the window.

They left Nilo tied up, hanging, upside down, outside the window over the cliff. (It was better than he deserved.)

"We have to catch up with Moustache and Chandani – and those sapphires," said Vaurienne. "I'm right behind you," said Maresh. "They can't go too fast with those heavy sapphires. We should be able to catch them," he added. They ran toward the door, but Vaurienne stopped short. She walked back to the negotiating table. She picked up her Blood & Sand, surveyed the room, and then she drank her closing drink. "Now the deal is done," she said, slamming the glass onto the table. The two Jaders ran out the door. Vaurienne reached out to Maresh. "Whoa. Let's slow down; don't want to attract any unwanted attention," she suggested. They slowed to a brisk walk and made their way down the hall and toward the exit of the Cobalt Chateau.

They arrived at the front just in time to see Mr. Moustache and Chandani finishing up the loading of the giant sapphires. Chandani was on top of the load, tying down the cover. Maresh climbed up inside with her. "Where the vamp have you been?" she asked. "We could've used some help loading up these monsters."

"I got held up," he said. Maresh climbed beside her. When she turned her head to see how Moustache was coming along, he coldcocked her. Chandani fell on the cover, looking for all the world like she was sleeping.

Mr. Moustache climbed into the floater and sat behind the wheel, with a mess of dried blood on the left side of his face. Vaurienne slipped into the passenger seat. "Thanks for waiting," she said as she pushed the derringer into his side.

"My, my Vaurienne. You are just full of surprises."

"Shut up and drive," was all she said.

When they were several hours outside of the Blue Oko and well into the green sands of the Donja, Gala told Mr. Moustache to stop and get out. "Maresh!" she shouted. "Get Chandani out of the trailer."

A moment later, Chandani was rubbing her head standing beside Mr. Moustache – or was he now Mr. Half-moustache? Or maybe just half-stache? "Give them a water flask, they'll need it in the Donja," she said to Maresh. He complied. "You can drive, Maresh," she said.

As they left the double-crossers in the desolate green sand, Maresh asked, "I know they deserve it, but are we just going to leave them to die in the desert?"

"We ought to. The bastards. Actually, they're only about a day's walk – or two – back to Glastalica. They should have enough water – if they conserve."

"Okaaaayyyy....Ummm, by the way, where are we going?" he asked.

"Head south toward the Petrified Forest Pass," she said.

"I don't know if I should say this, but -uuhhh," began Maresh.

"Maresh, just say it."

"I mean, I really love your hair. But…"

"But what?"

"If we're going to meet up with a bunch of Jaders, do you think they're ready for that?"

"Look!" she began… Upon consideration, she added, "Actually, you might have a point." Gala rummaged around in the back seat and found a scarf to hide her flaming locks.

"One more question."

"Vamp, what else?"

"What—what should I call you?" he asked. "Should I still call you Vaurienne?"

"No, from now on, you can call me Ruby."

She plugged her Hummingbird into the dash to re-charge it and then put her feet up.

Glitter-like green specks of sand floated in their desert wake. High above the Donja, Two gyptos circled Moustache and Chandani.

STORYTRAX: *The Warrior* - Patty Smyth

CHAPTER 43

Teach's Revenge

Gala and Maresh arrived at the Petrified Forest Pass at dusk with the massive Sapphires in tow. Gruun was waiting with an army of Jaders. There were more than 200 soldiers, all in those familiar green boots. Each was armed with a Browning Vel-T.

Though Gruun was briefly surprised to see Vaurienne, he was much more focused on the Sapphires. "You made it back with the sapphires, good. And right on time. We'll need to get through the pass and load these onto my ship so we can take them to Botan. I have a trading partner waiting for them. Did you have any trouble with the negotiations?"

"Trouble!? Did I have any trouble!?" she shouted. Gala jumped out of the floater before it even stopped and ran up to face Gruun (who had guards on both sides). "You low-down quatchee! You tried to sell me into Nilo's harem!" she screamed, even louder. Her anger had been simmering on the floater ride down through the Donja. Now all of that anger bubbled over. She drew her cuttas and waved them in front of Gruun's face, slicing off a few of his chin whiskers.

The Jade guards drew their blasters and pointed them at Vaurienne. She breathed heavily, but did not back down.

"I like what you've done with your hair, Gala," he said.

"Call me Ruby," she said. "That's my real name."

"Oh, you're giving up Vaurienne? But that's who you decided to become. Not through an accident of birth, but through hard work and sheer determination."

"That was all a lie and you know it. Stealing me from my family. Threatening me and them. I was just a child. I was afraid. I couldn't fight back. You - you brainwashed me. But now, I'm not afraid anymore. You can't control me anymore. You can't sell me to anybody! I am not your property!"

"Oh, Gala, don't be so self-important," Gruun said dismissively. "Everything's not about you. There are much bigger stakes at play here. I figured you would get out of the Blue Oko with the sapphires," he lied convincingly. "And here you are, safe and sound, with the sapphires. We should get going through the pass while we still have the night. We can arrive by dawn and be on our way to Botan," he said.

Ruby stared at Gruun, flanked by a dozen soldiers with their weapons still pointed at her. She was outnumbered, but she didn't care; she was seething at that poor excuse for a man. That man who stole her from her family and held her in a cage for more than a year. That perversely warped father figure in front of her. How she hated the sight of him. She wanted to slice him a dozen ways from Sunday.

As if he sensed her thoughts, "Gala, if you're going to try to kill me, you'd better get on with it. I really don't have time to waste right now. A new day will be dawning for the clans of Minos," he said. She raised her cuttas. The clicks of a dozen blasters cocking echoed against the Petrified Forest.

"My name is Ruby."

"Gala – er, Ruby," said Maresh from behind her. "You can't do this. Put the knives down," he added. "I'm sorry your Eminems; she's been under tremendous stress." He walked close to her and whispered, "You know I'm on your side, but this will just get you killed. Now is not the time; put your cuttas away."

She looked at Maresh, unsure of his intentions – and then back at Gruun, keenly aware of his intentions. Then she looked at the dozen blasters aimed at her.

"And there is still the matter of your old family – the ones on Botan. You do remember, I know where they are. I've left them alone while you worked for me, but your father still owes me money," Gruun said. "I can have an army get rid of them at any time....burn down that little house by the pond. Do you remember it? Your mother, father, brother – perhaps even your old – what did you call her, Gram?" Gruun threatened. "I wonder what blue ice cream bananas look like when they burn?" he asked aloud.

"Please," said Maresh. Ruby slowly sheathed her knives.

"That's more like it," said Gruun. "Kinti, make sure those sapphires are secured for the trip through the pass. I want to get them loaded onto the ship as soon as possible," he ordered. "And Vaurienne, I really am glad you are back with us. I would've hated to lose you," he said with a false smile.

Gruun patted her on the shoulder, then turned and walked away, barking orders. The guards holstered their weapons and followed him.

Ruby was still standing in the same spot. Though she had put her knives away, her anger was still at full boil. "He acts like he's not afraid of me. That makes me even more angry," she said to Maresh. "I can't let him keep doing this to me."

"You can't take them all on by yourself," said Maresh. "Let's just try to get along for the trip."

"What trip?" she asked. Then she realized that Gruun was taking all of them to Botan. She hadn't been home in more than a decade. So much had changed. She was so different. She wasn't even sure what home was supposed to be anymore. And her so-called family never even came for her. They had probably moved on. She wasn't sure she even wanted to go to Botan now.

Maresh put his hand on her shoulder. She glared at him, with fire still in her eyes. "We have to go," he said softly. The fire in those green eyes dimmed. "Will you come with me?" he asked. Ruby shook Maresh's hand off her shoulder. And she began walking toward the pass.

They walked through the night. The petrified forest was previously a forest of greenstalks, thousands of years ago, before the Donja was a desert. Now they were made completely of stone. They were frozen in time. A few were still a hundred feet high, but most had been worn down by the elements or simply toppled. Pieces were strewn all across the pass. These stone giants reminded Ruby of her childhood and the live greenstalks near Runyon Falls.

She saw Yuni, Two-teeth, Brown-teeth, and most of the Jaders she had known for years. But not Cassius. She caught up to Yuni and asked, "Where is Cassius?"

"That's not any of your concern, spare," Yuni replied, as she continued walking, not even looking at Ruby.

But Two-teeth, who was walking beside Yuni, was always eager to show that he knew what was going on, so he answered, "Cassius isn't coming with us. He disagreed with his father, said he didn't want to attack Botan. Gruun ordered him to go with us, but he refused. He got on a rammel and went into the Donja. Several Jaders actually followed him. I wanted to cut him down, but Gruun said we had to focus on the bigger picture. He said he was done trying to get Cassius to be a real man, so from now on, he considered Cassius dead to him, and dead to the Jade Clan. Gruun hasn't named a new deputy yet, but I'm angling for the job."

Most of the remainder of the march was uneventful. As the suns rose, the small army left the pass and heard the sound of the surf. They smelled barbecue. Around the corner, they saw the outline of *Teach's Revenge*. The tall ship, with its huge sails, was Gruun's pride and joy – added to his other ship (*Music* was her name – already docked off the coast of Botan) and *Wager's Access*, it meant that the Jade Clan could transport smuggled items across the sea without having to pay taxes, tariffs, or crossing fees to the other clan leaders.

Teach's Revenge was large enough to carry all of the sapphires, supplies, soldiers, and their weapons from Minos to Botan. Gruun had hired an experienced captain from the Blue Clan by the name of Ten Eel. This was a seafaring man to be sure. He had spent more than half his life on the oceans. Ten Eel wasn't his real name but that's what he'd been called for decades. Some said the moniker was due to his unusual hair. It looked like a bunch of greasy, slimy eels protruding from his captain's hat which he never removed. Others claimed it was because of his favorite food: Ten Eel Pie, a somewhat grotesque – and not at all sweet – dessert. Regardless, he was the most experienced mariner Gruun could find. But even with Ten Eel's experience, the journey was going to be a challenge; the Jade crew lacked seafaring exposure; they were green in more ways than their boots. Further, as lifelong desert-dwellers, most were afraid of water. None of them even knew how to swim. And they were also deathly afraid of the gravity geysers and gravity wells they'd heard about in the ocean especially because those dangerous occurrences were unseeable.

The only thing most of them knew about the ocean for sure was that it was where their leader, Gruun, had lost his arm to a devil-shark. Between the gravity phenomena, not knowing how to swim, general discomfort with water, and stories of devil-sharks taking men off the deck, there was a prevailing unease about their pending voyage.

The soldiers began preparing and loading the cargo. Gruun left Two-teeth in charge and he took Ruby, Yuni, and Maresh toward the tantalizing aroma of that barbecue. Built into the side of a cliff was the Lock & Bull – one of the few places that served food outside of the coastal okos. The massive wooden door was wide open but a big padlock (almost a foot across) in the shape of a bull's head hung on the handle.

The Lock & Bull Inn was known for one thing: Minosian barbecue (made from wild Caliga boars). Those boars had a naturally spicy taste to their meat. When roasted and paired with a special sauce, the dish was absolutely amazing. And no one could make it like "Big T" Bullock – the owner and head cook of the Lock & Bull. Gruun waltzed in like he owned the place. The smattering of patrons greeted him with low yells of "Gruuuuuuuuun."

Big T saw Gruun come in and rolled his eyes. He wasn't a fan of the Jade leader but as Gruun now essentially owned *Wager's Access*, he had tried to make nice. Big T approached Gruun and said, "Are you here to eat?"

"Of course we are!" bellowed Gruun as he slapped Big T on the back. (Big T was one of the few people that rivaled Gruun in sheer mass. Although Big T was as wide as Gruun, he was also a head and half taller.)

"Excellent. I'm glad to see you again, your Eminems," said Big T – with a fake smile (he had to choke back his disdain for Gruun). "How about this table?" he asked and pulled out a chair.

"No, I want that table," said Gruun. He walked to one side of the establishment and pulled a table right into the middle of the eatery, knocking down chairs with the effort. "This will do." He grabbed his own chair and plopped himself down. "Four plates of your best barbecued Caliga," he ordered. Gala, Maresh, and Yuni picked up their own chairs and joined Gruun at the table. "And bring us some of that famous sweet, red tea – oh yes, with those cute little hush puppies and honey goat butter! Haha!" he laughed heartily.

Gala was unsure why she was invited to the meal, as was Maresh. As they sat, Ruby took in the almost familiar feel of the place. Red and white checkered table cloths were the only thing that stood out – as nearly everything else was dark brown and made of wood. Even the massive staircase that went upstairs to the rooms for let.

"Gala," Gruun said, "I guess you're wondering why I asked you here." The Jade leader grabbed a cup of sweet red tea and held it aloft. "I want to toast my messenger, the famous Gala Vaurienne. Once again, as ever, you were successful in your task. The Giant Sapphires will change the history of our little planet. Oh, and –uuhhh– sorry about that harem thing. (He took a drink.) I want you to know that you will always be an important part of the Jade clan family." Gruun drank deeply of the syrupy red concoction and popped a handful of the still-steaming, just-arrived hush puppies from the basket into his huge mouth. Some crumbs fell into his bushy beard as he chomped. He slathered several with honey goat butter and it melted down into his forearm hair as he ate; he didn't notice – or didn't care – and grabbed another handful.

Maresh said, "Congratulations, Gala." He and Yuni both drank.

Ruby was still angry at Gruun but she didn't really know what else to do at the moment, so she drank the red tea as well. Then a waitress brought four huge plates of chopped, Minosian boar barbecue and set them on the table. The scent was captivating.

"Dig in everyone! My treat!" said Gruun as he grabbed a three-pronged fork and stuffed a huge mound of the finely diced meat into his mouth. The others were surprised – Gruun never treated. But they saw him in virtual heaven enjoying the barbecue. So they each began to eat...slowly at first. When they realized how wonderful that spicy, succulent meat actually tasted, they began to eat faster! While she was eating, Ruby began to wonder if she could really trust Gruun. As they were finishing their meal, a Jader walked in and whispered into Gruun's ear. He abruptly stood up. "The ship is loaded. Time to go," and he turned and walked out. Maresh, Yuni, and Gala followed him.

Big T noticed the Jaders leaving but he couldn't get out from the kitchen fast enough. He nearly knocked over two employees and several customers but by the time he got to the table, Gruun and company were out the door. He walked over to the table. Empty plates, empty cups, and empty baskets of hush puppies. "Vamp," he said to himself. "That quatchee Gruun didn't pay...again." Disgusted, he threw a hand towel over his shoulder and began to clear the table, throwing the dishes together. Ruby ran back to the table. She reached inside her belt and withdrew a roll of Gruun's money (that she didn't have to pay Nilo for the sapphires). She tossed it onto the table. "Thanks for the meal," she said.

Big T opened the roll and saw the money. His jaw dropped. "Thanks for the tip!" he said. Gala didn't hear him; she was already out the door catching up with Gruun and company.

As soon as the cargo was loaded and everyone was on board, Gruun nodded to Ten Eel.

"Cast off!" ordered the captain.

The novelty of being on a ship and out on the ocean was surprisingly exhilarating for most of them. But fairly soon, the novelty wore off. First it devolved back to general discomfort, which eventually gave way to a very specific discomfort: seasickness. Any number of Jaders were holding onto the deck rails and hurling over the side. They bobbed up and down like whack-a-moles.

Moments later, a shadow crossed the beach at *Wager's Access*. That shadow belonged to a lone floating figure. Finch looked at *Teach's Revenge* on the horizon. It was quite a distance from shore. He had come to follow his new adoptee, even though she didn't know it. Unfortunately, bullpars are not fans of water. Finch stared out to sea, watching the ship get smaller and smaller. The suns were climbing higher in the sky. It was now or never.

Finch set his sights on that ship. He started to proceed out across the waves...but then he retreated as a wave came in his direction. He mustered up his courage and tried once more, only to be 'forced' back again by the water that he so desperately wanted to avoid. He could not let Gala get away. He rose higher, put his head down, and ventured out into the blue. At first, he found it difficult to maintain proper height due to the rising and falling waves. He was not used to this - this - this….variability. Water was so frustrating and so… wet. He much preferred that the ground beneath him to be dry and stay at one level. Just as he got beyond most of the waves near the shore, a rogue wave came and soaked him completely. The wave dissipated, but Finch was soaked. He stopped and hovered there, dripping. He turned and looked back toward the safety of shore. Then he turned and looked toward the quickly disappearing *Teach's Revenge*. He leaned toward the ship and re-doubled his efforts, gliding as fast as he could. The water made it difficult for him to get any speed.

The further he traveled, the further the ship seemed to get from his position. He didn't seem to be making much progress. In fact, just the opposite. *Teach's Revenge* kept growing smaller and smaller. But Finch's focus was on that ship and his Gala, so he continued onward. As an occasional wave came near him, he had to try to dodge or rise above it. Several waves just missed him with a few grabbing at his now-hanging feet. It was all very unsettling for a creature used to going where he wanted, when he wanted. He was floating much lower than usual. Being wet seemed to weigh him down. Finally, the water before him seemed to calm down. He thought he might have a clearer path.

Without warning, Finch was sucked down underneath the ocean. In less than a second, he disappeared underneath the waves. He was just – gone. On the surface, the water rose and fell as it always did. But there was no Finch.

A gravity well! It had pulled the bullpar under the surface. A few moments later, and a few hundred yards away, Finch was shot out of the ocean and into the sky through a gravity geyser. It was as if he emerged from some gargantuan, invisible whale's blowhole. He surfaced choking for air. Finch had lived a long time and he was clearly a tough, old bird. But this shook him to the core. Water was not for him. He knew he would not make it to Gala.

But he couldn't think like that! Though he was in a heavily disheveled state, he tried to right himself and look for the ship. He turned on his imaginary axis. Unfortunately, *Teach's Revenge* was no longer in sight. He scanned the horizon – first this direction, and then another. There was nothing but ocean everywhere he looked. Finch stared intently at the horizon, not wanting to give up. The only direction that made any sense was back. Eventually, he acknowledged defeat, turned, and headed back toward land.

Once safely back on shore, Finch shook himself to get rid of that awful water. Droplets went spraying in a thousand different directions. How he loathed being wet. He glided until he was well out of reach of those dreadful waves. Finch looked around, turning as he went. Then he stopped. He just stopped in mid-air. Hovering there. Thinking.

He headed back into the Donja and then turned north toward the Scarlet Beach.

CHAPTER **44**

Treacherous Voyage

Ruby sat with Maresh on deck. She couldn't believe she was going back to Botan. This is what she had secretly longed for. All those years in Hamada. She wanted nothing more than to go home. Could she escape Gruun's clutches? Was there any way to defeat him? Was there even the slightest chance that she might get to see anyone she knew from her old life? Mother? Father? Even Baron. Perhaps her friends, Ho, and Mae-Ellen. Surely they were now grown as well. They had probably all gone on with their lives. Would they even remember her? Gruun said if they had cared, they would have tried to rescue her. But no one ever came from Botan. Not once.

Was it even worth considering? Was she just being selfish? She knew that acting on her personal desire to go home could put everyone she cared about in jeopardy. The risk was simply too great. Gruun literally had an army. Ruby only had her family and friends. It was just so unfair.

Years ago, Ruby had given up asking 'why me?' That query wasn't getting her anywhere. She decided to do the best she could with her new life on Minos. If she were going to be stuck there, she wanted to fit in. She wanted to make the best of a bad situation. After all, there was no way she could escape. Even if she had gotten away from Gruun and the Jaders, it would have been impossible for her to cross the great ocean. And the other clans weren't all that friendly either, so she wasn't likely to get help anywhere on Minos.

So, she set her mind to fitting in; it was the only thing she had control over. And she had been successful, rising to become Gruun's messenger. She adopted a new name: Gala (her 'old' middle name) and Vaurienne – a rascal or a scoundrel. She covered up the remaining vestiges of her old identity. She colored her red hair and blue lips to fit in. She always wore eye-guards to hide her green eyes. She had tried to make a few friends along the way. Alas, her efforts did not seem to have much impact.

Captain Ten Eel was doing his best to navigate the unseen dangers of the great ocean. Chief among them were the gravity geysers and gravity wells lurking beneath the surface. He had a map, although it was old. And these phenomena weren't always static; they sometimes moved. So Ten Eel had to focus on the map but also rely on spotters in the crow's nests. He had to be ready to respond in a moment's notice.

Gravity wells could suck anything underneath the waves – even a ship as large as *Teach's Revenge*. Gravity geysers, on the other hand, could lift that same ship right out of the water – high up into the air. Of course any forward momentum would likely continue, so if a ship passed through a geyser, it would then drop back down to the ocean like dead weight. Depending on the speed, it might skip like a child throwing a stone or it could simply smash itself onto the surface tension of the ocean. Ten Eel was doing his best to avoid either scenario while piloting the ship toward Botan's Giselle Bay.

Another challenge with the gravity disturbances was that they were almost completely invisible. A ship could sail right into one without warning. Sometimes there were subtle hints from the surface. Gravity wells generally looked like flatter, calmer sections of water, occasionally with a little concave appearance. Meanwhile, gravity geysers sometimes appeared to bubble and had more of a convex shape. Of course, other times, geysers left no doubt – as when they shot water, fish, and whatever else was in the water, forcefully skyward. Either way, one wrong decision could end a voyage prematurely.

The Jaders keeping watch high atop the masts had no experience whatsoever in identifying the gravity disturbances which inevitably led to a large quantity of false alarms. However, Captain Ten Eel faithfully guided the ship to avoid these disturbances – whether real or imagined. Luckily, the trip was unremarkable at first.

About halfway through the three-week voyage, the lookouts failed to notice a large gravity well until they were almost up on it.

"Well to port! Well to port!" the lookout shouted just before the ship was about to enter it.

"Well to port! Well to port!" repeated another.

The captain ordered the helmsman, "Hard to starboard! Hard to starboard!"

Teach's Revenge leaned hard to the right and started to veer away from the gravity well.

But the well was too strong. The ship was pulled back to the left. The captain kept the rudder hard to starboard but the well was pulling them left into a downward spiral. "Hold on everyone!" the captain yelled. "Tie yourselves down!" Those orders were repeated all over the ship. Everyone tried desperately to strap themselves in with whatever they could find.

As much as the wind was helping them – trying to nudge them out of the downward spiral, the gravity well was stronger. The ship began to circle around as if it were going down a drain in slow motion. *Teach's Revenge* leaned precipitously to port. Everything that wasn't tied down rolled or slid to the left side of the ship. As they made a second circular pass, the captain realized they were fighting an agonizingly slow – and losing – battle.

"It's got us," he said. "There's not enough wind to push us out, which means we're going to get pulled down. If that happens, we're done for. We might be able to fight this gravity well for a while, but we're not getting out of this one."

"What can we do?" asked Gruun.

"Maybe you didn't hear me; it's got us. There's nothing we can do. We're only holding on so far because the wind is full in our sails – pulling in the opposite direction. But that's just prolonging the inevitable. Maybe if we were going faster, we might have had enough momentum to help propel the ship past the well. But we don't have any speed at this point, so it's not gonna happen," said Ten Eel. He sat back in his captain's chair (leaning left) and lit a pipe.

"What are you doing!?" shouted Gruun. "Get this ship out of here!"

"First off, I'm the captain of this ship. So don't speak to me like that. Second, I would think it's fairly obvious that I'm smoking my pipe. If I'm going to die, then I plan to die a happy man. Third…" He puffed his pipe and blew out a long stream of cherry-scented smoke. "and third, let me be clear. We're not getting out of this. This ship is going down. It won't ever come back up – at least not in one piece."

Just then, Maresh and Ruby literally fell into the bridge, crashing in from the right side. (They had been unable to strap in and unable to hold on any longer.) They got a fresh grip on some railings.

"What's happening?" screamed Ruby.

"Caught in gravity well," said the captain calmly, still smoking his pipe.

"Can't you get us out of it?" asked Ruby.

"No, I'm pretty sure the ship will be sunk in a few minutes," Ten Eel responded. "The problem is that we don't have enough speed to get us away from the force of gravity pulling us down. We're fighting it, but that's just slowing us down. So, there's really nothing we can do. Just accept it, we're going to die." He puffed some more on his pipe and blew a smoke ring.

Outside on deck, as *Teach's Revenge* was circling ever downward, everyone was hanging on for dear life. Below deck was just as bad. Most had no idea what was going on, but it was probably best that they didn't have to stare into the mouth of that gravity well that was sucking them down.

"I'm not a sailor," screamed Maresh.

"Interesting," said the captain.

"If you don't get us out of here, I'll end you!" yelled Gruun, pulling out his blaster. The ship lurched forward; Gruun dropped his weapon as he had to use his hand and hook to hold on. Ten Eel chuckled.

"As I was saying," said Maresh. "I'm not a sailor, but if the problem is that we're going too slowly, why not just go faster?"

"You're definitely not a sailor, boy. The wind is what makes a ship go fast. And while we do have a favorable wind, it's not enough. It's not a floater, boy. I can't just push a foot pedal and accelerate. A ship is more like a sled going down a mountain. You land folks just don't understand the sea." He took another puff on his pipe. Although chaos was exploding all around him, the captain seemed unnaturally calm and ready to accept his fate. He exhaled slowly, puffing another ring.

"But instead of fighting the gravity well, couldn't we just turn into it to increase our speed?" Maresh asked.

"You want us to go down deeper into the gravity well? That would just take us down to our watery graves even faster," replied Ten Eel. "Jaders…Let's die faster" he mocked. "Faster," he said with another cherry puff. "Faster," he said slowly, turning the word around in his mind. "Faster…faster – waitaminnit!" he shouted. "There is a chance that might actually work… I mean, it'll probably just kill us more quickly. But, if we turned into the gravity well and used that force to increase our speed – and if the wind stays favorable – we might be able to lurch ourselves out of this mess. Then again, we would probably just hasten our demise," he said with yet another puff of his pipe and sat back in his captain's chair, calmly blowing another ring.

"Well, if we're going to die anyway, and if there's a chance to live, shouldn't we take it!?" yelled Ruby.

Ten Eel looked at Gala; a smile appeared across his lips, "What the vamp!?" he shouted over the roar of the spinning water.

The captain stood up and walked – with some difficulty – to the wheel. The helmsman had relinquished his grip several minutes earlier and was now pinned against the wall of the bridge facing out a porthole into the jaws of death (the gravity well that was about to swallow the entire ship). Captain Ten Eel turned the wheel hard to port – into the direction of the downward swirl from the gravity well. The ship began to speed up. After making a full revolution, it began to go even faster, but it was also descending more quickly.

"We're going the wrong direction, you loper!" yelled Gruun.

"Not quite enough speed yet," said the captain, ignoring Gruun. The ship made another pass; it was really gaining speed now. "Almost…." said Ten Eel. The ship was virtually sideways now. It was more than a minor miracle that they hadn't lost everyone on deck. The vortex of gravity was spinning them round faster and faster.

"I'm going to kill you!" shouted Gruun. Another pass; the ship was going faster than ever as Ten Eel ignored Gruun. Everyone on the bridge was leaning and many were losing their grips. "Now!" yelled the captain. He turned the big wheel fully to starboard (right), spinning and spinning in the opposite direction. He just hoped that they had enough momentum to ride straight up the side of the swirl.

Their speed was propelling the ship upward. But as they neared the top, their momentum slowed. It was not going to be enough. They were not going to escape. One sail ripped away from the mast, followed by a second – and then a mast collapsed. The ropes from those two sails got twisted together at their ends. Just then a powerful updraft caught those two sails and helped pull the ship upward, like a reverse parachute – and over the edge of the funnel. The forward momentum launched the ship out of the water and into the air. The spinning had stopped. They were out of the bottomless swirl! For a few seconds, they were literally floating in mid-air. The vicious roaring sound of the gravity well subsided as the whirlpool-like hole closed up. All was silent.

"Hurray!" someone shouted. And then another, and another. Before long, everyone was cheering. The ship was safe. They were all saved. "Hurray!"

"Well done, captain!" said Gruun. "I thought we were all dead."

"Get ready for impact!" yelled the captain. He knew that – gravity disturbance or not – what went up was bound to come down. The captain noticed that they weren't falling yet, but the fall was certainly coming. "Brace yourselves!" he shouted again. They were all rather disoriented from their recent spinning. But they definitely hadn't hit the ocean yet, and he was pretty sure they should have fallen back down by now.

The captain ran to the deck. "Oh no," he said. *Teach's Revenge* was surely not falling. Indeed, quite the opposite; it was rising. In fact it was already nearly fifty feet above the waves. They had launched themselves out of a gravity well and right into a gravity geyser. He ran back to the bridge and grabbed his map. Using his sextant and moving from their last known position, he ran his finger ahead to a marking on the map. It read: "Danger: Molly's Push-up." It was one of the most powerful known gravity geysers in the great ocean.

Outside on deck, the Jaders who were previously holding on for dear life, began to realize they weren't going to fall. They began to look over the railings and saw the water nearly 100 feet below. The poor passengers thought they were flying. They looked out and seemed to enjoy the ride. They had no idea what was coming.

From their current height of more than 150 feet, the plunge back to sea level would be violent. The captain realized that this time, unlike with the gravity well, they likely had sufficient forward velocity to propel them through the gravity geyser. This meant that pretty soon, they would probably – aaaaaaaahhhhhhh! The ship had obviously and suddenly passed through the geyser and was now falling back toward the ocean.

"Brace for impact! Brace for impact!" yelled the captain.

"Brace for impact!" was repeated across the ship.

The splash was ginormous. The ship's deck, which normally sat high above the waves, plunged below the surface, and was momentarily washed over. But then, just as quickly, she buoyed back up. *Teach's Revenge* bobbed up and down a few more times before coming to rest, or more accurately, adrift.

Almost everyone was wet, but – miraculously – it seemed that everyone had managed to hold on (or be held in some cases). "Man overboard!" one of the lookouts yelled. "Man overboard!" The second lookout had been thrown from his perch somewhere between the falling and subsequent bouncing of the ship.

Most of the passengers rushed to the port side to see a lone Jader struggling to keep his head above water. He was quickly being separated from the ship. "Helphhhssshh!" he tried to yell. They all watched.

"Someone has to save him!" Ruby yelled. She looked at Maresh.

"Not me," he said; "I can't swim." She went to Gruun.

"I'm not going into the ocean again," he said as he raised his handhook. "I've only got one hand left and I intend to keep it. If we only lost one man after that ride, I'd say we're doing pretty good."

Captain Ten Eel walked across the deck to see the struggling Jader. He lit his pipe once again – and, saying nothing, he puffed a few puffs of billowy smoke.

"Why is no one helping that poor man?" asked Ruby.

"You see, missy," Ten Eel began – and then he took a long puff from his pipe, "we have a bunch of Jaders on this ship. Jaders are desert people. I doubt any of them can swim," he said with another cherry puff from his still-lit pipe.

"Good grief," sighed Ruby. She took off her Jader jacket and her green boots. She turned to Maresh and said, "Get a rope for us." Then she climbed atop the railing, paused for a moment, took a breath, and dove in.

"She's just going to drown herself, and then they'll both be dead," said Yuni.

"This should be fun to watch," said Two-teeth.

It was true she hadn't swum since leaving Botan. But she did grow up with a pond outside her front door. She had learned to swim in that pond at the age of three. Some summer days, she spent hours in the water. Even after she lost her leg, Ruby was still an excellent swimmer. She had avoided water on Minos, mostly because of the desert culture and her desperate need to fit in. But also because she wanted to keep her red hair and blue lips under wraps. And, realistically, there just weren't many opportunities to swim on Minos. Of course, there were the beaches, but she knew that she had to fit in as a Jader. Anyway, none of that mattered now.

She swam out toward the struggling Jader. "It's okay, I've got you," she said as she got closer. "Help me! I'm drowwbbb..." the rest of the words came out as bubbles when he went under a wave. "I can't – I can't....swim!" he yelled, popping back up and thrashing around.

"Just relax," Ruby yelled. "I can bring you back to the ship. Quit splashing so much!" she yelled. The panicked Jader lunged for Ruby and pulled her down with him.

He was a big one, at least twice her size. She was pretty sure she could pull him back to the ship, but all bets were off if he drowned her first. Ruby fought back to the surface and gasped. After she'd gotten one gulp of air, she felt the Jader's hand on the top of her head. In trying to push himself up, he was pushing her down again.

Ruby struggled to get away. But the lookout now had a firm grip on her hair. This was not going to work. She didn't want to let him drown, but she wasn't planning on letting him kill her, either. She pried his fingers from her curly locks and pulled away – out of his reach – to catch her breath and decide what to do next. Breathing was high on her list. Without thinking, Ruby instinctively did something she had explicitly avoided for nearly 12 years: She reached down and scratched her leg. Then she swam toward the struggling Jader. When she got close enough, she leaned backward with her feet toward him. Then she kicked the crap out of him, knocking him out cold – sending a few teeth flying into the salty water.

Unconscious, he was much easier to handle. Ruby grabbed him from behind and pulled him on his back. Then she swam in the direction of the ship. While she was dragging this huge Jader back through the waves, it occurred to her that Two-teeth could've used those chompers that were now likely sinking to the bottom of the ocean. She chuckled to herself. She was half-exhausted by the time she reached the rope. Some of the guards dropped down a loop to pull the semi-conscious lookout up on deck.

Ruby held onto the other rope for a moment to catch her breath. She bobbed in the water for a bit, feeling the wetness. She didn't recall being fully submerged the entire time she was on Minos. Ruby pulled herself partially out of the water, and then let her body fall back in. She was enjoying the feeling of floating. But she knew she had to get back on board the ship. She grasped the rope and took a deep breath – then disappeared beneath the waves – leaving a trail of bubbles. She did not surface.

Ruby didn't know what had happened. She was being pulled with great speed underneath the ship. Her body was twisting and turning under the water. It was extremely disorienting. What was happening? Could it be another gravity well? It took a few seconds for her to catch her bearings. But this was no gravity well. As she passed from underneath *Teach's Revenge*, the light penetrated beneath the waves and she saw it. A devil-shark had grabbed Ruby's leg and was pulling her away. It was a fearsome creature. Its front fins were webbed and trailed back to its body. It had long, razor sharp teeth with two extra-long fangs. Pointy horns protruded from the beast's head. The animal's black body was streaked with jagged, red stripes. Ruby almost marveled at the sight of this underwater creature. But she had more urgent matters to attend to – like staying alive!

Luckily, the shark had grabbed her left leg, so there was no blood. And thankfully, she had just taken a deep breath, but that would only last her so long. This animal was taking her down. She had to do something – fast! She tried to wiggle free, but the shark's jaws were clamped on too tightly. She thought maybe she could kick the shark, but she couldn't get any leverage because even though her leg was powerful, it was stuck in the animal's jaws; she could only push against water. And she was being pulled deeper.

The pressure was building in her temples and she could hear her heart thumping in her chest. She had to do something soon. The devil-shark wasn't likely to offer any assistance. She pulled out her curved blades and began to hack at the devil-shark's hide. But the creature's skin was so thick that her cuttas were having little effect. It seemed to be getting darker. Was the shark taking her that deep? Or was the lack of oxygen affecting her perception? She put her knives away.

Time – and air – were running out. She hated shooting an animal, but she had no choice. Ruby reached into her hair and pulled out her hummingbird. She blasted at the shark...but the blast dissipated and had no effect. The water had somehow refracted the laser from the blaster. She fired a second time, but with the same result. She was still being pulled deeper. She shoved the hummingbird back into her hair. Ruby reached for the surface as some air bubbles escaped from her mouth. The bubbles rose toward the light. The pressure was closing in on her.

Ruby felt her heart beginning to pound more loudly in her chest. She could hear every beat – louder and louder. But then she felt her descent slow. More air escaped from her clenched lips. The water no longer seemed to be rushing past her. Had everything slowed down in her final moments? The darkness seemed to be closing in but also fading away at the same time. Was it beginning to get lighter? She couldn't hold her breath any longer; her lungs felt as if they would surely burst. More bubbles escaped from her mouth. She barely noticed that now she was rising instead of going deeper.

Her body continued to rise as the last of the air escaped from her lungs. Ruby and the devil-shark broke through the surface of the water. But being thrust into the air, where it could not breathe, surprised the shark and caused it to let go of Ruby's leg. Both of them had been pushed upward, caught in another gravity geyser. The fresh air jolted Ruby back to consciousness. She coughed up water and gasped. For a moment, both Ruby and the shark were floating in the air above the waves. They twisted and turned in the air – facing one another just inches apart. The shark snapped his huge mouth at her but only chomped on air. Passing through the geyser, both Ruby and the shark then fell back into the water. They were now on the far side of the ship. The devil-shark stared at Ruby but really didn't seem to have an appetite for her anymore. It turned and swam off in a zig-zaggy daze.

Thankfully, the current was actually pushing back her toward *Teach's Revenge*. Her leg seemed to be working although her pants were in shreds and barely hanging on. Meanwhile, everyone on deck was still looking over the other side where she had disappeared just moments before. Everything was happening so quickly. She swam to the side of the ship and grabbed onto some rigging. Though she was nearly exhausted, she managed to pull herself back up to the deck. She walked over to the side of the ship where so many, including Maresh, were looking over the railing for her.

She couldn't resist, "What are you looking for?" she asked Maresh. Without turning back, Maresh said, "We're looking for Gala Vaurienne. She just rescued the lookout, but then she vanished beneath the waves."

"Uh-huh," she responded. "Do you think someone ought to dive in after her?"

"I don't think anyone else knows how to swim," said Maresh. "Okay," said Ruby, "then maybe we should just leave her for the Devil-sharks."

"No, we can't do that. She's Gala Vaurienne. She just saved that man!" he turned to face the person who would say something so unfeeling, so uncaring.

"Gala!" he shouted, and picked her up and hugged her.

When Maresh shouted her name, everyone else turned and saw her. Cheers began for Vaurienne, Gruun's messenger, the fearless savior of Jaders. But, almost as soon as the cheers began, they started to fade. Literally everyone was staring at Ruby. Most had not seen her red hair. And now – the bandana was gone, her eye-guards had fallen out in the water, and there was no black left on those shocking blue lips. Red hair, green eyes, blue lips…

"Is that Vaurienne?" someone asked?

"She's not a Jader," said another.

"What the heck is she, with those lips?" asked Raja.

"And that hair…." There was lots of yelling.

Even though she was now pulling on her green boots, it was clear that this was definitely no Jader. She felt – for just a moment – like a little girl wearing a hat that clashed with her hair – and her blue lips. Maresh handed her a towel. She wrapped herself in it and went below deck for the remainder of the voyage.

Her signature Jader pants were tattered; she found a skirt below deck…Not her first choice, but….

STORYTRAX: *Find Your Way Back* - Starship

ACT VI ~ ARRIVAL

CHAPTER **45**

Diversion

Botan.

Before departing from *Wager's Access*, Gruun had ordered another volley of missiles aimed at Botan. The target was the continent's northernmost city of Severu, in the clord region. This attack served dual purposes. It was a final test of range and accuracy for his missiles prior to the main offensive. But it was also designed to draw attention away from the south and Giselle Bay where Gruun was planning to land *Teach's Revenge* with his forces. The strike was scheduled to hit the day before Gruun and the Jaders landed.

Three missiles reached their targets in Severu. Two were for navigational purposes only, but the third contained a warhead. It hit the port and caused significant damage and casualties. Severu was considered a likely target for an attack from Minos for two reasons: First, it was the most industrialized city on Botan, so damage there would have an outsized impact on manufacturing and production of all types. Second, it was considered to be a likely sea landing from Minos' main naval operations at Pelican's Point.

When the attack hit Severu, the Botanian Assembly requested General Salinger and the *Vasco Da Gama* to redeploy to the north. Tanner Clemens agreed to stay on board and help the decimated crew and his friend Jalen. They took off for Severu the evening of the attack.

Gruun's plan had the desired effect. The IDC contingent (what was left of it) and the Botanian army were all focused on Severu – with virtually no attention given to the resort area of Giselle Bay, where *Teach's Revenge* would soon make landfall. If the high-tech spaceship *Vasco*, with its blast cannons now operational, had stayed near Wedding-Shi, it could have made short work of the wooden sailing ship now approaching Botan before the Jaders could even set foot on the coast. But that was not to be.

Captain Ten Eel sailed the ship south of the bay to a spot just offshore. The Jaders loaded into longboats and made their way to shore. They were especially careful loading into the boats as none wanted to fall in and risk drowning – or meeting up with devil-sharks! Gruun and Brown-teeth took the floater (and the sapphires) over the shallow water to land. Ruby, Maresh, Yuni, and the others followed in the longboats.

When they were all on shore, Gruun gathered his troops. "Today, my friends, you join me in the dawn of a new age. Now, we Minosians will no longer play second fiddle to the Botanians. The Jade clan will be..." he began. Ruby wasn't listening any more. She was trying to think of a way to get home. She didn't care about the risk; she just wanted to see her family. Gruun kept jabbering about the future and taking over the 'weaklings' of Botan. Ruby she was from Botan. And she didn't consider herself particularly weak.

After all, she was kidnapped from her home as a child. She never finished school. She was beaten and tortured. But she – a svelte figure of little more than five feet in height – managed to become messenger to a clan leader and a member of the Minosian Council. She was respected by many, feared by some. She was clever and a good fighter. *Perhaps*, she thought, *Gruun might be underestimating the potential resistance from Botan*.

Gruun continued jammering from atop a rock, "We will march to the ternium mines to meet up with the first wave. We will camp there tonight. Make preparations to march in 30 minutes!"

He climbed down from his rock and motioned to Two-teeth. Two-teeth, in turn, collected Yuni, Maresh, Ruby, and a handful of others. "I have a special mission for you. I'm appointing Two-teeth in charge of this scout squad," he said, looking at Ruby. She glared back.

Things with Gruun were obviously not going to get any better. "There is a special store of high-grade ternium at a site west of here. We'll need that extra ternium for our blasters; with it, we will be virtually invincible," he said.

"What's our target?" asked Ruby.

"You are to follow Two-teeth. He knows the destination. Get your gear ready. I want you on your way in 15 minutes."

"Two-teeth, Yuni, I want to talk to you," Gruun barked. Two-teeth turned to Ruby and the others. "Pack up, we'll be back in a few minutes." He and Yuni walked over to Gruun. They stepped away so that the others in the squad couldn't hear them.

Ruby was angry. "How dare he leave me out of the conversation!? I should be leading the mission!" she said to Maresh.

"Gala – uuhhh, sorry, Ruby – I don't think things are going to be the same from now on," said Maresh. "You should probably watch your back," he added.

"I thought that's what I had you for," she said with a smile.

Gruun whispered to Two-teeth and Yuni: "Our Gala Vaurienne has served her purpose. The spare who became messenger. She served me well, but I have other things to focus on now. She has become a distraction. Do I make myself clear?" he asked with a nod.

"You want us to watch her now?" asked Two-teeth.

"No, you ignorant quatchee, I want you to kill her," said Gruun in a low, determined voice. "Take her on this mission – she might prove helpful. She is originally from Botan, after all. Play with her, have a little fun...but afterward, see to it that she does not come back with you. This will be the last mission for Gala Vaurienne."

Two-teeth smiled his nasty, decrepit smile.

Yuni nodded. "Got it boss," she said.

"What type of resistance should we expect?" Two-teeth asked.

"None," said Gruun. "I hit this amusement park several weeks ago with a few of our IDC missiles. But we can't be too careful. So, after you get what you need, I want you to blow the rest of it off the map."

The scout team headed west on foot. They began making their way inland. After walking for more than an hour, Ruby caught up to the front of the group and asked, "Now that we're on our way, would you mind telling me where it is that we're going?"

"We're going to an amusement park to get back-up ternium for our blasters," said Two-teeth. Yuni elbowed him in the side.

"What?" he whispered. "It doesn't matter what she knows, she's not going to tell anyone."

Ruby fell back to talk to Maresh at the rear of the group. "What did Two-teeth say about our mission?" asked Maresh.

"I don't know. I can't tell if he's lying, playing me for a fool, or if he's just a loper," she said. "The quatchee said we were going to an amusement park."

CHAPTER **46**

Gravity Park Deux

The Jader scout squad, under the command of Two-teeth, arrived at its destination. As they walked through the massive, deserted parkbay, Ruby had a strange sense that she had been there before. There was a huge pile of twisted, crumpled metal on the ground near the entrance. It was scorched with burn marks. As she walked by, Ruby could make out some writing on a scorched sign: 'tainment at its finest.'

The scout squad walked through what appeared to be the remnants of a formal entrance. There were still remains of gates, but they were mostly destroyed. The Jaders had to climb over rubble and dodge still-smoldering wreckage.

"What are we doing here?" asked Ruby.

Two-teeth pulled out a map and studied it. Yuni walked up beside him and turned the map right side up. They talked and pointed – seeming to disagree. "I'm in charge, you loper. We go where I say," he said through gritted teeth (metaphorically speaking).

Yuni pulled Gala and Maresh aside. Meanwhile, Two-teeth gathered the rest of the squad together. He handed the group his map and pointed them in the direction of *Experimental Fusion Alley* to search for ternium. Then he turned his attention to Ruby, Maresh, and Yuni.

Two-teeth and Yuni both opened their packs. They were loaded with explosives and a single long coil of fuse. "The four of us are going to rig this place to blow sky high. Gruun said that there is one location inside this complex that would cause the most destruction. He said that low gravity would enable the explosion to cause more devastation," said Two-teeth.

"Finally, we get to do some real damage," said Yuni.

They walked down a path toward the target. Ruby couldn't shake a familiar feeling about this place. She passed a sign that read 'Gravity G-For.' She couldn't make out the rest. "G-Force…?" she said softly to herself. *I know that. Where have I seen that before?* she thought. "This looks like a children's amuse... Why exactly are we blowing it up?" she asked.

"Need to know basis," said Yuni, frowning.

"Maresh," she whispered. "I think I've been here before."

"Well, if you know your way around, you might want to slip away now," he whispered back.

"Why would I do that?" she asked.

"I overheard Gruun order Two-teeth and Yuni to kill you here," he said. "They don't plan on bringing you back with us."

"What are you two talking about?" asked Yuni?

"Just wondering what you want us to do," said Maresh.

"I want you to follow orders," she barked.

"Gala, take this pack and catch up with Two-teeth. I need to talk to Maresh," said Yuni. Ruby took the pack and caught up with Two-teeth. Yuni and Maresh hung back.

"What's up?" asked Maresh?

"Sssshhhh." She placed her finger in front of her lips. "Follow me. We need to go somewhere more private. I don't want anyone else to hear." Yuni walked into what appeared to be a partially demolished snack stand.

Maresh followed. "What's with all the cloak and dagger stuff?" he asked her. Yuni looked around. Maresh looked around as well. When he turned back to face Yuni, his body suddenly jerked and stiffened. His eyes opened wide. He gasped. He put his hands on Yuni's shoulders.

Yuni plunged her knife into his stomach again and again, deeper and with more force on subsequent thrusts. Maresh slumped to the ground. "We know you've been helping Gala," said Yuni. "But you're not going to help her anymore." Maresh was lying on the ground, bleeding out with too many stab wounds to count. He gasped, but was unable to speak; his eyes were still wide open. He coughed and reached up for Yuni; she knocked his hand away as he fell back onto the ground. Yuni stared at her now-motionless former comrade – sliced his throat. Then she wiped her blade on his shirt. Finally, she emptied his pockets, putting the few levs she found into her own pocket.

A few minutes further down the path, Ruby and Two-teeth approached their destination. *Did Maresh know what he was talking about?* Ruby wondered. Not that she was completely surprised.

"Here we are," said Two-teeth.

It didn't look like much. In fact, a lot of whatever-this-was before was now in pieces on the ground. There were sections of a wall still standing. They were almost 12 feet high marked with a big, yellow stripe at the top. A big red stripe on the ground seemed to be marking a boundary of something. Ruby felt she had been here before; she just couldn't remember why this place felt so familiar.

Two-teeth opened up his pack. "Here, place these three charges at the base of those columns. Then run the fuse back across that red line."

Ruby did as she was told. She didn't want to believe that her adopted clan would really kill her. That could not be true. She tried to do as she had always done; focus on the mission and fit in. She was Gala Vaurienne, Gruun's messenger. *I just have to focus – complete the mission – and everything will be fine.* she told herself.

When Yuni caught up to them, Two-teeth was planting the remaining charges. She nodded to him. He showed his characteristically disturbing smile.

"Where's Maresh?" Ruby asked as she walked toward the red stripe with her fuses.

"I sent him to go and help the others. We can take care of the demolition – and that other thing," Yuni said, with a half smile.

Ruby looked around as Two-teeth and Yuni ran the fuse from their side. If Maresh was right, she didn't have much time – and with Maresh not here, she was definitely on her own. She noticed an abandoned ice cream stand – tiny rivulets of blue ice cream banana ice cream were dried on the ground. There were a few dragon-fliers buzzing around the sticky mess.

She remembered this place, didn't she? She stared at the remnants of the wall with the red and yellow stripes. She shook her head. Gravity Park... Gravity G-Force Accelerator... Her mind began to piece it together... Jumbo bag of chocolate-swirled clord candy...stomach ache. She tilted her head and half closed one eye — it was as if a memory were fighting to make its way up from deep within her brain. She stared at the red line. A jumble of images and sounds filled her head. Running from Jaders. Baron. A smashed bug re-inflating itself. Looking out of the bars from Gruun's cage. Her parents. Streaking across the sky in a floater. Passing out.

Her head slowly straightened and her eyes widened. It was all coming back now. The first time she saw Mr. Moustache... Baron and the Reverse Gravity Cloud Arena – with the big red stripe! Ruby remembered this place. Strange how she had put it out of her mind. But now she knew exactly where she was.

She looked back inside the red stripe; only now did she recognize the toys strewn on the ground. Odd that she hadn't noticed them before. There were gold boxes and a huge iridium satellite, not to mention a barbell labeled 100,000 pounds. Then she saw the heavy metal balls...zaffers. She was not ready to accept the fate that Gruun wanted to dish out. She was going to fight back. And then, Ruby had an idea. A wild and crazy idea. *I'm not going to die today*, she thought. *And I'm not going back to Gruun. I'm going home.* The whole plan wasn't yet fully formed in her brain, but she decided then and there that she was going to take charge. Ruby Gala Vaurienne Clemens was not a victim; she was a survivor.

"Hey, Yuni," she called. "Want to play catch?" Ruby walked over and picked up a zaffer. "Do you remember on *Teach's Revenge* a few days ago when we got caught in that gravity geyser – right after we escaped the gravity well?" she asked.

"Yeah, you mean the one that almost swallowed the whole ship and killed everyone?"

"Yeah, that one," Ruby replied. "The well sucked us down and the geyser shot us up."

"So?"

"This whole place is a gravity geyser, just on land instead of out in the water."

Two-teeth walked up beside Yuni. "Those things don't exist on land. They only happen in the water," he said.

"Maybe on Minos, but Botan is different. You forget, I am from here." She bent over and picked up a zaffer, tossing it up in the air to herself. It floated down more slowly than a heavy metal ball should have. "You see this? It's called a zaffer. This one weighs more than a thousand pounds," she said, still tossing it to herself.

"Clearly it does not. Throw it to me," he responded. Ruby threw the zaffer (underhand) to Two-teeth. It sailed over his head. He laughed at her. "You can't throw very well." He picked it up and threw it back at her (overhand) as hard as he could. The zaffer hit Ruby in the stomach. "Oooommmpphhh!" Even though the gravity was light inside the arena, that still hurt. Ruby was doubled over in pain. Two-teeth laughed.

"What are you doing?" Yuni whispered to him.

"Remember what Gruun said?" he whispered back to her. "'Play with her...have a little fun' – and then you can kill her. So that's what I'm doing. First, I'm playing with her. Then we can kill her."

Yuni smiled, then she picked up her own zaffer and began tossing it up to herself. As Ruby straightened herself, Yuni yelled, "Pick it up!" Ruby slowly bent down to pick up the zaffer. That's when Yuni fired her zaffer, hitting Ruby in the head. Ruby yelped as she fell to the ground, grabbing her skull.

This time, Yuni and Two-teeth both laughed heartily. "I guess she can't catch very well, either," said Yuni. "What a loper!"

Ruby pulled her hands from her head; they were wet with blood. She puked on the ground at the sight.

"Get up!" yelled Two-teeth. "I want to play catch some more." This was no longer a game – not that it ever really was. Ruby stood up and wiped her hands on her pants.

"Come on, throw the balls to us, little girl!" taunted Yuni.

Ruby bent over and picked up both zaffers, one in each hand. She threw them back at the same time, underhand – hard – to her tormenters. Both zaffers sailed over their heads.

"You are terrible at this game!" yelled Two-teeth. "You can't throw *and* you can't catch!"

Yuni walked back to retrieve the zaffers and handed one to Two-teeth. They looked at each other, then at Ruby. They wound up and threw both zaffers *at* her – not *to* her – at the same time. Yuni's zaffer struck Ruby in the side. Two-teeths' throw beaned Ruby on the hip. They were both enjoying doling out punishment to Ruby.

"I think the spare's time is almost up," whispered Yuni to Two-teeth.

Ruby scrounged in the dirt for the zaffers. While she was getting them, she noticed something else. It was an old screen – one like she used to have when she was a child. Except this one was cracked and dirty. She tried to turn it on. The light came on for a second – she thought she heard music briefly, but then the light went out. She shoved it in her shirt as she got up.

"I can too throw!" Ruby shouted. "Just back up a few steps." They moved backward. She picked up both zaffers and threw them at Two-teeth and Yuni again. Yet again, the zaffers sailed over their outstretched hands. Two-teeth told Yuni to get the zaffers again. He was laughing so hard, he could barely talk. He was enjoying himself more than – more than he could ever remember. He thought it was a shame that his fun would end soon.

"Can we just go ahead and?" Yuni whispered as she brought the zaffers back.

"This is too much fun," he said. "Why stop now?"

Yuni fired off a throw that caught Ruby in the shoulder. Two-teeth rifled his throw at Ruby as hard as he could, but his aim was too low;

his zaffer hit Ruby in her (artificial) foot. As he had missed, he said to Yuni, "Well, the fun couldn't last forever. We do need to get back to Gruun. We might as well finish the job." Two-teeth began to reach for his blaster

"Wait," Ruby yelled again from a distance. "I really can throw! Please give me one more chance."

Yuni looked at Two-teeth "Just shoot," she said in a low voice. "Oh, we will kill that lousy spare, but you know what? I'm in such a good mood, I think we should treat this as the last request of the condemned. Let's let her throw again. I don't know when I'll get another chance to laugh like this."

"I can do this!" Ruby yelled. Two-teeth was having the time of his life. Yuni just wanted to kill Ruby and get back to camp. "Just take a few more steps backward... That's it. Keep going past that red line... Perfect." Ruby hoped her last few throws had allowed her to judge the distance and trajectory appropriately. She reached for the screen inside her shirt. She tapped it a few times – and the light returned. Ruby just wanted to hear music; she didn't care what kind. It had just been so long. She couldn't really read the cracked, dirty screen, but she knew from memory where the play button was.

So she pushed the button and shoved the screen into her pocket. The music began. The song was *Werewolves of London* by Warren Zevon. Ruby closed her eyes. She pictured herself back at home, playing softball with her friends. She saw her pitches go high every time. She heard Ho saying, "You can do it. Just focus." She tried to remember all those nights throwing softballs against Father's workshop. Ruby wound up – with a zaffer in each hand – her arms looping around, looking for all the world like two back-to-back windmills.

"I don't think you can throw this far!" shouted Two-teeth. He and Yuni laughed again. Ruby let loose of both zaffers at the same time. Her aim was directly for their chests. But she threw high – again. Just as she knew she would. She couldn't help it.

The heavy, dense zaffers flew in a slowly-rising line. They looked sure to float over the outstretched arms of both Two-teeth and Yuni. As the projectiles came closer – and as it became clear that Ruby's throws would yet again be way over the mark – Yuni dropped her hands and started to reach for her blaster. In a slow motion arc, the zaffers continued to rise – that is, until they reached the red line at the edge of the gravity cloud. That's when their trajectories changed abruptly. They immediately assumed a different curve…decidedly downward and accelerating quickly due to their sudden, massive increase in mass. Three thousand pounds of collective force and momentum and velocity and anger and vengeance – accelerated by gravity – hurtled toward the two Jaders in an instant.

Initially, Ruby's throws looked high. But she had counted on that. Based on the sudden shift in gravity as the zaffers crossed the boundary line of the arena, the path of her throws was altered dramatically. While the Jaders stood there waiting, they were still snickering and criticizing her ridiculously high throws again. With their crooked smiles and miserable laughs, they continued to make fun of Ruby. They didn't notice how the speed and direction of the zaffers had suddenly changed. The altered courses took both zaffers straight into the chests of Yuni and Two-teeth. Their faces had looks of shock and surprise. Needless to say, neither one of the Jaders caught these suddenly-much-heavier-and-swifter projectiles. The zaffers continued their accelerated, much-more-rapid-than-expected, breakneck descent – like personal missiles – straight through the bodies of the two Jaders with two quick successive, sickening, *schlip-fooosh* sounds.

And Ruby... watched. Yes, Ruby watched. But this time... This time, she did not turn away.

"Draw blood," came the lyrics.

STORYTRAX: *Werewolves of London* - Warren Zevon

CHAPTER **47**

Collision Course

Ruby shook her head. This was crazy. She had to figure out a way to get home. The rest of the Jade scout squad was surely the next obstacle to her escape. She had to find Maresh and tell him what she was doing; she owed him that much. Her mind was going a million miles a minute. She had to focus. Deep breaths...deep breaths.

She began to run back the way she came. She would find Maresh and maybe he could help cover for her. She soon slowed her run to a deliberate, purposeful walk. Something caught her eye up ahead. She saw a puddle on the ground. As she approached, she noticed that the color of the puddle was deep, dark red. *Is that blood?* Instinctively, she started to turn away, but stopped short. Instead, she steeled herself and intentionally walked toward the puddle. A few steps away, inside the snack bar, she found Maresh lying on the ground; his stomach was a bloody mess. He was lying there dead with his pockets turned inside out. Ruby knew immediately that Yuni had killed him.

She felt sorry for Maresh. He had helped her. She hadn't even thought he could have been at risk, but she realized that he had likely known. She knelt down and closed his eyes. Ruby had seen a lot of death in recent days. Unfortunately, she had a feeling that more was coming her way. But she didn't want death; she just wanted to go home. *Was that even possible? If they killed Maresh, would they ever let her leave? After all, he was a natural member of the Jade Clan, born and raised.* She knew now that Gruun would never let her go.
"Aaaaaaaagggggghhhh!" she screamed. That release felt better. Her head was clearer now. *Focus on the problem at hand*, she thought. She would surely have a better chance against a small scout squad than against Gruun's entire army.

She took stock of her situation. She was in a deserted theme park. The only other people around were half a dozen Jaders that had orders to kill her. She was miles and miles from anywhere – and she had no transportation. She had a hummingbird hidden in her hair, but that had only two shots. Oh yeah, and Gruun had fired multiple barrages of missiles – possibly igniting an intercontinental war. Staring down at her green boots, she realized that she pretty much looked like a Jader – and was, of course, here with a scout squad to blow up the place. If the Botanians came, would anyone believe that she wasn't the enemy? Wouldn't she be shot just as easily as the other Jaders?

If there were only some way she could communicate to someone...anyone. Her parents maybe? She looked at the rubble that was left of the snack stand. There were pieces of a shattered landline phone receiver on the ground. What if one of the other rides or shops had a phone? She ran to the Gravity G-Force Accelerator. She looked around for a door. It was open – and the service shack was still standing! Ruby pushed her way in. There was a phone! She stepped forward and picked it up off the base. Alas, the cord was cut; the phone was dead.

How could she be so close and have no way out? She could try to fight the rest of the scout squad, but she was outnumbered and more than outgunned. She was so frustrated. What she wouldn't give for her old screen. What would Gala Vaurienne do? She slammed the broken phone down. In doing so, she hit her finger on the counter. "Owwww!" she whispered loudly. She shook her fingers up and down – and then rubbed them on her pants. That's when her fingers hit it. The screen she'd found earlier. It was in really bad condition. She pulled it out of her pocket and looked at it. She turned it over in her hands.

The front was cracked, shattered really, with hundreds of jagged lines; she could barely make out anything. And then she remembered, it had played music – just a few moments ago! Only now it seemed dead. She shook it – as if the waving motion of her hands might somehow magically bring it back to life. But wait, she was walking around with a mobile power source. She had kept it hidden for years; she hadn't exposed that to anyone for so long. There had to be a way.

Ruby pulled her skirt part way up and tapped her leg a few times. Her father had told her many years ago about the power source in her leg. She had never gotten a chance to use it before she was abducted by Gruun's goons. Afterward, she'd never really needed to power much of anything in Hamada. Not to mention that she tried so hard not to stand out in the clan culture. A few more taps on unseen buttons and a translucent electrical watermark appeared. And then it disappeared. She was not doing it right.

She tapped a few more unseen buttons. The electrical watermark appeared again. Ruby placed the screen on top of it. Then she waited. Was she supposed to do something else? She couldn't remember. While she was waiting, trying to figure out what to do next, the screen began to glow softly. The glow slowly became brighter! Make no mistake, it was still trashed. She could barely make out anything through all that shattered glass. But at least it had power.

She tried touching the screen. Nothing happened. She tried again. Something happened. But she wasn't sure what. The background changed. But it was hard to make out. She stared at the screen concentrating her attention. It was coming a bit more into focus....a shape of some sort. It looked vaguely familiar. Was that a boot? Yes, it was a boot going into a mouth...KikTalk!?

If she could get to the KikTalk app, she could get to something else, right? It only made sense. She tried to slide the top of the screen. No dice. She tapped a few more times. Nothing. It was stuck on KikTalk. Ugh. She never really cared for those inane videos that Baron posted. Besides, she'd been gone so long, did anyone even use that anymore? Only kids used it before she was abducted, but all the kids she knew weren't kids anymore. The screen flashed off. It went black. Ruby hung her head.

Then she heard a beeping sound. The power returned a few seconds later. This thing surely couldn't have much life left in it. Ruby was desperate. Maybe she could use this piece of junk to communicate somehow. She remembered the KikTalk app. At least it was worth a try. She pointed the camera at herself – although she had no idea if it was working. Baron was the only one she knew that used KikTalk – or at least he did a decade ago. It was definitely a longshot, but she didn't have a slew of other ideas. She straightened up and spoke to the screen:

"This is a message for Baron Clemens. It's me, Vaurienne–uhhh– Gala... I mean, Ruby...Ruby Clemens. (That felt strange to say.) I was kidnapped by the Jade Clan 12 years ago. But now I'm here on Botan in the Gravity Park. Baron, Mom, Dad, if you see this, I'm... here."

She paused for a second and looked around; then she added, "And I think there's a war coming." She looked at the screen and she thought it said 'uploading' for a second.

But the screen faded to black. Ruby shook it and then tried to charge it again with her leg, but this time it was really dead. Just like Artax, just like Maresh. She had no idea if the message was even sent. Or if it was sent, she had no idea if anyone she knew would ever see it. Her plan for escape wasn't working out so well. She pulled her hair back, hard with both hands. She just wanted to scream again. So she did. "Aaaaaaggggggghhhhh!" Then she threw the screen as hard as she could against the wall of the shack. This time, it broke in half and fell to the ground.

One thing she knew for sure is that there were half a dozen Jaders in this park and they would probably be coming for her. She had to stay alive. She had to have a plan. Ruby got up and brushed herself off. She ran back to the remains of the Reverse Gravity Cloud Arena.

The first thing she did was to drag Yuni and then Two-teeth (he was heavy!) inside the arena. She propped them up sitting against two of the metal boxes, facing away from the entrance. From outside the red stripe, it looked as if the two might have been talking, perhaps having a picnic. She looked at the ice cream stand with its sticky blue ice cream melted on the ground and the dragon-fliers still buzzing around. She continued working.

A few minutes later, she saw the rest of the squad approaching. She stood and waited for them. "Did you get the ternium?" she asked.

"Yeah, we got it," one of them said.

"You're Raja, aren't you?" Ruby asked. "I recognize you from the Summit at Hamada Castle."

"Yes, Vaurienne. Are you ready here? Did you and Two-teeth set the explosives?"

"They're almost ready," said Ruby.

"Where are Two-teeth and Yuni?" asked Raja.

"They're in the arena over there. I think they're having a picnic," she said.

"What!?" said Raja. "We need to get this ternium back to Gruun."

"I agree, Raja. But Gruun put Two-teeth in charge of this mission – as he repeatedly reminded me. He said that he and Yuni were going to have a green beer there on the sand before they blew up the place. Because he was in charge and he could do it if he wanted. And then they were going to lay the final charges."

"Oh, he did, huh?" asked Raja.

"Yeah. You know, I'm pretty sure he had at least 10 beers in his silver cooler. You guys ought to make him share. If I were you, I'd go get some beer before he and Yuni drink it all."

"You know, Gala, that's not a bad idea. Tell you what. You stay right here – and we're gonna go get us some beer." Raja walked right up to Ruby – with his face just a few inches from hers and whispered as he passed by. "You do know what happens next, don't you?"

"I'm not afraid," said Ruby.

"I guess that's why Gruun made you his messenger. All the way to the end… I almost feel sorry for you...spare. I'll bring you back a beer as a last request." He chuckled. Then Raja and the crew went to see Two-teeth and Yuni.

Ruby watched them walk into the ruins of the gravity cloud arena. She bent over and picked up the fuse, but she suddenly realized had no matches. She looked around and noticed the dragon-fliers buzzing around the melted ice cream. She leaned over and grabbed a dragon-flier by the leg. She held it up to her face and it blew smoke rings at her. "What a cute little beastie," she said. Then she swung it around in big, looping circles, trailing a tiny stream of fire, almost as if she were dancing with the smoky insect. Then she held that dragon-flier right up next to the fuses and it blew a tiny breath of fire. As the fuse sparked and burned, Ruby spun herself around and swung the dragon-flier up and down, making big, looping trails of light and smoke. Eventually, of course, the dragon-flier grew tired of Ruby's game and it nicked her finger with its sharp tail. "Vamp!" she said softly. She let go and watched as it flapped slowly away. "Sometimes, you just gotta let go and dance," she said softly to herself, with a grin. It had been so long since she'd danced.

The fuse continued to burn. About that time, the rest of the Jaders reached Two-teeth and Yuni. They realized the two were not having a picnic. "What the...?" said Raja. He slapped the lifeless Two-teeth on the shoulder, knocking him to the ground. Everyone looked at Raja. There was a brief moment of silence. Then Raja screamed, "Run!"

Ruby picked up one of the packs and slung it over her shoulder. Then she looked at her finger. It was bleeding.

The scout squad started running out toward the edge of the arena, but they were in too deep.

As Ruby walked away, she sucked the blood from her finger.

By that time, the fuse had burned all the way down. What was left of the gravity cloud arena – and the scout squad – blew up in a massive fireball behind her.

Gruun's messenger continued walking.

STORYTRAX: *Turn the Page* - Bob Seger

    The Day the Music Died - Don McLean

    Dance the Night Away - Van Halen

****

Baron received a notification on his screen from KikTalk. He glanced at the flashing boot-in-mouth icon. He swiped it away, deleting it. "Vamp, nobody uses that anymore," he said to himself.

****

Mom was coming back home after picking up Gram. Gram picked up her screen to see if there was any news about the war. She had a notification that she hadn't seen in many years. She clicked on the logo of the boot going into an open mouth. The video began to play. Gram gasped! Her mouth dropped open. "Oh my God, Oliva. We have to go to the Gravity Park, right now!"

"The what? That placed closed years ago. Why would we go–?" asked Liv.

"Ruby is there!"

"What!?"

****

Mom and Gram arrived at the now-even-more-destroyed Gravity Park. "We'll cover more ground faster if we split up," said Mom. They went to different sections of the park to look for Ruby. Gram took the path toward the *Experimental Fusion Alley*. Mom made her way toward the big rides – and the huge, still-rising plume of smoke.

"Ruby!" Mom yelled as she ran toward a distant figure. She couldn't believe that her daughter might actually be alive. And that she might actually be here, so close. "Ruby!" she yelled again. Was this crazy? Her daughter had been gone for 12 years. Her little girl. Mom began to cry. "Ruby!"

The video that Gram saw certainly looked real. Even if it had been 12 years, Mom would know her Ruby Gala anywhere. Sure the girl (woman?) in that video was older but that's about how old Ruby should be. That hair, those eyes, those outrageously blue lips! It had to be Ruby. "Please God," she said to herself. "Ruby!" she screamed.

Mom stopped running. The figure in the distance was running toward her now. "Ruby?" she yelled. The figure continued running toward her.

"Mom!" yelled Ruby.

Mom began running again. Those few seconds of running toward each other felt like a painful, slow-motion lifetime. They continued yelling as they approached each other.

"Mom!"

"Ruby!"

"Mom!"

"Ruby!" They kept repeating each other's names. As they got closer, their voices softened.

"Ruby?"

"Mom?"

They fell together in a full-body hug. It was long and tight. Neither one wanted to let go. Ruby smelled her mother's perfume. She drank it in. Oliva stroked her daughter's hair. "I missed you so much," said Ruby as she loosened her grip enough to take a breath.

"Oh, Ruby, we didn't know you were alive. Oh, sweetie, I've missed you so much," said Mom.

Their hug parted but they still held onto each other's hands. They gazed into each other's eyes. "How I've longed to see those beautiful green eyes. I can't believe you're actually here. I have so many questions," said Mom. "Are you okay? Where have you been? How did you get here?"

"Mom," said Ruby. "I love you so much."

"Oh, honey, I love you too," Mom replied.

A secondary explosion rocked the park. They instinctively embraced each other again. As they pulled away after a few seconds, Ruby looked around nervously, "We have to get out of here, now."

"I'm taking you home, but we have to find Gram."

"Home," Ruby thought. That word had such a simple and yet complex meaning to her. The home in which she grew up was a distant memory, but she was beginning to feel those memories rekindle. Images, sounds, voices, emotions that she had long suppressed were beginning to find their way back into her consciousness.

"Wait – did you say 'Gram'?" Ruby asked in disbelief.

"Yes, she was the one who saw your KikTalk video. She came here with me to get you," said Mom.

"Vamp…." Ruby said. "Mom, I came here on a ship with the Jade Clan. They're planning to start a war with Botan."

"I know sweetie. Your father's already helping the IDC fight them."

"Dad?" Ruby asked softly. "Where is he?"

"He's not here, sweetie, but you'll see him soon. Come on, I'm taking you home."

Ruby Gala Vaurienne Clemens. She had not been a little girl for a long time. She had been a messenger for one of the Clan leaders of Minos. She fought and negotiated and drank and had adventures. She was a girl – now a woman – who was forced to grow up too soon. Yet in that moment, she was glad to listen to her mother. They still held hands while they ran back toward the entrance to the Gravity Park.

As they neared the exit, Mom slowed. She was breathing heavily. "This is where Gram and I split up." Gram was coming back toward them.

"Ruby!"

"Gram!"

There were more hugs – and more tears.

"Gram, I missed you so much!"

"Ruby, my angel. My heart was broken. But now it is overflowing," said Gram.

Mom looked over at Maresh, lying face up with a puddle of blood around him. "Guys, we all have lots of questions, but this probably isn't the safest place," she said. "Can we go now?"

Gram had one arm around Ruby's shoulders and with her other hand, she patted her big pocketbook. "I think I have everything I need."

CHAPTER **48**

Motley Crew

Back on Minos, *The Emancipation* was docked at Pelican's Point. It was no longer in dry dock. It was resting in the water next to the pier – and it was bustling with activity. People were going up and down the gangplank. Carpenters were repairing things; sailors were climbing masts, rigging sails, attaching new lines; painters were touching up the trim.

Supplies were also being loaded. One crate, in particular, was larger than ten men. It was being rolled onto the ship – very slowly.

"Is that the one?" asked Captain Ferrus.

"Yes, it is," said Cassius.

"Be careful with that one, boys," said Captain Ferrus. "Take it straight to the bridge," he ordered.

At the stern, Holland and Sampson were hanging from ropes while they (and several others) attached large, metal cylinders to the rear quarters of the ship. The eight shiny silver cylinders looked out of place on a wooden sailing ship.

Ferrus had put those gold bars and Roden's big ruby to good use. Nia was there, too. Oshi observed from her perch on the pier. She nodded to Faron and he handed a box full of levs to some workers, then they shook hands. Oshi had assigned Faron and a few dozen dozen gold sailors to join the motley crue. Cassius had brought about 30 Jaders. Nia had even received permission from Roden to bring a few red guards. Along with a few old boatmen that Ferrus knew, they had the makings of a halfway decent crew.

The workers were finishing up and leaving the ship. It was time for the crew to board. Cassius and Ferrus assembled them all on the dock. Cassius jumped up on a box. "Gentlemen – and ladies," he began. "I am Cassius, deputy of the Jade Clan. You are about to join a historic mission. Our goal is to stop a war. Minos and Botan are a rammel's sneeze away from escalating a conflict that has already begun. We have a chance to stop it. But it will not be easy."

"We have, on our crew, members from the Jade Clan, the Gold Clan, and the Red Clan. We don't have many experienced sailors, but we do have fighters. We don't know each other, but if we can overcome our differences and work together, we have a chance to avoid carnage – literally on a planetary scale. Your families and your homes, your very way of life are all at risk. The Interplanetary Defense Corps has already landed one of their most advanced battle cruisers on Levon. This conflict has the potential to get very bad, very quickly. And although the attacks have begun on Botan, they are certain to come to Minos with a vengeance. But we – all of you standing here – are the one last chance our planet has to avoid such a disaster.

"Our first challenge is to get from here on Pelican's Point to Botan. And we will have to go fast. You'll notice the new thrusters attached to the rear of *The Emancipation*." Everyone looked at the stern. "These are missile thrusters that could have been used for the war, but they have been re-purposed to propel our ship faster than ever thought possible," he said. "Thanks to Oshi for her support," he waved in her direction. She waved back.

"But the crossing is not without risk. As every ship has done for centuries, we will have to avoid the gravity wells and geysers," said Cassius. "And to help us in that effort, I want to introduce you to the captain of *The Emancipation*, Captain Ferrus."

Captain Ferrus walked to the front of the group and stood up on the box after Cassius stepped down. "We'll need to navigate tricky waters, but I have an excellent navigator. And *The Emancipation* knows the way as well. She already holds the record for the fastest intercontinental sea crossing. So, for her, this'll just be breaking her own record," said Ferrus. "Any questions before we shove off?"

"Who are we fighting?" asked one red guard.

Cassius hopped up on another box beside Ferrus. "We will be fighting a rogue contingent of the Jade Clan army who is trying to start this war. They are led … by my father, Gruun." There were murmurs among the crew. Some of the gold sailors looked at the Jaders in their midst. "But those of us here today can be a force for good. We can avert a war. We can save thousands of lives."

"Crew, I want you to introduce yourselves to each other," said Ferrus. "If you're from the Red Clan, introduce yourself to a Jader. If you're from the Jade Clan, introduce yourself to a gold sailor. Shake hands and tell each other your names," he added. Most of them looked sheepishly at each other.

"Do it NOW!" Cassius barked. The men and women introduced each other and shook hands.

"Hey!" yelled a gold sailor. "Why don't we have anyone from the Blue Clan?" she asked.

"Those represented here today seek to avoid war and to pursue a path of peace. But not everyone has those same desires," said Cassius.

"I have a question," said a Jader. "Do we really have enough soldiers, enough supplies, and weapons to stop Gruun's army?"

"We don't need to stop an army, just barely one regiment. Besides, the IDC is already there, and we'll also have the Botanian security forces on our side. Oshi, as a member of the Council, has already sent a message that we are coming to offer assistance," said Cassius.

Ferrus held his hat aloft and everyone saw that red feather blowing in the breeze. "The wind's with us boys. All we need now is a little luck – and everything will be all right."

"We're going to need more than just a little luck," said one red guard.

As if on cue, a blob approached from the end of the pier coming out from behind some boxes; it knocked a few over. Ferrus, eyeing opportunity, added "And there's our good luck, right on time!" Everyone turned to look at the bullpar gliding slowly in their direction. They all watched silently as Finch floated right up to their assemblage. There was pointing and several smiles as the virtual embodiment of good luck came into their midst.

(While everyone's attention was on Finch, Mr. Moustache slipped aboard ship and hid himself. He meant to join this party – but his goal was certainly not to avert a war. He had one thing on his mind: vengeance.)

"All Aboard!" shouted Captain Ferrus. Everyone boarded the ship and began preparing for departure. Everyone that is, except for Finch. He followed everyone right up to the edge of the gangplank. Bullpars did not like water – not one bit. He had already braved the ocean for Ruby and failed miserably. He was not looking forward to repeating that error. He froze at that location for several minutes. Bullpars were very good at not moving.

He seemed to shake his head. And then the bullpar turned the opposite direction. He began to slowly float away from *The Emancipation*. As everyone else was preparing to cast off, Ferrus watched Finch. He yelled over the railing. "That's all right Finch. We don't need you. I know you're afraid of the water. It's okay. I'm sure Gala doesn't need you either."

Finch stopped again in mid-air.

"When we get there... If we survive, and if we find Gala. And if we can save her from Gruun, I'll be sure to tell her that you said 'hello.' Why don't you go on back to the Tavern? That should be fun," said Ferrus. He turned around and headed toward the bridge. Finch took a deep breath. His whole body expanded and then seemed to de-inflate. A snarl grew on his face. Finch slowly spun in place and returned to the ship. He glided up the gangplank and onto the deck. He floated past the sailors and the captain onto the bridge. Ferrus smiled and nodded at the bullpar.

The captain stepped onto the bridge. "Cast off!" he ordered. Supporters on the dock untied thick ropes and tossed them onto the deck. *The Emancipation* slowly drifted away from the dock. Ferrus guided the ship toward the open water. "Holland, are you ready with the engines?" he asked.

"Ready, sir!" responded Holland. Ferrus stuck his head into a hole in the huge crate beside the wheel. In a muffled voice, he said "Okay, are you ready? You'll need to tell me when to turn. We're going to be traveling faster than you ever have. Are you sure you can do this?" There was some sort of animal sound. Ferrus removed his head from the box and said, "Good."

"Attention! All hands! All hands! We are about to engage engines. Find yourself a seat! Batten down the hatches!" Ferrus yelled. He turned to Cassius, "I've always wanted to say that." Then he addressed everyone else, "Strap in! All ahead, full!" Ferrus ordered. The missile thrusters lit up and began to push the ship forward. Slowly at first, then picking up speed. The wind was blowing hard through the hair of those left on deck.

The ship began to go faster and faster as the Levonian suns looked down upon the 'motley crew.'

STORYTRAX: *The Final Countdown* - Europe

CHAPTER **49**

Farmhouse Stand

Mom, Gram, and Ruby stopped in front of the garage at the farmhouse in the still-red family floater. Ruby was ecstatic, but she was also kind of numb. She had been gone for more than 12 years – longer than she was alive before that. More than half her life had been spent with other people in another place and a completely different culture. Was this even her home now?

She looked at her father's old workshop next to the garage. She got out of the floater and looked down at the pond. She remembered it being so much bigger. Had it shrunk? Or had it just grown larger in her dreams?

"I'm sure someone else wants to see you, too," said Mom.

A man walked out of the house. At first, Ruby thought it might be her father. But he would be older now. Still, it did look like her father. "I thought you said dad was off with the IDC," Ruby said.

"He is, honey. I'm going to try to contact him now. Nothing could keep him from coming home!" said Mom.

Ruby stared at the man walking toward her. She thought she recognized this person, but she wasn't sure who it was. As she searched her memories, the realization hit her like a ton of bricks: Baron.

"Baron!" she screamed. "Beeeaaaaaaaaarrrrrrrrrrrr!" She dropped her pack and ran toward her brother.

"Ruby....Ruby..." was all he could say. He picked her up and spun her around and they hugged.

For the tiniest of moments, Ruby was 10 years old again. As her mind adjusted to the new reality, she stepped back and took stock of her brother. She noticed that Baron was much bigger now; he had grown into a man. "You're so big," she said, laughing softly.

Mae-Ellen and Ho walked out of the house to greet their old friend. They all screamed each other's names and fell into a three-way hug. There were tears of joy.

****

The scout squad hadn't checked in well after Gruun's lookouts spotted the large smoke cloud from the direction of the Gravity park, so Gruun dispatched Rogan and several other fighters to investigate (and to clean up if necessary). Rogan found Raja hanging on to life – but only barely. With his dying breath, Raja informed the others that Gala had escaped and blown them up. Rogan returned to camp to report back.

Gruun was quite angry at this turn of events. He surmised that Ruby had likely gone to her family's home. "I told her that if she tried to escape, her family would pay the price," Gruun said to Brown-teeth. *Botanians*, he thought, *especially women...are so predictable.* "Brown-teeth, send a ground strike team to her house. No survivors. Kill everyone there – even the animals. Nothing left alive. And I want her boots; she doesn't get to wear Jade Clan boots anymore – not even as a corpse."

"Ummm – the animals?" Brown-teeth asked?

"Everything that lives."

The way Gruun gave those orders was stoic, cold and without emotion. He just ordered multiple deaths – even animals – matter-of-factly. Surely he was angry and even offended, but he showed no emotion – he just stared straight ahead when he uttered those words. Did Ruby really mean nothing to him? He practically raised her – in his own twisted way. He promoted her above many naturals to be his trusted messenger. But, in the end, you were either with Gruun and the Jaders or you weren't.

"You want me to go with the strike team?" asked Brown-teeth, jarring the leader out of his stare.

"No," said Gruun. "I need you here. We need to prepare for the assault on Wedding-Shi."

Rogan led the ground strike team to attack Ruby and her family at their farmhouse. He was accompanied by Bandit, Shantu, and seven others. Gruun had evidently known the location of Tanner's home for some time. But, for a while, he was content to have Ruby instead of the money he was owed. Gruun figured that he'd get around to dealing with Tanner at some point. But the years got away from him and he hadn't been back to Botan for quite some time. In addition, he justified his delay (to himself) because he was planning a much larger effort. However, given the situation – and the opportunity – not to mention the proximity – Gruun wanted his full measure of revenge.

The strike team closed in on the blue ice cream banana orchard. They, of course, had their Browning blasters. Ruby, Baron, Mom, Gram, and friends had no weapons. They were sitting in the living room. Mom brought Ruby a big glass of clord juice in the tiny soda bottle she drank from when she was a girl.

"Umm, thanks Mom, I haven't had this since I... left, but I could probably just use a regular cup," Ruby said. Anyway, she took a looonnnngggg draught.

"You didn't leave, honey; you were stolen from us," said Mom.

"I know. It just sounds so weird to say 'kidnapped,'" Ruby said. "I can't believe I'm home. I missed you all so much," she added.

"We didn't know what happened or where you were," said Baron. For a moment, there was an awkward silence.

Ruby sat her drink on the table. "Why didn't you look for me?"

"Oh, honey, we did. We looked for months and months. There were search parties, the police, even the Botanian Guard looked for you. Your picture was on everyone's screen," said Mom. "I'm so sorry we didn't find you. And your father...." she said. "The authorities told us that you were gone and officially considered dead. The speculation was that you had been cut and bled up on Runyon Falls and possibly eaten by shaving leeches. But even then, your father wouldn't give up.

He kept looking. He called on his old friends in the guard and even back on Earth. For almost three years, he nearly drove himself crazy."

"And he actually didn't even give up then," said Baron. "For almost four more years, every Saturday, Dad and I would send out emails, messages, and search around Runyon Falls. We just wanted some sort of sign, maybe a scrap of clothing, or some indication of you."

"Tanner even asked the Jade Clan. He offered to pay any kind of ransom – or exchange himself for you. But they said they didn't have you," said Mom.

"We had your funeral," said Gram, with tears streaming down her face.

"Oh Ruby, my baby! I'm so sorry for what happened to you!" Mom hugged her daughter. They hugged… for a long time. "Honey, can you tell us what happened?" Mom asked. "But it's okay if you don't want to talk about it," she added.

"No, I want to tell you. It's just – it's a lot. Twelve years. I'm not even sure where to begin," she said. "The Jade Clan abducted me from Runyon Falls that day I went back to tell the Storyteller that I was declining his offer – just like you Gram," Ruby said.

"Oh no, the Jade Clan!" Ruby said with her eyes as big as saucers. "They'll be coming for me. They have an army! We have to hide!" she said as she looked around like a crazy person.

"Where's Father!?" she asked. The situation was gravely serious. Ruby was so glad to be home, but she knew they were all in terrible danger. Why did no one else seem concerned? She stood. "Guys, get up. We need to leave now. I know they are coming for me. And I'm afraid of what they'll do to everyone here."

"Ruby, I know that the Jade Clan has come to Botan. Your father told me. But he's with the IDC now – and they are going to stop the Jaders up north in Severu. They have a battle cruiser. You're home now. You'll be safe here," Mom said. "Besides, they don't even know where we are."

"Mom, you don't understand. The Jaders are preparing for war. But they're not in Severu; we landed at Giselle Bay. The Jade Clan leader

– his name is Gruun – he thinks he owns me. He's not just going to let me walk away. When you picked me up at the Gravity Park, they had just killed someone who was helping me. The only way I could get away was to kill several of them," she said.

"Honey, what do you mean?" Mom asked.

"Did you see that explosion?" Ruby asked.

"The huge plume of black smoke," Gram said softly.

"That was me. I had no choice. Gruun already stole me away from my family. He kept me in a cage. He tried to sell me into slavery. He – he – he's a monster. He won't stop until he gets what he wants. And what he wants is me – and probably all of you now. I should never have come home!" she screamed and ran out of the house.

"Guys," Mae-Ellen said. "I know this sounds a little extreme, but I think maybe Ruby might be right."

Ho stood up. "I agree," he said. "We need to go."

"Well, you always had some sort of special affection for Ruby; I can see why you'd agree with her," said Baron.

"No, that's not it," Ho said. He pointed out the window. "I see a group of armed men coming up from the banana orchard."

Blasts shot through the windows.

"Get down!" yelled Baron. "Everybody down!"

Ruby was already outside – she dove off the porch. More blasts hit the home and shattered more windows. Ruby looked in through a now-broken side window. She yelled through the hole, "Everyone, get around to the back of the house. Get to the garage and Father's workshop!"

Another round of blasts. Everyone in the house ran out the back door.

Ruby got to the garage first. She grabbed the Spin Doctor sitting in a corner. A little puff of dust swirled around when she picked it up.

"Everyone follow me up to the top of the hill by the pond," she said. They all followed her, except Baron.

He had remained behind in the house. Several of the ground strike team had made it up to the front porch. Baron came flying out of the kitchen with a frying pan in each hand and a big pot on his head. He was trying to use it as a makeshift helmet. He whacked one of the surprised Jaders with a frying pan – sending the home invader flying off the porch with a blow that smashed his nose flat. The other Jader blasted Baron in the head. The shot hit the pot. The pot flew off and Baron fell backward.

The Jader took another shot – and hit Baron in the chest. Baron stumbled backward. The Jader tilted his head and stared at Baron. (Baron had put a steel cookie sheet in his shirt.) Baron stumbled a bit more – forward this time. Then he began to sway. He dropped one of the frying pans onto the porch. The Jader watched. Baron swayed forward, then backward, and then forward again. On this final forward sway, Baron launched a frying pan uppercut with everything he had. The Jader's helmet flew off; most of his teeth flew out of his mouth; blood shot up onto the ceiling. Then the Jader fell down to the floor of the porch with a thud.

Shantu was making his way around the house to the garage. He found the family floater and snuck up to it. Then he bent down to attach something to the underside of the vehicle.

Baron picked up his pot (helmet) and put it back on his head. Several more blasts just missed him. He ran down the hill toward the big oak tree leading the Jaders away from his family. More blasts followed him. The remaining members of the strike team, including Shantu, followed after him. Rogan hoped that Baron would lead them to Ruby, but as Gruun said, his mission was to kill everything alive at the farm. And Baron was, for the moment, alive. Luckily for Baron, the Jaders were not very experienced running and shooting at the same time, so their shots missed. Baron wasn't sure exactly where he was going; his only thought was to lead them away from his mother, his Gram, his friends – and his sister. She had only just gotten home. He couldn't let them take her again.

Lying in the grass at the top of the hill by the pond, Ruby and the rest saw Baron's courageous act. But they all knew it wasn't going to be enough. They were outnumbered and outgunned. It was just a matter of time.

"If only we could get back to the floater," Mom said.

"We'd be killed before we got halfway there," said Ruby.

"Look," Ho said. "Baron has bought us some time. We better make good use of it."

Mae-Ellen chimed in, "What's the plan?"

Everyone looked at each other.

"I'll take the Spin Doctor and roll down to where they are, past the old oak tree. I still own the record for the longest roll," said Ho.

"The Jaders will get you," said Ruby. "No, the barrel will protect me and they'll follow me. Then I can run away. I'm faster than all of you so I have the best chance of escaping. Then you guys can make for the floater," he said. But Ho wasn't very convinced himself that this was a good idea.

"Are you forgetting what happened after you broke that record the last time?" asked Ruby. "You couldn't walk, much less run away. You fell down and lost your lunch."

"Yeah, that's not a very good plan," said Mae-Ellen.

"I'm the one they want," said Ruby. "I'll go."

"No," said her mother. "I just got you back; I'm not going to lose you again."

"Mom, it's the only way."

"Young lady, your brother is out there fighting for you – for all of us. He's trying to distract them so that we can get away. That can't be for nothing. We can't lose anyone else."

"There has to be another way," said Gram softly.

"We need a weapon, something to fight with," said Ho.

They looked around.

"There are tools in the garage," said Mom.

"I don't think a sonic screwdriver's gonna cut it against eight Jaders with blasters," said Ruby. "We need something bigger."

"Yeah, something more powerful," said Ho.

"What, like a bomb?" asked Mae-Ellen.

"Yes," said Mom. "That would be great – a bomb...or maybe a missile."

"or a hand-grenade?" asked Gram.

"But we don't have anything like that," said Mom.

Ruby stared down at the Jaders blasting at her brother – sacrificing himself with only pots and pans as protection.

"We need something with a lot of power," said Ho.

"We have something with a lot of power. I have a leg. A leg that could be a bomb," said Ruby.

"What?" said Mom.

"Remember crisis mode?" said Ruby. "Life or death."

Mom knew her daughter was right. Ruby sat down on the ground and pulled back her skirt. She touched a few invisible buttons and her artificial leg separated from her body. "Ho, bring the Spin Doctor over here," said Ruby.

She rubbed her leg. It had been good to her. But she needed more from it right now. Ruby punched a few unseen buttons. Several translucent buttons appeared. She pushed the red button three times then entered 4-2-1. The green light was flashing. "Everybody ready?" Ruby asked. "When I push this green button, put my leg into the Spin Doctor. Then you guys have to push it as hard as you can down the hill."

"Then what?" asked Mae-Ellen.

"Then, hit the ground and put your hands over your ears," said Ruby.

Meanwhile, at the bottom of the hill, near the old oak tree, one of the Jaders managed to hit Baron in the head, again knocking off his pot. He fell down and disappeared from view. The Jaders all fired on the place he fell – or at least in that general direction. Smoke and dust rose from the ground in that spot.

"Noooo!!!" yelled Ruby, as she pushed the green button. It stopped flashing. All of the buttons disappeared. A little red warning sign appeared across the middle of the thigh and began to blink slowly. In big letters, it read 'Danger: Crisis Mode Activated.'

"Here! Put it in as far as you can. Just leave the boot at the edge."

Ho took Ruby's leg and pushed it all the way into the barrel. Then he, Mom, and Mae-Ellen began to roll the Spin Doctor. They started running and gave one last shove as they all fell down in the grass.

The Spin Doctor took off. Their aim was true. It was headed right toward the Jade strike team. Ho, Mae-Ellen, and Mom crawled back up the hill and crouched behind a boulder with Ruby and Gram.

"What now?" asked Mae-Ellen.

"Pray," said Gram.

"Then put your heads down and cover your ears," said Ruby.

The barrel continued rolling down toward Baron and the Jaders. Until, that is, it hit a rock and changed course. The new course took it to the right of the oak tree. It was going to miss the Jaders. And when the barrel hit that rock, it popped up with a loud smacking sound. The Jaders heard it; the element of surprise was now forfeited as well.

First one Jader, and then another, fired on the rolling barrel. They weren't very good shots and most of them missed. But at least one hit the barrel – turning it even farther away. Another of the blasts hit immediately in the path of the Spin Doctor causing it to bounce high into the air. If Ruby's leg fell out, their only chance would be ruined. But somehow her leg remained inside. When the Spin Doctor landed, it continued to roll. And it kept rolling. In fact, it was a new record – not that children's records mattered just then. Inside the barrel, the red warning sign flashed faster.

The barrel was running out of steam. When it finally slowed, one side caught a fallen branch and spun around so that only the broad side of the barrel was visible to the strike team – while the other opening was cloaked in shade. What was also visible to the strike team was a shiny, green boot poking out the other side. That shiny green boot (attached to Ruby's leg) was the only thing visible outside of the barrel.

"Rogan, look, a jade boot!" said Shantu.

Rogan saw the shiny green glint from the late afternoon sunslight. "That wasn't very smart, Vaurienne. You can't get away from us," he said softly. "We've got her, now," he said. "Bandit, Shantu, spread out. Don't let her get past," Rogan ordered. "Where's Bandit?"

"He's on the side of the porch with his face smashed in. I think he might be dead. The pot guy did it," said Shantu.

"Vamp," said Rogan. "We'll deal with pot guy later, if he's not already dead. First, we get Gala Vaurienne." He motioned signals with his hand. The other Jaders looked at him; they had no idea what he was trying to communicate to them.

"What?" said Shantu.

"Ugh," said Rogan, looking up at the sky. "Let's go get her, okay?"

Inside the barrel, Ruby's leg was nearing overload. The red warning signal began to flash so quickly that it appeared to be on continuously.

The strike team moved in. They fired a few warning shots over the top of the barrel. They made their way closer, wary of any surprises. Rogan was certain that Gala had tried to escape. But he was also certain that they had her now. He was going to kill her. He would get her jade boots and then kill the rest of the people – and animals – on the farm. He smiled to himself. Gruun would be proud.

Rogan held up his hand in a stop motion when the strike team got very close to the barrel. (That sign they understood.) He wanted to be first. When he got to the front of the group, he motioned the others to gather around all sides of the barrel. But from their standing positions, they still couldn't see inside the Spin Doctor. And inside, the red warning sign was not only solid, the entire leg itself began to glow amber, indicating imminent overload.

The Jaders closed in around the barrel. Ruby's leg did not move. "That spare is probably so dizzy from the ride down in this barrel that she passed out. She's still not moving," Rogan said. "I'm going to drag her out by her jade boots and yank them off her feet," he said.

As he bent down to grab Ruby's green boot, a shrill, whistle-like blast came out of the barrel. Rogan's hand reached for Ruby's boot.

Then Ruby's leg, the Spin Doctor, and the Jade Strike team all exploded into a massive fireball – with the force and fury of a ternium fusion reaction. The blast left a hundred-foot circle of scorched ground – and no survivors.

Mom, Gram, Ho, and Mae-Ellen took Ruby to the garage. After they all piled into the floater, Mom got out and put something into the trunk. When she got back into the floater, everyone was silent.

"Baron?" Ruby asked. "Is he...?"

"I'm sorry, Ruby. The Jaders blasted him repeatedly, and then that explosion. Nothing could have survived that," Ho said.

Mom started to cry silently; a single tear rolled down her cheek. She had just gotten her daughter back. And now she had lost her son. Fate was cruel indeed.

"And now they'll probably send more Jaders after me. Just leave me here. You guys need to get away," said Ruby. She tried to crawl out of the floater.

"Oh, no, you don't," said Ho as he pulled her back.

"You don't understand!" she yelled.

"No, YOU don't understand. Your brother didn't sacrifice himself so that you could just give up," Mom said. No one else said a word. Mom's screen flashed; it was Tanner.

"Tanner!" Oliva said. "I need you. The Jaders attacked our house. I have Ruby; she's with me now. But…" she began to sob.

"What did you say? It sounded like you said you have… Ruby? Oh my God," he said.

"Tanner, the Jade Clan attacked us at our house!" she said. "And they –" she began.

"Are you okay? Is anyone hurt?" he asked. "We're on our way back, right now. The northern strike was a false alarm; probably a diversion – and we fell for it."

"We can't stay here, Tan. We got rid of the attackers, but Ruby said they'll probably send more."

"Get out of there, then. I'm sorry, but they're going to engage the arc engines for a jump. It'll get us back faster, but at that speed … down here in the atmosphere, we'll have no communications."

"Where should we go?" Mom asked. The static began. "Oh Tanner," she said. "They ki…." (more static)

"Runyon Falls!" said Father. (more static) "Go to Runyon Falls! I'll meet you there as fast–" he was cut off in mid-sentence. Only static remained. "Tanner!" More static. The call was dropped. Mom hung up. She pointed the floater toward Runyon Falls and accelerated. No one said a word.

When they arrived at the falls, it was eerily still and quiet. They realized that none of them had ever visited during the day (none of them, except Ruby, on the day of her offer.) Mom parked and they all got out, all of them except Ruby.

Ruby looked up the path to the falls. "I – ummm. I think I'll just stay here," she said. *If Baron were here*, Ruby thought, *he would have probably said something like "Quit whining…Why don't you just hop?"* Ruby smiled.

Mom opened the trunk and grabbed Ruby's X-frame silver crutches. "You can't stay here. We're exposed out in the open," said Mom.

"You're right," said Ruby. Her messenger experience was kicking in. "If we head up to the falls, we'll have the cover of the cliffs and the greenstalks. At least that's something," she added. "Then we'll have a better chance to defend ourselves."

At the top of the hill and the end of the path, they noticed that the rain had soaked the fire pit. Everything was wet. "We need to look for a place to hide," Mom said.

Moments later, Gruun arrived at the parkbay with the rest of his men. He had decided to postpone the attack on Wedding-Shi and instead follow the tracker to put an end to his Vaurienne problem.

STORYTRAX: *Blinded By The Light* - Manfred Mann

CHAPTER 50

Blood on the Falls

The Emancipation arrived at Botan in record time! They knew they had to hurry, so Captain Ferrus ran the ship aground at Garden Shore Beach – the closest point to Runyon Falls and to Ruby (according to their talented navigator who was still hidden in his crate). Mr. Moustache stealthily slipped over the side and dropped into the waist-high water. He stepped gingerly, but quickly, to shore and stole a floater from a Botanian who was visiting the beach. Moustache raced to get to Runyon Falls ahead of the 'motley crew.'

****

Before entering Runyon Falls, Gruun pulled out a screen. A blue dot indicated where he was standing. And a flashing red dot was right on the spot where the Clemens' red floater sat across the parkbay – close enough to spit on. The Jade leader smiled and put his screen away. He looked around and saw the trail. "Up that path," he ordered. He and his men proceeded up the pathway toward the storyfire. The fire pit was still wet and silent. The Storyteller (himself) was nowhere to be seen.

Mom and Gram were hiding behind some brush on one side of the falls. But the space was small, so Ho, Mae-Ellen, and Ruby had to hide in a different spot on the other side of the falls. They saw Gruun and the Jade fighters make their way out from the path and into the open.

"Find them!" yelled Gruun. "I know they're here somewhere. I want Gala Vaurienne!" Jade soldiers scurried about.

Back at the parkbay, the *Vasco da Gama* landed. When Father disembarked, he saw his old family floater and lots of muddy footprints. "Jaders," he said.

Salinger walked up. "Looks like a lot of 'em," he said. "Leave a guard detail on the ship. Everyone else, on me, prepare to engage the Jaders. But be careful, they may have hostages."

Gruun's men were searching the area when Tanner, Salinger, and the IDC troops emerged from the path. Blaster fire immediately erupted from both sides. (Evidently, blasters were not affected by the strange phenomenon that disabled most electronics at Runyon Falls.) Most of the Jaders ran past the falls to get to higher ground. Most of the IDC troops, including Tanner and Salinger, pursued them.

A few of the Jade fighters were pinned down behind some rocks by the IDC troops. The Jaders were in front of, and just below, Ruby's position. The Jaders had the advantage as they had cover and the high gound, while the IDC troops were out in the open.

"They're going to get slaughtered. We have to help them," whispered Ruby.

"What can we do?" asked Mae-Ellen.

"What about these?" asked Ho. He just found a treasure trove. What looked to be at least a dozen old, dark yellow eggs with black swirls.

"Waah-waah eggs!" said Ruby. "Those look really old," she said.

"Are we going to make them breakfast?" asked Mae-Ellen.

"These are old and rotten," said Ho. "That means they're filled with – ."

"Acid!" said Ruby. "It'll be like throwing toxic, stinking, burning, acid grenades."

"Yeah, that works," said Mae-Ellen, nodding her head.

"I can stand up just over here, right behind the part of this rock that juts out. Ruby, you can hand the eggs to Mae-Ellen. Mae, then you can feed them to me and I can let 'em have it," said Ho.

"Why do you get to throw these newfound weapons?" asked Ruby.

"Well, I can't throw that far," said Mae-Ellen.

"And you always seem to miss," said Ho.

"Not always," said Ruby as she thought of her final throws at the Gravity Park. But she couldn't stand and throw at the same time with her crutches, so she knew Ho was right.

Ruby carefully handed Mae-Ellen an egg. Mae carefully passed it on to Ho. Ho took aim and let loose with a shot right on the shoulder of one of the Jaders. It got his attention and he turned around to see what was on his shoulder. "Ooooohhh, what is that smell?" he said. The Jader reached up to wipe the mess from his shoulder just about the same time that the acid had eaten through his jacket and shirt. He immediately began screaming because both his shoulder – and now his hand – were burning from the acid. "Aaaaaaagggghhh," yelled the Jader.

Ruby handed Mae-Ellen another egg. She passed that one to Ho. He wound up and threw another one at the Jaders below them. This one hit a second Jader on the head. As he wore no helmet, the acid began to eat his hair and dripped down his face. He ran screaming into the blasts of the IDC. Ruby handed a third egg to Mae-Ellen. But the egg was old and brittle; it cracked in Mae's grasp and fell back into Ruby's lap.

That egg broke and spattered an acidic goo onto Ruby's leg. That goo immediately began to eat away at Ruby's leg. She wanted to scream more than she had ever wanted anything. But she knew that would give away their position and likely get all of them killed. She gasped and bit her cheeks – hard – cupping both hands over her mouth. The pain was almost unbearable. Ho climbed down from his gunnery position and held Ruby's face against his chest.

Mae-Ellen tried to wipe the acid away with water from the falls but the damage was significant. She burned her hands trying to wipe it away from Ruby's leg. Because she was scooping water for Ruby's leg, she didn't notice the acid on her hands at first. But when it began to burn, it almost seemed to sear right through her. She started trying to shake off the painful liquid; it didn't work. She didn't mean to, but she let out a small scream. Not very loud. Just a tiny one – barely a whimper, really.

But the Jaders heard her. About that time, another group of Jaders – who had circled around behind the falls – came up from behind the small contingent of IDC fighters who had remained. The IDC fighters were now caught in a crossfire. They had no chance.

It turns out that Gruun was in that second group. When the first group came out from behind their rocks, they grabbed Ruby, Ho, and Mae-Ellen and took them down to Gruun. "I think we've found what you're looking for, Gruun," said one of the Jaders. He was pulling Ruby by the hair. She didn't have her crutches and her second leg was badly burned. It was really a nasty mess – with skin burning and peeling off.

Gruun leaned down to look at her. "Well, my dear. You are a challenge indeed. I told you what would happen if you tried to escape again." Gruun pulled his hookhand back and stabbed it down into Ruby's acid-torn leg. He then dragged his skewered messenger to the front of the fire pit. Pain seared anew throughout her entire body. Ruby could only breathe with short, quick, half-gulps of air.

Gruun withdrew his tri-hook. This time, instead of plunging straight down into her leg, he raked it from her thigh down to the knee – tearing acid-burnt strips of flesh from the bone. Ruby stared at Gruun. He stared back at her. His black eyes; her green eyes. Gruun stepped back to survey his work. "I'm enjoying this already," he said. "Imagine what I'm going to do to your father. I bet you have a mother around here somewhere, too. And we don't want to forget Grammy, do we?" Gruun laughed. A great, big belly laugh – with all of his rotund body shaking.

Ruby had had enough. She pushed herself up against the edge of the fire pit. She reached up into that matted mass of curly red hair – and pulled out her hummingbird. She was going to end this. Two shots. It would only take one. From this distance, she couldn't miss. How long she had waited for this. She took aim while Gruun's self-absorbed laughter rang in her ears.

"Leave my family alone!" she yelled as she fired.

She squeezed the trigger; but only a clicking sound came from the tiny weapon. She had not charged it after her run-in with the devil-shark! Still aiming at Gruun with her arm outstretched, she fired again.

Click.

The hummingbird was snatched from her outstretched hand. She whipped her head sideways. Mr. Moustache! He scowled at Ruby. Even through all her obvious pain, Ruby noticed how funny he looked. She giggled. "Hey half-stache," she managed to get out. "You look lopsided."

"Thanks Moustache," Gruun said as he recovered from his fit of laughter and saw Moustache holding a blaster aimed at Ruby. "I always knew I could count on you. But don't shoot her. Vaurienne is mine. What happened to your face?" Gruun pulled out his own full-sized blaster and pointed it at Ruby. This has taken more than enough time already. I have important things to take care of. I'm done with you." He fired at his former messenger.

Finch arrived just in time. The blast ricocheted off his hardened body. Gruun was surprised to see a bullpar, but he was just as surprised that his blast had no effect. He shot again. That blast bounced off Finch as well. A third shot. Which also glanced off of Finch with no effect – or no effect on Finch, that is. The ricocheted blast hit one of the other Jaders.

Frustrated, Gruun shot several more times – in quick succession – at Finch's virtually impenetrable outside. These shots bounced off Finch and found their way to the cliffside where they blasted off huge slabs of rock. The ensuing rockslide fell onto a group of Jaders that was watching Gruun, trapping them. One of the blasts ricocheted back to Gruun knocking him down.

Finch surveyed the situation. He saw four other Jaders with weapons pointing at Ruby's friends. He glided around and took one of them out with a quick bite. As he ventured toward the second, that Jader blasted Finch several times on approach. Of course, Finch was unharmed, but he chomped on the shooter, shutting him down permanently. The other two Jaders ran away.

Finch returned to check on Ruby. Moustache went to help Gruun up. After Moustache helped him, Gruun shook him off.

"I can handle this bullpar," said Moustache. He pulled out a big clord from his shirt and waved it in front of Finch. Finch's eyes followed that clord back and forth as Moustache waved it. Like a hypnotist with his patient, Moustache swung that clord slowly side to side. When he was sure he had Finch hooked, Moustache tossed that clord over the cliff. Finch was unable to resist following that tasty treat.

Now Ruby was defenseless. Gruun picked up his blaster. "This time, no one is going to save you," he said. The storyfire lit behind Ruby. The Storyteller, himself, rose up behind it. As he rose higher, the fire became brighter. Gruun – and everyone else – watched – transfixed at the sight of the Storyteller underlit from the fire with his long, flowing beard and robes. "Leave this child alone, Gruun!" boomed the Storyteller with that voice that pierced through everyone who heard it.

"Long time, Storyteller," said Gruun.

"I guess that's relative. Gruun of the Jade Clan. I do remember you," said the Storyteller. "You have committed many crimes. And I do not think you will see tomorrow."

"I want the Tenso Bakas," said Gruun.

"They are the stuff of legend," said the Storyteller.

"You said your stories were true. I think you still have them… And I that's why you've been able to live so long."

"You will never get them, Gruun."

"I think I will," said Gruun. If you won't help me, I'll just take them. He blasted the Storyteller just below the waist. There was a black blast mark on the Storyteller's long, white robes. The Storyteller looked down at the hole. He took a deep breath. "It is not wise to engage with forces you do not understand, Gruun. Such actions are not likely to end well for you."

Gruun blasted the Storyteller again, this time just a few inches below the first blast. Then a third shot, just to the side. Three blasts, three black holes. The fire dimmed. The light on the Storyteller darkened as he slowly floated down and into the shadows.

"No," said Ruby softly, reaching her hand in the direction of the Storyteller.

"And now, little girl," said Gruun. "It's your turn. There's really no one left to save you now, Vaurienne." He looked around just to be sure. "You will die tonight, alone, disgraced. And I – Gruun – I will take over Botan. I will rule both continents. You will be nothing more than a bad dream, a distant, faded, crippled, memory. A worthless spare. That's all you ever really were in the first place."

"But..." Ruby began, "you said... you said you loved me. You said..."

"That I was your new father? Haha! Don't believe everything you hear Vauriene," Gruun responded. He raised his blaster. But then Gruun's expression changed. He looked at Ruby and began to lower his blaster.

A waah-waah egg flew through the air and struck Gruun on the leg. He spun and saw Ho standing there ready to throw another one. "Leave Ruby alone!" Ho shouted. Gruun shook the acidy goo from his leg and shot his blaster at Ho, striking him in the foot. (None of the Jaders were very good shots.) Though his leg was covered with acid and bleeding, Gruun wasn't going to be distracted again.

"Enough of this!" shouted Gruun. I will have Botan.. And I will have it now!" He turned back to face Ruby, still sitting against the rocks by the fire pit.

Mom ran between her daughter and Gruun. "Leave my daughter alone!" she yelled as she fell in front of Ruby.

Then Mae-Ellen ran up beside them. "Yeah, leave Ruby alone."

Ho limped to their side as well. "Why don't you just go away. Nobody wants you here."

"I never liked you Botanians. I'll just kill all of you now. A few days early won't matter." A leaf fluttered down onto Gruun's shoulder. He shook it off. Another floated onto his face. As he was holding a blaster with his left hand, he brushed it off with his airy forearm. It fluttered to the ground. But it wasn't a leaf, it was a bug – and an odd-shaped one at that. Gruun looked down at the bug, shook his head again and stepped on it. Yellow blood oozed out of its tiny body.

Gruun turned his attention back to Ruby, her mom, and Mae-Ellen. He didn't notice the bug re-inflate itself by sucking the yellow blood back inside its body. Still something else hit him in the face.

"Damn bugs!" he said. In frustration, Gruun reached up with his hookhand and wiped this one away, accidentally scratching his face. The blood streamed down from the cut on his cheek. A drop fell onto the re-inflated insect. "Vamp!" he shouted. "One more reason to kill the lot of you."

He raised his blaster again. Then yet another bug fluttered onto him. Another shaving leech. Then another, and another. More leeches began to bombard Gruun – who began swatting frantically. Gram was standing a few feet above him on a boulder wearing a big pink glove (with black lightning bolts) and holding a purple pouch marked "Dangerous." She dumped the last few shaving leeches onto Gruun. Aroused by the blood, the vicious little insects from that purple pouch began to slice into his face and his neck. They began to make an eerie singing sound. Gruun continued in a vain attempt to swat them away, but it was no use. He dropped his blaster to try to pry them from his cheeks. He stepped on a few. No sooner did he pull one off than another latched on. The squished leeches re-inflated themselves and attacked again. Their song became louder.

Hearing the call, a swarm of shaving leeches native to Runyon Falls – attracted by the blood and the call of the others – rose from the cracks and crevices and descended upon Gruun. They were all over him now. The sight was not a pleasant one. He screamed, covered in the leeches, while some even went into his mouth. He struggled to spit them out - his mouth oozing with yellow goo. Gruun stumbled forward and wavered, teetering back and forth, then, almost completely covered with the insects, he fell head-first into the storyfire. Just as he fell over the edge of the fire pit, the fire roared back to life and consumed him. The storyfire blazed higher and brighter. A moment later, several shaving leeches flitted away. Then a triple hook reached up over the edge and the steel claws scraped the stones of the fire pit. The storyfire blazed up again, flipping the hook over the top and onto the ground where it rolled to a rocking stop. It was scorched, blackened, smoking, and disembodied.

STORYTRAX: *In the Air Tonight* - Phil Collins

CHAPTER **51**

The Arm, The Watch, The Leg & The Locket

The IDC and the remaining Jaders continued to fight near the top of the falls. Blaster-fire echoed off the cliffs below. The IDC was getting the upper hand. The Jaders recognized that fact and split up. General Salinger took a team after the first group and Tanner took another team after the second, smaller group of Jade fighters.

The second group of fleeing Jaders split again. Tanner found himself alone chasing three combatants. When they realized that it was three against one, they turned to engage him. He fought courageously and bested all three of them – just barely. Then he stopped for a moment to catch his breath. Brown-teeth snuck up from behind and hit him on the head with a rock, knocking Tanner out cold.

Brown-teeth stared at Tanner on the ground. "That's a nice watch," he said. "You won't need it anymore." He took that Space Force watch – Tanner's only memento of his time on Earth. Brown-teeth put the watch on his own wrist and admired it. As his blaster was lost, Brown-teeth decided he would just throw Father off the cliff. He grabbed his Botanian enemy under the shoulders and dragged him to the edge of the cliff. Brown-teeth paused a moment to look over the edge and catch his breath.

It was a long way down. *Better get on with it*, he thought. *There's still more fighting to come today.* Brown-teeth bent down to put his arms around Father again. He looked up and he saw something rising from below the edge of the cliff. It continued to rise upward. The shape was partially obscured because it was rising in front of the now-setting beta sun.

When the shape came out of the halo of the fast-fading smaller sun, the shape that was Finch came into focus. "A bullpar?" muttered Brown-teeth. Finch floated around Brown-teeth and Tanner. Though they had never met, he could tell that this was Ruby's father by his scent. He growled at Brown-teeth. "Get away from here, you stupid quatchee," Brown-teeth said with a wave of one of his hands – as he dropped Father to the ground on the precipice. Finch's response was another low growl.

Brown-teeth stepped away from Tanner, leaving him lying perilously close to the edge of the cliff. The body began to slowly slide downward. Brown-teeth turned his attention to Finch. "Look, you mangy bullpar. I told you to go away." Brown-teeth shooed Finch with both hands. Finch didn't flinch. Brown-teeth threw a few rocks at the bullpar. Finch's response was to glide closer – right up to Brown-teeth's face, staring him down. Brown-teeth pulled out a knife and stabbed Finch in the side.

Except he didn't really stab Finch. Instead, the knife blade broke – and fell, clinking down the side of the cliff. Of course, Finch didn't think that was very nice. So he opened his huge mouth and chomped down hard on Brown-teeth's arm. Of course Brown-teeth screamed – a great deal – and dropped the knife. But that didn't phase Finch either.

Finch turned so that he held Brown-teeth dangling over the edge of the cliff. "Noooo!" screamed Brown-teeth. "Noooooooo!" Finch Continued to revolve until Brown-teeth was back over the ground, but the arm was still held tightly in those powerful jaws. "Aaaaaarrrrggggghhhhh!" screamed the hapless Brown-teeth. "Lemme go! Lemme go!" But Finch didn't let go. Instead, he began to spin. He spun round and round – faster and faster. Brown-teeth thought his arm might rip out of its shoulder socket. He flailed trying to grab at his own shoulder. Finch and Brown-teeth were becoming a spinning blur. Until… Finch stopped… Suddenly…Abruptly; the bullpar was immediately stationary in mid-air. The centrifugal force separated most of Brown-teeth from the arm that remained firmly in Finch's jaws. The Jader's body went flying over the cliff. Finch floated back from the cliff, dropped the nasty arm on the ground, and glided away.

There was a rustling sound in the bushes approaching the site. Salinger arrived and saw an arm on the ground. That arm had a Space Force watch on it. "Oh, no," he said. "Tanner…" Salinger looked over the edge of the cliff and back at the disembodied arm. "I'm so sorry, buddy."

"Hey," a voice came from somewhere out in the abyss. "You can be sorry later; help me up now," said Tanner.

Salinger walked a few steps toward the voice and saw a hand reaching up over the edge. He helped his friend up and away from the cliff. "Tanner! I thought that was you...your arm."

Tanner rubbed the back of his head. "What are you talking about?" he asked.

"That's your watch over there," said Salinger.

"Vamp," said Father. "That quatchee Jader conked me on the head; he must've stolen my watch, too."

"General Salinger! General Salinger!" came a call from down the path.

"That's Lieutenant Cartney," said Salinger, as he looked down at the arm on the ground and then back at Father. "I have an idea," he said. "Tanner, do you trust me?"

Tanner, still a bit woozy, looked at Salinger; he looked the general up and down. "Yes, I trust you."

"Then I need you to hide in that cave. And don't say a word."

"Okay, but – "

"We don't have time. Just go, please."

"All right, Jalen," Tanner said as he leaned over to get his watch.

"No!" whispered Salinger. "Leave the watch. Get in that cave now!" Father stumbled, but rushed as best he could into the cave.

"General Salinger!" called Cartney.

"Up here, Cartney!" Salinger responded.

Cartney came into view with a few other IDC troops. "Are you okay, sir?"

"I'm fine, Cartney. I followed some Jaders up here."

Cartney looked around and saw three Jaders on the ground. "I guess you won, sir."

"That I did, Cartney."

"What's this?" Cartney asked.

"What is what, Lieutenant?"

"An arm, sir," Cartney responded.

"Excuse me Lieutenant?" Salinger replied.

"An arm, sir and a great deal of blood. No one could lose this much blood and still live," said the lieutenant as he bent down to examine the arm.

"Well, these Jaders all have their arms," said Salinger looking at the Jaders on the ground.

"I don't think this belonged to a Jader, sir. There's a watch on the wrist. It's a Space Force watch – just like yours," said Cartney.

"No!" shouted Salinger. "I think Tanner did come up this way; I saw him earlier chasing one of those splinter groups."

Cartney removed the watch and turned it over. "Sir, there's an inscription. 'For meritorious service, Tanner Clemens, Dec. 6, 2264.'" Cartney stood up. "I'm sorry sir. I know he was your friend." Cartney handed the watch to the general.

"Yes, he was. But he was also a deserter. I guess that saves me the trouble of taking him back to Earth," said Salinger. Clutching the watch, he added, "I can give this to his wife. It's the least I can do."

"Sir?" asked Cartney.

"Yes, lieutenant."

"What do we do with the arm, sir?" he inquired.

"Give it to me, lieutenant," said the general. Salinger hurled it over the cliff.

****

Back down by the fire pit. Mom and Gram were tending to Ruby. Ho and Mae-Ellen went back down to the floater to try to call for help from Mom's screen.

"I don't we can save her leg," said Mom.

Gram nodded. Ruby had given up her artificial leg; now, between the acid and Gruun, she was going to lose the other one. She had passed out from the pain.

"Sweetie, can you hear me?" Mom asked as she tried to give Ruby a drink of water.

"Ohhhhhh," groaned Ruby. She drank thirstily. "Mom, I'm so thirsty. Can I have some more please?" she asked.

"I'll get it from the falls," said Gram. She took the canteen and hiked over to the falls to fill it. Ruby closed her eyes and put her head on her mother's shoulder. Then she felt an odd thump.

Mr. Moustache had hit mother on the head with the butt of a blaster that he had picked up from one of his fallen comrades, knocking her out. Ruby lifted her head and watched her mother's limp body fall to the ground. "Mom!" she shouted.

Ruby looked up to see Moustache. "Gruun was right about one thing," he said. "No one can save you now. You're nothing but an impostor, just a spare. And we don't need you anymore."

Moustache walked up to Ruby. He kicked Mom aside. Then he bent over and yanked Ruby's remaining jade boot off her severely burned and shredded leg. "You don't get to wear this anymore." Ruby gasped several shortened breaths and groaned. The pain had been positively searing but it was beginning to go numb. And she really didn't have the energy to scream, so she just sat there and endured it. What else could she do?

Moustache stepped back. He looked down at what was left of her scorched and ripped leg. "Hehh. It looks like you won't be needing boots of any kind any more. You don't need boots if you don't have any legs, huh Vaurienne? Yes, the great Gala Vaurienne. You're not so tough." Moustache fired his blaster a little to the right of Ruby's head. She flinched as bits of rock flew from the impact.

Moustache stared at Ruby. Ruby stared at Moustache. Ruby reached into her voluminous red curls. She felt around. "Are you looking for this?" Moustache asked. He held up her hummingbird. In her delirium, she had forgotten he had taken it from her earlier. Moustache laughed. "You're becoming forgetful, my dear. I think we should just put you out of your misery," he said. He shot at the other side of her.

Gram was returning from getting water for the canteen. "Get away from my granddaughter!" she yelled.

Moustache turned and fired in her direction. His shot missed Gram but hit the rock wall beside her, triggering another mini-landslide that trapped Gram. "Well, isn't that nice, Grammy gets to watch," he said with a laugh, returning his attention to Ruby. He shot her leg with his blaster. She didn't react because she didn't feel anything. That made him even angrier, so he fired at her leg again.

Moustache grabbed Ruby. He snatched her up and threw her against the rock wall opposite the fire pit where she had been sitting. Then he saw a glint in the fading twilight. It was something gold around Ruby's neck. He focused on the large locket that she wore. He turned his head sideways, remembering he had seen that somewhere before. "Where did you get that locket?" he asked.

"It was a-a gift… from Oshi," said Ruby.

"What!?" exclaimed Moustache. "You really are presumptuous. You don't get to have anything from Minos. You're just a spare. You're not of the Jade Clan. And you're not from the Gold Clan either." He walked up to her and ripped the locket from her neck. Then he threw it, smashing it against the rock wall beside her. It fell into pieces on the ground beside Ruby.

Moustache looked down on his Gruun's former messenger, towering over her. He put his face right in front of hers and stared into her eyes.

All she could see was evil in the black pits of his eyes. "I'm going to kill you," he said, taking heavy breaths and spewing his foul breath into her lungs. "And I'm going to enjoy it." He slapped her face with the back of his hand. Then he ripped her shirt. He started to turn away, but then swung back and struck her in the face with the blaster. She fell to the ground – with her face among the broken pieces of Oshi's locket.

Ruby's eyes were closed from the blow. "Just get it over with," she said softly. She was in pain. She also didn't want anyone else to suffer because of her. Mom, Gram, her friends….Baron. They were all fine before she came back. Ruby kept her eyes closed. She actually clenched them tighter.

And then, one green eye opened wide, barely peeking through piles of curly, red hair. That one eye darted back and forth – quickly and erratically. Ruby was in a blurry state of pain and numbness; she losing consciousness.

There were blasts and shouts and commotion all around her. The pain began to crowd out her other senses. She knew she was at Runyon Falls. It was supposed to be a good place – a place of fantasy and stories – but she could barely move. It was a mistake to come here…

Ruby prayed. "Please, God. Just let this be finished," she said. She began to cry quietly; tears rolled down her cheeks. She thought of her beloved Artax. Maybe she would get to see him again.

"Oh, isn't that sweet. The girl with the red hair and ridiculous blue lips. Gala Vaurienne – or whatever your name is. The girl with no legs. Well, you can cry for yourself, because no one else will. You're just getting what you deserve," said Moustache. He fired his blaster at her, just missing her prone body. Again, rock fragments sprayed around. And this time, a cloud of dust spurted into the air. Ruby coughed. She reflexively covered her mouth and then wiped her eyes. When she opened them, she assumed for the last time, she noticed something. There on the ground in front of her. Inside the remains of Oshi's locket was something metallic. Oshi had said that she hoped the locket might serve as a sort of protection. But Ruby didn't think the leader of the Gold Oko meant that literally.

As the dust cloud was clearing, Ruby reached out and grabbed the hummingbird that had been hidden in the locket. She shot into the dust cloud where she thought Moustache was standing. He blasted back in her direction. She shot again, this time at the spot where she saw the blast come from. After a brief delay, Moustache blasted back again shooting far over her head. Ruby tried to shoot once more, but the tiny hummingbird only had two rounds. She just pulled the trigger again. *Click...* and again... *Click.*

The dust settled and there was an eerie silence. Moustache was standing there looking at Ruby. She fired again. *Click.* Moustache didn't move. He just stood there. Ruby dropped the spent hummingbird. Moustache continued to stand and look at her. "Just shoot! Do it!" she yelled. "Do it now! Just get it over with!"

Moustache was stiff as a board with his arm extended and blaster pointed at Ruby. He still refused to move a muscle. Ruby just stared at him. "What is he doing?" she asked herself. His fingers started to twitch. His grip loosened; the blaster tilted downward, barely hanging onto his trigger finger. The weapon slowly dropped from his hand and fell to the ground. There was a hole in his chest. Ruby watched his black eyes flutter; then they rolled upward and back into his head. His body grew limp and he slumped to the ground. Everything got blurry for Ruby and she slipped into darkness.

STORYTRAX: *Stairway to Heaven* - Led Zeppelin

CHAPTER 52

Late to the Party

After marching as fast as they could, and eventually thumbing a ride on the back of a train of longbeds, Cassius showed up at Runyon Falls along with the motley crew of *The Emancipation*. Together with the IDC troops, they gathered up the remainders of the Jade invasion force and tied them up, forcing them to sit on the ground. Cassius and Nia ran to Ruby.

She was still with her eyes closed. Ruby had somehow pulled herself into a sitting position, leaning back against the wall, but now she was not moving.

"Gala!" Nia shouted, as she ran toward her friend.

"Gala, are you?" Cassius dropped to his knees by Ruby's side and put his arms on her shoulders. "Gala," he said softly.

Ruby opened her green eyes slowly. "Cass," she said.

"Gala, are you okay?"

"Well, I'm alive. I think I may have lost my other leg," she added.

"Oh, Gala," Nia said. "I'm so sorry."

"It's not that bad," she said.

"Well, you pretty much look like shaka, you loper," said Cass.

"If I'm alive, that's pretty good. To tell the truth, I really didn't think I'd make it this far. I need to tell you something: Gruun's dead."

"I can't say I'm surprised. I know he probably earned whatever he got, but he was my father. I know it may sound morbid, but I'm kind of glad that I didn't have to be the one to kill him," he said.

"I think I understand that," Ruby said. "I know with my family, I... My family! Gram! Cass, my grandmother is trapped under some rocks over there. Please help her."

"Holland! Sampson!" Cass called. "Help me free Gala's grandmother. Over here! Up by those rocks!"

Captain Ferrus walked up and looked down at Ruby. "Gala Vaurienne, you don't look so good." "Is there anything you need?"

"I'd really like some water," she replied. "I think I can manage that," he said.

"Mom!" Ruby saw her mother on the ground. "Mom!" she screamed.

Mother rolled over and tried to sit up. Her head was aching. Captain Ferrus returned with the water. "Please help my mother," Ruby said.

Ferrus helped Oliva over toward Ruby and they sat together.

Ho and Mae-Ellen returned from the parkbay following a group of the crew from *The Emancipation*. "Are you guys okay?" Ho asked.

"We called for the MedAlert," said Mae-Ellen.

****

Back up on top of the falls, General Salinger sent his crew down to the base with their prisoners.

"We'll take these Jaders down and ready them for transport to Wedding-Shi," said Cartney. They turned to go. "Aren't you coming sir?"

"Thanks, that will be all, Lieutenant. I'll be down in a bit. I just want to take a minute," replied Salinger.

"Yessir!"

After they left down the path, Salinger walked over to the cave. "Tanner!" he called softly. "Tanner, it's me, Jalen." Tanner came close to the entrance to the cave. "I need you to stay here for a while. Do you have your screen?" he asked.

"Yes," replied Tanner. "I'll ping you as soon as we take off, then it'll be safe for you to come out."

The friends shook hands. "Until we meet again," said Tanner.

"Yes, brother," said Jalen.

"Thank you. Jalen, I heard what you did. I can't begin to… Just - just tell your mom I said, 'Hi,' – and that I really appreciated her making me feel like family," said Tanner.

"I will," said Salinger as he hugged his old friend. Then the general turned and ran down to the base of the falls. Tanner pulled out his screen, but he remembered it didn't work here at Runyon Falls. He would just have to wait.

The general caught up to the rest of his team and the Jaders as they emerged from the path. The IDC crew immediately saw some other Jade Clan members, along with some Red Clan and Gold Clan members. Cartney and several others from the IDC drew their weapons. "Stand down, men!" said Salinger. He walked up to Cartney. "Lieutenant, look." said the general.

"I see them sir. Those boots – more Jaders. I'm not sure about the others. But we can take them," he said.

"No, son. I mean, look at them – really look closely. Do you see what they're doing? They're helping – not hurting. I don't think they're a threat. These may be the ones that the ambassador told us about," he said. General Salinger walked up to Oliva. He knelt down. "Are you all right?" he asked.

"I think we're going to be okay, but Ruby's been injured. Do you have someone who can look at her leg?" Mom asked.

"Certainly," said Salinger. He called for a medic.

"This – this is your daughter?" the general asked.

"Yes, she's come home."

"That's fabulous news." The medic arrived. He began to attend to Ruby.

"Jalen, where's Tanner?" Mom asked. Jalen looked at Mother. "Where is my husband?" she asked more forcefully.

Jalen leaned over to her and whispered. "He's fine, Oliva. He's hiding in a cave. You do know there's a warrant out for him from the IDC? We have to pretend he's dead." The general looked her straight in the eyes. Mom looked back. "He and I have a plan. He just has to stay in that cave for a while longer. After we're gone, he can rejoin you and your family. Then no one will come looking for him ever again. But we have to keep this quiet. Do you understand?" Mom nodded slowly.

Stepping back, the general asked "Now, what about this group that just arrived? Are they peaceful?"

"Yes," said Ruby. "They're my friends. They've come to help stop the Jaders from attacking." Salinger looked at her.

"General Salinger, if my daughter vouches for them...," said Oliva.

"Ruby, this is General Salinger. He's one of your father's old friends from Earth," Mom said.

"Hi, Ruby. I need to know if these new arrivals are a threat," he said.

"General, please, these are my friends," she said. Cassius stood.

"General Salinger, I'd like to introduce you to Cassius, Deputy of the Jade Clan. Cassius, meet General Salinger of the IDC," said Ruby. They shook hands – eyeing each other.

"Why are you here, son?" Salinger asked Cassius.

"Not all Minosians want war," Cassius said. "I brought members of the Jade, Gold, and Red clans together to help stop this attack."

The medic stood. "General!" he called. The medic whispered something to Salinger. Salinger nodded. "Can it be done here?" he asked.

"Yessir."

"Then get ready," said the general. Salinger knelt down and whispered to Ruby.

"I know," she said. "I'm ready." Two IDC soldiers arrived and carried Ruby to a big, flat rock.

"Where are you taking my daughter?" Oliva asked.

Salinger knelt down to talk to Oliva. "Ruby's leg is dead and needs to be removed quickly. The acid and the blast wound were too much. There's a danger that the acid could get into her bloodstream."

"I understand. Take me to her. I want to be there with her." Captain Ferrus escorted Oliva to her daughter's side.

Meanwhile, Salinger talked to Cassius. Cassius nodded, then he ran over to some of his crew. He sent two members of the red clan up the mountain. Then he sent two members of the gold clan back down to the parkbay. Salinger pulled out his screen and tried to tap out a message, but his screen wouldn't work at Runyon Falls.

Cartney put the rest of the Jade attack force prisoners on the ground all together.

Over at the flat rock, the medic removed Ruby's damaged leg with a laser that both cut and cauterized it at the same time. (Functioning on the same principle as a ternium blaster, the laser was one of the few advanced tools that actually worked near the falls.) Ruby passed out from the procedure. She was surrounded by her mother, Gram, and her friends, Nia, Ho, and Mae-Ellen. She was going to live.

The gold clan members returned from the parkbay, leading a large animal. They walked that animal up to Ruby.

"What the?" Mom said, shielding her daughter from the huge beast.

"It's okay, ma'am. She will want to see him," said Cassius.

Mom warily stood aside. The huge beast approached Gruun's former messenger. He stuck out his monstrous, wet, yellow tongue and licked Ruby's face. Her green eyes opened. She looked up to see a fuzzy ball of brown. She tried to focus her gaze. Just as it was beginning to become more clear, there was another yellow tongue swipe covering her face with wetness. Ruby wiped her face and rubbed her eyes. She looked again.

"Artax?" she asked. It was Artax, her beloved rammel. "Artax!?" she screamed. "But how?" For the moment, she didn't care. She flung her arms around his great neck, at least as far as her slender arms could go around that gargantuan neck.

"I tried to tell you," Cassius said. "Several times....but you wouldn't listen. I couldn't scream it out loud necause I was defying Gruun's orders."

"But I thought you took him into the desert to die," she said.

"That's what I've been trying to tell you. I did take him into the desert," said Cassius. "But I didn't leave him there to die. I got him water and asked a friend to take care of him. I think you probably know my friend; I asked him to help you as well. His name is Maresh."

"I'm sorry, Cassius. Maresh did help me. But Yuni killed him," Ruby said.

"And where is Yuni?" asked Cassius.

"She's never going to hurt anyone else," said Ruby.

"Understood," said Cassius and he nodded.

It was completely dark now. The storyfire had burned down to embers but was still glowing softly. The eerie light illuminated the falls. The Storyteller arose and floated toward the fire; as he did so, the flames began to grow and burn more brightly, lighting up the entire area.

The Storyteller's robes were burned from laser blasts. He floated to Gram. "Are you unharmed Samantha Caulfield Clemens?" he asked.

"Yes, I'm fine," said Gram.

"But my granddaughter…"

"Yes, I know this one," he said. He floated to Ruby. As he stood – or hovered – above her, he asked, "Are you all right, my child?"

Ruby looked at him and said, "I think... But I lost my other leg."

"That is not a problem. You are alive; that is what is important," he said in his big, booming voice.

"But wait, Gruun shot you," said Ruby. "He shot you – three times," she said as she pointed to his scorched robes.

"I am quite uninjured, my child."

"But–" Ruby began...when she was rudely interrupted.

The sound of a foghorn blew – loudly. One of the sailors said, "That sounds like a foghorn, but we're nowhere near the coast. There can't be any ships that close."

The low, piercing sound blasted again. "It could be more Jaders; maybe they have a secret weapon!" shouted Lt. Cartney.

"Attention Troops," added Salinger.

Captain Ferrus chuckled, "Settle down gents. That's no foghorn."

Holland began to laugh. Nia looked at him and started to snicker; she put her hand to her mouth. Finch glided in toward the storyfire. All eyes were on the floating bullpar. He cut loose with another foghorn burst just as he passed the storyfire. Flames shot out more than 20 feet behind him. Holland fell down laughing so hard, he almost cried.

"I see Finch has gotten into the clords," said the Storyteller.

"Wait...how do you know Finch?" asked Ruby.

"Aaaah. We are old friends, indeed," said the Storyteller. "But that is a story for another time."

Finch let a final foghorn escape and shook his lips like a horse. Then he just hovered there. The Storyteller hugged Finch, waved his hand in front of his nose, stepped back (figuratively speakimg), and began to laugh. Everyone else joined in on a good laugh, too. They all needed to let off some steam – though most of them did it far less conspicuously than Finch.

CHAPTER 53

Parting Shots

The IDC troops marched the remaining Jade invaders down to the *Vasco da Gama*. Meanwhile, three Red Clan members came down from the top of the cliff. One of them was wearing only his underwear. The three of them stood at attention while the IDC soldiers continued down the trail to the parkbay.

"Load those prisoners into the brigg!" ordered Lt. Cartney.

General Salinger observed the Jaders marching into the ship. "Where is Lt. Noffler?" he asked.

"I haven't seen her in quite a while," said Cartney. "Lt. Noffler, report," said Salinger into his radio. No response.

"I saw her up by the falls, sir," said a soldier. "She was double-checking for stragglers; she said she would be down in a minute."

Within a few minutes, the ship was ready to depart. "Is everyone on board?" asked General Salinger.

"All present and accounted for, sir," said Lt. Cartney.

"Prepare to lift off," ordered Salinger. "Destination: Tansin Base, Wedding-Shi."

"Roger that," said Corporal Aronda.

The *Vasco da Gama* was on its way to the Botanian Guard base near the capital.

"Corporal Aronda, you have the bridge. Lieutenant Cartney, get Lieutenant Noffler and meet me in my office in ten minutes."

Ten minutes later, Lt. Cartney showed up. "I can't find Lieutenant Noffler, sir. She's not responding to her page," said Cartney.

Salinger picked up a microphone. "Lieutenant Noffler, report to the general's office. Lieutenant Noffler, report to the general's office." No response. "Where the hell is Noffler?" asked Salinger. "The last I heard she was back at the top of the falls," he added.

"I saw her outside the ship before we departed, sir," said Cartney.

There was a knock on the door of the general's office. Cartney opened the door. "What is it, soldier?" he asked. "Sir, this appears to be Lieutenant Noffler's radio and shield. We found them next to the main hatch."

Just then, an alarm sounded. "Incoming! Incoming!" came Aronda's voice over the intercom.

Salinger and Cartney rushed to the bridge. "Report!" shouted the general.

"Sir, we just picked up a dozen missiles coming across the water. They appear to be headed toward the capital – in tight formation," said Aronda.

"Move to intercept," ordered Salinger.

The *Vasco* streaked toward the missiles with orange exhaust trails.

"Coming into range, sir," said Aronda.

"Prepare to fire FirstStrike missiles," barked Salinger. "Missile on missile should take them out quickly enough."

"Targeted all 12 bogeys, sir," said Cartney.

"Fire," ordered Salinger. Cartney pushed the launch button. Nothing happened. He pressed the button once more. Again, nothing happened.

"Unresponsive, sir!" yelled Cartney.

"This can't be happening!" yelled Salinger. "Are our blast cannons operational?" asked the general.

"Yessir, they've been repaired," said Cartney.

"Then let's go get 'em one by one," said the general. "It'll be like laser tag."

"What's laser tag?" asked Aronda.

"Before your time, son," said Salinger.

"Take us in, Aronda. Dartan, Cunis, you're up, gunners," ordered the general.

The *Vasco* headed straight for the missiles. "Fire," ordered Salinger. As the Vasco flew past the missiles, the gunners opened fire and hit seven missiles on the first pass. Their tight formation made them easy targets. The huge explosions made it clear that these were no decoys.

"Bring her around again," ordered Salinger. But as the ship came up behind the missiles, the targets separated. "Stay on the port targets." The gunners fired and hit two more missiles, leaving three racing toward Wedding-Shi.

"Sir, the strain on the remaining engine is causing it to overheat," reported Corporal Aronda.

"Turn us about, we still have three more targets to take out," ordered the general. "Hard to starboard! I need more speed; we have to catch up to those missiles or thousands could die. It's time to earn our paychecks."

The *Vasco* closed in on two more missiles – even as the engines were in the red. "Fire!" shouted Salinger.

The gunners fired. Dartan hit his target. Cunis missed. "I need to get closer!" shouted Cunis.

"Those vamping missiles are so fast. If we only had both engines, this would be no problem," said Cartney.

"I need more speed!" shouted Salinger.

"Sir, we're already dangerously close to burning out the reactor," said Aronda.

"Thousands of people are in danger," said Salinger. "We have to catch those missiles. Only two left."

The Vasco's engines began to whine. Red lights flashed all over the place. Cunis fired but missed again. Dartan fired; he missed as well. The ship was shaking violently, it was hard to get a clean shot with the cannons.

"We're getting close to the city, sir," said Aronda.

"Give me everything you've got, Aronda," said the general. Aronda pushed the drive lever all the way forward. "That's it, sir, but she won't last long," he said.

The *Vasco* began to gain on the remaining two missiles. "We're almost in range," said Cartney.

"We're running out of time," said Aronda. "Wedding-Shi is just ahead."

"We're gaining, but still not in range," said Cartney.

"We're gonna have to take our shots. Fire!" ordered Salinger. Cunis fired – and hit! One missile remained. Cunis fired again, but did not connect. The engine whine was at a fever pitch now. Dartan fired, no dice. There was a loud pop. The whining began to slow; the ship began to lose speed. Dartan fired again; missed.

"We're not going to be able to get back into range," said Cartney. Dartan fired a burst of shots in a last-ditch hope that he might get lucky. Eight shots missed their mark. But the ninth (and final) one – was a hit! The missile exploded in the sky high above Wedding-Shi. "Hurray! Huuuurrrrraaaayyy!" the ship erupted in cheers.

"Good job team!" said the general.

"Sir, the engines are spent. We might have enough power to get to Tansin base, but it won't be fast," said Aronda.

"Make it so," said the general. The ship turned toward the base. Aronda let out a sigh.

"Uh-oh," said Cartney. "Sir, there's another missile!"

"I thought we got all 12," said Aronda.

"We did," said Cartney.

"Why didn't we know about this one before?" asked Salinger.

"It was lagging far behind the first wave; my guess is that the plan was to use the others as a diversion. There's only one missile this time, but we're in no shape to do anything about it," said Cartney. "General, it's headed toward Runyon Falls."

****

Noffler had observed the explosions in the sky. Gruun's plan almost worked. When she left Minos and the Jade Clan all those years ago, she was willing to sacrifice everything for the Jade Clan. And sacrifice she had. She had given up her home, her name, and her clan to join the IDC. She developed an entire network to smuggle weapons to Levon. Gruun's idea for a delayed launch almost got to Wedding-Shi. Nadine Imaelka Noffler had no idea that her sabotage would have been overcome so quickly. The damaged engine, the cannons, even removing the launchers from the FirstStrike missiles. Her former colleagues were resourceful. She had to give them that. But they were out of options now.

She could tell that the *Vasco* could never get back to stop the final missile from destroying Runyon Falls. The Jade Clan was not going to take over Levon today, but at least Runyon Falls would be no more. How she despised the place – and all that it stood for. Stories! "Hmmmppphhh," she said to herself. She pulled on her other green boot and began to walk toward the rendezvous on the coast. *Next time...next time, they would have to do better*, she thought.

****

The final missile raced toward Runyon Falls. It left a single orange streak in the sky.

Back at Runyon Falls, one of the red clansmen (not the one in his underwear) approached Oliva and Ruby. When he removed the hat (which was pulled way down, covering his face), it was Tanner!

"Ruby? Is that you?" he asked.

"Father!" Ruby yelled. Father ran to hug his daughter. Oliva and Gram joined in a great, big family hug. They were all together!

...except for Baron.

The Storyteller floated higher. He gazed off into the sky. He saw, in the distance, that final, orange streak headed toward them. "Finch!" he bellowed in his booming Storyteller voice. "I'm sorry to ask, my friend, but we will all need your help."

The Storyteller floated down. Finch glided over toward him. They touched foreheads for a long moment. "I will do my best," the Storyteller said to Finch. Finch turned and floated over to Ruby.

"Mom, Dad, Gram, this is Finch. He's a real, live bullpar. He's the best," she said.

"I can see that," said Gram. Finch nuzzled Ruby. She patted his head. "He's saved my life more than one time. He's my friend," she added.

"What a magnificent creature," said Father.

"Thank you, Finch. Thank you for saving my daughter," said Mother.

Finch floated away. He began to rise, floating higher and moving faster. "Where are you going?" Ruby asked.

Finch floated further toward the sky. He was going up and up...toward the missile. The missile was screaming toward Runyon Falls. Finch was growling right back at it. Finch's skin was almost indestructible – at least to blaster fire. But no one knew – not even Finch – how he might fare against a FirstStrike missile. Finch gritted his teeth and leaned forward. He was going up. The missile was now on its way down. They were headed straight for one another. Neither would veer from its course. The missile could not; Finch would not. Closer. Faster. Closer.

They met in a flaming ball of fury that lit up the night sky. When the smoke cleared, the sky was empty, save for a thousand stars. Ruby began to cry softly. She buried her head in her father's chest.

ACT VII ~ ASSUMPTION

CHAPTER 54

Homecoming

Three days later.

The *Vasco Da Gama* was repaired and General Salinger sent word to Oliva that he was headed back to Earth. (He couldn't communicate directly with Tanner, who was officially dead.) Cassius, Captain Ferrus, and the rest of the 'Motley Crew' were still on Botan, but they were preparing to head back to Minos on *The Emancipation*.

Cassius was now the official leader of the Jade Clan because Gruun had named him deputy at the last Summit. As such, Cassius signed a peace treaty with the Botanians. Because of that agreement, and General Salinger's official IDC testimony that the 'motley crew' had come to stop the invasion, they were allowed to return to Minos in peace. The attack force was considered a rogue group and not officially representing Minos.

The motley crew camped on the Clemens farm in the field across from the blue ice cream bananas. They absolutely loved those sweet blue treats. So much so that Nia and Holland made an exclusive deal with the Clemens family to import them to Minos. Captain Ferrus would be in charge of shipping.

Mother had gotten Ruby a new screen. She'd copied over all her favorite ancient earth tunes onto the new device. Ruby was thankful for the music. It sort of helped her escape emotionally. Of course, she had just escaped from Gruun and her terrible twelve-year ordeal. She was happy to be back on Botan. But she knew that this wasn't the end; it was the beginning of something else. Although she had no idea what.

Nia visited with Ruby at her house several times. Sometimes she brought Holland and Cassius. It was surreal to Ruby. Her friends from Minos who had helped her were now here in her old home on Botan. The home she had almost completely hidden from herself, even from her memories. Her two totally different worlds had collided. Ruby sometimes felt like she was at the center of that collision; sometimes she felt it was imploding and at the same time.

One day when Nia came to visit, she came alone. "Nia, please tell Oshi how much we all appreciated her help – especially me," Ruby said.

"I'm so sorry I never knew that you were on Minos against your will. Taken from your family as a child. I wish I had known," said Nia.

"And what could you have done?" asked Ruby.

"I don't know," Nia responded. "Perhaps, at least, I could have been a better friend."

"You were – *are* – the best friend," said Ruby.

"We have to leave for the coast tomorrow," said Nia.

"I'm going to miss you," said Ruby. "You know, you could come and visit," Nia suggested.

"I've never thought of that," said Ruby. "Honestly, when I wasn't just trying to survive, I was thinking about how I might get away one day. Now that I have, I'm really not sure how I feel about going back to visit voluntarily."

"Well, you know that Oshi would welcome you. And of course, Cassius. I'm pretty sure Roden would probably be okay with a visit. If not, you could stay with Holland and me. But I'd still probably stay away from the Blue Oko if I were you," Nia said.

They hugged and said their goodbyes.

CHAPTER 55

Déjà vu

One month later...

After the incredible excitement of an invasion, missile strikes, escaping from Gruun, and the battle for Runyon Falls, a semblance of normalcy was starting to set in, or at least what one might call a routine. The contrast was stark. Truth be told, Ruby actually found herself getting bored. Yes, life had returned to normal for most of her family, but not for Ruby. She wasn't even sure what normal meant anymore. She was struggling to get used to having no legs, and just being a regular person. It wasn't easy. She didn't have a job or a plan really. She was basically an unemployed adult...with no legs. She wasn't a messenger anymore. But she was a survivor.

Father was working on three new limbs – two legs and an arm – but they wouldn't be ready anytime soon. The money from the exports of the blue ice cream bananas would surely help. Psychologically, Ruby could handle the wait, but it was much tougher on Baron. Yes, Baron had survived the terrible shooting of the Jaders – and even the explosion from Ruby's old leg. The pots and pans mostly protected him from the Jaders' shots but several blasts did destroy one of his arms. He had fallen into one of the holes he had helped Father dig for a new oak tree. That meant that the explosion from Ruby's leg went right over him. He was stranded... alone, out in the field for almost a whole day, but now he was recovering nicely.

The laser blasts cauterized the arm so he didn't bleed out, but now he was going to have to learn to deal without it. As hard as it was, both Ruby and Baron knew that Father's inventions would give them back much of their capabilities at some point. At first, they both spent a fair amount of time in bed, and then, later, quite a bit of time on the couch.

They also did a lot of catching up – and telling each other stories! But they both wanted to go outside so much. They often sat on the front porch and looked at the farm, drinking it in and appreciating it (in different ways). Of course, Ho and Mae-Ellen came to visit. They even went swimming in the pond! That was a hoot.

Mother took care of them so wonderfully, but she wasn't too easy on them. She tried to help them heal by making them do more and more on their own. "Just because you can't walk right now – or only have one arm, it doesn't mean you can't pull your own weight around here," said Mom. Ruby was building up good callouses from walking on her hands. Baron was trying to learn to use one hand; he often used his mouth as well. Baron even got Ruby into lifting weights to help with her recovery.

Ruby rode Artax quite a bit. She loved that rammel. He was a trusted friend, as well as her new primary mode of transportation. Baron and Ruby built a sort of ramp together for her to get onto Artax. And Father made her a special saddle. Ruby was definitely having trouble re-adjusting to life on the farm. Life on Minos under Gruun was no picnic. Sometimes it was horrible – and sometimes even worse. But it was never boring.

She had been the messenger for the leader of a clan. She was a spy, a negotiator, and a representative. She rode across deserts and gambled with kings. She fought battles as Gala Vaurienne. She did many important things.

But now, she sat on a couch a lot. She was mostly recovered physically, so that was no longer an excuse. She knew that her current problem was mostly in her mind, but… She didn't know what she was going to do with her life. For so long, Ruby had wanted nothing more than to come home. And she was so glad to be here. But, even though she was home, it was as if part of her was still lost.

One of the ways that Ruby tried to deal with the feeling of being lost was actually to go get lost. She would ride with Artax for hours. She would get lost on purpose. While she was finding her way back home (sometimes Artax's natural navigation proved extremely helpful!), she would think. Being out and about, whether on a trail, on some road, or in the greenstalk forest, made her feel better. It wasn't that she was actually going anywhere, but Ruby felt like she was making progress on some kind of voyage. She just didn't know what her destination was.

One day Gram arrived for yet another visit. She seemed to come around more often than Ruby remembered. She made breakfast and everyone enjoyed it. Pancakes with warm clord syrup – still Ruby's favorite!

After breakfast, Ruby took Artax out for another adventure. She was gone for hours and hours. She had gotten lost in her thoughts. It was past the point where she should have begun trying to find her way home. While trying to get her bearings, she came upon the parkbay at near Runyon Falls!

Ruby hadn't been back since the attack. She hadn't wanted to visit. So many memories…of Finch, Gruun, Moustache, and the battle. It was too much to deal with. It was terrible and violent. But it was also something else. She wouldn't characterize it as happy, even though they did win. There was something positive in the victory. They stopped the invasion... Gruun got his; and Moustache, she did nail that quatchee. There was also the loss of her other leg. Her emotions were jumbled; she guessed it would take a while to put everything into perspective. It was too soon; too raw. But now, for some reason, despite wanting to avoid the place, she felt compelled to go up the path to the storyfire anyway.

Both suns were low in the sky as dusk approached. The place was filled with children. The Storyteller was finishing the one about Sherable Josiah. Ruby stayed far enough away so that she didn't interrupt the story or disturb the children. When the Storyteller finished, the parents came and took their 10-year-olds away.

The Storyteller floated over to Ruby. His robes were new and clean and white. "I wondered when I might see you again, Ruby," he said. He used his softer, conversational voice, not the big booming storytelling voice that went right through you.

"How did you know I'd be back at all?" she asked.

"I just had a feeling. After all, Gala Vaurienne is an adventurer. I didn't expect you to stay away forever," he said. "Follow me. Let's talk," said the Storyteller. He made his way back to his cave home. The Storyteller floated while Ruby followed on Artax.

When they got to the entrance, Artax couldn't fit in. But the Storyteller didn't stop. "Ummm, helloooooo!" said Ruby. "We can't fit through that hole. So, whatever you want to say to me, you probably need to say it out here."

"No," said the Storyteller.

"What?" Ruby asked.

"I said 'No,'" said the Storyteller. "If you want to hear what I have to say, you need to come in and sit down with me. I'm tired and I'm not coming back out tonight."

"Ugghh," said Ruby. "I'm not climbing down that hole on my hands!" she yelled after him. "

Two thousand one hundred and twenty-six," said the Storyteller – in his big, booming voice.

"Huh?" said Ruby.

"Two thousand one hundred and twenty-six," said the Storyteller again.

"That's what I thought you said. Is that supposed to mean something to me?" she asked.

"Yes," he said. "Two thousand one hundred and twenty-six is the answer."

Ruby rolled her eyes and leaned her head back, as she let out a sigh. "And what," she asked, "is the question?"

"The question you asked me," said the Storyteller. "You asked me how old I was. I am two thousand one hundred and twenty-six years old."

"I didn't ask you anything," said Ruby.

"The last time you were here, you asked me how old I was," said the Storyteller.

Ruby remembered her 10-year-old self asking the Storyteller how old he was. He didn't tell her then – 12 years ago. But he was answering her now. *Why tell me now?* she thought. *There was no way this guy was over two thousand years old.*

"Are you coming?" the Storyteller asked.

"Part of her didn't want to climb down that hole and walk on her hands, but there was another part of her that couldn't quite resist. So she climbed down from Artax onto a rock and made her way into the cave. She walked on her hands until she came to the great room. She saw the Storyteller sitting on a chair. He threw some crystals into the fireplace and it began to glow. "Sit with me, my child," he said, offering her a chair. Ruby climbed up into the soft, comfortable chair.

"Now, where were we?" he asked. "The last time you were here, I recall making you an offer. And you were going to think it over. But you never got back to me," said the Storyteller.

"Well, I was kidnapped and held captive on another continent for 12 years," Ruby said.

"You were here a month ago, when we fought to stop the attack on Botan," said the Storyteller.

"We were kind of busy," Ruby said.

"Well, that's no excuse," he added. "I'm still waiting for your answer." Ruby thought that was pretty rude. Although he did try to help her when Gruun was going to kill her – and he got shot three times. "My dear, I'm growing cold. Would you mind getting me the blanket on the wall behind you?"

Ruby thought that the Storyteller could just float over and get it himself. Besides, she would have to walk on her hands. *Old people,* she thought. *Well, he did claim to be about a thousand – scratch that – two thousand years old.* And she was taught to respect her elders. "Sure, I'll get it for you," she said with a sigh. Ruby made her way to the wall; she stopped for a moment to yawn on the way. It was getting late indeed.

Ruby pulled the blanket down. When she did so, it exposed two massive horns sticking out of the wall. It looked like someone might have carved the horns out of the rock to use for a coat rack. They were enormous. But whoever carved them should probably have made them smaller. They were really too big for that space. She began to carry (drag) the huge blanket back to the Storyteller.

Then she stopped dead in her tracks. She let go of the blanket and turned around to stare at the horns in the wall. She looked at them long and hard, turning her head sideways. "Those can't be…" she began, shaking her head slowly.

"Yes, they are Caligula's horns," said the Storyteller. "I'm getting a chill. That blanket would be nice about now," he added.

Ruby could hardly believe that the horns from the story she heard at the age of 10 and the horns in the cave wall in front of her were the same horns.

She threw the blanket over her shoulder and brought it back to the Storyteller. "Here you go," she said.

"Thank you so much, child," he said. Ruby climbed back in her comfortable chair.

"Who are you?" she asked.

"I am the Storyteller," he said.

"I mean, do you have a name?" Ruby asked.

"Of course I have a name. Everyone has a name," said the Storyteller. "My name is Shiloh."

Ruby's eyes got wide. "You – you're – you're Shiloh. Shiloh-from-the-story-Shiloh? Really?" she asked in a shaky voice.

"The same. Now, about the job of storyteller," Shiloh said. "You have the gift, my dear. You would be exceptional. But you really have to want to do it."

"How – how are you so old?" Ruby asked. "Wait, wait. You can't be Shiloh. The real Shiloh – if those stories aren't just myth – had his legs bitten off by the demon Caligula."

"Yes, it's true. I have no legs," said Shiloh. He slowly pulled back the blanket. Ruby stared at where his legs should have been. Then she stared at the man – who was the toddler Shiloh. Her mind was processing as fast as it could go.

"So, when Gruun shot you, he didn't actually hit you," she observed. "Well, he could have hit me. He was just a terrible shot. And anyway, he ruined a perfectly good set of robes. They were barely over a hundred years old."

Ruby was still processing what she had just learned. *If this were really Shiloh, and if those were really Caligula's horns...and if he was really two thousand years old, then the stories were true.* "They're not just stories; this is our history," she said softly.

"Yes, indeed," said Shiloh. "And if you look hard enough, you can see the lessons in our past. Because if you don't listen to the past, as an Earth philosopher once observed, 'you are condemned to repeat it.'"

Ruby was overwhelmed with the feeling that she really did want to be the next Storyteller. Indeed, as she searched her heart, she realized that's what she had always wanted. "I do want to tell the stories, so much! I do, I do!" she said. "But what about my family?"

"You can see them whenever you want. You'd still live with them; at first, you could come here on weekends – if you like."

Suddenly, cold feet set in. She got up from the chair. "I – I just don't know. I think this is what I want to do with the rest of my life, but.... For so many years, I didn't think I'd have any choice at all – and certainly nothing like this. Can I talk to my parents first?" she asked.

"Yes, of course you can, my child," said the Storyteller...his voice waning.

"Thank you. Thank you," Ruby said as she 'walked' down the hallway toward the entrance.

"Indecisive child," said Shiloh to himself. He closed his eyes.

Before Ruby got to the hole, she turned around. She knew that she wanted to be the Storyteller. She didn't need to ask her parents. She wasn't 10 years old anymore. Ruby knew exactly what she wanted to do and where she wanted to be. She wasn't going to let this opportunity slip away.

When she returned to tell Shiloh the good news, she found him resting –too quietly. "Shiloh?" she asked softly. There was no response. "Shiloh?" she called more loudly. Still no response. Ruby's eyes grew wide with concern. Her blue lips began to tremble. Did she wait too long? Was Shiloh still alive? He was not moving. He didn't even appear to be breathing. "Storyteller!" she yelled. But Shiloh did not move. Ruby fell down at the foot of the chair and began to cry.

"You can't be gone. I need you. I don't know the stories. I'll miss you so much. I know you want me to tell the stories, but I can't do it without you. You can't be gone; you just can't." She buried her head in the blanket on his lap and cried.

Shiloh took a deep breath as his eyes opened. He put his hand slowly on Ruby's shoulder. "Dear child, I haven't gone anywhere." He smiled down at the young lady as she looked up at him with those huge green eyes and incredible blue lips. "I told you I was getting tired. After all, I am a wee bit ancient; and I do seem to enjoy a good nap more than I used to. But don't worry, I still have much to teach you." He smiled. She laid her head down on the floor on that big blanket. They both drifted off to sleep in front of the glowing fireplace.

****

The next morning...

"Good morning sunshine!" said the Storyteller. "You should get back home, Your parents might be worried." Shiloh reached out his hand; he pulled Ruby up effortlessly. They hugged. "The stories I have told you so far are only the beginning. There are a great deal more for you to hear. Why, I wouldn't be surprised if it takes a hundred years to teach you all of them," said the Storyteller. "And you now have some of your own stories to teach me as well! There's some clord juice on the table, then you should probably get home and check in."

Ruby struggled across the stone floor on her hands. Then she looked up that tunnel to the top of the hole. This was going to be tough. She took a deep breath. "Let me help you. You can glide with me," said Shiloh as he reached for Ruby. When he touched her hand, something strange and wonderful happened; She began to float. They glided up the passage together.

"This must be what it feels like to fly," Ruby said. Artax was waiting for her out in the morning sunlight. It was a gorgeous Spring day; birds were flying and flowers blooming. Runyon Falls was alive and framed in majestic greenery. The rushing sound of the water was omnipresent. Ruby found it quite satisfying.

Shiloh let go of Ruby. "Ooohhh," she said with a gasp, afraid she would fall without his help. But she didn't fall. Ruby was now gliding by herself. She looked back at the Storyteller and smiled.

He smiled back at her and said, "Now, about those blue lips of yours…"

Ruby suddenly felt the blood drain from her face. *No*, she thought. *Not now. Not from the Storyteller*. She whirled around with indignity as she glared in his direction. Perhaps this wasn't as welcoming a place as she had thought.

Ruby steeled herself and asked "What's wrong with my lips?"

"Nothing's wrong with them, my dear. Don't you know why you have them?" She had been preparing for a confrontation, not a question.

"No, I – I was just born with them," she replied a little surprised. "Do you know something about my lips?" she asked as she touched them with two fingers.

He nodded his head. "Why, yes, I do," said Shiloh. "But that…is another story…for another time." He floated past the former Jader with a smile. Ruby's eyes widened and she followed the Storyteller. Artax was close behind.

STORYTRAX: *Brighter than the Suns* (Inspired by *Brighter than the Sun* - Colbie Caillat)

The End

CARTOGRPAHY

The planet Levon consisted of two large continents separated by a great ocean in addition to tiny polar ice caps, along with a smattering of small islands. Ruby and her family lived on the continent of Botan. Botan was the larger of the two continents and had extremely fertile soil. In fact, agriculture was one of the primary industries on the planet – and it was centered firmly on Botan. Governed by an elected assembly, the entire continent was a single nation. More than eighty percent of the planet's population lived on Botan.

The smaller continent of Minos was about half the size of Botan and much more sparsely populated. Minosian soil was sandy and rocky. Different plants, mostly smaller – and not commercially attractive – were better adapted to that type of soil. Minos did have fabulous coastal areas – beaches with great, wide swaths of sand and shorelines with rocky cliffs kissing the sea. In the middle of the continent, there was Hamada. From a distance, it looked like a lush, fertile valley with green stretching to the horizon. But looks can be deceiving. What appeared to be the hue of plants and a tropical paradise, was actually an enormous desert – consisting largely of green sand. Although this central desert area was officially called Hamada, everyone usually referred to this arid wasteland as 'The Donja.'

Minos was divided into four territories that governed the continent. The four territories were each run by a clan with strong familial connections. Three of these territories (Red Oko, Gold Oko, and Blue Oko) rimmed the outside of the continent on the shores. Each of the 'Coastal Okos' was run by a clan of corresponding color. The Red Clan ran the Red Oko; the Gold Clan ran the Gold Oko, and the Blue Clan ran the Blue Oko. The sand in each territory matched the color of the ruling clans, thus giving them their names. The fourth territory (the almost completely landlocked Hamada) contained 80% of the land mass – almost entirely within the Donja. Hamada – with its dark green desert – was run by the Jade Clan.

The primary industries on Minos were tourism and gambling. (However, those were just the legitimate businesses. There was also an open and substantial organized criminal enterprise that underpinned the entire Minosian economy, mostly smuggling and arms. Accordingly, laws were less strict and often unenforced on Minos – especially in the

Donja.) Politically, Minos had a ruling council consisting of the leading members from each of the four ruling clans.

The Great Ocean between the two continents contained a few small islands of varying sizes – and were mostly uninhabited. The few inhabitants of the islands considered themselves fiercely independent and unaligned with either Botan or Minos. Travel across the seas was treacherous. An unpredictable series of gravity geysers (that minimize gravity – or push up) and also gravity wells (that intensify gravity – or pull down) made sea voyages extremely risky business. These gravity disturbances often existed in yin and yang-like pairs. This meant that intercontinental travel was relatively rare.

Sea crossings had to be negotiated by sailing ship. Floaters couldn't make the journey. For one thing, they didn't have the range. But they were also unlikely to be able to withstand the pressures – and unpredictability – of the gravity wells and geysers. Not to mention, the natural gravity phenomena interfered with the basic operation of an anti-gravity transport. The crossing was too dangerous for airplanes as well because the geysers and wells extended far into the atmosphere, but that didn't really matter in practice as that particular technology (air travel) was virtually banned on Levon.

Together, the Botanian Assembly and the Minosian Council formed the Levonian Planetary Coalition that represented Levon in interplanetary matters, although the Coalition hadn't met formally in years. This planetary coalition was also the body that established the policy of controlling and limiting advanced technology on Levon. The two continental participants each had different reasons for restricting technology. The Botanians wanted to limit technology because they mostly believed that it would help reinforce the importance of agriculture and put a greater focus on family and simpler living. They accepted space travelers, somewhat grudgingly, but did not allow space-faring craft to be based on their planet. They were also concerned about 'future shock' or rapid technological change that could cause unintended impacts on the culture without proper time to adjust. (However, the Levonians did love their floaters, especially in the larger Botan.)

Meanwhile, the Minosians agreed publicly that restricting technology might be better for the environment, tourism, and a more historically Levonian simpler way of life. (Privately, they also felt that technology might interfere with their less 'public' enterprises. However, these stances did not dissuade them from trying to import advanced weapons – against their own rules.)

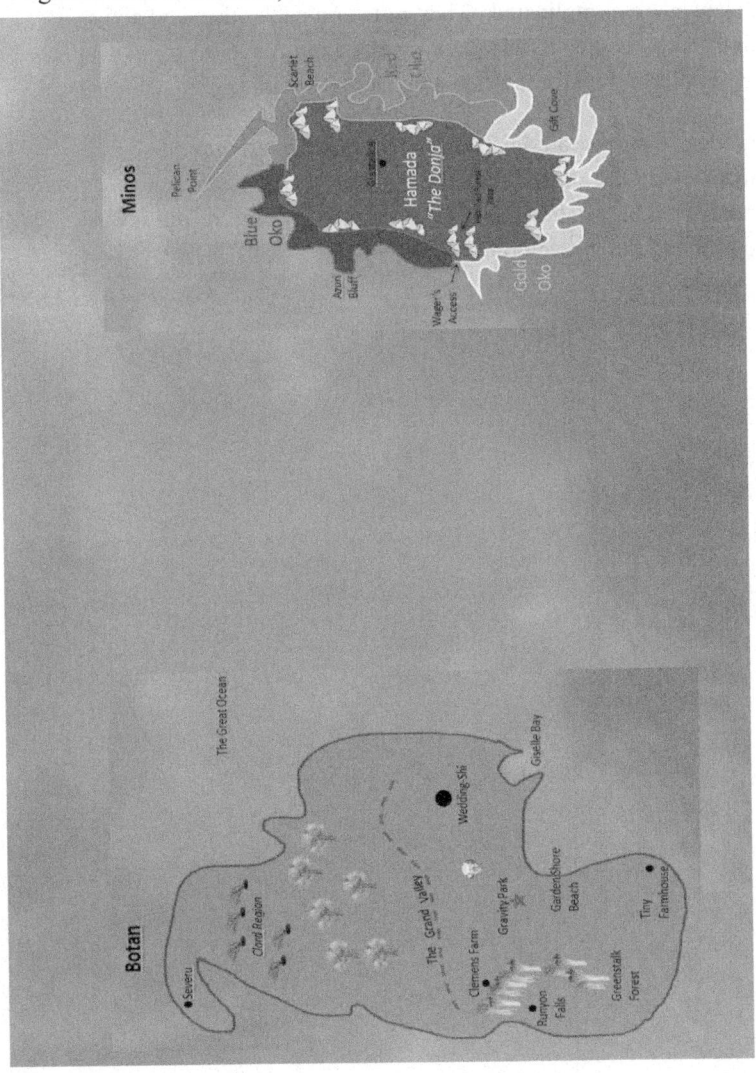

Oshi was the leader of the Gold Clan. Roden was the leader of the Red Clan. Nilo was the leader of the Blue Clan. Gruun was the leader of the Jade Clan. The Minosian clans usually worked together and were generally in agreement even if they didn't always trust each other. Cheating and double-dealing were not uncommon and mostly considered part of the culture.

But clan always came first, so any business dealings were considered unfettered by political or legal obligations. The relationships between the clans were complicated. They relied on each other and actively traded – even if they didn't always have a high level of trust. But more than anything, they were allied against the Botanians.

In modern times, sporadic efforts were made in attempts to build bridges and make shared connections between Botanians and Minosians. One such effort was an exchange program but it was discontinued due to lack of interest.

PRIMARY CHARACTERS

- CLEMENS FAMILY:
    - Sister: **Ruby Clemens**
    - Brother: Baron Eryx Clemens
    - Father: Tanner Clemens
    - Mother: Oliva (Liv) Clemens
    - Grandmother: Samantha (Sam) Caulfield Clemens, aka Gram
- MODERN BOTANIANS:
    - **The Storyteller**
    - Ambassador Kimea Imahori
- HISTORICAL BOTANIANS:
    - Sherable Josiah
    - Prince Trajan
    - Empress Giselle
    - Judge Paxton
    - Shiloh
- JADERS:
    - **Gruun** (Your Eminems, leader of the Jaders)
    - **Vaurienne**
    - Brown-teeth
    - Two-teeth
    - Mr. Moustache
    - Yuni
    - Cassius (son of Gruun)
    - Maresh
- MINOSIANS:
    - Oshi (Your Majesty; leader of the Gold Oko)
    - Faron (Oshi's butler/Deputy)
    - Roden (My Lord; leader of the Red Oko)
    - Neptunia (Roden's messenger, aka Nia)
    - Nilo (Sire; leader of the Blue Oko)
    - Cyrus (Head of Nilo's guard/Deputy)
    - Holland
    - Captain Nigel Ferrus
    - Mung & Kive (blue guards)

- INTERSTELLAR DEFENSE CORPS:
    - General Jalen Salinger
    - Lieutenant Nadine Noffler
    - Lieutenant Mark Cartney
    - Corporal Niko Aronda

STORYTRAX *'The Soundtrack of the Story'*

(Available on Spotify. Playlist: Runyon Falls StoryTrax)

1. Prelude: *Miracles* - Jefferson Starship
2. Ch. 1: *Witchy Woman* - Eagles
3. Ch. 3: *All Along the Watchtower* - Jimi Hendrix
4. Ch. 5: *My Ruby Blue* - **TBD** (John Waite???)
5. Ch. 5: *Dance the Night Away* - Van Halen
6. Ch. 19 *Crimson and Clover* - Joan Jett & The Blackhearts
7. Ch. 22: *99 Red Balloons* - Nena (English version)
8. Ch. 23: *You Make Me Feel Like Dancing* - (Adam Levine & Franki Valli???)
9. Ch. 23: *What I Like About You* - The Romantics
10. Ch. 23: *Eine Kleine Nachtmusik* - Wolfgang Mozart (London Symphony)
11. Ch. 23: *Contra Stand* - Slimba PRTY
12. Ch. 29: *Flight of the Valkyries* - Richard Wagner (London Symphony)
13. Ch. 38: *Adders in the Sand* - **TBD**
14. Ch. 40: *My Girl* - Chilliwack
15. Ch. 41: *Some Like It Hot* - The Power Station
16. Ch. 42: *The Warrior* - Patty Smyth
17. Ch. 44: *Find Your Way Back* - Starship
18. Ch. 46: *Werewolves of London* - Warren Zevon
19. Ch. 47: *Turn the Page* - Bob Seger
20. Ch. 47: *The Day the Music Died* - Don McLean
21. Ch. 47: *Dance the Night Away* - Van Halen
22. Ch. 48: *Final Countdown* - Europe
23. Ch. 49: *Blinded By The Light* - Manfred Mann
24. Ch. 50: *In the Air Tonight* - Phil Collins
25. Ch. 51: *Stairway to Heaven* - Led Zeppelin
26. Ch. 55: *Brighter Than the Suns* - **TBD** (Colbie Caillat???)

Original Tunes of Inspiration

1. *My Baby Blue* - Badfinger
2. *You Make Me Feel Like Dancing* - Leo Sayer
3. *Riders on the Storm* - The Doors
4. *Brighter Than the Sun* - Colbie Caillat

Bonus 'Finger Dancing' Songs

1. *I Can't Wait* - Nu Shooz
2. *Let's Groove Tonight* - Earth, Wind and Fire
3. *Crazy Little Thing Called Love* - Queen
4. *Wild Thing* - Tone Loc
5. *Gonna Make You Sweat (Everybody Dance Now)* - C&C Music Factory

Made in the USA
Middletown, DE
31 August 2024